HAMMURABI'S
CODE

CHARLES
KENNEY

SIMON & SCHUSTER
New York London Toronto
Sydney Tokyo Singapore

SIMON & SCHUSTER
ROCKEFELLER CENTER
1230 AVENUE OF THE AMERICAS
NEW YORK, NY 10020

SIMON & SCHUSTER AND COLOPHON ARE REGISTERED
TRADEMARKS OF SIMON & SCHUSTER INC.

DESIGNED BY PEI LOI KOAY
MANUFACTURED IN THE UNITED STATES OF AMERICA

1   2   3   4   5   6   7   8   9   10

LIBRARY OF CONGRESS
CATALOGING-IN-PUBLICATION DATA IS AVAILABLE.

ISBN 0-671-89697-0

THIS BOOK IS DEDICATED
TO THE MEMORY OF MY MOTHER,
ANNE L. KENNEY

ACKNOWLEDGMENTS

I am grateful to a number of people who read my manuscript with a critical eye: Dayton Duncan, Jody Hotchkiss, Richard Kletter, Scot Lehigh, Lisa Driscoll Tuite, and Robert L. Turner. I am grateful, as well, to Sean Mullin.

For their support I thank my father as well as my brothers Michael, Thomas, Patrick, John, and Timothy.

My wife, Anne, read the manuscript in numerous stages and gave me much good advice and encouragement. I received loving support from my children, Charlie and Elizabeth.

I feel particularly blessed by my association with the two people who gave life to this novel: Laurie Bernstein, my superb editor at Simon and Schuster, and Flip Brophy, my wonderful agent at Sterling Lord Literistic. I am unable to convey to either how grateful I am.

"So we beat on, boats against the current, borne back ceaselessly into the past."

—*THE GREAT GATSBY,*
F. SCOTT FITZGERALD

CHAPTER

1

On a warm summer night, a man seeking vengeance set out to kill the most beloved individual in the city of Boston. Councillor Philip P. Stewart was reclining in a padded lounge chair on his porch listening to a Red Sox game and smoking a Pall Mall while a man approached Stewart's home with the intent of shooting him through the heart.

The man, who concealed a pistol in the pocket of a light windbreaker he wore over a T-shirt, walked along a quiet residential street toward the councillor's home in the Moss Hill neighborhood of Boston. A soft summer rain fell, a cleansing rain whose drops glistened on the leaves of lilac bushes that lined the street. The rich, earthy fragrances of summer hung thick and heavy in the air. The man approached Councillor Stewart's house from the rear of the property, which bordered a dead-end street and was marked by an eight-foot privet hedge that gave Stewart's small backyard a country feel. As the man with the gun cut through the hedge he could hear the faint sound of Red Sox announcer Joe Castiglione coming from the radio. The man with the gun paused for a moment and peered carefully through the trees and shrubs bordering the Stewart property on either side.

He was not acting on impulse. He had considered this act carefully. This would not be a moment of insanity triggered by a flash of madness. The man felt deeply aggrieved by Stewart, yet powerless to resolve his anger in any legally appropriate way. And so, without any legitimate outlet, his anger had grown and brought him to this time, to this place—on a mission of vengeance. Over time, during the many months in which he had considered the action he was about to take, the man had grown increasingly comfortable with the idea. In planning for this moment, there were many considerations, not the least of which was the question of whether he could get away with it. The man who stood in the shadow of the hedge working to calm the sound of his own galloping heart believed that he could. That he would.

He brushed against the hedge, soaking one side of his shirt. He peered across the yard at the Stewart home, a gray, Cape Cod–style structure with white shutters. The house was small but more than sufficient for the needs of a single man living alone. Peering through the leaves of a sturdy elm, the man saw yellow light spilling from the porch onto a small flagstone terrace. With a quick swipe at the sweat on his brow and a gasp for breath, he pushed away from the hedge and crossed the yard toward the house, smelling the sweet fragrance of a Pall Mall as he reached the terrace. To avoid startling the councillor, the man spoke in a soft voice.

"Clemens pitching?" he asked.

Stewart was startled, but only momentarily, for it was not unheard of for him to receive unannounced visitors at home. The "poor souls," as he called them, who constituted his political flock—alcoholics, the mentally ill, the homeless—had often visited through the years. Though most had come to his City Hall office, some had appeared at his home seeking food, medical care, a warm coat. Some he ministered to personally, others he took to a hospital, clinic, or shelter. Legend had it that he had never, in all the years, turned anyone away.

Stewart did not recognize the voice out of the darkness. His tired eyes were not what they had once been. He squinted against the glare of the porch light, looking up and seeing the form of his visitor come through the screen door.

"We're leading in the bottom of the eighth," said Stewart. "Clemens went six and two-thirds. Pretty sharp." He looked up from his seat, squinting and holding his hand up to shield his eyes against the porch light as he studied his visitor. "Sit down,"

Stewart said with as much cheer as he could muster.

The man did so, moving out of the shadows and into the light, and it was then that Stewart saw the man, saw the face that was familiar to him. Stewart felt a knifelike fear slice through his chest. He tried not to betray it.

"What do you want?" Stewart demanded.

"Only to talk," the man lied.

Stewart fumed. "For a moment," he said. "I am very tired."

The man sat down in the chair across from the councillor and gazed intently at Stewart. Beyond the fear in his face, Stewart did not look well. Beneath his sunken eyes were deep circles. His face was lined with creases, his eyes yellowed. His hands trembled and his skin had taken on a grayish pallor. His thinning hair had long since turned gray. When he spoke, a click from his tobacco-stained dentures could sometimes be heard. He seemed terminally weary.

"Do you know why I'm here?" the man asked.

Stewart sighed heavily, a mixture of weariness and disgust. "To talk, you said."

"Do you know what about?" the man asked.

Stewart glared. He reached to the table at his side and tapped a Pall Mall out of its package. He lit the cigarette and took a deep drag. "Why don't you enlighten me," he said.

A Red Sox runner advanced to second. The announcer's voice took on an edge of excitement. The evening air, earlier heavy with tropical humidity, had grown slightly cooler with the passing shower. Stewart wore a sleeveless sweater over a short-sleeved sport shirt, yet he seemed chilled and folded his arms over his chest. He drew on the cigarette again, not as deeply this time.

"Do you ever consider what comes next?" the man asked earnestly, almost brightly.

Stewart appeared stumped.

The man half smiled. "In the broadest sense," he said.

Stewart shook his head. "I have trouble enough with tomorrow," he said. A flip remark.

The man did not smile. "I mean it as a serious question," he said.

Silence.

"Do you ever dare look into the great abyss?"

Stewart sat silently, fear swelling in his chest, pressing against his lungs. His breathing grew slightly labored. He was sweating now. And trembling. Some instinct from deep within urged him to make a run for it, but it seemed his legs could not move. He could see no weapon but he could feel it, sense it, knew it was there somewhere covered by the man's windbreaker.

Stewart's voice was shaky. "I thought this was in the past."

The man seemed remarkably calm. "What would you do if you were me?" he asked Stewart.

Stewart steadied himself. "I would leave immediately," he said. "Before there was trouble."

The man nodded, as though thinking about that, considering the option.

"You concede," the man said, "that you are not the saint you are considered to be?"

Stewart rubbed his eyes with the fingers on his right hand. He drew on the butt again, deeply this time.

"In fact, isn't it true that you are an evil man?"

Stewart frowned.

The man nodded. Then he rose from his chair. "I am going to leave," he said. He stepped into the kitchen, just a few feet past Stewart, and took a hand towel from a rack.

He took the gun from inside his windbreaker and wrapped the towel around it with his left hand while he held the weapon with his right.

Stewart recoiled in shock. He threw up his hands. "For Chrissakes calm down," he said loudly, a note of panic in his throat. He moved to get up.

"Stay there," the man ordered and Stewart obeyed.

A chilling breeze blew through the screen, gently rattling the door. Stewart shivered.

"I am only doing what I have a right to do," said the man. He quickly reached over and turned the radio dial to the right, raising the volume on the game as the announcer shouted out news of a Sox hit and a runner driving toward the plate. As Stewart began to move forward in an effort to rise the man fired twice, burning a hole through the towel and exploding two slugs into Stewart's heart, killing him instantly. The man dropped the towel on the floor, placed the gun in his pocket, and vanished into the night.

The Boston *Post* was housed in a vast, sprawling red-brick building in the Dorchester section of the city, set on a plot of land bordered on one side by an aging, congested interstate highway, on another by a heavily traveled secondary road, and on a third side by an inlet running from Dorchester Bay. On the ground floor, at one end of the building, were loading docks— nine hundred feet long—where every night, beginning at 11:30, dozens of dark-green box trucks were crammed with papers and dispatched to thousands of locations. Beyond the docks, and taking up most of the rest of the ground floor, were massive, high-speed presses. The building's second floor contained scores of offices housing hundreds of employees who worked in advertising, circulation, accounting, personnel, and promotion. On the third floor, at the front of the *Post* building, were hushed, spacious, wood-paneled offices of the company's senior managers—the publisher, chief financial officer, and others engaged in balancing the accounts.

In the back half of the building's third floor was the editorial operation, home to the reporters, editors, researchers, clerks, and secretaries who put the newspaper together each day. The editorial department was divided into various divisions—sports, arts, national and foreign—but its center was the local news operation. Local reporters were spread throughout the city room, a vast space without ornament where the walls and ceiling were white, the lighting harsh, and the air stale. It was a room that seemed to go on and on, with row upon row of desks and computer terminals piled high with books, reports, and yellowing newsprint. Some desks were so laden with junk saved through the years that the stacks served as barriers to hide the reporter hunkered within.

Toward the rear of the room was the paper's nerve center— the city desk, home to the editors in charge of local news. The desk was U-shaped, with a half dozen assistant city editors positioned around the U and the city editor, Howard Berman, at the head of the desk facing out over the room. His was an unbroken view all the way to the sports department 110 yards away.

The city desk was like a small village unto itself. Within the U were seats for a half dozen student interns who performed a variety of tasks, nearly all of them poorly. The interns answered the thousands of phone calls that came into the city desk each day. They handled the scores of calls from crackpots and lunatics—from people who claimed to be Jesus Christ to those who said they'd found Hitler's children living in a bank vault on Beacon Hill.

Within the six hundred square feet inside the perimeter of the city desk were fax machines that spewed an endless roll of paper twenty-four hours a day. Most of the faxes were either thrown away inadvertantly, lost behind the machines, or distributed by the interns to the wrong people. There were two coffee machines, both with coffeepots whose bottoms were thick with sludge. It was that layer of scum, Berman insisted, that gave the city desk coffee its unique character. There was a small refrigerator that, when opened, emitted a stench so powerful no one could get close enough to the machine to clean it. There were computers and copiers and phones and faxes and so much machinery that the tangle of wires that lay under the feet of those at the desk was like the thick cable of a ship's anchor. Strewn around the desk were discarded pizza boxes, sandwich wrappers, paper cups, Coke cans, and hundreds of old newspapers.

Along the three walls of the city room were glass offices housing the paper's senior editors and a few columnists. Berman had an office along one wall, but rarely used it, preferring instead his perch at the city desk. Berman's job was to oversee the reporting and editing of all local news. He was in charge of the reporters and editors who covered politics at the State House and City Hall; oversaw feature writers, specialists in education and medicine, and he led a large crew of general assignment reporters who wrote about accidents, fires, and, most of all, crime. Crime stories were the staple of the city desk and Berman loved them—stories about crimes of passion, cold-blooded crimes, victimless crimes, stupid crimes, brilliant crimes, heartbreaking crimes. He loved these stories whether they came from the city's sewers or corporate suites, for these were the unvarnished stories of life and death in the city.

Berman was an intense, nervously energetic man of thirty-five. He was short, with the wiry, nearly gaunt physique of an English rock musician. He had held the city editor's job for four years—longer than was traditional at the *Post*. It was the most grueling job at the paper and the editorial department was littered with the burned-out carcasses of former city editors who'd cracked or wilted under the pressure. (One former city editor, long since reassigned to another department, spent each day hunched over a terminal wearing a ski hat, wool scarf, and goggles.) No matter how good the package of local stories was on any given day, they were forgotten within twenty-four hours when a new *Post* hit the streets. When Berman's group put out a stellar effort, he rarely heard from his superiors. But when the *Record-American*, the *Post*'s slimy crosstown rival, beat them on a story, Berman heard a great deal.

Unlike so many of his predecessors, however, Berman had not allowed the job to drag him down. He had, in fact, thrived by taking the only rational approach to making it work: he eliminated the rest of his life. Berman had accepted the job, after six successful years as a reporter—three covering local news and three as a foreign correspondent in Central and South America. Berman had a knack for languages—he spoke French, Spanish, and had picked up Creole—which had been of immeasurable value when he covered the political turbulence in Haiti. When he took the city editor's job he had decided that if he were to do it, he would devote his every waking moment to it for five years in the hopes it would lead to a significant promotion—perhaps to managing editor. Berman knew that anything short of an all-out commitment to the job would be a prescription for failure. He succeeded because he worked harder than anyone else in the newsroom—a minimum of twelve hours a day and usually more. Berman kept a cot folded in the corner of a utility room at the back of the news operation and a week never went by that he didn't pull it out and sleep within earshot of the city desk. During his first summer on the job he slept by the desk an average of three nights a week, and one morning he had appeared at a meeting with his assistant editors wearing only pajama bottoms. His sometimes eccentric behavior was tolerated because Berman handled the most thankless job in the building with nothing less than distinction.

Berman's capacity for endless hours of work was essential to his success. But he also had an unerring instinct for news, and an uncanny ability to deal with the varying characters who populated the newsroom. The daily bread of newspapers such as the *Post* was local news coverage, yet the more experienced and polished a reporter was, the less likely he or she was to be assigned to the metro reporting staff. The best reporters—those who proved to be fast, industrious, accurate, and stylish—were invariably promoted to the national or foreign desks or to living/arts, the Sunday magazine—anywhere but the metro staff, which was widely viewed as the lowest point on the journalistic food chain. Yet Berman managed to produce a consistently quality product. He coaxed out of hiding a reporter who had previously spent most of his time hunched under his desk whispering on the telephone. He brought peace between two older reporters who had engaged in fistfights over annoying noises each made—snorting, sneezing, etcetera—from their neighboring desks. He took his band of kooks, retreads, incompetents, and barely literate interns—along with a handful of excellent reporters—and made them into a metro staff that somehow got the job done day in and day out.

So the Boston *Post* had Berman's diligence to thank on the morning of July 12, 1994, when he became the first newsperson in the city to sniff out one of the hottest stories in Boston since the 1950 Brinks robbery.

Many editors ignored the police scanners that sat atop the city desk and crackled obnoxiously throughout the night and day. But Berman listened. Part of the reason his attention span was so short, a characteristic that drove the reporters and editors who worked for him to distraction, was his constant monitoring of the normally mundane scanner traffic.

"It's like panning for gold," Berman would say. "You sift and sift and sift some more and, bingo!—a nugget."

On this particular morning, as the harshly accented voice of the Boston Police Department dispatcher croaked through the static, Berman struck a rich vein when he heard a call for a squad car to number 112 Moss Hill Road in Jamaica Plain. He knew, because he made it his business to know such details, that it was the address of Boston City Councillor Philip P. Stewart.

"Why would a car be going to Stewart's house?" Berman asked no one in particular as he moved closer to the scanner. "Jesus, I wonder if he's getting chauffeured around town by the cops now. Are the cops driving Stewart around, or what?" Berman asked a row of assistant editors. "Can't we find that out? And who gave them the authorization? Kids are killing each other in the streets but they can spare a cop to drive a fucking councillor around? Cut the shit."

Approximately ten minutes later the dispatcher called for an ambulance to be sent to "the Jamaica Plain address previously mentioned."

Berman swiveled away from his terminal and faced the radios. "They're hiding something," he said. "Address previously mentioned. They only say that when they don't want anyone to pay attention. They never say it! What's going on over there?"

Berman rose and began pacing the wide area behind the city desk where the cheap, burnt-orange carpet was worn through from his incessant striding. He was disheveled in blue jeans, high-top Reeboks, and a button-down shirt with the tail half hanging out. He peered out over the city room searching for a reporter.

"Kimmy," he shouted to a reporter sitting at her desk reading the paper and drinking coffee. "Kimmy! Come on." The young woman rose reluctantly and walked up to the center of the U on the desk and faced Berman.

"Sorry to wake you," he said. "Get over to 112 Moss Hill Road in JP. Councillor Stewart's house. Something might be wrong."

"Like what?" said the reporter.

"They sent an ambulance is all I know," said Berman. "Hurry. And call me soonest."

He grabbed his phone and dialed the photo department.

"Jerry, we need a camera at 112 Moss Hill Road in JP. Councillor Stewart's home. Pronto. Something's up."

Donald Deegan was not thinking kind thoughts on this summer morning. He had never thought kindly about the High and Mighty One. For fifteen years Deegan had been forced to curry favor with Philip Stewart, and he had never liked it even a little bit. As was the case with many other politicians in town, Stewart regularly turned to Deegan for political counsel. And on this morning Deegan had been asked to breakfast with the High and Mighty One to discuss some political problem. Deegan had told Stewart when he called that his health was poor, that straying from his home was uncomfortable. But the High and Mighty One paid no attention. He asked Deegan to be at his house at nine A.M.

"We need a talk," Stewart had said. "A talk" meant there was a problem. "A talk" meant a strategy session, perhaps a lengthy one, a tiring one. When the councillor had phoned Deegan the afternoon before, he had sounded subdued. Deegan wondered whether it had been more than that. Had the sour note in his voice been that of fright? In recent months Stewart had not looked well. He had appeared sallow and dissipated. His body was older than its years, and Deegan wondered whether the bad cells had invaded the High and Mighty One.

Deegan thought of this as he dressed in a wrinkled blue wool suit that had not seen the dry cleaners since midwinter. He wore a white shirt and a black-and-gray-striped bowtie. Deegan was short and gaunt. His large round head, noticeably out of proportion to his body, and his oversized ears gave him the look of a leprechaun. In years past, his step had a spring to it, his voice a lilt. No more. A half million cigarettes had taken their toll. The elasticity in his lungs was gone, the bacilli covered in a thick layer of accumulated tar, not unlike a seabird after a tanker spill. His breathing was labored. Deegan used a portable oxygen machine. A hose ran from a small box that was attached to a mask which, when he felt the urge, he placed over his nose and mouth for reinvigoration. On this morning, he left his house and placed the machine in the car on the front passenger seat. He drove slowly in his black LTD up along Centre Street in West Roxbury, past the Holy Name Church, through a corner of Brookline and into Moss Hill. He parked in front of Stewart's house, a modest-sized cape, well kept, with a small patch of lawn in front. In the warm morning air, bees buzzed around the chrysanthemums and dahlias in the yard.

Deegan knocked on the front door and then again. He pressed the bell repeatedly but there was no answer. He was about to return home when he thought of checking the rear porch where Stewart spent much of his time in summer. Deegan moved slowly, following the flagstone path around the side of the house. He rounded the corner to the backyard and glanced over toward the screened-in porch. Over the shrubs, he could see Stewart's head. The arrogant prick wouldn't even get up off his ass to come answer the door, thought Deegan. Deegan turned the corner and followed the path to the porch and only then did he look up, and it was at that moment that he saw Philip Stewart slumped in the chair, a mass of dead weight collapsed into a heap, his head hanging back, mouth and eyes open, a sizable stain, reddish-brown, on the front of his shirt and sleeveless sweater.

Donald Deegan's heart pounded within his chest. Later he would sit back at home in his red leather easy chair, a generous tumbler of Glenlivet in one hand, a Marlboro in the other, and permit a half smile to crease his face. The High and Mighty One cold and white and stiff, his dick like the stem of an umbrella under his trousers. What a sight! It was later, after his duty had been done, that Donald Deegan sat in the privacy of his own home and raised a glass to the demise of Philip Stewart.

But at the moment Deegan did his duty. He went next door and called the police department liaison to the City Council, a man he knew well, and asked him to send a car. The man complied without question and it was that radio call which Howard Berman heard on the scanner. And it was the next call, made by the first officer to arrive at the scene, which brought an ambulance to the house.

The *Post* photographer arrived in time to capture on film two

EMTs, led by a paramedic, carrying a stretcher with Stewart's body covered in a black plastic sheet. The photographer clicked away as they loaded Stewart's body into the back of the ambulance, and shut the doors. Kimmy Brooks, the reporter, got no comment on the record from either of the cops on the scene, though they did confirm off-the-record that the body was indeed that of Philip P. Stewart, and that he had been shot at least once, probably twice, in the chest. When she heard that, she raced to a pay phone and broke the news to Berman.

Upon hearing this stunning bit of information, Berman strode quickly to the corner office belonging to the *Post*'s editor in chief, Roy Johnson.

"Roy, terrible news," said Berman, his heart racing. "Phil Stewart has just been found dead at his home. Murdered, apparently."

"My God," Johnson gasped, slumping back in his chair as though he'd been hammered in the stomach. "Who could do that to such a man?"

"Two shots to the chest," said Berman. "We've got a pic of the EMTs carrying the body to the van."

Johnson was a veteran newsman, a tough man who'd seen every news story imaginable, but he sat, thunderstruck. Johnson had known Stewart well. He had liked and respected the man. Johnson sat at his desk, looking up at Berman, searching for some explanation.

"*Why?*" he implored Berman.

Berman shrugged. "No idea," he said. "Nothing from the cops yet."

"Now I've seen everything," he said quietly. "There is no point below which human beings will not stoop." He shook his head and stared out the window. "Insane."

Berman nodded. He knew that Johnson and Stewart had been friends. He did not want to appear crass, but he was far more interested in how his newspaper covered Stewart's death than in the fact that the councillor was dead. Berman had an immense amount of work ahead of him and was itching to move. "Think we can get two clear pages inside, Roy?"

Johnson nodded absently.

Berman turned and half ran toward the city desk. This was big, he thought, adrenaline surging through his body.

This would be a great news day.

Det. Thomas McCormack of the Boston Police Department Homicide Division was beeped the moment the EMTs arrived. He was there in minutes. McCormack asked the EMTs, two uniformed officers, and Donald Deegan to wait outside for him. He liked to study a setting alone, in the still that always settled over a murder scene after the fact.

He stood by himself on the porch and took it all in. There was a padded lounge chair facing out toward the backyard and another chair opposite. On a side table next to the padded chair was an ashtray, three-quarters of a pack of Pall Malls, a book of matches, and an empty Moxie can. On another table was a radio. McCormack noted that it was tuned to WRKO-AM. On the floor halfway between the two chairs was a hand towel. McCormack picked it up by a corner and examined it. There was a small hole and powder burns. The towel, it was clear, had been used to muffle the shots. McCormack went into the kitchen. It was small and neat. On the table was another ashtray and more Pall Malls. There was a portable television on the counter next to a microwave. On the far end of the counter, next to the hallway leading from the front of the house, was a set of keys and a wallet, which McCormack opened. It contained Stewart's driver's license and assorted credit cards in his name. McCormack counted the cash—eleven one-hundred-dollar bills, three fifties, assorted twenties, tens, and singles—more than $1,300 in all. A great deal of money for a city councillor earning $38,000 a year.

McCormack pulled a plastic bag from his suitcoat pocket, placed the wallet inside, and sealed it. He would call in a variety of investigators and they would comb every inch, quite literally, of the house and the yard. They would knock on every door in the neighborhood. They would write page after page after page of reports. And what would they conclude? McCormack wondered.

McCormack thought the scene rather odd. How would he describe it in his report? He looked around the room. Nothing, save for the towel, was out of place. Nothing had been disturbed. The matches were stacked neatly on top of the red Pall Mall package. The Moxie can, though empty, was upright. On impulse, McCormack picked up the can and placed it into a plastic bag. Then he slid it inside his jacket pocket. He looked around the porch and out into the kitchen. Clinical was the word that came to mind. Clean. Neat. No muss, no fuss.

McCormack went outside to the ambulance and had the EMTs fold back the plastic cover partway. The detective looked at the face of the dead councillor. His lids had been rolled closed by an EMT but his mouth remained open. McCormack walked over to where several officers had gathered by the side of the house. They had brought out a chair for Donald Deegan, who did not appear well. Between McCormack and Deegan, long-time acquaintances, there was mutual distrust. McCormack asked the others for a moment alone with Deegan. Deegan explained that he was scheduled to meet with Stewart that morning and had arrived for their discussion when he found the councillor dead.

"What was the meeting about?" McCormack asked.

"He didn't say," said Deegan. "He just said he wanted to have a talk."

McCormack nodded toward the house. "You touched nothing, I assume?" he said.

"The doorknob," said Deegan.

McCormack nodded. Wiseguy.

"Where were you last night?" McCormack asked.

You prick, thought Deegan. "At home," he replied.

"With anyone?" asked the detective.

Deegan paused for a moment. "Christie Brinkley," he replied.

McCormack looked at the ugly little man who seemed more dwarf than not, looked at his gray pallor and his withered face and couldn't help himself. He laughed quietly.

Deegan smiled.

"As you know, detective, I live alone," said Deegan. "I'm always alone. Except for a visiting nurse now and then."

McCormack nodded. "Any thoughts?" he asked.

Deegan considered the question and smiled. "The town will

mourn him," Deegan said. "They think he's a saint."

McCormack looked down at his shoes and nodded, a frown on his fleshy face.

Deegan smiled. "We know different," he said. "Not many knew him, really. Very few saw his other side."

"Did you do it?" McCormack suddenly asked.

Deegan studied the detective. He shook his head slowly and smiled again, mischeviously this time. "No, detective," he replied. "Did you?"

"Let's meet!" Berman shouted out to his assistant editors stationed around the city desk. "Gather round."

Five of the six were there at that moment and they assembled in a huddle around Berman at the head of the desk. "Philip Stewart is dead, shot in the chest twice," he said.

There was a collective gasp from his assistant editors.

"They just found him at his house," said Berman.

"How do we know?" one asked.

"There were a couple of radio calls to the house—cruiser, then an ambulance. I sent Kimmy. She confirmed it with the cops. We have a photo of the EMTs with the body."

"Was anyone else there?" asked another editor, referring to other newspapers or television stations.

Berman shook his head, clearly pleased that the *Post* had a jump on the story and an exclusive photo.

"Obviously, we'll blow it out tomorrow," he said. "We've got two clear pages inside. How's this for a package: main news story on the death, cops stuff, etcetera, which we should put two, maybe even three people on. Let's put both the City Hall guys on it, plus someone working the cops. We'll do a backgrounder on his life—in effect a long obit. Also we'll need a highlights box with a chronology of the major events in his life. And a big react story including pols, businesspeople, clergy, community activists, and so on. And man-on-the-street."

"We should also do a page-one box giving the basic information on arrangements—wake, funeral, any memorial service, whatever," said one of his assistants.

"Good. And let's bear down on the reaction story," said

Berman. "Lots of voices. He was an authentic hero. The activists *loved* this guy. So the react story will have real people and pols."

"What about a sidebar on the day at Spruce Street," someone suggested. "What if we have someone go down and just record what happens? Write the scene from the moment people hear the news through the rest of the day?"

The Spruce Street Inn was the city's largest and most important homeless shelter. Stewart had risen from once having been a guest there—a broken, homeless alcoholic—to being chairman of the board of directors and its political champion in the city. His was a Lazarus-like tale. He had risen from near-death, defeating alcohol and overcoming hopelessness. Even as a member of the council, he was at Spruce Street several times a week checking on operations, serving food to the needy, washing clothes, or doing a variety of menial tasks. He still served in a volunteer capacity as chairman of the Greater Boston Shelter Coalition, a position which gave him substantial control over the disbursement of millions of dollars annually.

"Good," said Berman. "Let's get someone over there now so they'll be there when word gets out. One more thing," said Berman. "Who's going to do the bio piece? It should be mostly from the clips but with some fresh quotes. It's got to be well written. Who can do that?"

"Cronin would be perfect for that," someone suggested, referring to Frank Cronin, one of the *Post*'s best reporters, who specialized in long investigative and feature stories.

"Damnit, he's away," said Berman. "Vacation."

Early that afternoon, word of Stewart's death spread throughout the city like a prairie fire in August heat. The local TV stations broke into scheduled programming with bulletins. Throughout Boston people collected in front of radios and TVs as they numbly sat and watched or listened. There were, of course, those to whom Stewart was merely another pol whose face they'd seen flash by on the evening news, but to thousands of other Bostonians, Stewart was an icon whose death left them stricken with grief.

By late afternoon a crowd of several hundred people had gathered on the sprawling brick City Hall plaza three stories below the windows of Stewart's Council office. Another fifty or more stood stiffly on Moss Hill Road in front of the councillor's home, which was under siege from Boston police searching for clues. Off to one side of the crowd, behind police lines marked by bright yellow tape, was a group of media people—a half dozen print, TV, and radio reporters and three cameras from the city's network affiliates. As afternoon gave way to early evening and workers began leaving downtown, more and more people gravitated to City Hall Plaza, where the crowd swelled to nearly a thousand.

As he did every night at six o'clock, Berman interrupted the predeadline rush in the city room to watch the evening news on the local television stations. Perched on a platform raised slightly above his desk were three small Hitachis, each tuned to a different station. He watched all three, shifting the sound up on one and down on the others as a story would catch his eye. On this night, a dozen reporters and editors formed a half circle behind Berman, watching stories on the murder.

All three stations led with it and all dedicated almost ten minutes of their airtime to the story. The parade of people appearing on the screen to offer words of praise for Stewart included both of Massachusetts's U.S. senators, the governor and lieutenant governor, the cardinal, and the mayor of Boston. Stewart's colleagues on the City Council seemed particularly stricken. One poignant scene showed two council members, Eddie Keaveney of South Boston, an arch conservative, and Jamal Lewis of Roxbury, a liberal black—two men who had battled for years and whose enmity had verged on physical violence at times—weeping and embracing in the Council chambers.

As dusk gave way to darkness over the sorrowful city of Boston that night, a couple began passing among the crowd at City Hall Plaza distributing candles. Soon the throng began moving slowly down Tremont Street, gathering mourners as the procession made its way through the city, past the Common, and into the South End. When word reached the Spruce Street Inn that the crowd was headed there, volunteers backed a flatbed truck up to the front of the building, across from a city park. Powerful klieg lights from the TV trucks illuminated the makeshift stage while the mourners' candles cast a soft glow into the night sky. Police department technicians hastily rigged a sound system, and within a few moments of the crowd's arrival, the Inn's chaplain, Father Tom McHugh, offered a brief prayer for the repose of Phil Stewart's soul. He then introduced the mayor, who had been out jogging when he had been tracked down and given the news that morning. He had immediately gone to the scene of the crime and was still in jogging clothes when he took the stage. The mayor was a tall, athletic man who had built his political career through his relentless work on behalf of neighborhood groups.

"We have lost today, because of an act of brutal and senseless violence, perhaps the finest, the most decent citizen of our city, a man who well lived the Christian life, who was the embodiment of that to which many of us aspire. To have risen from the depths of despair, from the clutches of alcoholism, to become one of the most effective, if not to say beloved, members of our Council was in itself an achievement of Herculean proportions. But even more inspiring to me was Phil's incredible ability to maintain a caring attitude toward others. He and I worked together closely on issues of housing and homelessness, issues of health care, crime and drugs, alcohol rehabilitation. And I cannot remember a single instance, not one, when he placed his own interests ahead of the interest of someone in need."

The mayor paused and gazed out over the hushed crowd of mourners.

"Many of you may be familiar with this story," he said. "To me, it so perfectly represents what Phil was all about . . ."

Some in the crowd, knowing well the story that the mayor was about to tell—for it had become part of the Stewart lore—began sobbing.

"It was a number of years ago now, back when Phil and I were serving together on the Council. It was in Dorchester, after a community meeting. And we were walking along when a young fellow approached us. It appeared he was going to speak with us, but, instead, he suddenly charged forward—it was a freezing cold winter day, a bitterly cold morning—and the young man, who we later found out was disturbed, without warning charged forward and assaulted Phil. He punched him in the face, knocking him into a frozen snowbank. It just so happened that the community meeting had been on a matter related to the police department and several officers were on the scene immediately restraining the young fellow. The poor soul had been deinstitutionalized, as it turned out. He was sitting there on the ground, being restrained by an officer and wearing only an old workshirt, no hat or gloves or jacket.

"The officers were about to arrest him but Phil interceded. He would not permit it. 'He'll get worse in jail, my friends,' Phil said. 'I'll take him down to the Inn.' And then what did he do? What did this decent man who has been today taken away from us with such brutality? He took off his overcoat and draped it over the man's shoulders. *He gave him the coat off his back!*"

Hundreds of Bostonians in the candlelit park joined their mayor in weeping openly at the loss of Philip Stewart.

The mayor turned abruptly from the microphone, his head bowed, and walked quickly from the platform. He was followed by other speakers who similiarly praised Stewart.

When it grew late and the crowd had dwindled some, and Father McHugh returned to the stage for a final prayer to close the evening, a remarkable thing occurred: People Stewart had helped through the years spontaneously came up out of the audience to tell of his effect on their lives. A balding, middle-aged man in a suit recalled his days as an alcoholic street person and said it had been the shelter of the Inn and personal counseling from Phil Stewart that had enabled him to turn his life around. An older man who appeared to be approaching seventy had a similiar story. And a young woman said she had escaped a life of drug abuse and prostitution with Phil Stewart's help. The testimony continued late into the night, beyond the time Berman had to put the final touches on his package for the morning paper.

By eleven P.M., the layout editor had put together page one, which included a main news story and a long reaction piece with quotes—and wails of sorrow—from people in virtually every neighborhood of the city. Also on page one were two pictures:

one of the candlelight vigil and another of Stewart's body being carried from the house. On the inside pages to which the front-page story jumped were additional photos of the vigil, the mayor, and two shots of Stewart. There were also inside stories on the day at the Spruce Street Inn—a touching feature on the profound sense of loss suffered there by the staff and guests alike. There were sidebars on the spontaneous gathering at City Hall that led to the vigil at Spruce Street. And, finally, there was a piece about his life.

Late that night, after the first edition had rolled off the presses, Berman slumped back in his chair. He thought about the next day and the direction the *Post*'s coverage would take. He wondered who would do such a thing and why. Earlier in the day, another editor speculated that it was a random killing. Berman dismissed that possibility out of hand. Random killings were rare. People killed for very specific reasons, usually money or sex. In most cases, murderers were acquainted with their victims, often they were related. Berman believed Stewart was killed for a reason, and he wanted desperately to know that reason. He wished Cronin was around. He would know what to do, how to approach the story. Cronin was his best reporter, not his best writer or stylist but his best reporter. Cronin went into the trenches and dug and dug and dug some more until he unearthed the story. He was not fashionable, but he was effective. Frank Cronin always delivered.

CHAPTER

2

"Suspects?" asked *Post*'s editor Roy Johnson.

Berman shook his head. "Not as of five minutes ago." The two men were in Johnson's corner office, shortly after eight A.M. on Thursday, just shy of twenty-four hours since the discovery of Stewart's body.

"I don't want to get beat on this," said Johnson. "You know how these things go. They'll have nothing for a few days, even weeks, then, bang. Arrest, arraignment, all big news."

Berman nodded. "There'll be white heat to bring someone in fast."

"Are they speculating on motive?"

"They're mystified," said Berman. "I'm not sure they know any more than we do."

"Which is nothing," said Johnson, sullenly.

"Which is nothing."

Johnson drew back in his chair, propping his chin on his hand. "What do you think, Howard?"

"I honest to God have no idea," said Berman. "I really didn't know the guy, except by reputation."

Johnson nodded in disgust. "He did more damn good for the unfortunates of this town than anybody." Johnson said it as though challenging Berman to disagree.

Berman fidgeted, then rose from his seat and paced across the room. "Everybody's asking the same question," said Berman. "Why would anyone kill such a sainted one? It's all over the talk shows."

"Unless they were deranged," said Johnson.

The editor frowned and shook his head. Though he knew this was painful for Johnson, Berman was not known for his bedside manner. "I don't mean to seem indelicate, Roy, but I'm frankly more interested in our coverage of this than anything else right now. And that means who do we assign to chase it for the foreseeable future. All my best reporters are on projects. I'm covering the city with kids."

Berman wanted Frank Cronin to cover the story, but Cronin was on vacation, and when he returned he was planning to continue working on a series Johnson had proposed on the financial exploitation of the elderly. Rather than asking bluntly to shift Cronin off that, he wanted Johnson to see they had little choice.

"Who's wired into the cops these days?" Johnson asked.

"Cronin," said Berman.

"DA's office?"

Berman nodded. "Cronin."

"Well, shit, he's our best digger, no?"

Berman nodded again.

Johnson did not appear pleased. Cronin had already invested a month in Johnson's project. At a daily newspaper, where a week is considered too long to work on almost any story, a month was considered indecent.

Johnson screwed up his face, then relaxed. "Do we have a choice?"

"I don't think we do," said Berman, rising and heading for the door. He could not place the call to Vermont to track Cronin down soon enough. The thought of getting beaten on any aspect of the story by the city's television stations or the *Record-American* made Berman feel physically ill.

Berman was close to the door, bidding Johnson goodbye when the editor stopped him and asked, "What's the deal with Cronin, anyway?"

Like most editors, Johnson spent the bulk of his time meeting with other editors. He had had little more than perfunctory contact with the paper's reporting staff (except for the Washington and a couple of foreign bureaus, which got him out of town for a few days). Save for a couple of meetings on the series about financial exploitation of the elderly, Johnson had had little to do with Cronin. Johnson was relatively new on the job. Years earlier he'd worked at the *Post,* then gone off to *Time* magazine. Now he was back as editor. But so much had changed in the days he'd been gone that he still didn't have a good grasp of which reporters were best suited for certain stories.

Fortunately for Berman, just as his hesitation to respond grew uncomfortably long, Johnson's phone rang. The editor of the Boston *Post* was a sophisticated man, but he had one glaringly rude habit for which Berman was suddenly grateful: Johnson often held protracted phone conversations while one of his employees sat in his office waiting to continue a discussion.

The question posed by Johnson—what was the story of one Frank Cronin—had been asked of Berman many times, yet he had never quite mastered an answer. While Johnson talked on the phone, Berman considered the matter.

To start with, Berman thought, Cronin was the best reporter at the paper. In ten years, Cronin was the only *Post* reporter to have won a Pulitzer Prize. The award had come for a series in which Cronin had traced the perilous passage of a Vietnamese family from Saigon to Boston.

But what made Cronin a character of such intrigue around the *Post* was a far more dubious distinction. Three years earlier he had been suspended for a month from the *Post* when it was determined that he had violated the paper's ethics rules. Since no one had ever been fired from the *Post* for any reason, suspension was the closest thing to professional capital punishment that existed at the paper. Cronin's transgression had come in the midst of an investigative piece he was doing on the superintendent of the city clinic, a woman who had a mattress address in Boston but who actually lived in the suburbs. Were she to be found out, she would likely be fired. During the period in which Cronin was working on the story, a night cleaning woman at the *Post* approached him in tears. Her name was Geneen Ouelette and Cronin had become friendly with her years earlier when they had been on the overnight shift together. She was in her early fifties and had survived a series of disasters in her life, struggling always to keep her family intact. She had lived through separation and reconciliation with her husband, his year-long layoff, the cerebral palsy of a daughter. But now she had told Cronin she feared she was on the verge of losing her nineteen-year-old son, Daniel. He had become a drunk, and she had been told that by far the best facility in the area was at the city clinic, but she discovered there was a six- to nine-month waiting period for the program. She learned from a friend who worked as an orderly at the clinic that most of the patients got in through political influence. Word was, the friend told Geneen, that none of the twelve people then in the program had ever been on the waiting list; all had been placed through politicians.

When Geneen explained the situation to him, Cronin saw that it was a great potential story. The idea that one needed the intercession of a state representative or a city councillor to secure a steel-frame bed for someone suffering from DTs was despicable, a perfect example of the venality of Boston politics. But to Geneen, this was hardly the point. She cared not at all for the systemic problem; her concern was her son. As a reporter, it was Cronin's job to look at the situation differently. By writing about the need for political influence at the clinic, he knew that, overnight, he could alter the admissions process. It was a stark choice; the correct course for a journalist was obvious.

Geneen believed Cronin had influence, that he knew important people in the city government. It wasn't really true, but she didn't know that, and so she asked for his help; she asked him to make a call, talk with whomever needed talking to and to get her son into the program. And quickly.

It would be seen later, by those who admired Cronin, as an aberration, a temporary lapse in judgment. But he never felt that way. When Berman asked him much later what he would do if he had it to do over again, he said he wouldn't change anything, he would still help Geneen.

He knew the consequences would be serious, but he went to the clinic, nonetheless, and had a private conversation with the superintendent. He told her that he knew about her mattress address but that he would ignore it if she would place Geneen's son in alcohol rehab. She readily agreed.

That very night space was made in the clinic for Daniel

Ouelette. Once he was admitted, Cronin went to Berman and confessed his transgression. It was a corrupt act and he knew it. Berman was furious and demanded an explanation. Cronin said he thought it over and decided that he could not use the information Geneen had given him for a story. It was a private matter. He learned about the political nature of the clinic not by reporting but in the context of a plea for help from a friend. To turn around and not only refuse to help the friend but then to also use her information for a story would have been unethical, he argued. More important, he told Berman, Geneen was desperate. This was her son, her child, they were talking about.

"She's kept that family together through hard times, Howard," Cronin had said. "It's more than you or I have ever done."

Berman was stunned by the whole matter and felt sure Cronin would be fired. Cronin did not, Berman recalled, seem to care terribly what the punishment was, though Berman knew Cronin would have been deeply hurt by a dismissal. Some senior editors said anything short of firing would be unthinkable for such a grievous error, but the tradition at the *Post* was that everybody got a second chance, no matter the transgression.

After the suspension, Cronin achieved a kind of celebrity status within the building—venerated by some as a hero who had subsumed his personal and professional interests for the good of another; scorned by others who saw him as one who had sold his journalistic integrity. Through it all, Berman had marveled at Cronin's equanimity. He had made his decision and then, with a Zen-like calm, he lived with it.

"So what's with him?" Johnson asked abruptly, hanging up the phone.

"How do you mean?" Berman asked.

"Just generally," Johnson said. "I don't feel like I know him really."

"He's hard to get to know," said Berman. "He loves his work, you know that. He's a nut about jogging, pumping iron. Single, never married." Berman paused. "I don't know what else to say."

"Is he as arrogant as they say?"

Berman felt a surge of anger. Johnson was trying to bait him for some reason. Cronin was hardly arrogant, though the politically correct crowd at the *Post,* the self-satisfied crowd that had so disapproved of his help for Geneen Ouelette, peddled the notion that he was.

"Aloof," said Berman. "Distant. Reserved."

Berman knew a good deal more about Cronin than he told Roy Johnson. He knew, for example, that Cronin's greatest passion, outside his work, was his farmhouse in the hills of eastern Vermont. Berman knew Cronin had been a hockey star at Dartmouth and had been drafted by Boston in the National Hockey League. Berman also knew that, once or twice a year, Cronin drank himself into a stupor over a long weekend. Berman would not have known that unless he had once been called upon to bail Cronin out of jail in upstate New York, where he had gone on a bender and gotten into a scrape with the police. He knew that Cronin gave money to people at the paper who needed it, loans where repayment was never expected. Johnson's phone rang again, and this time when the editor began to chat Berman quietly slipped out of the office. As he returned to the city desk Berman thought that he knew Frank Cronin better than anyone else at the *Post.* And still, Berman realized, he didn't *really* know him.

Cronin was difficult to reach in Vermont, something that had long frustrated Berman. Cronin had no telephone at his ramshackle farmhouse and had resisted Berman's entreaties to have one installed, even at *Post* expense. Cronin's explanation had been simple: "If it's easy to call me, you'll call me, Howard," he had told Berman. "And when I'm in Vermont, I don't want you to call me."

Cronin had once given Berman the number of a fellow who ran a small dairy farm a few miles down the valley from Cronin and said he could try and reach him through the farmer in an emergency. Right after his discussion with Johnson, Berman called the farmer and left a message for Cronin to call back. Late that afternoon, Cronin phoned in. He had just seen a story about Stewart in the Rutland *Herald.*

Berman was tense. "We need you on this right away, Frank," he said. "Can you come right now?"

"What happened exactly?" he asked Berman.

"Nobody heard or saw anything," said Berman. "They found him on the porch Wednesday morning. Cops estimate he'd been dead about twelve hours."

"How'd we get it?" Cronin asked.

"I heard a call on the radio—squad car, then ambulance to the address," said Berman. "I knew it was his house."

"Pretty good," said Cronin, impressed that his friend had sifted it out of the radio traffic.

Berman smiled. "Yeah, we had a pic on one of the body being carried to the ambulance. Nobody else had it."

"Suspects?" Cronin asked.

"Nothing so far," said Berman. "None yet. They're at a loss as far as motive goes." Pause. "Look, we need you on it, Frankie. Right away. We can't get beat on this. The heat's on here."

This was what Cronin did. This was who he was. His mission was to dig beneath the surface, to find facts and motives and drama—the stuff that made the smudged ink slopped on newsprint each day reach up and grab readers' attention. Cronin reveled in the process of digging, of finding new information and being the first to report it. There were others who were brilliant analysts of political or world events. There were gorgeous stylists whose feature stories could move even the stoniest heart.

Cronin was different. He was a man who gathered facts, wove them into a coherent package, and put them into the paper.

"What do you have in mind?"

"Just jump in," said Berman, speaking rapidly. "Jump in and see what there is. Follow the trail. Scrounge around and see what you come up with. What have the cops got, motives, suspects, anything. I don't care what angle you come at the story from, Frank, I just care that you come at the story, attack it. Get us something."

Berman hesitated, then said, "Sloane's on it." He was referring to Assistant District Attorney Susan Sloane.

Cronin was silent. He could picture her in his mind. He often did that, often thought back to their times together, quiet moments they had shared. He recalled their vacations together, informal dinners at her place or his. It had been a long time since he had seen her, and he thought that encountering her now while working on this story would be difficult for both of them.

"You there?" Berman asked.

"I'm here."

"She'd talk to you, maybe steer us in the right direction."

"Howard, don't be so crass."

Berman's voice betrayed his nervous tension. "I'm telling you, Frank, we can't get beat on this story," he said. "They'll rip my head off if the *Record* has something we don't."

"What do you think he was really like," Cronin wondered aloud.

Berman sounded annoyed. "What's that supposed to mean?"

"Just that," Cronin said. "I wonder what he was like. Underneath it all."

"Well, isn't it possible he was really like what he *appeared* to be really like?" Berman asked.

"Of course," said Cronin. "But even if that's what he was like most of the time, I wonder what he was like the rest of the time? What else did he do with his life? What would make somebody want to kill him?"

Berman shrugged. "What the rest of us do," he said. "Watch the Sox. Smoke cigarettes. Take walks. Get laid."

"That's not what I'm talking about," said Cronin.

"Jesus, Frank, you can pry at the depths of his soul later," said Berman. "I'd just like to know who killed him and why."

"I'll drive down tonight," said Cronin. "See you in your office in the morning."

"We cannot get beat on this, Frankie," said Berman, pleadingly. "We just cannot."

Cronin woke shortly after five A.M., four hours after he'd arrived from Vermont, to the sounds of birds chirping in the pine trees outside his apartment window. He rose, quickly showered, dressed in khaki pants and a blue-and-white-striped dress shirt, and went into the kitchen where he made coffee. He moved quietly in the early mornings in the hopes that he would not wake his landlady, a frail, elderly woman. Cronin's apartment, which was the second floor of a two-family, consisted of two bedrooms, a kitchen, and gumwood paneled living room. The house was set in a well-kept section of the Roslindale neighborhood of Boston, where the houses tended to be close together, each separated by a compact, neatly trimmed lawn or garden. The neighborhood was a mixture of two- and three-family houses occupied, for the most part, by Italian and Irish Americans and Greek immigrants. Many of the Irish and Italians worked at the gas company, or for the government—the Post Office, fire or police departments. The Greeks owned stores, restaurants, and sub shops.

At 5:40 A.M., Cronin walked quietly down the back steps and drove to St. John's Chapel, a small stone church on the grounds of what was once a monastery on the edge of an arboretum in Jamaica Plain. The chapel was staffed by Jesuits from Boston College who lived in a large tudor-style home next door. There were seven of them, all doctoral candidates in various disciplines, principally theology. Each man celebrated Mass one day a week at six A.M. On average, Cronin went three or four mornings a week, and generally saw the same faces each day: an older man, in his early sixties, who carried a black lunchpail and wore a Boston Bruins jacket; three elderly women well into their seventies who wore veils; a cop who lived around the corner; a husband and wife who appeared to be his own age. Occasionally there were others, though he had rarely seen more than a half dozen people there on a given day.

Cronin arrived a few minutes early, as was his custom, and took his usual seat against the cool stone wall in the last row. The chapel was ancient and musty, with worn oak pews and tattered red-leather prayer books. The windows, of authentic stained glass, depicted various biblical scenes. Waterstains appeared in spots on the granite walls, and in winter, the wind whistled through cracks in the door and window casings. In the air was the smell of incense, of burning candle wax. Along the walls, carved into the stone by some long-dead mason, were the Stations of the Cross, the sacrament in memory of each stop on Christ's road to the Crucifixion. The detailed stone carvings depicted Jesus's being condemned to death. They showed him weighted down with the Cross as he climbed Calvary. They showed Christ being nailed to the Cross, dying, being removed and placed in the sepulchre.

Somehow, in the hush of the chapel, the depiction of this terrible violence committed against Christ seemed coolly lacking in passion. The fourteen stations, seven carvings along each sidewall, served as silent ornament, no threat to the tranquillity of the holy place. There was a refugelike quality to this chapel for Cronin. He felt less judged in the presence of God than in the presence of man.

Cronin arrived at the *Post* a few minutes after seven, and went directly to the weight room to workout. In forty minutes, he could complete the circuit of Nautilus machines twice. It was a decent workout and, along with jogging three times a week, kept him in good physical condition. In shorts, tank top, and sneakers, Cronin had the well-muscled look of an athlete and appeared bigger than he did in his normal workclothes of loose-fitting dress shirt, jacket, and khaki pants. Fully dressed, hands stuffed into his pants pockets, slouching by his desk chatting with coworkers, Cronin looked smaller than he was. But in gym clothes, he looked every bit his six feet two inches, 195 pounds. Cronin had always been big and powerful. As a kid, he had been a power-hitter in baseball. He had also been a moderately successful Golden Gloves boxer and a feared power forward in hockey. In college, his hockey teammates, noticing his bulging forearms, had nicknamed him Popeye.

Cronin's appearance was otherwise unremarkable. He had a short scar that ran at a slight angle away from his left eye, a remnant of the hockey wars, and a thin nose that was slightly too prominent. His jaw was set in a strong, square line and his thick, jet-black hair formed a widow's peak high on his forehead. His eyes—a deep, rich green that in some light appeared to be a luminous black—were his most attractive feature. Though he was not a strikingly handsome man, not one women noticed in a crowd, he was attractive enough, and had grown more so with age.

Cronin showered, dressed, and was at his desk in the city

room by eight A.M. He looked around and saw that he had virtually the entire place to himself. One assistant metro editor monitored the radio traffic at the city desk, and one student intern slept in a chair nearby. Cronin liked the early morning quiet of the newsroom. It was the only time of day when there was a letup from the constant din of the place. Throughout the rest of the day there were dozens of people chatting, laughing, arguing, shouting back and forth across the room. Cronin found the quiet of the early morning the most productive time to plan and organize. As he sat at his computer terminal Cronin could hear the hum of cool air being forced through the duct above his head. And from beyond a cluster of desks sixty feet away came the sound of a vacuum cleaner. Soon, with the vacuuming done and the worker moved on, he could hear only the whoosh of air through the vent. The room was eerily silent. He gazed around and saw dozens of terminals perched on desks, the square heads of aliens, the cursors on their screens blinking on and off in a sickly green color.

His desk was piled high with stacks of documents he had gathered for his now aborted series on the financial exploitation of the elderly. He recognized that the topic was important and the sort of thing a major newspaper should tackle, but it had bored him and he was glad to be rid of it. There were piles of documents stacked so high they shielded him from the woman at an adjacent desk. Cronin didn't have much space, nobody in the city room did, but what he had was tucked into the quietest corner in the room, a modest but welcome perquisite of his stature at the paper. In another profession, someone of Cronin's worth would be rich with material rewards—hefty salary and bonus, stock options, and more—but in the newspaper business, where reporters were, on a comparative basis, poorly paid, the stars were rewarded differently. The ultimate perk was the freedom to write on topics of one's own choosing.

Cronin had earned his stripes not because he was possessed of a magnificent natural gift, but because of his dogged determination. He approached his work with passion and drive, working whatever hours were necessary, including nights and weekends, until a story was completed. It appeared to his colleagues at the newspaper that he had little in the way of a private life, though they did not know for sure.

Cronin ignored the internal politics of the *Post,* a consuming occupation for many reporters and editors there. He preferred the work of newspapering. There was no aspect of reporting that put him off. Even sifting through documents, a tedious but often crucial process, held a certain fascination for him. He had learned through the years how to coax stories out of people. With primary sources—people who help a reporter gather the basic building blocks of an article—the key was to get the person to tell his or her story. There was a difference between persuading someone to answer questions and convincing them to tell a story. This was a crucial distinction many journalists did not fully grasp. To tell a story people had to feel a certain empathy from a reporter, and Cronin conveyed that feeling naturally, without artifice. Through the years, he had cultivated many good sources in the city, including a number of law enforcement people. In the Stewart story, none would be more crucial than the lead homicide detective on the case, Tom McCormack.

Cronin had become acquainted with Detective McCormack a number of years earlier, when Cronin had written a series of articles about a case on which McCormack had worked that involved a man wrongfully convicted of murder and imprisoned for sixteen years. The combination of McCormack's investigation and Cronin's articles had resulted in the man, B. D. Edlund, being freed from prison and given a half-million-dollar annuity by the state legislature.

Cronin had not easily won McCormack's trust. The detective had a visceral aversion to the *Post.* Like many people in the city, McCormack resented the newspaper's having crusaded on behalf of forced busing back in the 1970s. McCormack did not quarrel with the federal court's determination that the Boston public schools had been willfully segregated and, as a result, that the system denied equal opportunity to thousands of black children. McCormack passionately supported equal access for all children. But he agreed with many others in the city—who were, to their sorrow, eventually proven correct—that the busing order as implemented by the courts was catastrophic. It drove tens of thousands of stable middle-class families to the suburbs, never to return. But the *Post* never understood the legitimate views of the working ethnic families in the city. The newspaper had been condescending and sanctimonious throughout the busing ordeal. Perhaps worst of all, the *Post* editors and reporters who worked for the imposition of busing on the city were personally unaffected by it. They lived in the suburbs and were not subject to the busing decree.

But McCormack saw Cronin in a different light. The detective had been impressed with Cronin's dogged work on the Edlund case, and he had come to view Cronin as a *Post* aberration—someone not guided by liberal orthodoxy. In the years since the Edlund case, McCormack had helped Frank Cronin on a couple of stories.

Cronin rarely approached McCormack, for he felt that a source so valuable should only be tapped on the most important stories. There was no question that the Stewart matter qualified. And so it was that on Friday, the day of Phil Stewart's funeral, Frank Cronin called Detective McCormack and they agreed to meet that evening at Larz Anderson Park in Brookline, just a few miles from police headquarters in Boston's Back Bay. McCormack was particularly fond of the park's vantage point on a hill with a sweeping view of the city. A couple of nights a week, after leaving work, Tom McCormack would drive out to the park and smoke a cigar while idly gazing out over Boston.

At the appointed time, Cronin saw McCormack turn into the parking lot in a black Crown Victoria. He pulled himself out of the car and began walking the hundred or so feet to the nearest bench. It was a short, but painful journey for Tom McCormack. Cronin could see that his limp had worsened. McCormack's right leg had been seriously injured in a shootout during a raid just two years earlier.

McCormack made his way to the bench, where he sat sideways, positioning himself so that he had a full view of the city skyline. He was wearing a rumpled gray suit and wingtips, and he carried a brown paper bag from which he removed two bottles of Sam Adams. He popped the top off with a church key and handed one to Cronin, who gratefully accepted it. He opened the other and took a long sip. McCormack seemed old to Cronin. The detective was only in his early sixties, but he didn't look well. He was pale, too heavy, and, judging from the lines in his face, Frank guessed that the pain made him grimace too often. McCormack had a broad forehead, a sharp beak of a nose, and a full head of curly salt and pepper hair. His skin was flushed and the veins around his nose had begun to show through. His eyes were kind.

The two men gazed out toward the northeast. On a long hill that sloped away in front of them kids were playing Frisbee with a dog. In the playground off to one side, beyond the grove of trees and picnic tables, a half dozen parents watched over their little ones. One mother pushed a giddy little boy higher and higher on a swing.

"I was sorry to hear about your wife," said Cronin. "That was very sad."

McCormack nodded. "I appreciated your note," he said. "It means a lot."

McCormack looked out across the city as the setting sun cast a softer light on the landscape. In the distance, planes from Logan, as though in slow motion, rose soundlessly into the air or glided gently to earth. McCormack sipped his beer. From Cronin's angle, he could not see whether the detective's eyes were fixed upon some object in the distance or whether he was taking in the full horizon. But Cronin could hear McCormack's deep, rhythmic breathing, almost as though he was asleep. His tie was loosened at the neck. Finally, he shifted his position and recrossed his legs.

"Dot and I would come up here often, especially in the early years," McCormack said. "I gave her her diamond up here." He turned to Cronin and smiled.

"Still not married, are you?"

Cronin shook his head.

"How about you and Sloane?"

Cronin paused a moment, then said simply, "It didn't work out."

"I like her," McCormack said. "And there's nothing like marriage. A good one. Happiest years of my life, by far. We just fit. We rarely exchanged an unpleasant word. 'Follow your bliss,' they say. Dot was my bliss." He turned and studied Cronin's face. "I know. Widowers romanticize. But believe me, we had something."

McCormack finished his beer and limped over to a bathroom next to the skating rink that was shut for the summer. He returned and sat heavily on the bench.

"Dot and I talked about you just before she passed away," he said. "I told her you reminded me of myself in a way." Cronin reacted with surprise. McCormack chuckled at the recollection. "It's true. I told her, 'If you think about it, detectives and reporters commit similar sins. We take the truth and make it black and white.' 'What's wrong with that?' she asked me. I said, 'The problem with that is the truth is often gray.' "

He sighed. "By then she was too far gone to follow much of what I was saying." He shifted his weight, seemingly unable to get comfortable, and ran a hand through his mop of hair.

"It was breast cancer?"

"Started there," McCormack replied. "Then it metastasized." He shrugged as though to say, nothing you can do then.

He shook his head. "It goes so *fast*. Then, when you *want* it to accelerate, when you need it just to be the end, it stalls." He had a quizzical look on his full face as though he was groping to understand all of this. "They linger, suffering."

McCormack resumed his stare out over the city as the sun dipped in the sky. He was quiet for a moment, and then, as though snapping out of a sort of reverie, he slapped his thigh and turned toward Cronin.

"Afterward, they give me time off," said McCormack. "So I head out to my sister's in San Diego. Husband's a retired ensign. I spend six weeks with them."

"How was San Diego?" Cronin asked, trying to lighten the conversation.

"Too sunny for my taste," said McCormack. "Sunny every day. No letup." He was serious.

"They asked you to come back for this?" Cronin asked.

43

McCormack shook his head. "No need to ask," he said.

They sat silently for a moment. "So what do you make of it?" McCormack asked.

Cronin shrugged.

McCormack sipped his beer. "You know what I wonder?" he said.

"What?"

"I wonder why someone would want to do this fellow if he was the saint he's made out to be?" He eyed Cronin. "If he's so perfect, where's the motive?"

"Right," said Cronin.

"The commissioner thinks it's a whacko, some homeless mental patient, someone along those lines," said McCormack. He shook his head, dismissing the idea.

"The place is undisturbed. No food, clothes, not a thing. His wallet was on the kitchen counter in plain sight. As you go in from the rear, through the porch, there's a doorway into the kitchen, then, just off that, there's a den, study-type room. He used it as an office. It was packed with stuff, photographs covering the walls. Pictures of him and various pols—Kennedys, McCarthy, McGovern, Jesse Jackson. All the lefties."

"Anything interesting in the wallet?" Cronin asked.

"Credit cards, license, you know," he said.

"Money?" Cronin asked.

"About thirteen, fourteen hundred bucks," said McCormack.

Cronin did some quiet calculations in his head.

"That's almost three weeks pay for him," said Cronin. "Three weeks take home pay."

McCormack studied the reporter. "We're clear on the terms of this discussion, right?"

"It's off-the-record," Cronin said. "I attribute nothing you tell me to you. Anything you tell me I use in a story is attributed to an official familiar with the investigation." McCormack nodded. He knew Cronin would protect him.

"The wallet was just a fraction," said McCormack.

"Of?"

"I'm telling this for your own information," said the detective. "I don't think you should use this because so few people know.

Could be traced back to me. But he had a strongbox in the bedroom closet."

"How much was in it?"

"That we've found so far, almost seventy grand," McCormack said.

"Jesus!" Cronin exclaimed.

"Any idea where it came from or what it was for?" Cronin asked.

McCormack shook his head. "We're lost," he said. "He was up to something, exactly what we don't know. We know of one scam only. The feds almost grabbed him on it, in fact."

"You're kidding."

"Best-kept secret in town," said the detective. "I don't know myself until yesterday when the feds filled me in."

"What happened?" Cronin asked.

"Evidently this woman walks in off the street," he said. "Shows up at the U.S. Attorney's office with a story to tell. They sit her down with one of the young turks in there and she claims Stewart's holding her up. For years. Says she's tired of getting squeezed."

"Recently?"

"Three, four months ago."

"Who is she?

"DiMasi's her name, Arlene DiMasi," said McCormack. "She and her husband have a little restaurant in the North End. They also do some catering for the city. Napoli Catering, it's called. Arlene handles the business side. Husband does the cooking. She goes to the feds on her own—the husband doesn't know. She says they're paying Stewart off for seven years. In exchange for contracts. She says she'd been after her husband to go to the law but he wouldn't consider it. She goes to the grand jury and tells the whole story."

McCormack pauses. "They're ready to indict and she chokes. Says she won't testify at trial."

"You're sure of this," said Cronin. It translated into: "I'm going to use this in a story and I must be absolutely certain it's right."

"Positive," said the detective.

McCormack struggled to his feet with a sharp intake of breath as he placed his weight on his bad leg. He began limping slowly back toward his car with Cronin alongside.

"Phone me at home if it's necessary, but it's best to talk here," McCormack said. "I'm here two, three nights a week, anyway."

They walked slowly toward the parking lot. McCormack unlocked the Crown Vic's door and leaned on the roof with one elbow.

"This is a strange one," he mused. "An unusually antiseptic scene. The money still in the wallet. Sitting there in plain view. A common criminal doesn't leave thirteen, fourteen hundred bucks behind. This was planned. Thought out. I don't think the way to crack it is to go out looking for a killer. We need to retrace Stewart's steps. Who did he screw over? Who did he hurt? We go back and look and find his victims, whoever and whatever they were, and we'll find ourselves a killer."

McCormack lowered himself in behind the steering wheel, then closed the door.

Cronin leaned on the door frame. "I want you to know I appreciate your help," he said.

McCormack nodded. "Happy to do it," he said.

"Just one more question," said Cronin. "Why?"

"Why what?"

"Why are you helping me?"

McCormack started the car and revved the engine. He looked up at Cronin and said, "Because I like you. But, also, to tell you the God's honest truth, because I think Phil Stewart was dirty." And he drove away.

CHAPTER

3

Cronin spotted Arlene DiMasi walking briskly along Day Boulevard in South Boston. She was a slender woman who, it was clear, took great care with her appearance. Though it was just after seven A.M., her platinum hair was carefully arranged and her face meticulously made up. She wore a black Nike jogging suit with pink trim and pink Reeboks. A Sony Walkman was tucked into her jacket pocket, a wire running up to her earpiece. She strode rapidly along and turned onto the causeway leading out across the water toward Castle Island.

After she passed, Cronin drove farther out the boulevard toward the island and parked near Kelly's Landing, a small, informal restaurant. He pulled his car over into the far corner of the lot and walked around the back of the huge stone fort from which troops had guarded the entrance to Boston Harbor in the seventeenth and eighteenth centuries. Jets on their final approach to Logan, just a thousand yards across the water, roared low overhead. Arlene DiMasi's route would take her out along the causeway and then bring her back around behind the fort before completing her walk in front of Kelly's. Cronin selected a wooden bench with a commanding view of the harbor, yet tucked in behind the fort out of sight of most passersby.

He waited. Twenty minutes later, she came around the bend, arms pumping, faced flushed. When she was forty feet away, Cronin called to her, but she did not hear. Then just as she was walking past where he stood, he called her name more loudly.

She stopped abruptly and turned, removing the earphones.

"Did you say my name?" she asked.

"Arlene DiMasi?"

"Who are you?" she asked.

"My name is Frank Cronin, Mrs. DiMasi. I'm a reporter for the *Post*. Here's my identification." He extended his press card toward her. She took it warily, inspected it, and handed it back. She edged a step away from Cronin.

"What do you want?"

"I'd like to talk with you. I need your help with a story I'm working on."

She looked him up and down. Arlene DiMasi was distrustful by nature. "Why the frig should I help you? I don't even know you."

There was a harsh edge to her voice and when she studied him, she did so with eyes narrowed and a look of distaste on her face.

"Please give me a minute to explain. Just sit down and listen to me. For a moment." Cronin motioned toward the bench.

He had seen the look many times before. She was wary, slightly frightened, yet she was also intrigued.

"How do I know you're not a friggin' rapist?"

He smiled. A clean-shaven, unthreatening, all-American boy. "Presenting his ID?" Cronin asked.

She eyed him.

"Please sit down," he said offering her a seat on the bench.

"Let's hear it," she said, as she crossed her legs, and pulled a pack of Marlboro Lights out of her jogging jacket. She placed one in her mouth, snapped a pink Bic lighter, and took a deep drag.

He leaned forward on the bench, elbows on his knees, his hands flat together in front of his face as though he were offering a prayer. He would drop the news on her abruptly and gauge her reaction.

"Mrs. DiMasi," he began carefully. "I am investigating corruption in the life of Philip Stewart."

She seemed, suddenly, paler, but she did not respond. She drew again on her cigarette and exhaled slowly, aiming her smoke out over the bay.

"I know that you know precisely what I'm talking about," he said.

Suddenly she rose to leave, dropping her cigarette to the ground and crushing it with her heel. "I've heard enough," she said, as she hurried away. Cronin scrambled after her and fell in step as she headed toward the parking lot.

"Please, I already have the story. I know you went to the feds. I'm writing an article about it. But I may be able to protect you and your husband."

She stopped abruptly and turned angrily toward him. She tilted her head to one side as though challenging him to a fight. She moved to within a foot of his face and spat out her words. "So you've come to do me a favor, huh?"

"I may be able to help you," he said softly.

She laughed a hard, hollow laugh. "I was born at night, Mr. Cronin, but not last night."

"It's not absolutely necessary that your name or your husband's name be in the story," he said. "But to do that I need your help."

She looked at him skeptically. "This I do not understand," she said.

"Please," Cronin said, motioning toward the bench. They both sat down.

"Here are the basics," he said. "Here's what I know. I know that for years Stewart extorted money from you and your husband. You paid him because you knew that if you didn't, you would lose contracts with the city. And you needed the contracts because the restaurant hasn't been doing particularly well. I know that you went to the U.S. Attorney's office and told them you were being extorted, that they took you seriously and proceeded to the grand jury. I know you testified at length before the grand jury but that when time came to indict you said you would not be willing to testify at trial."

She shook her head, a look of utter disbelief spreading across her face. "I cannot believe I'm hearing this," she said, gazing off toward the east and slowly shaking her head in disbelief.

Arlene DiMasi was a hard woman, toughened by the years, but the strain of it all was too much for her. She felt a burning sensation behind her eyes. She turned away and let out a deep, weary sigh. She sat pensively looking out over the water and lit another cigarette. She was humiliated in front of a perfect stranger, a newspaper reporter. She had gone to federal authorities in the strictest of confidence and now a man she had never before laid eyes on was accosting her in a public place and telling her he knew the darkest secret of her life. How could this happen, she wondered? This *violation?* The assistant U.S. attorneys had guaranteed her that her information would be held in the strictest of confidence.

It was as though Cronin could read her mind. He had found through the years that people in her position were invariably shocked that information they had shared in confidence with law enforcement officials had somehow leaked. The sense of betrayal was palpable and, to Cronin, understandable.

When she spoke again her voice had lost much of its defiance.

"We'll be ruined," she said. "Destroyed. If this gets out." Her voice cracked, but, again, she caught herself. She spoke as evenly as she could manage. "We had no choice," she said, turning and looking at Cronin, as though trying to gauge whether he believed her. He listened carefully. "We panicked. The thought of losing the business, our house, *everything.* We couldn't bear it." She took a deep breath.

Suddenly, she seemed terribly annoyed with Cronin.

"Why would you do this to us?" she asked. "If you know so much about us then you know we're not well off. We struggle. We friggin' work ourselves to exhaustion. It's always been that way for us. Nothin' has come easy to us. And now you've come to destroy us."

Cronin shook his head. "That's not my intention."

"Then leave us alone," she snapped.

Cronin was silent.

She waved him off in disgust and spat out her words. "You could give a shit less about us."

She glared at him.

Cronin spoke quietly. "I want to expose him for what he was," he said.

"What does it matter now?" asked Arlene DiMasi. "He's dead. What could it possibly matter now?"

"The truth matters," he said.

She scoffed at the notion, emitting a bitter laugh. "And you're fuckin' Dudley Doright, huh?"

Cronin looked to the northeast. A few sailboats rode the light breeze just offshore. In the distance was a cargo ship, making for open waters.

"This is what I do," he said simply.

"You mean invade people's lives."

"Do you think you and your husband were the only people he held up?" Cronin continued. "You think somebody who did what he did to you, over a period of years, never ever did it again to anyone else? You find that believable?"

She clamped her mouth shut as though she was trying to get newly applied lipstick even on her lips.

"There are two choices," Cronin said. "One, I can write a story based on what I know now—that he extorted money from you and your husband in return for catering contracts. That would include your names."

Her reply was defiant, each word bitten off and spit out: "No fuckin' way."

"But if I know the full story with detail and color, then I could tell the story without naming Napoli or you or your husband."

She screwed up her face, at a loss to understand what Cronin was talking about. "I tell you what happened, and you put that in the paper, but you don't put our names in? You're lying. It's a sleazeball trick to get me to spill my guts."

Cronin sat impassively.

"And if I don't tell you the story you put our names in the paper?"

"I'd have no choice."

A look of disdain crept across her face. "So this is how it works? This is how the press does its dirty business. This is very friggin' revealing."

It wasn't something Cronin was terribly proud of, though the reality was that the news business was extremely competitive, and to succeed, reporters had to play by the rules, even when they might not find those rules particularly attractive. Many reporters in town, Cronin knew, went far beyond what he considered ethical boundaries. There were reporters who, having been invited to a state senator's home for his annual press party, snuck away from the gathering and rifled files in the man's private study. At the *Record-American* there were a number of reporters who bullied and threatened people for information. Their technique involved intimidation. They told public officials who refused to give them information that they would write disparaging items about them in a weekend column. Arlene DiMasi was in a corner, but she did have a choice, one that many other reporters would not have offered.

"Mrs. DiMasi, with all due respect, I did not pay bribes to a public official," said Cronin. "Please don't portray me as too great an ogre."

"You could let the whole thing go."

Cronin shook his head. "That's not an option."

"Oh, right," she said sarcastically, "the *truth*."

Cronin betrayed an edge of impatience. "Mrs. DiMasi, there are some reporters who would have already written the story. You'd get a call at five o'clock the night before the story appeared to see if you wanted to make a comment. Or, more likely, you'd see the story in the paper with a line saying you could not be reached for comment even though nobody had ever *tried* to reach you for comment."

She took his rebuke in silence. She looked away from him, back toward the city where, in the distance, the North End could be seen. She spoke in a whisper he barely heard. "He was an evil man."

Cronin was silent, half expecting her to say more, but she seemed lost in her own thoughts—in her confusion and passionate hatred for Philip Stewart.

"There's another alternative here," said Cronin. "You could put the whole thing on-the-record—your name, your husband's name, Napoli. Everything."

She shook her head. "It would be insane," she said.

"There's only one thing left that you can get at," said Cronin, "but it was the most important thing to him—his reputation."

She seemed to seriously consider it for a moment, but then shook it off. "It would be humiliating," she said, "to expose ourselves that way."

"A lot of people would understand, I think," he said. "It wasn't as though it was your idea to pay him off. You didn't hatch a scheme to get rich. He put you in an untenable position. People will see that you had no alternative."

She was lost. She didn't want to believe him, but he could tell that what he was saying made some sense to her.

"I don't want to put you under any more stress than you're al-ready under," he said. "All I will tell you is that a story with you on-the-record and with full details would be immensely power-ful. It would change the way or begin to change the way people think of Stewart. It would blot the legacy. Appropriately.

"The other thing to consider is that in cases like these, there's a certain inevitability to the leakage of names," he said. "As you can see, law enforcement agencies don't keep many secrets. In a case like this, there's no real chance that you and your husband will escape having your names in the media. So if it's going to happen eventually anyway . . ."

He rose from the bench, pulled a card from his pocket with his phone numbers, and handed it to her. "Think it over," he said. "I'll do nothing for a couple of days. We'll publish nothing. You have my word. Think about what I've said. Talk it over with your husband if you wish. If I don't hear from you within forty-eight hours, I'll know your answer. But if you'd be willing to talk, please give me a call." He paused. "I'm sorry that this is the way it works. I don't want to hurt you. I hope you believe me."

One of the first lessons Cronin had learned as a young re-porter was that an astonishing amount of information es-sential to good news stories was sitting in public buildings waiting to be picked up. Often, newsworthy information re-mained secret because reporters didn't bother to look for it, or didn't know where to look. And because of the Freedom of In-formation Act, millions of government documents were avail-able for public inspection.

Most reporters Cronin knew rarely searched documents. When he would say he was headed to the Registry of Deeds or the secretary of state's office or the Office of Campaign and Po-litical Finance or the city clerk's office, most of his colleagues looked at him as though he was a bit off his game. The thought of sitting in a dusty closet pouring through faded onionskin hour after hour, sometimes day after day, was distinctly unappealing to modern journalists. Reporters much preferred to have sources hand the goods to them.

On a story such as the Stewart matter, documents were essential. To write about allegations that Stewart had extorted money from the DiMasis, Cronin had to determine with certainty that Napoli did, in fact, have catering contracts with the city for the amounts she specified at the times she stated. He headed to City Hall as much to cover himself as to check Arlene's DiMasi's credibility.

Searches were nearly always an adventure at the Hall. The public records division was housed in a series of vast, windowless rooms where documents were often haphazardly dumped rather than filed. Persons doing a records search of any kind were required to sign a ledger book in the office with their name and a description of what they were looking for. Cronin had been burned before because of the ledger. He had learned the first few times he had done records searches here that the journalistic bottom-dwellers that were the reporters from the *Record* regularly searched the log to see what their competitors from the *Post* were up to. The *Record* reporters would then dig up the same documents searched by the *Post* and throw some sort of story together.

Cronin signed in under a broken fluorescent bulb. He made sure nothing he wrote was even remotely legible. He walked to the end of a lengthy cement counter behind which a half dozen clerks lounged. He stood waiting, as none of the clerks made even the slightest move to come to his assistance. After a while, one bored young man offered to help. Cronin told him that he was looking for records on city catering contracts. The man rolled his eyes, went into a back office, consulted with a senior clerk, and returned. He opened a wooden gate and beckoned for Cronin to follow him back into the dimly lit recesses of the Hall. The clerk gestured unspecifically to a stack of several dozen cardboard boxes and walked away. "That should be everything back five years," he called over his shoulder. And he was gone.

Shortly after nine A.M., Cronin settled in and began reviewing the voluminous files. He quickly found that, though the documents were arranged in a vaguely chronological way, there was no other rhyme or reason to them. He had hoped that some files would be cross-referenced by vendor, which would put all the Napoli records together. Cronin thought that if the records were computerized, he could type in a request for all references to Napoli and within literally seconds receive everything he wanted. But that was not the case and he dug in and was soon filthy. The files were covered with thick dust—an indication that thay hadn't been touched in years. He pushed on, thumbing through hundreds and hundreds of salmon-pink forms. By 4:30 P.M., when the records office closed, he had culled out twenty-seven Napoli contracts.

The following morning at nine he returned to complete his work. By two that afternoon he had located a dozen more Napoli contracts. He went back to the *Post* and laid out the documents on his desk. He went through each one carefully, scribbling notes on a separate sheet of paper. Finally, he had a clear picture of Napoli's history with the city. He found that in each of the past seven years Napoli had done in excess of $100,000 worth of business with the city. For the city of Boston, with its billion-dollar budget, the money was a pittance, but for a small, family-owned North End caterer, it was a substantial sum.

The documents also showed that nearly all of the catering had been done at City Council–sponsored events. All but two of those were paid for out of the City Council's administrative budget, over which Stewart had had substantial control. The range of services Napoli provided was broad. Some called for Napoli to prepare antipasto for a dozen, others required canapes for three hundred people, still others demanded full, sit-down dinners for fifty. Napoli had catered everything from low-budget retirement parties for city employees to extravagent celebrations for two space shuttle astronauts. There had been breakfast for homeless veterans, lunch for the Gay and Lesbian Political Alliance, and dinner for the Ancient Order of Hibernians.

Cronin planned to write a story based on his information from McCormack and the documents, but when he went home that night, Cronin found a message on his answering machine from Arlene DiMasi. She wanted to meet the next morning at Kelly's Landing.

Arlene DiMasi was sipping tea at a corner table when he arrived. She wore a red Adidas jogging suit with black trim and white Nikes with a red stripe. Her hair was carefully done and her nails, long and shiny, were lacquered with polish that matched her outfit. A ring of red lipstick circled the filter tip of a butt that lay in the ashtray. She was heavily madeup, but even that could not fully conceal the deep circles under her bloodshot eyes. She appeared exhausted, and Cronin thought she had perhaps not slept at all the night before. And who knew how much she had cried. She sipped her tea and tapped an inch-long ash from the end of her cigarette and took a drag. She turned away from him and, when she exhaled, the bluish smoke drifted toward a nearby window.

"I'm glad he's dead," she said, turning back and looking directly into Cronin's eyes. "He was a pig."

It was clear she expected a response of some kind, perhaps reprobation. Something. But he was silent and would remain so for as long as necessary. During his career as a reporter, Cronin had endured many protracted, uncomfortable silences. He knew that if he spoke next it might break her momentum, get her off the track. He was sure that if he held his tongue, she would continue her story. He placed his elbows on the table, clasped his hands, and folded them together. He rested his chin on his folded hands and waited.

"I want you to understand some things before you write your article," she said. "Am I allowed to tell you things not for the paper? Just so you understand them?"

"Why don't you tell me whatever you feel I should know," he said. "Then, after that, we'll figure out what to put into the paper."

She nodded. "I've decided to tell you the whole story," she said. "With our names included. My husband doesn't agree with me, but he goes along with what I want usually. He didn't try to stop me from coming here. I told him, 'Hey, it's going to come out sometime anyway.' And I figure if I explain it all, maybe you'll understand and maybe people will see that we're not evil."

She shrugged. "It's worth a try, anyway," she said. "So tell our story. But please do it in a way that people can see how we were put in a position where we really had no choice. We committed a crime by paying the money. I get it. No squawks. We did it. Technically, we didn't have to do it. We could have said no and walked away. We *should* have said no and walked away. If he came up to me today and made the same deal I'd spit in his fuckin' face. We're guilty of a crime. I understand. But it's not that black and white." She shook her head and half smiled. "I'm sorry, but it's just not. And anybody who thinks it's nice and simple, black and white, has their head up their ass."

She lit another cigarette and thought for a moment. "I *am* glad he's dead," she said evenly. "He was a bad guy. That no-good bastard hurt us. He hurt my Gabriel. He hurt me. He hurt our marriage." She stared down into her cup. "You don't know what it's like. Day after day with this. It's like a friggin' nightmare. Like a giant weight on your neck all the time. Just when you think you've gotten used to it you remember it and it wrecks your day, day after day after day. I'd wake up in the night sometimes terrified we were about to get caught. Sometimes I'd say I can't stand it anymore, it's not right and we have to stop. We were going to stop a million friggin' times. But then we'd look at what would happen if we lost the contract. It's what has kept us afloat. The restaurant never worked out. We always thought we were on the verge of breaking through but it never happened. The catering paid the bills. It was the difference between staying in business and losing it all."

She leaned forward, hands on the table, palms up, beseeching him to understand. "We didn't have any choice. I just hope people see that."

She studied Cronin and shook her head. "This is like a goddamn nightmare."

"You can change your mind," he said.

"You said more people would believe the story if our names were in it?"

"No doubt about it," he said.

"That's what I want," she said, nodding her head. "I've been feeling this terrible feeling for a long time, like a dirty feeling. Like I was violated. That no-good son of a bitch *hurt* us. I want to hurt him."

Cronin returned to the *Post* and wrote his story:

> Officials of the U.S. Justice Department in Boston have investigated allegations that the late city councillor Philip Stewart, who was murdered last week, extorted tens of thousands of dollars from a Boston catering company over the past decade, according to law enforcement sources and the catering company owner.
>
> The investigation, which was conducted by two assistant U.S. attorneys, occurred several months prior to Stewart's death, the sources said.
>
> The probe centered on Stewart's relationship with Napoli Catering Co. of the North End, which for a number of years has had contracts with the city.
>
> Arlene DiMasi, who with her husband, Gabriel, owns Napoli, said during an interview with the Post that Stewart had extorted money from them for seven years. She said Stewart said that if they did not pay him they would lose their city contract.
>
> Stewart's death, which plunged the city into mourning last week, is currently being investigated by Boston police, who have refused to comment on the progress of their investigation. To date, police have not disclosed whether they have a suspect or a motive for the killing. Stewart was shot twice in the chest at point-blank range.
>
> Federal officials began the investigation into Stewart when Arlene DiMasi went to the U.S. Attorney's office in Boston and complained that Stewart had demanded cash payments in return for renewal of the firm's city contract.
>
> During an interview with the Post, DiMasi said Stew-

art demanded cash payments three to four times a year. Payments ranged from a few hundred dollars to several thousand.

DiMasi said that during the past seven years, Napoli catering paid Stewart in excess of $19,000. DiMasi said that Stewart insisted in being paid with $50 bills and that the cash was invariably delivered to Stewart's Council office in an order of takeout food. DiMasi said that the bills would be wrapped in tinfoil and placed at the bottom of a brown bag containing the food.

Stewart once complained that sauce had leaked onto the bills, said DiMasi.

"He was very bold, very arrogant," she said. "It was like we owed him this money, like he had worked for it."

DiMasi said she and her husband were aware that they were making unlawful payments but they felt trapped. She said that proceeds from their restaurant, the Domini Cafe, were unsteady and revenues from the catering business kept the restaurant afloat.

DiMasi said that on many occasions she and her husband decided to break the arrangement, but never followed through for fear of losing their livelihood.

"We felt we were in too deep to get out," she said.

The story continued on at some length, laying out background information on Stewart, his life, his record, and his death.

"Holy shit!" Berman squealed as he read the story on his computer screen. "Fifties wrapped in tinfoil! Great detail!"

Moments later, after having read the entire story, Berman looked up from his screen and studied Cronin. Cronin knew Berman would challenge him. It was how Berman operated. Even on stories he found all but flawless, he often challenged a reporter with questions.

"Powerful stuff, powerful stuff," Berman said, leaning back in his chair, hands behind his head.

"You're sure about all this?"

"I'm sure," said Cronin.

The scanners on the city desk crackled in the background. Berman got up and closed the door to his office. He slumped down in a chair across from Cronin and sat silently for a moment.

"Who's your primary source?" Berman asked.

"I've got someone inside," said Cronin.

"Mind telling me who it is?" Berman asked.

"Yes."

Berman frowned.

"The story's on the record," said Cronin. "It doesn't hang on a source. What's the problem?"

"No problem," said Berman. "The person who tipped you to this is good?"

"Inside," said Cronin, who had no intention of telling anyone at the paper or elsewhere who his source was. McCormack would be known as Cronin's "guy" to *Post* editors. Cronin had seen many cases where reporters told editors who their sources were and learned to their horror that their editors soon blabbed the source's name all over town.

Berman switched gears. "You think he scammed others?" Berman asked.

"I'd be very surprised if he didn't," said Cronin. "Just like these people—small vendors who depended on city contracts."

"If we go down this road," Berman said quietly, "we will get an epic amount of heat. Epic. There are people who will go fucking ballistic. To even raise a question about Stewart is blasphemous to some people in this town. To suggest he was a thief . . . Jesus." Berman shook his head. "We've got to be sure, Frank. If there's even a hint of doubt . . ."

Cronin shook his head. "There's no doubt, Howard" he said. "He was dirty."

"OK, let's say you're right," said Berman, jumping to his feet and pacing. "Let's say I concede that. Stewart was dirty. OK. So what? He's dead. In the ground. Buried. He's fucking *dead*, Frank."

"Howard, there were two Phil Stewarts. The one everyone saw. And an exceptionally well concealed dark side."

"So you're on this investigation that may produce a couple of stories, it may produce a dozen stories. It may be months of work. For what? You're investigating a *dead* man."

"No, Howard," Cronin said forcefully. "I'm investigating a *reputation,* a legacy. Stewart's reputation lives. It thrives. He has been glorified, all but canonized. I'm not after the man. Now I'm after something much bigger. The reputation. Because it's a lie."

CHAPTER

4

A cool rain swept across the city, washing away the heat of the day. Looking out across Boston from the highest point in Larz Anderson Park, Cronin could see darker, more ominous clouds in the distance, moving steadily eastward. The heavy weather was just a dozen miles west of the city and would hit within an hour. As the breeze picked up the temperature dropped. Cronin had hoped to catch up with McCormack, but the detective did not appear at the park on this evening. A couple walked a dog on the grassy hill beyond where Cronin had parked, but no one else braved the increasingly chilly rain. Cronin waited until after seven o'clock before giving up on the possibility that McCormack would show. The wind out of the west was more persistent now. Heavier clouds had moved over the city and the rain came harder and colder. From atop the park's hill, Cronin could see it sweeping in sheets across the landscape. It was chilly and forbidding, but Cronin saw it as cleansing as well, for it was growing into the sort of torrent that would wash away the city's accumulated summer grime and send it pouring into the sewers and out to sea.

Cronin left the park and headed back out through Brookline to West Roxbury. As he drove, thunder rolled in the distance and he saw a flash of lightning. After a short drive, he turned off the main road through a gate and continued past hundreds of rows of gravestones. He followed a narrow unpaved roadway back around a small stone chapel to a corner of the cemetery where thick oak trees shielded the grounds from the outside world.

Cronin squeezed his car over to the side of the road, past the grove of trees and up against an old wooden fence that surrounded the back portions of the cemetery. He zipped up his Goretex jacket, put on his baseball cap, and headed back toward the deepest reaches of this place that he knew so well. In the older part of the cemetery the years had smoothed the edges of hundreds of slabs of chiseled granite. Some listed one way or another, bent by the winds of time. On one side of the narrow roadway was the original section where graves were eighty, even one hundred years old. He moved on to a plot where the graves had been dug and the stones set in the early 1960s. He made his way past several rows to the rear of the section, the last row, where the stones, shades of black and gray, sat stiffly in the whipping wind and rain. He was in a protected area at the back of the cemetery, a section nearly surrounded by trees. The sound of the rain on the leaves grew louder as the full force of the storm struck. Branches swayed wildly in the wind as flashes of lightning lit the skies only seconds after great claps of thunder.

He walked to the end of the line and turned to face the final headstone in the second to last row. He stood still for a long moment, his eyes fixed on the grave marker. Soon, Cronin fell to his knees, soaking his dungarees and sneakers. He bowed his head, made the sign of the cross, and prayed.

For Cronin, prayer was remembrance.

He saw things so vividly, sometimes fully, sometimes only in flashes. She seemed tall to him, though in fact she was not. But for all of their time together, he looked up at her. He would lean against the corner of the refrigerator as she worked patiently over the stove, cooking their supper. Her skin was fair and freckled around her nose. She joked that they were a sign of beauty, but she silently cursed the Celtic genes that sentenced her to live with a freckled face. Her hair was thick and auburn and she cared for it so meticulously that it looked lustrous no matter the occasion. She was attractive enough, though hardly the great beauty he considered her. Her nose was slightly too big, her skin too chalky. But what he remembered more than anything else about the way she looked was her smile and its radiance. She smiled that way only for him, and, later, for the baby. Never for the father or anyone else. It was a smile of boundless love and warmth and he was mesmerized by it. Often, as he gazed up at her, she would reach down and pull him close, squeezing him hard and telling him that she loved him "more than the sun and the moon and the stars."

With his face pressed close, he could smell the freshness of her skin, and the hint of roses that came from her soap. She would joke with him in the evening, telling him stories about her work in a diner in the center of town. She would tell him of the idiosyncracies of coworkers, including one who always ate his lunch in reverse order—first coffee and two oatmeal cookies, a sandwich next, and then a cup of soup. He and his mother would howl with laughter over these and other stories. For the boy, it was not so much what she said that engaged him, but the music of her voice. It was light and lilting, full of laughter. There was no sound he more enjoyed. But he noticed that whenever the father visited, her voice grew heavier and lost its joy.

The father was a great hulking man, enormously powerful, with muscular arms and thick, heavily calloused hands. He remembered his father arriving now and again on freezing winter nights, sometimes parking a huge logging truck out front. His travels in search of work, at lumber camps from Maine to the Canadian Rockies, gave him a life entirely apart from theirs. He appeared rarely as the years passed, returning for a night or two, here or there, and then, as abruptly as he arrived, he would be gone.

And so, with the father away, it was he and his mother. And that is how they both preferred it. For Christmas one year, he had used glue and popsicle sticks to construct a pencil box for her. When he had presented it to her she acted as though he had bestowed upon her the Crown Jewels, but to her, of course, the small box with its crooked lines was far more precious than any jewel could possibly have been.

He was suddenly flooded with the sweet memory of one summer they had spent together on Cape Cod, one blissful summer where it was just the two of them. It was the summer when she found a job as a cocktail waitress at a resort on Cape Cod, a job where she would make good money that would help them through the winter. He had been only five years old at the time, but he recalled it so clearly as he knelt there, remembered that they had risen in the very early morning, before the sun, and gone to the bus station in Coaticook, Quebec, where they lived. He stood with her, holding one hand, while she lugged a heavy duffel bag in the other. At the ticket window, she carefully counted bills out of her purse, paying in exact change, to the cent, for two tickets. Soon, they boarded a Trailways that took them south through the bright early summer day down into Vermont, through Burlington and the Green Mountains, southeast along Interstate 89. By midafternoon they had reached Concord, New Hampshire, where they changed buses and she bought him lunch of a frankfurt and milk.

"A lot cheaper than in Boston," she had said to him, smiling at her own little bit of wisdom.

They rode to Boston, where it was muggy and dusty, where the traffic seemed as though it could not budge. The station was wild there and she clenched his hand until it hurt, keeping him off to the side away from the crowd and the strange-looking people in filthy clothing who muttered to themselves or shouted out loud, invoking the name of the Lord.

They boarded their third and final bus of the day in early evening and crept through traffic for the better part of an hour, headed south. After a while, ever so gradually, they gained speed and the road grew less congested. After an hour and a half there were few cars and no longer any buildings on the sides of the road, only stands of scrub pine. They crossed a bridge spanning the Cape Cod canal, up and over and on down past Hyannis where she said the Kennedy family lived in summer, to a small town called Chatham. It was a quiet place of narrow streets; pretty, weathered-shingle summer homes; a quaint business district of a single block. The bus driver let them off on Main Street, in front of the newsstand, and in the cool of the evening she told him to breath the air. They stood on the sidewalk by the duffel and she looked up to the sky, closing her eyes and taking deep breaths of the salt air, laughing as she did so, giddy at their adventure together.

With directions from the man at the newsstand, they walked

up Main Street only two blocks and then turned, and they knew
they were headed toward the ocean, for a cool breeze, laden
with salt, blew directly into their faces. She lugged the duffel bag
and he walked alongside her, moving as swiftly as his little legs
would carry him, not wanting to slow her down. They walked
five blocks until they came to the entrance to The Inn, a driveway
marked by a modest sign. They went through the gate and up the
drive and arrived at a grand sweeping staircase leading to a wide
porch that wrapped around a massive Victorian structure. On
the deck people were sitting on white wicker chairs and love
seats. Frankie's first image of the place would stay with him always. As they trudged up the stairs, he saw an older gentleman
reading a newspaper. He was dressed in a seersucker suit, fresh
white shirt, and navy blue bowtie. His hair was white and thinning and he wore a white mustache. He looked over the reading
glasses perched on his nose and smiled benevolently as she held
her little boy's hand and guided him through the hotel entrance.
Inside, the lobby was hushed. A huge Oriental carpet covered the
floor. In various spots around the room were small clusters—a
coffee table, easy chairs, a sofa, reading lamps—where guests
could enjoy a drink or sit and read. There were people scattered
about having cocktails, and others already seated for dinner.

Upon their arrival, they had been led from the grand lobby,
back behind the registration desk, out through the back door,
past a large garbage dumpster containing slop from the kitchen,
across a back parking lot to a small, narrow, two-story barracks-
like structure. This was the dormitory where the help lived for
the summer. Their room was small, just large enough for two
single beds, a dresser, and one chair.

He woke during the night, frightened, unsure where he was.
She gathered him in her arms and brought him in to bed with
her, pulling him close so that his head was under the curve in her
chin, his face against her chest. In her arms, he soon fell back to
sleep.

Every day that summer they would breakfast together, hang
out a while, then head for the beach. She knew to slather him
with sunscreen and she did it every day and then again if he went
in the water for any length of time. Unlike many of the other

children he saw that summer, he never got a sunburn. As June turned to July, both he and his mother turned slightly brownish.

They spent hours in the sand, digging holes to China, building elaborate sandcastles surrounded by moats that were deep and wide. The moats were always her idea. "For protection," she would say. After a while he didn't need to be reminded that a moat was needed and he would dig them as intensely as he built the castle and its walls.

They would go up to the kitchen for lunch some days, although usually they would pack a lunch in the morning, pour some juice into a thermos, and eat right there on the beach, never leaving the sand all day long. This for Frankie was the most glorious of times. How could he possibly have been happier? He had her all to himself literally all day long, day after day after day. She would work with him on the castles, or bury him in the sand up to his neck if he asked. She would swim in the ocean with him and buy him ice cream from the Frosty man who came around with his truck in midafternoon. Sometimes they would lay together on their towels, side by side, the same towels every day, and he would doze off with her arm around his shoulder. Sometimes he would use the crook of her shoulder as his pillow and close his eyes and dream, and when he would wake up he would find he had been dreaming of doing exactly what they were doing at that moment in that place. In late afternoon, often after he had taken a nap on the beach, she would give him juice and a cookie and they would walk slowly along the sand, way down to the point, where the Coast Guard manned a lighthouse, and they would search for shells and sand dollars. They would bring a fresh plastic bag each day, and in late afternoon they would return to their room with the bag sagging under the weight of their sandy, wet prizes.

He could see her back in the kitchen of their trailer back home in Canada, at the small table by the window, the curtain blowing in on the breeze, pressing against the screen, the smoke from her cigarette drifting toward the refrigerator. He was six when she told him that he would soon have a baby brother or sister and, within months, a little boy was born and she shed tears of joy when she returned from the hospital and laid the infant in his arms.

She knelt beside the sofa where he sat, the fully swathed infant, red-faced and asleep, feeling heavy against his chest. He did not know what to make of this creature, though he was excited about his arrival. She knelt and leaned over to kiss the baby's head, then she took his face in her hands and kissed him, too. She spoke softly to him.

"You're such a big boy now, Frankie," she said. "You're a big brother. Isn't that exciting?"

"Am I still your favorite, Mom?" he asked.

"Darling, I love my boys more than I can say, more than anything. But Frankie, I want you to do something very special for Mom, OK?"

She caressed the infant's cheek and kissed him again. She placed her hand on his shoulder. "I want you to promise me that you will always love your little brother, and that you will always be kind to him and try to help him. Will you promise me that, sweetheart?"

He nodded. "I promise, Mom."

"Frankie," she said, her voice taking on a note of urgency. "This is *very* important to Mommy, sweetie. I want you to *promise* me that you will *always* love your brother."

"I'll be the best big brother ever, Mom," he said. "I promise."

She pulled them both to her bosom and held them. He could barely hear her whisper "thank you." And he could feel her warm tears fall from her face onto his own.

The child brought him and his mother even closer together. They played with him and cared for him and laughed at his attempts to form words, to crawl, and then to walk. He and his mother found great joy with the child, who was shy and easily frightened by others. He seemed to take comfort only in the presence of his mother and brother.

Frankie liked it best when the baby was sick, not seriously ill, of course, but feverish. His skin would become hot to the touch

and he would become listless and his thirst would be unquench-
able. It was at such times that he and his mother, sitting on the
sofa, would place him on a pillow between them so that the little
boy's head lay on his mother's lap, his feet on his big brother's.
As the baby got older he would sometimes ask to reverse his position, placing his head on his brother's lap.

They grew to be inseparable. The baby became a little boy
who worshiped his older brother. When the baby was four, and
Frankie was ten, the little boy asked him one day, "Are we best
pals, Frankie?"

"Of course we are," said Frankie with a laugh.

But the little guy was deadly serious. "Are we the best pals in
the whole world, Frankie?" the boy asked earnestly.

"You bet we are," his brother replied.

"For ever and ever?"

"For ever and ever," said Frankie, as his best pal broke into a
smile.

One day she was gone.
An automobile accident. He cried the first few days, remembered nothing of the wake or funeral. No one knew where
their father was. A distant cousin of their mother's, an older
woman from Boston whom they had never met, came to the
house and stayed with them for a week. Since she was the only
adult relative available, it was left to her to decide on arrangements. She chose to have the burial in Boston. The little boy was
left behind, with neighbors, when Frankie traveled to the funeral. All he recalled was standing on the soggy ground as she
was lowered into the earth.

Their father's sister lived in West Texas, and she and her husband were contacted and asked to take the boys, but they had
four of their own and barely got by. And so a woman from the
provincial government arrived. At the time, Frankie was eleven
and the little boy was five. She gave them each a bag of M&M's
and drove them out to the interstate. More than an hour later
they stopped in front of a boxy gray house in a subdivision. She
told them it was their new home. Upon hearing this, his pal be-

gan to cry. Frankie wanted to cry as well. He fought the burning behind his eyes, the tingling feeling in his nose, the heaving in his chest. He battled what felt like a physical need to cry. He learned that if he shut his eyes as tightly as possible, and clenched his teeth and his fists hard, he could ward off the urge to cry. He would use that technique hundreds of times in the next seven years, during which he and his pal would be shunted to eleven different foster homes. After their mother was gone, Frankie watched his best pal turn sullen.

For many years thereafter, Frank would experience a nightmare. It would come once a week or so all the way through college. Then it came less frequently and had dwindled to the point where, after he turned thirty, he experienced it only two or three times a year.

He had dreamed that she was missing, alive somewhere. He dreamed that he undertook a frantic search and that he had found her living in England. She would be dressed in a gray wool skirt and jacket, and she would receive him politely but coolly. He told her he had been looking for her and had come to bring her home. He told her that he and his best pal needed her. He begged her to come back. But she would not. She was adamant. She had started a new life.

At this point in the dream he would experience a searing pain in his chest, a pain so sharp that he would wake up in a moment of agony.

For years, the dream tormented him. The pattern was the same. He would go to bed and sleep soundly for two to three hours. Then he would experience the dream. Upon finding her, he would heave and weep and cry for joy, but she would be standoffish. And it would become clear that she had known of his search, had known that he had long been at it, yet she did nothing to help him. She had no wish to be found, she told him. It was nothing against him, particularly. It was just that she had found a new life.

He would beg her to come home with him. He would plead with her. But she would not. She would merely shake her head, no, and that was that. He would go away wondering whether she had a new husband, whether she had children. And he would return to the spot—in London, Surrey, Cornwall, wher-ever—to find that she had vanished.

In spite of it all—the loss, the deterioration of his best pal, the pain of remembering—Frankie moved forward. He persevered. He carried on even though his heart had been broken by his own life.

CHAPTER

5

Susan Sloane, chief of the homicide division in the office of the Suffolk County District Attorney, walked briskly through the courthouse hallway, the heels of her black pumps clicking hard on the polished granite floor. She walked with purpose and determination, and those who lined the hallway walls—witnesses waiting to testify, police and court officers, lawyers in other cases, and families of the victims and the accused—took note of her as she strode toward courtroom number sixteen, where it was her mission to revoke forever the freedom of a twenty-three-year-old killer. Those who watched her noticed no one trait in particular—not her dark hair, chopped clean at the neck, not her shapely legs. They did not see the warmth and beauty of her smile, because in the courtroom she rarely smiled. Her job as chief prosecutor of murder trials in a murderous city was grim business. But in the seconds it took her to move across the hallway and into the courtroom, the people who caught a glimpse of her noticed a sense of urgency, an energy. Those able to see her green eyes—narrowed, focused—saw her determination.

Courtroom number sixteen, long ago stripped of its art deco ornament, was her domain. The walls were unattractively paneled with dried-out walnut curling at the edges. Hanging on one wall, slightly crooked, was a clock. At the front of the room, set above all else, was the judge's padded black-leather high-backed chair. In front of the judge were positioned a court stenographer and clerk. Then came two aged pine tables, six feet long, two and a half feet wide. The tables, one in front of the other, were spaced about six feet apart. The one closest to the judge was reserved for the prosecution, the other for the defense. The jury box was to the right of the tables and, in the back of the room, were a few rows of benches for spectators. When Sloane arrived, there were a dozen spectators, about the usual number. These were cases that attracted desultory if any attention beyond the families of those involved in the terrible proceedings.

Before she took her seat, Sloane went to the end of the first row of spectators. There, seated in cushioned armchairs identical to those used by the jurors, were the wife and two teenaged daughters of the victim in this case. Stephen (Benny) Bennett had been shot dead thirteen months earlier. His wife and daughters had grieved mightily during that time; their lives broken in ways that could not be repaired.

But now their moment had arrived. Here in this courtroom they were treated with the greatest respect. Sloane took pains to care for the victims' families. She ensured their transportation to and from court, paying for cabs when necessary. She provided for their morning coffee, for their lunch, for a comfortable, private area where they could spend the interminable hours waiting during the course of indictments, pretrial motions, jury selection, the trial itself, and then, finally, the always agonizing wait for a verdict.

With the family settled, Susan Sloane proceeded to the prosecution table where she sat reviewing her notes one last time. Detective McCormack entered the courtroom from a side door and took a seat among the court officers.

Sloane glanced to her left, saw McCormack, and got up from her seat. She went into the side hallway reserved for court personnel and McCormack followed. They stood together off to the side of an ancient elevator, a cage used to transport jurors and prisoners. The space was cramped and dusty.

McCormack, a head taller than Sloane, leaned down so his ear was close to her mouth. She started to whisper something and then stopped.

No matter how many times she closed a murder trial, this moment always made her nervous. The momentous nature of what was happening struck her with particular force prior to the closing.

Sloane had done this dozens of times. She had always prepared thoroughly and performed well. She knew, deep down, that she would do the same this day. But in spite of that confidence, in spite of her experience, she inevitably grew jittery on the day of a closing.

It was on such days that she felt particularly comforted by Mack's presence. She would have performed perfectly well without him there, of course, but she was more comfortable when he was. It was his friendship and moral support she needed at such times, not his ability as a cop.

McCormack understood. He had come to know her well in the nearly four years they had worked together. They seemed an improbable team. Sloane was petite, exceptionally fit, strikingly pretty, from a background of privilege. McCormack was a lumbering physical presence, overweight, a grayish pallor, a product of humble beginnings. Yet they were a formidable team, smart and relentless, and together they had solved dozens of murders.

They had been rewarded in this case, where the leads had been cold day after day, week after week, until, finally, McCormack had found a young man to whom the killer had confessed in the moments after the murder. McCormack had brought the young fellow in and he and Sloane had worked with him and soon enough the pieces had fallen into place. And now had come the day of triumph for the Commonwealth, for today was the day on which Sloane would recount for the jurors the case against the defendant.

Sloane had rehearsed her closing argument the night before in her office, McCormack her audience. Over pizza and diet Cokes, Sloane had gone through her closing once with the aid of notes, then again without notes. She had performed beautifully, he had thought. He was always awed by her preparation, the ease with which she retained in her head countless details, bits of evidence and testimony.

Though her first run-through had seemed nearly perfect to Mack, it had not been good enough for Sloane. She had done it a second time and then a third.

McCormack insisted after that that she go home and go to bed, and she had done so, but she had tossed and turned for half the night unable to get out of her mind the terrible images this case evoked.

She had thought, as she had for many months, about Benny Bennett, whose life was so cruelly taken from him. She had thought of his wife, a sweet woman who now seemed rather lost in the world. She had thought of Benny's two daughters, good, stable girls who had been very close to their father. And she had thought of the grandmother of the accused, a heavy woman with mournful eyes who had sat in the back of the courtroom throughout the trial. Sloane had thought that the woman must fear for this boy, this child of her child, this young man she loved so dearly, whose savagery was unknown to her.

"Take it nice and slow," said McCormack.

Sloane nodded. She glanced back into the courtroom toward the defense table and saw the defendant sitting there. He was twenty-three years old, and if Sloane did her job well this morning, he would never again taste even a moment's freedom.

Sloane squeezed Mack's hand and he nodded his head ever so slightly. A sign of affirmation, a wish good luck. They returned to their places and soon the jury filed in. The court officer announced the judge's arrival and all present rose. The judge seated herself, then nodded toward Sloane.

"Is the Commonwealth prepared for summation?" she asked.

Sloane rose. "We are, your honor," she replied.

"You may proceed," said the judge.

Susan Sloane walked toward the jurors, stopping a foot shy of the wooden railing that separated them from the rest of the courtroom. She appeared businesslike in a dark green suit, skirt to just above the knee, sheer stockings, an off-white silk shirt buttoned at the collar. She wore simple gold earrings and very little makeup.

Though she had been out of school for years, she could have passed for a college senior. She was fortunate to have inherited her mother's flawless skin. Sloane was arrestingly pretty, with thick, jet-black hair clipped short. She had a bright smile and seductive green eyes. In a sleeveless dress, Sloane's powerful shoulders and upper body, verging on muscular, were evident, vestiges of having been an avid sculler in college. She had made the women's team, although she had never been very good. At five feet three, she had been too short to excel, but she had been, as she was in so many other aspects of her life, dogged. She won a fair number of races and lost more than she cared to remember but none by a wide margin. Since then, though she still rowed once or twice a week, her upper body had gotten smaller, but her athletic build was still noticeable.

"Ladies and gentleman of the jury," she began, standing with her hands folded in front of her, "in the past nine days you have seen dozens of witnesses sitting in that chair answering thousands of questions. Now comes the time to decide which of those statements make sense, which witnesses were telling the truth. Let me be clear at the outset: we, the Commonwealth, bear the entire legal burden in this matter. We must prove to you beyond a reasonable doubt that this defendant murdered Benny Bennett outside of his liquor store a minute after closing time on the night of May 26, 1993. The defense has no obligation whatsoever to prove that this defendant is without guilt. So we have presented witnesses to you in an effort to do that. You have heard from a variety of people, good people, friends and neighbors of Benny's and his family. You heard Chico the stockboy testify that on the day of the murder, the defendant entered the store in the late afternoon without a shirt and that Benny told him he needed a shirt to be in the store, that nobody was allowed in without a shirt; that there was a sign to that effect on the front door. You heard Chico say that when the defendant asked why he needed a shirt, Benny replied, 'because this is a nice store.' "

Sloane paused for a moment as she glanced down at the floor. "Because this is a nice store," she continued. "Benny had worked hard for that store. He bought it just three years ago. His own business. His lifelong dream realized. He was proud of that store. 'Wear a shirt,' he asked his customers. Not so much to ask. But you heard Chico testify, and Kitty Fernandes testify that the defendant let loose with a stream of invective, a stream of filthy language, violent language, aimed at Benny. You heard Chico and Kitty testify that at that moment a young woman, Carla, entered the store and that the defendant began rubbing up against her in a sexually suggestive way, and that Benny in the strongest possible terms said, 'I will not allow that in my store.' And he ordered the defendant out. And you heard Carla and Kitty and Chico testify that before leaving the defendant said, 'I'll be back.' "

Sloane stepped back and to the side, watching the jurors as she did so to see if their eyes remained upon her. They did. She had their attention. They were listening closely. Did they know she was telling them the truth? she wondered.

"And within an hour he was back," she continued. "You heard Chico testify that the defendant returned wearing a long, baggy shirt, that he went up to the counter and confronted Benny, that he raised his shirt showing the grip of a gun sticking out from the waistband of his pants, and that when he showed that gun to Benny the defendant said these words: he said, 'I'll blow your head off.' "

She looked down at the floor, then quickly back up and scanned the jurors, her brow knitted, her mouth set. She repeated it, slowly, drawing out the words. "I'll. Blow. Your. Head. Off.

"You heard testimony from Chico and from Andrew Parks, the last customer of the night in Benny's store, that was identical. Both men testified that they walked out of the store with Benny that night and stood chatting as he pulled down the heavy metal grates and locked them in place. And both Chico and Andrew Parks testified that no sooner had Benny locked the grates than a shot rang out hitting the grate. And then a second shot rang out. A second bullet, forty-five caliber. It was that slug, that second shot, which struck the head of Benny Bennett. It entered his skull and pierced his brain. And it took his life away. You heard the first EMT responding to the scene testify that Benny died right there on the sidewalk in front of his store."

She turned away from the jury now and looked into a corner of the room to compose herself. Her hands were folded in front of her face, as though she was praying. She could hear the soft, muffled sobs coming from Benny's wife and daughters.

"Ladies and gentlemen, you heard the testimony of Tyrone Miller, who was with the defendant that night down by the tracks, not five hundred yards from the shooting. And you heard Tyrone Miller testify—Tyrone Miller, a friend of the defendant—that the defendant came down to the tracks in a state of agitation shortly after eleven P.M. and said these words, chilling words we will never forget. He said, 'I hadda buck him twice.'

"Buck him," she repeated. "Ladies and gentlemen, you didn't know what he meant by that and I didn't know either, but we heard testimony that in the talk of the street these days that term has one meaning and only one meaning: to buck him is to shoot him."

Sloane folded her arms across her chest and walked slowly away from the railing in front of the jurors, back across the courtroom, passing directly in front of the defense table. She looked down at the floor as she walked. She circled around behind the defense table, taking a position three feet directly behind where the defendant sat. The man who murdered Benny Bennett stiffened. The room was hushed. Sloane stood silently, looking over the defendant's head at the jurors. She repeated the words again, more slowly this time. "I had to buck him twice."

There was a barely detectable mocking tone to her words now. "The defense will tell you in closing that we have not proven our case, ladies and gentlemen. They will tell you that we presented no eyewitnesses. No one who actually saw this defendant point a gun at Benny Bennett and pull the trigger. They will tell you that we do not have a murder weapon. That we were unable to find the gun. And both of those things are true. Nobody saw him shooting. We do not have the gun.

"But ladies and gentlemen, you have heard the witnesses. You have heard good people, people with no ax to grind, no criminal history, nothing to gain. You have heard Chico and Kitty and Carla and Andrew Parks and Tyrone Miller. And you heard them testify as to the threats made by this defendant against Benny. You have heard the testimony that the defendant carried a weapon, threatened to blow Benny's head off, promised to come back to the store. You heard the testimony that the defendant said to Mr. Miller, 'I hadda buck him twice.'

"The defendant offered no testimony during this trial. He is not required to take the stand. He is not required to prove where he was at the time of the killing. But where was he? If he was elsewhere, why haven't we heard about it?

"And the reason we haven't heard about it, ladies and gentlemen, is because he was on the edge of the park across from the store with a weapon in his hand aiming and firing at Benny Bennett, not once but twice, first missing but then pulling the trigger a second time and driving a slug into the brain of Benny, sending Benny crashing to the sidewalk. Killing him. Murdering him. In cold blood. Because Benny told him to wear a shirt in his store."

Her voice dropped down to a whisper. "In his 'nice store,' " she said.

She walked slowly back to the railing and looked at each of the twelve jurors and the two alternates, pausing a second to make eye contact with each. "I implore you, ladies and gentlemen, to deliberate with wisdom and to return the only verdict warranted by the set of facts you have heard here in this room: guilty of murder in the first degree. Thank you."

After the closing arguments and the judge's instructions to the jury, the jurors were led off to the airless room in which they would be given lunch and then asked to conduct their solemn deliberations.

Sloane retreated to her office with McCormack and Benny Bennett's widow and daughters. The office was long and narrow, and in one corner, leaning against the wall, was a massive, twisted chrome bumper from an Oldsmobile. On a table next to it was a metal curling iron, nine inches in length. On the table near the iron lay a kitchen knife, and alongside that, was a Hillerich and Bradsby thirty-three-ounce baseball bat. All four items had various color tags affixed to them. All were crucial pieces of evidence in pending cases, for all had been used to commit murder.

Benny Bennett's wife and daughters settled in around the small conference table in Sloane's office. Soup and sandwiches were brought in for the Bennett family before Sloane left them in the care of a court matron.

It was a ritual, observed by Sloane and McCormack, that on the day one of their cases went to the jury, they would go out for lunch together to the same spot. They rode down the rear elevator to the subbasement, where McCormack's car was parked. They walked together, wordlessly, across the cement garage floor to the Crown Victoria.

"Hungry?" McCormack asked as they rode down Cambridge Street toward the Charles River.

Sloane shook her head.

"Me neither," he said and she turned to him and smiled, for she knew that of course he was hungry. Mack was always hungry.

"Buzzy's," she said, and he pulled into a parking lot on the right at Charles Circle and ordered a roast beef sandwich and coffee.

Sloane waited in the car as McCormack stood at the window, hands in his pockets. With his suit jacket pushed back she could see the edge of the shoulder strap holstering his gun. She could see his beeper and his ample stomach.

"I thought you were on Jenny Craig," she said when he got back into the car.

"They were all women," he said. "In the class. I was the only man."

"So?" she said.

He glanced at her as he drove across the Longfellow Bridge into Cambridge and turned west on Memorial Drive.

"So?" he said. "What do you mean so? Have you ever tried being the only fat guy in a room. It's not easy."

She smiled.

Mack pulled the car over under a tree on Memorial Drive. They got out and walked to a park bench that looked out across the river. The gold dome of the State House glittered in the midday sun.

Ever since their first murder case together four years earlier, when Sloane had been so jumpy about the jury's verdict that McCormack brought her to this place to calm her down, they had come here when deliberations began, for just an hour or so, to watch the sailboats glide across the water, to clear their minds, calm their nerves.

Sloane sat on the bench and put her head back, enjoying the warmth of the sun on her face. McCormack spread waxed paper out on his lap and took a bite of his sandwich. He sipped his coffee.

"That was some closing," he said to her. He nodded his head, glancing at her with a look of admiration. "You could talk a dog off a meat wagon."

She turned toward him and tried to smile. She could not. McCormack knew his role here, knew that time and time again, in trial after trial, Sloane had the same reaction on the day of the closing argument: her heart bled.

McCormack had worked with a dozen or more prosecutors through the years and he had never known anyone as tough as Sloane. Some of the guys he'd worked with had had a swagger or an attitude that portrayed a kind of toughness, a machismo. But Sloane was mentally tough. She was unrelenting. She would do whatever it took, within the law, to get a guilty verdict. She never suppressed evidence or issued phony warrants. She played by the rules and she played with an almost brutal will to win. Her job was to represent the innocent citizens of the Commonwealth against those accused of the worst possible crimes. And the people of the state had no idea how well they were represented in these matters, McCormack thought. No idea.

When she had first taken over homicide prosecutions, she had made some strategic mistakes typical of beginners—negotiating a plea when she need not have done so, refusing a plea bargain when she didn't have the evidence to go to trial. Back then, some of the detectives had begun to whisper that she wasn't up to the job. But it had not been long before Sloane had grown into the position. She sized up cases after one read of the file and almost always chose the correct strategic course. In the murder trials she had personally prosecuted, she had won thirty-three guilties in thirty-three attempts. Under her leadership, the department had won guilty verdicts in 412 of the 441 cases they had tried during her tenure.

She was witheringly efficient in her prosecution of cases, fueled by a passion McCormack had rarely seen in an assistant DA. She despised people who hurt the innocent. She made a moral distinction in her own mind—one she was reluctant to acknowledge—between the murders of innocent people and murders of criminals. To her, taking the life of an innocent person was the worst sin a human being could commit. She was far less interested in the prosecution of drug dealers who killed other drug dealers. It was not that she was content to permit the urban war to rage unabated, but she was limited in the amount of manpower she had available and in her store of moral indignation. She was required to prosecute every murder committed in the County of Suffolk, Commonwealth of Massachusetts, nearly one hundred per year. But she could not possibly devote equal time or resources to each. As a result, she targeted cases where the victim was more innocent than not. She had little interest or time for shootouts between gang members where a homicide resulted. But when a nine-year-old girl in a schoolyard was killed in the crossfire of a gang fight, she pursued the shooters with a vengeance. She had become obsessed with that one, had bypassed the other ten lawyers in her office and assigned it to herself. She had put three detectives on it—which was unheard of—and had pushed and wheedled and bullied until she was satisfied that the three young thugs under suspicion were in fact the guilty parties. She went to trial, eviscerated the defense, and won guilty verdicts against all three.

For all of her toughness, however, Sloane could never avoid, as a trial drew to a close, reflecting on the lives of those involved. Including the lives of the accused and his family.

She turned toward McCormack and spoke with sadness in her voice.

"Have you seen the woman in the back of the court, the older woman?" she asked.

McCormack nodded. "The grandmother," he said.

"Can you imagine it?" she asked.

He thought about it for a moment then said sadly, "No, I cannot."

She shook her head in bewilderment. "That boy's entire life is about to be gone. In prison forever." She rubbed her fingers over her temple. "Jesus," she whispered staring off across the river.

Sloane was showing the strain, as was McCormack. But in

time they would come back, in a matter of weeks or months they would be on the trail of someone who had hurt someone else, and they would come in and seek, through the system of justice, to avenge that terrible death. And they would, Mack knew, succeed.

McCormack had a piece of his sandwich left and he handed it to Sloane. She thanked him and ate it. They sat together for a while absorbing the warmth of the day. Then they drove back to the courthouse to await the jury's verdict. They were not kept in suspense long.

At 4:19 P.M., the jurors returned and pronounced the defendant guilty of murder in the first degree. The judge set sentencing for a week hence but she had no discretion. The sentence could only be life without parole. Barring a successful appeal or a gubernatorial commutation or pardon, this killer would die in prison.

In her office, Sloane accepted congratulations from the district attorney and from colleagues and staff members. She was embraced and profusely thanked by the family members, by Benny Bennett's wife and daughters, all of whom were in tears when they entered the cab that Sloane called to take them home.

McCormack arrived after staffers in the DA's office had finished their congratulations. He peeked in and saw Sloane signing papers that had accumulated during the trial.

She smiled upon seeing Mack and sat back in her chair, tossing her pen onto the pile of papers. She was worn out, glad the trial was over.

"Happy birthday," McCormack said, handing her an envelope.

"You remembered!" she said, delighted. "Thank you, Mack. This is so sweet."

She ripped open the envelope and found two Red Sox tickets. Box seats.

"Oh, Mack, you are so thoughtful." She went to him and reached around his neck and hugged him.

"You are the world's nicest man," she said. "How about joining me for the game on the . . . ah, let's see," she said looking at the tickets, "on the fifth. How about it?"

He dismissed the idea with a wave of his hand.

"Take somebody younger and thinner," he says. "How about Frank?"

She frowned at him. "No engineering my private life, Mack, remember?"

"I'm only trying to help speed up the inevitable," he said. "I saw him the other night." McCormack paused. "He asked after you," he lied.

Sloane eyed him. "He did?"

"Really," said McCormack.

"You're quite a bad liar, Mack," she said. "But thanks."

CHAPTER

6

In the twilight, Sloane watched Canada geese coast out of the sky and land with barely a ripple on the surface of the pond. She gazed past the water and saw a fox move hesitantly across the seventh fairway, heading for the woods. She remained still, watching him trot more confidently as he approached the cover of the forest, where he disappeared.

She had stood on this very spot hundreds of times. Her father had brought her and her sister, Alice, here when they were very young, and through the years they had accompanied him on countless nature walks. He would bring them along when he played a few holes on this portion of the club grounds, where an extra nine holes were laid out.

Suddenly, a cooling breeze swept down the sloping ninth fairway, and blew Sloane's dark hair back. It had been a hot, humid day, but since she had strolled down to the far end of the golf course the air had dried out. Sloane saw that the sky had turned a rich blue, nearly dark. She realized she'd been standing there for some time, daydreaming.

She remembered the first time they had met, four years earlier. At the time, Sloane was dating a man named Tom Dillon, who, it turned out, had been a classmate of Cronin's at Dartmouth. Sloane and Tom had gone to a party in Cambridge and, to Tom's surprise, run into Frank there. When the party ended early due to an acute beer shortage, Tom and Sloane had joined Frank and some others at the Club Casablanca in Harvard Square. Sloane remembered distinctly that they had taken up a position at the end of the bar and poured quarters into the juke-box until closing time at two A.M.

At the time, Sloane was quite happy with Tom and she had be-lieved that they would wind up getting married. Still, there had been something about Frank Cronin she found appealing. He possessed an easy self-confidence, a calmness that suggested a maturity beyond his years.

Tom told her later that Frank had been the star of the Dart-mouth hockey team for three years running, had been its captain in his senior year. Tom told her that Cronin had been the team's fastest skater and highest scorer. He had also been the team en-forcer—when someone on an opposing team singled out one of the smaller Dartmouth players, Cronin had been the one to step in. He'd been drafted by Boston in the National Hockey League; after that, Tom had gone off to medical school in New York and lost track of Frank.

Sloane remembered a particular moment late that night at Casablanca. The crowd at the bar had thinned out some and the group was soon to head home, but they wanted to wait until their songs were finished playing on the jukebox. There was a particular song that Frank had been waiting for and she remem-bered that when it had come on he had smiled broadly and looked straight at Sloane and held her gaze for just an instant longer than she would have expected. And then she remembered hearing the sweet strains of Sinatra lazily singing "Summer Wind."

By that fall, Sloane and Tom Dillon had drifted apart. Several months later, after Cronin and Sloane ran into each other at a judicial conference that Cronin was covering, they began dating.

It had been a blissful time.

Soon after they began seeing one another they became all but inseparable. They would spend rainy spring weekends in Cam-bridge bookstores or seeing old movies at the Brattle Theater. They spent some evenings at seedy clubs around Boston listen-ing to the hottest new rock 'n' roll bands. Other nights they would go out to a cheap restaurant or have dinner at Sloane's apartment on the flat of Beacon Hill.

In the summer they made trips together to the Cape to visit

friends, to Martha's Vineyard where they went surf casting for bluefish off Chappaquiddick Island.

But the highlight of that giddy period of early love came when they went on vacation together for two weeks to Frank's old farmhouse in Pomfret, Vermont. The house itself had seen better days. There was a pleasant living room with a fireplace, and three bedrooms, two quite small though the other rather spacious. The kitchen was hardly more than serviceable. But the property on which the house sat was spectacular. Cronin had a dozen acres of land in the hills, most of it heavily wooded, but some of it open meadows and streams. Across a field behind the house was a pond fed by a natural underground spring.

Frank had bought the place not long after he had gone to work for the *Post*. He had come to know the area by visiting the family of his Dartmouth roommate, Dan Linden. The Lindens lived in Darien but had a sprawling, beautifully designed vacation home in Pomfret. Frank's place had originally been part of the Linden property, and Dan's father, who had developed a strong relationship with Frank when the boys were in school, sold him the property for far below market value. The house had been used only occasionally for guests, anyway, and the Linden property contained more than two hundred acres, so they could surely afford the loss of a dozen.

Sloane loved the place. She and Frank had taken long walks, six or seven miles, up over Hewitt Hill and across to Galaxy Hill. From the top of Galaxy Hill they could look north and west for miles and miles and see nothing but forest, nothing but a carpet of lush greenery. On warm days they swam in the pond and spent their afternoon reading on the porch. They drove into Woodstock for dinner a couple of times and in to Hanover once. But most nights they would cook up some pasta or grill chicken or lamb from George the butcher in Woodstock and sit out on the porch of Frank's place and watch the trees sway in the pleasant evening breeze.

There was no doubt that they were in love, happily, contentedly in love.

Initially, it did not trouble Sloane that Frank did not express his love for her verbally. She knew from being with him—by the way he looked at her and spoke to her and listened to her—that he loved her. She knew by their passionate lovemaking the intensity of his love.

The fact that he was showing his love was far more important than his saying the words, she reasoned to herself.

But then the vacation was over and they returned to Boston and soon enough she saw Frank begin, inexorably, to drift away from her. She could feel him pulling back. He seemed hesitant, anxious. She raised the subject and he shied away from it saying time and again that he cared very much for her, but never going beyond that. For periods of weeks and even months all seemed well, but it became clear to Sloane that the future of their relationship was, at best, uncertain.

Sloane had been approaching thirty at the time. The ideas of stability, commitment, and children were very much on her mind. But Frank was far from being in the same place.

And so, sadly, they had parted.

And though it had been a long time, she still missed him as much on this, her thirty-first birthday, as she did on the day they separated.

She shivered against the breeze that swept across the course and as she began walking back toward the clubhouse, her thoughts turned to her parents.

The Sloanes were quiet, private people. They had taken pains through the years to teach their daughter, even at an early age, that with privilege came responsibility—"a duty to God," as her mother put it—to help others. This did not mean, they had taught her, attending a few black tie charitable functions annually, but rather making aid to others part of one's life. Even now, as she held down the demanding job of chief of homicide in the Suffolk County District Attorney's office, Susan Sloane rose before dawn every Wednesday morning to serve breakfast to homeless women at a downtown shelter.

She had learned well from her parents, from these two people who had helped nurture within her a sense of fair play, a curiosity about the world, and tolerence for differences among people.

Sloane had seriously considered following her father into international corporate law, but with only minimal exposure in law school, she had developed a passion for the flesh-and-blood reality of criminal law. She had been struck by the idea that society was invested with the power to deprive a person transgressing certain rules of their liberty. And even, in some states, of their *life*.

During the summer between her second and third years of law school, Sloane had taken a job as a public defender in Chicago. Like so many other eager, young law students, she became an ardent advocate for her clients. Upon graduation the following spring, she went to work at the public defenders office in Boston. She was assigned to Roxbury District Court, where she worked on standard district court fare—robberies, armed assaults, motor vehicle offenses—misdemeanors and minor felonies.

Like any other resident of a major American city or its environs, Sloane knew from reading the newspaper that the inner city was plagued with violence. She knew intellectually of the deprivation, the pathologies, the widespread incidence of young, uneducated, single women giving birth to children whose fate would often be the same. She knew, intellectually, that too many young black males fathered children and then abandoned them. She knew that the economy of the inner city had failed and that a staggering percentage of the young males had encounters with the criminal justice system.

But to witness it firsthand, to see the reality of it, had been harrowing. She had been appalled at how many innocent people were hurt, in one way or another, by the violence of the city streets. And after a year and a half on the job, she had abruptly quit. She had awakened one Saturday morning and realized what she had known subconsciously all along: that the overwhelming majority of the people she defended were guilty. And most had lengthy histories of violent acts. She decided within a matter of hours that she could no longer go into a courtroom and try to win freedom for people who had hurt others and who would, in all likelihood, go out again soon and hurt someone else. It had all come crashing in on her that day. Faced with the knowledge that she had become an advocate for some of the most vicious people in the city was too much. She had to stop. The following Monday morning she submitted her resignation and, two weeks later, she was gone.

She had taken some time off, audited a couple of courses, increased the amount of her volunteer work, did some traveling, and read voraciously. Over time, it had become clear where she was headed. Her mother saw it first. Amid much talk of working for various advocacy groups—litigating on behalf of children, the environment, battered women, and more—Emma Sloane had seen quite clearly that her daughter was destined to become a prosecutor. Susan believed deeply in the rule of law. She believed that a civilized society needed clearly prescribed rules. She believed that the great majority of people (who were good, in Sloane's view) could only be shielded from the tyranny of the few (who were bad), if the rule of law was upheld fairly and consistently.

Other than sitting on a bench draped in a black robe, said Emma Sloane, the only place a lawyer can work to protect the good from the bad is as a prosecutor. Both Susan and David Sloane reacted with surprise to the notion. Susan had never seen herself in such a role, but after talking about the idea only briefly, she felt a certain enthusiasm. After looking into it more deeply she decided to give it a try.

Six years later, Sloane had risen through the ranks to become chief of homicide at the Suffolk DA's office, where she was responsible for the investigation and prosecution of the murder of Councillor Philip Stewart.

After a shower in the women's locker room, Sloane dressed in a navy blue raw silk sleeveless dress. She slipped on a raspberry-colored blazer and headed toward the clubhouse, where she was scheduled to meet her parents for a birthday dinner. She left the locker building, a small but elegant brick structure of Georgian design, and strolled across the practice green, past rows of red clay tennis courts and the swimming pool, to the ramshackle clubhouse. It was a large clapboard building, white with dark green shutters and trim, set on a slight hill just behind the eighteenth green. The structure had aged gracefully and retained a slightly worn but polished look. The clubhouse was furnished with old oak and cherry, muted chintz and red leather. The main hallway was lined with golf memorabilia, with the framed scorecards from past events, including two U.S. Open championships. Wooden-shafted clubs from seventy years ago and gutta-percha balls—all used in World War I–era tournaments—were displayed in a glass case. The first floor included a large, informal dining room used mostly by families, as well as a library and reading room, a slightly stuffy yet comfortable formal dining room, and the men's bar. On the second floor were several private dining rooms that could be reserved for weddings and other events, as well as bedrooms for overnight club guests.

When Sloane arrived, her parents rose from the dinner table and hugged their daughter.

"Happy birthday, dear," said her mother.

Her father poured her a glass of champagne and raised his glass. "To our dear girl. A happy birthday and prayers for many, many more." The three Sloanes clinked glasses and sipped.

"And to Alice," her father said quietly. They raised their glasses again and sipped. There came a moment of silence. It had long been a family ritual that at the start of any family gathering they would pause briefly and remember Alice. Alice the soccer star. Beautiful, funny, irreverent Alice. Alice the artist whose paintings had dazzled her most demanding teachers.

Alice had been two years older than Sloane, a girl with so much energy, such zest for life. But when she was barely twenty-one, she had been hit by a drunk driver and killed.

In Sloane's world, all was well. All was perfect, in fact. She had grown up amid splendor and wealth with every conceivable opportunity. She had lived in the most exclusive area of Boston, summered in Maine, wintered in Hobe Sound, gone to Dana Hall, Wellesley, Harvard Law School. Everything in her life was perfect except what mattered most. Alice. Alice had been the center of the family, the passion and soul of the Sloanes.

And when she died she had left a gaping hole in Sloane's life, a hole in the family, a hole, Sloane believed, in the world.

Alice had always said that they would both get married in their twenties and have their babies simultaneously so that they could walk them together in new strollers, around Jamaica Pond and around and around, and they would have lunch together every day and discuss the issues of the day and Alice would watch Sloane's baby while Sloane did her law work, and Sloane would watch Alice's baby while Alice splashed paint across a canvas. But it was not to be.

It had been twelve years since Alice was gone. Twelve years of missing Alice.

They chatted over crabcake appetizers, laughing at ancient jokes that her father told over and over again through the years. During a dinner of grilled salmon, Emma Sloane turned the conversation to Susan's work. She told them about the Bennett case she'd won earlier in the day. They listened intently to the details, which she summarized as quickly as she was able. Though both her mother and father were intensely interested in the case, Sloane had had enough. She wanted to put it behind her. Her mother, sensing this, turned the conversation to the Stewart murder.

"I suppose this terrible Stewart case is taking up your time?"

"And with pathetic little result, frankly," said Sloane. "I've got others to keep me hopping as well, of course. Just in the past week I've got a gang execution of a boy all of fifteen years old. And I have the weekly case of a crazed ex-husband with stacks of restraining orders who got drunk and killed his ex-wife."

"Dear God," said her mother.

"What happened?" her father asked.

"Oh, Dad, you truly don't want to know," said Susan. "Grisly stuff."

David Sloane grimaced.

Susan nodded. "These jilted men are walking time bombs. They're set to go off but nobody knows when and all the restraining orders in the world won't stop them. Theirs is a savagery unlike any other. It's sheer bloodlust. A passion to kill. But this latest fellow we have cold. Every conceivable piece of evidence. We'll convict him on first degree I'm certain. And what he gets when he's in prison is precisely what he deserves, if you ask me."

"Susan!" exclaimed her mother.

"Would you care to see photographs of the woman's body, Mother?" Sloane asked, an edge to her voice. "Or perhaps you'd like to meet the children, three of the little buggers under seven, who are now motherless. Or perhaps you'd like to see the photos *and* meet the children."

"Speaking on your mother's behalf," said David Sloane to his daughter, "she yields."

"I do," said her mother, "but that tone of yours sounds a little bloodthirsty itself, if you ask me."

Sloane looked to her father. "You call that yielding?" she asked, a tone of mock horror.

David Sloane smiled. "Has your mother ever not gotten the last word, dear?"

They all laughed.

"Oh, I know what I wanted to ask you about, honey," her mother exclaimed. "This story in the paper that there is some inkling that Philip Stewart was somehow corrupt. Could that possibly be true?"

Sloane considered the question. "I don't suppose much of anything would surprise me anymore, Mother, though I admit I was a bit taken aback when I read it. You knew him, Dad, what do you think?"

"Not at all well," replied David Sloane as he swirled wine in his glass and reflected for a moment. "We'd met, you know, and talked. He struck me as a decent man." He shook his head and frowned as he looked across the table at his daughter. "Perhaps it's a function of having practiced law for so many years, where you see, for good and ill, people stripped of their pretensions. But I'll tell you I am reluctant to say that anyone is *truly* a certain type of character. There is so much we don't know—even about people who we may think we know rather well. There is so much that is unknowable unless, of course, a particular individual chooses to reveal whatever it is he or she is hiding.

"Who knows what *really* goes on inside any man," David

Sloane continued. "He could have lived another life for all we know."

"That's what Mack thinks," said Susan, "that Stewart may have had some sort of subterranean existence that he brilliantly concealed."

"How is your friend Mack, Susie?" her mother asked.

Susan sipped her wine. "Very well, really," she said. "Considering."

"Yes," said her mother. "His poor wife. That was so very sad."

"Mack's strong," said Sloane. "He's a survivor."

"Well, if he's correct about Stewart having some other life," said Emma Sloane, "then it was *exceptionally* well concealed, wasn't it?"

"Yes, and frankly, I wonder," Susan replied, "whether it's possible for such a public person to have successfully hidden something as wretched as this. Some other life in which he pillaged and plundered."

"Theoretically, it's certainly possible," said David Sloane. "The practicality of it is another matter, of course. But he was single, wasn't he?"

Sloane nodded.

"Well, that would certainly simplify matters, wouldn't it?" he said.

"How's that, exactly?" asked his wife.

"Well, it would be far easier to camouflage a separate life if you don't have to spend your time worrying about deceiving the people with whom you live."

"And the story said he extorted money from this very small catering company," said her mother. "That's the sort of thing that used to go on all the time in the city, years ago."

"But you know, Mother, the set of facts presented could conceivably lead to a different conclusion, at least legally," said Sloane.

"How could that be, dear?" asked her mother. "I would think extortion is extortion is extortion."

"We've questioned people close to Stewart, members of his council staff, close political supporters, and they insist this was fund-raising rather than extortion," said Susan. "They concede it appears shabby—*was* shabby—but they vehemently deny that he was a corrupt man."

David Sloane spoke up. "Couldn't it be argued that the system of fund-raising for political campaigns is de facto extortion? 'Under color of official right,' the statute reads. In other words, if a public official uses the color or power of his office to seek financial gain, it's extortion. Well, isn't that what perfectly legal political fund-raising is?"

"I don't quite see that," said Emma Sloane. "Raising money for a campaign strikes me as quite different from stealing funds from a helpless little family company that does a bit of city work."

"But how do we know the money wasn't proferred by the helpless little family company in the first place?" Susan asked.

"Well, they've complained in the newspaper," said Emma. "I don't think someone who initiates such an arrangement would talk about it publicly, do you?"

"One wouldn't think so," said Sloane.

An elderly waiter cleared the table and presented the Sloane's with a small carrot cake topped with a birthday candle.

Sloane went to blow out the candle but her father stopped her.

"Make a wish first, Suz," said her father.

Sloane paused for a moment. She thought of a wish, blushed slightly, and blew out the candle.

"What was your wish, dear?" Emma Sloane asked.

"Don't you dare tell," said her father. "That ruins it."

After dinner they moved into a comfortable sitting room for coffee and David Sloane asked his daughter whether she'd had any luck with her investigation thus far.

Sloane sighed. "It's not gone nearly as well as I'd hoped, actually," she said. "It's been maddening. We scoured the neighborhood—nothing. It was raining, so people weren't out strolling, but, still, nobody saw anything unusual. Nobody was seen running from the home, or yard, or the street."

"Any forensics?" asked her father.

Sloane shook her head. "Nothing. No prints, no fibers beyond what you'd expect—denim, cotton. Needless to say no weapon."

David Sloane saw an old friend across the room and excused himself to go say a brief hello. His wife saw it as an opportune moment to question Susan.

Emma Sloane was reluctant to raise Frank Cronin's name with Susan, but she could not help herself.

"I was wondering," she asked in a hesitant voice, "whether you'd had any contact with Frankie?"

Sloane stirred her decaf absently and shook her head. "Not really," she said. "We've exchanged polite notes. I congratulated him on a story he'd written some months ago and he sent me a nice card when that case was affirmed on appeal. But other than that we haven't talked. I've not seen him in, oh, it must be nearly ten months now."

Sloane's smile was brave, but she was pained by it all, her mother knew. Emma Sloane had always been reluctant to advise her daughter on matters of the heart, had always believed adults should be left to their own devices, but she fidgeted with her silverware in a way that suggested she was struggling with whether to speak.

"What is it, Mother?" Sloane asked. "I'd appreciate you sharing whatever thoughts you have."

Her mother had had two glasses of wine, Emma Sloane's limit, and was less reticent than she might otherwise have been.

"Well, I only hope you've not given up on him, Susie," said her mother. She hastened to add, "It is your business entirely, darling, of course. And I respect that. But I'd be disingenuous if I feigned disinterest. Your father and I obviously care very deeply for your well-being and I must say I cannot accept in my own mind that you two have given up on your relationship . . ."

". . . Such as it is," Sloane interjected.

"Such as it is," agreed her mother. "But I wonder whether it's been given a fair chance. Really, I wonder whether it has. He's a very fine man, Susie, you know that and I wonder whether it's not simply a matter of timing, really."

Sloane shook her head. "No, Mother," she replied. "Timing is part of the problem, but it's vastly more complicated and, I'm afraid, more difficult than simply timing."

She sipped her coffee and paused, reflecting. "I don't know precisely what the problem is myself, although more than anything else Frank is a man for whom commitment to a relationship isn't merely frightening, it's terrifying. He cares very much for me, Mother, and I for him. We share many mutual interests, delight in each other's company, but all of that doesn't necessarily make for a full, whole relationship. Not in our case, at any rate. You know, Mother, when you date someone either the relationship grows or it dies. You either peel the layers away that reveal the person or you don't. And in the time we were together he began to get to know me pretty well. I was very comfortable with him and I revealed a lot about myself. But it never came the other way. Quite honestly, Mother, it comes down to being ready and willing to share my life with him and him not being ready or willing to reciprocate. Why? Who knows. I'm not at all sure he knows. I *do* think his life had been complicated. Strained in some ways. I've told you how skillfully he steers clear of discussing his past, his childhood and family and upbringing and all that. Who knows what might have happened back there?"

"May I ask rather bluntly, Susie, whether you've given up on him?"

She seemed surprised by the question. "Oh, I don't think I have, Mother," she said. "I certainly hope not."

When she arrived home after dinner, Sloane found a cone-shaped package leaning by her rear entranceway. She picked it up and felt flowers. She carefully peeled back the green and white paper and revealed a half dozen beautiful peonies. Her favorites. Her mother making sure she ended her birthday on a pleasant note, no doubt. But when she opened the card she caught her breath: "Sloane, Happy Birthday, love, Frank."

Love, Frank.

She poured herself a glass of wine as she placed the flowers in a tall vase and set them in the center of the kitchen. She sat admiring them as she read and reread the card.

She sat looking at the flowers, sipping her wine, and she wanted to give in to the almost irresistible urge to talk to him. To hear his voice. Surely she should thank him for this gesture. She reached for the phone, then stopped. Perhaps the flowers meant something more than happy birthday. Perhaps he was sending a signal. He had always been so elliptical in the way he communicated. It had been so difficult for him to convey affection.

Could he possibly be signaling that he was ready to try again?

Whether he was or not, Sloane was touched by the flowers. It was after ten o'clock, but she could not resist. She picked up the phone and dialed his number. It fell easily from her memory.

He answered on the second ring.

"They're beautiful," she said. "Thank you."

"Oh," he said, genuinely surprised to hear her voice. "Your welcome."

"I didn't wake you?"

"No, no," he said. "I was just reading."

"What?"

"DeLillo."

"Not *Libra* again?" she said.

He laughed. "I'm afraid so," he said.

There was a brief, somewhat awkward pause.

"So you've been OK?" she asked.

"Yeah, I've been OK," he said. "You?"

"Fine," she said. "Lot of work."

"I'm sure."

Another pause.

Sloane sighed.

"I'm sorry," she said. "I shouldn't have called."

"No, no," said Frank, "I'm glad you did. It's good to hear your voice."

"I'll let you go," she said, clearly regretting that she had phoned. "I just wanted to say thanks. So, thanks."

"Happy birthday," he said.

"Good night," she said.

"Good night," he said.

She went upstairs to her bedroom and undressed. She was warm, flushed. The night air was tropical. The laziest of breezes blew, carrying the sweet smell of the new-mown field beyond the pond. She put on a silk nightshirt that fell just above the knee, and returned downstairs to lock the doors and flip on the alarm.

She went back upstairs to her bedroom. It was large, the result of a wall having been knocked down and the joining together of two smaller rooms. On one side, across from her bed, was a chintz love seat and comfortable chair in front of a small coffee table. In this room, Sloane felt as though she was locked away from the world; hidden in the most private of places.

She switched off most of the lights in her room. A small bedside lamp across from where she sat remained lit, casting a muted yellowish glow. Moonlight flowed in through the glass doors that lead to a small balcony.

She stretched out on the love seat. The cushions were goose down, luxuriant. She sipped her wine and set the glass on the table. It was nearly eleven P.M. on her birthday and Sloane was alone.

She slid the nightshirt up above her waist. With her right hand, she began to massage, ever so slowly, with infinite patience. She cleared her mind, relaxing herself. She was calm and deliberate. There was no rush, no urgency. She smiled at the recollection of a comment made by a friend: "Who you have sex with is your business, especially if it's yourself."

The rhythm was so slow, just as she wanted it. In time, the tension built. She seemed to tighten somewhere inside. And then there came a moment of wonderful relief. It was not sharp or quick. But fulsome and satisfying. And she hung on to the sensation for as long as she could until she sped up her rhythm slightly to coax it along and, suddenly, felt a second wave more intense than the first. She could hear herself groaning quietly, her head back, eyes closed. She shuddered and it was over and soon, in her bed alone, she fell into a deep sleep.

CHAPTER 7

"Follow the money" had been the mantra of Watergate investigators Bob Woodward and Carl Bernstein in the early 1970s, and Cronin believed that by pursuing the same trail he would find the real Philip Stewart. Berman, however, betrayed some impatience with this approach. To him, the key questions were who murdered Stewart and why. The issue of whether Stewart had extorted money was secondary. He wanted Cronin to spend his time dogging police, making sure the *Post* had the latest police suspicions on suspects and motive. Berman's overriding concern was not getting beat by the *Record*. As was the case with many editors, he was obsessed with the fear that the other paper would contain a scrap of information the *Post* did not have. Cronin had no such fear. He believed that his relationship with McCormack was an insurance policy against getting scooped by the *Record*.

The two men were in Berman's cramped, glass-walled office just off the city room. Berman was disheveled in blue jeans and a T-shirt, having raced in to work during the night to supervise coverage of a gang war in the city's streets. Cronin was dressed neatly in lightweight khaki pants, dress shirt, and sport jacket. It was shortly after nine o'clock, but already Cronin had been to Mass and worked out.

"Let's just stay focused on the cops and what they're doing," said Berman. "Why can't we do that?"

"They are doing routine, boring things that have zero news value, Howard," said Cronin. "They are running lab tests on fibers from the house. Examining prints. Interviewing neighbors. The usual stuff only more of it. It's slow and tedious and, so far, without result."

"They have nothing?" Berman asked, incredulous.

"Howard, you know, they're not interested in your itchiness for news," said Cronin. "That is not their overriding concern."

Berman rose from his desk and began pacing. "I would guess that in seventy-five percent of the murders in this city they make an arrest within two weeks, right?"

Cronin considered this for a moment and said, "I'd guess maybe half."

"Whatever," said Berman. "The point is that this is the most high profile case in history probably, they've got three times as many people on it as they normally would, and they've got diddly so far. Nada. What gives?"

Cronin pulled out a notebook and flipped through it. "I'll walk you through every conversation I have with my guy," said Cronin, in reference to McCormack. "He says it will take time. They have very little." He continued to thumb through his notebook, scanning for nuggets of interest. As he went through, he read aloud bits of information he had jotted down while talking with McCormack. "Lots of forensics, but nothing of consequence . . . believe it was carefully planned, well executed . . . no fibers that matter . . . print on radio dial but serrated edge obscures." Cronin flipped through more pages. "None of what gets early break—weapon, witness, forensics."

Cronin closed his notebook and looked at Berman. "So we can sit around waiting for the cops to stumble on something, which my guy says could be months, literally, or we can go out hunting," said Cronin. "I say we hunt."

Berman folded his arms across his chest and sighed. "For what exactly?" he asked.

"For who Stewart really was," Cronin replied.

Berman screwed up his face, appearing as though he had just bitten deeply into a lemon. "This is a newspaper, Frank, not *Psychology Today*," Berman said.

"Howard, my guy thinks that if you find the people he hurt then you'll find a killer," said Cronin. "If we get to really know this man, maybe we learn some things."

Berman listened carefully. He was in his usual devil's advocate stance. It could be annoying—in fact, it drove some reporters to angry rages—but Cronin didn't mind it. It was simply Berman's way of making himself comfortable with an idea.

"So where would you go from here?" Berman asked.

Cronin shrugged. "Have you ever heard of a dirty politician who crossed the line just once?" Cronin shook his head. "It doesn't work that way. There's a pattern. There's *always* a pattern. They do it once, it works, they do it again. And again."

Berman nodded his agreement.

"So back to the records," Cronin said.

Berman grimaced. "Looking for what, exactly?" he asked. "Jesus, we're talking about literally thousands and thousands of pieces of paper."

"But there's a profile to search for," said Cronin. "Obviously, we look only at contracts under the control of committees he chaired."

"Which were Transportation, Capital Administration, and one other," said Berman.

"Health Care," said Cronin.

Berman frowned. "Three huge areas with who knows how many contracts each."

"Thousands each," said Cronin. "At least over the past few years."

"So where do we start?" Berman asked.

"We learn from the past," Cronin said. "Crooked pols tend to focus on people who need them desperately, people who would basically go out of business without the public contract. So we look for people who have that level of dependence. That effectively eliminates any really big deals. IBM, for example, may sell the city mainframes, but Stewart would have no real leverage with a company like that. If he tried to extort them they'd go to the law or walk away. They don't need the city's business."

Berman looked skeptical. "You're describing a man with a base, predatory instinct. That's pretty far removed from what people knew."

"People knew the image, Howard, not the man," said Cronin.

"So you think he went after the most vulnerable?" Berman asked.

"Such as the DiMasis," said Cronin. "So we look for middle-sized deals, a half million up to say four or five million. And not a corporation—a small company run by one or two individuals. Companies with those sized contracts, who depend on the city for a good chunk of their revenues and who do some sort of work in health care, transportation, and—well, with capital administration it could be anything. But mostly contractors."

Berman eyed him. "Could take a while," he said.

"Two or three days in the archives is my guess," said Cronin. "With two or three good long days of fast sifting in the files I'm sure I can come up with a few dozen prospects. It won't be the entire universe but it'll be a sample."

"Then?"

"Then I start making the rounds, talking to them all, seeing what if any dealings they had with Stewart directly, whether he ever asked for anything."

"You don't want to spook them," said Berman.

"If somebody seems like a prospect, I'll point out that he's dead and there'll be no extortion prosecution," Cronin said. "That should help."

Shouts came from the city room for Berman. There had been a shooting in Roxbury. Another kid was dead on the streets. Berman moved quickly from his office heading for the city desk.

"Good hunting," he shouted back over his shoulder.

T he list turned out to be shorter than Cronin expected. He had anticipated digging up a dozen or more companies that met the critera, but after nearly twenty-seven hours over three days inside the vast, dusty catacombs of the City of Boston Public Records Division he had emerged with Xerox copies of contracts the city maintained with just six companies. All were owned by an individual or family, all relied heavily on the city (each contract document included an estimate from the vendor of the percentage of revenues the company received from the city), and all the contracts were small or medium-sized.

Cronin sat at his desk, going over the list. There was a small trucking company that had been hired by the city to plow snow.

There was a health-care company that had a contract with the city to supply mental health services to twenty-two neighborhood health centers. There was a transit company with a contract to transport special-needs students to and from Boston public schools, a collection company with a contract to computerize and collect all of the city's parking ticket revenues, a small firm that designed and installed playground equipment, and a contractor who organized the city's summer camp for the mentally retarded.

To Cronin, they all seemed decent prospects. In Boston, the disbursement of plowing contracts had long been a patronage haven. The competition was fierce from dozens of contractors with fleets of trucks that stood idle throughout the winter when construction all but ground to a halt. Others were good prospects as well, though.

Cronin was drawn to Urban Mental Health Services, which held a contract to provide mental health services in neighborhood health centers. The competition for such work was cutthroat, and in recent years there had been mounting fraud in medical services. Sandler Financial interested Cronin for the obvious reason—there were tremendous opportunities for abuse in the collection of tens of millions of dollars annually in parking fines. Two of the firms on his list were utterly dependent on the city. Both Camp Jubilee Enterprises, which ran the city's summer day camp for the mentally retarded, and Wrightways Transit, which had been contracted to transport handicapped children to and from school in specially equipped vans, relied on the city for 100 percent of their revenues. Without those contracts, they would be out of business overnight.

But when Cronin cross-checked his list of companies against the donors to Stewart's last reelection campaign, he found that the only name that showed up from any of the six firms on his list was the owner of PlayThings, Robert Dooley.

The PlayThings office was in South Boston, across Summer Street from a massive Boston Edison generating plant. It shared a long, low-slung industrial building with a plumbing supply company. Cronin arrived in the late morning of a gloriously sunny day, temperature in the high seventies and no humidity in the air, a rare day in Boston. When Cronin rang the doorbell at the PlayThings office, a man dressed in a plaid shirt and faded blue jeans, with a graying ponytail and beard, answered the door. It turned out to be Dooley, an aging hippie with a thin face and a mournful expression.

Cronin introduced himself and said he wanted to talk about Stewart. Dooley, clearly surprised, took a moment to answer. "Why me?" he asked.

Cronin had on his most ingratiating, least threatening face. This was a crucial moment in any interview—getting in the door to talk with someone who nervously or even suspiciously greeted the arrival of a reporter.

"We're talking to people about Councillor Stewart and noticed that you contributed to his last campaign," Cronin said, "and we thought we could ask you some questions about him."

Dooley seemed genuinely surprised. "I guess," said Dooley. "Come in."

The room into which Dooley led Cronin was long and narrow with a red-brick wall lined with large plants on one side and, in one corner, a drafting table and a stool. Across from it were two mismatched easy chairs and a beanbag chair, little more than a lump of leatherette on the hardwood floor. Dooley cleared some papers from one of the easy chairs and motioned for Cronin to take a seat. Dooley pulled his stool over away from the drafting table and sat down.

"Those look like fun," Cronin said, indicating bright color photos on the walls of various play structures.

Dooley nodded. "Yeah," he said with evident satisfaction. "Those are all in Austin. We got hired by a group of private companies down there a few years ago to build a series of structures. One of the folks down there had heard a talk I gave about the concept of emotional safety being as relevant as physical safety for kids. You notice the one on the right there, the yellow one, is scaled down, more comforting to a smaller child. That's specifically for toddlers. They don't react well to structures for bigger kids. They're not threatened on that like they are on a normal-sized structure."

The two men gazed at the photograph for an uncomfortable

moment. "But you're interested in Phil Stewart," said Dooley.

Cronin nodded. "I am," he said. "And I wonder whether you could tell me a little bit about how you got to know him?"

Cronin was fishing as he often did at the beginning of an interview. He did not want to let on until he had to what he was looking for.

"There isn't much to tell," said Dooley. "I was active in tent city, back in, oh, it must be twenty-plus years ago," he said, referring to a group of radical community activists and their efforts to build low-income housing in the city. "And Phil was an ally. So I knew him a little bit back then. But after that, I was gone—Cuernavaca, Berkeley, Missoula, eventually, where I finished school."

"But then you moved back here at some point," said Cronin.

"Oh, yeah, that was just four, five years ago," said Dooley. "I first got into this work in Missoula, but I had always figured I'd wend my way back here."

"And you started your business then?" Cronin asked.

"Not really," said Dooley. "I mean, I had started it already in Montana. I just really moved it here."

Cronin nodded. "And you hooked up with Councillor Stewart when you got back?"

"Not really," Dooley said. "When I came back I set up shop here and just continued with my business, you know, just as I had in Montana. Nothing much changed except the location."

Cronin wanted to be careful not to offend Dooley. "You got the big Boston contract when, a couple years ago?" Cronin asked.

"Two years ago," Dooley replied. But then he seemed annoyed. "What does that have to do with anything? I thought you were interested in Stewart?"

"I'm very interested in him," Cronin said innocently. "I just assumed he helped you get that contract."

Dooley was silent for a moment, evidently trying to figure out where Cronin was headed. "He really had next to nothing to do with it," Dooley said.

Cronin knew that Stewart had, in fact, signed off on the contract. He had a copy of the document with Stewart's signature next to Dooley's. But just as Cronin was beginning to believe that Dooley was intentionally trying to conceal that information, Dooley said: "He was there for the signing, that's it," said Dooley. "It was ceremonial. A PR event by the Parks Department. He knew nothing about the details of it. He had no memory of me until I reminded him of our Tent City days."

"So you didn't deal with him at all when you were bidding on the contract?" Cronin asked.

"Never," Dooley said.

"And your contribution to his campaign, $500 I think it was, came after that?" Cronin asked.

Dooley was red-faced. He fumbled for an answer. "Look, I design the stuff, then hire local contractors to build it. This deal is like eighty percent of my business right now, and one of the contractors asks me a while back how much money I had donated to different pols and I told him none; he advised me as an insurance policy—that's what he called it—to donate a sizable check to somebody. He said it may not guarantee you keep the deal, but it will make sure you have access to get into his office and appeal it if someone's trying to take it away."

"So he never asked you for any money?" Cronin asked.

"Stewart?" There was a look of genuine surprise on Dooley's face.

Cronin nodded.

"No," Dooley said. "Never. I just sent it in."

Cronin shook his head. "Not the campaign contribution," he said. "I meant did he ever ask for any other money?"

Dooley seemed at a loss. "What for?"

"Did he ever try to extort money from you?" Cronin asked.

Dooley appeared stunned. "Jesus, no," he said. "Are you serious?"

Cronin nodded.

"Absolutely not," he said. "Why would you even ask?"

"There was an incident reported in the paper the other day," Cronin said, "where he did that. Extorted some money from some people who owned a restaurant."

"Oh, yeah," said Dooley. "I heard about that. I couldn't really believe it. But, hey, what does it matter anyway. The guy's gone. He's dead. Leave well enough alone."

• • •

107

Cronin's visit to Randall Trucking yielded similar results, though his encounter at Randall struck a distinctly unpleasant note. Cronin had learned through the years that there were some people who had a visceral hatred for reporters. Paul Randall, owner of Randall Trucking, was among them. When Cronin arrived at the company's office and told a receptionist who he was, Randall, a heavyset man in work clothes and with an air of menace about him, promptly came charging out of a back office, opened the front door and said to Cronin: "Screw."

Cronin hesitated.

Randall did not. "You heard me," he barked. "Screw. Get off my property."

"I only wanted to ask you a few questions about Phil Stewart," Cronin said. "If you'd give me a minute I'd appreciate it."

"Screw!" Randall shouted. "Get off my property or I'll throw you off."

Cronin could see signs of progress for the city and the *Post* in Randall's reaction to him. It wasn't too many years earlier that he would have been dismissed as having come from the "nigga' loving" newspaper.

Cronin started for the door. "If you change your . . ."

". . . Get the fuck out," said Randall. "Don't even fuckin' talk to me."

When Cronin stepped outside Randall slammed the door only inches behind him.

It was certainly the least pleasant aspect of being a reporter. He had been greeted with similar hostility—and worse—many times throughout his career.

Though Cronin encountered more civil receptions at Urban Mental Health Services, Sandler Financial, and Camp Jubilee Enterprises, he uncovered no new information on Stewart. This surprised him. He did not expect a major story of corruption to tumble into his lap, but he had anticipated that one of the companies on his list would yield something, however tenuous.

He visited the last prospect, Wrightways Transit, with no real expectation of success. Wrightways was housed in a run-down concrete garage in one of Boston's worst neighborhoods. Next to the garage, which had about it the look of abandonment, was a parking lot of cracked cement through which dandelions and other weeds sprouted. The yard was surrounded by a twelve-foot chain-link fence topped with barbed wire. In one corner sat an abandoned kitchen table and a sofa bed, the stuffing pushing through slashes in the fabric. Lined up in the center of the yard were sixteen yellow Wrightways vans.

Raymond Wright was an affable man who, on this day, wore plaid Bermuda shorts and a Red Sox T-shirt. He was obese, barely able to squeeze into the tattered lawn chair he used in his office. When Cronin arrived and introduced himself, Wright, though immediately friendly, did not rise. Cronin got the sense that the man was so fat that if he tried to stand up the chair would remain attached to him. Wright's office was a tiny, cramped space barely large enough for a desk and small refrigerator. When Cronin arrived, Wright was smoking an El Producto panatella and drinking from a sixteen-ounce bottle of A&W Root Beer.

Wright explained that his company, which consisted of himself and various relatives, had a contract with the city to transport handicapped children to and from school.

"And somehow, in the process of getting the contract, I take it you met Phil Stewart," Cronin asked.

"Only the once," Wright said. "At the bid opening when I got the contract. It was just me, him, and a guy from the city clerk's office. To make it official."

"Why was Stewart there?" Cronin asked.

"They said something about him being chairman of the Transportation Committee," Wright replied.

Wright laughed and his body shook like pudding. "I was the only bidder! Nobody wants the work. It's a terrible headache, crazy zigzag routes, individual attention at each stop. With these kids, you know, the driver's got to stop, get out, go up to the apartment, help the poor mother bring the kid down, then load the kid onto the bus. And there's always changes. Schedule changes, route changes, and on and on. It's a terrible headache. The last two guys who had the contract lasted a year. Both lost money."

"So why do you do it?" Cronin asked.

"Look at this place," Wright said, waving his arm around, pointing toward the garage and the yard. "Look at it. This is everything, for me. This is it. My empire." He laughed heartily. "For twenty years I ran a garage out of here—repairs, body work—and what do I have to show for it? Some guys are born with a knack for business. Some have it, others don't. Me, I don't. I figured I'd try something new. The last guy who had the contract—I repaired his vans—told me how he wasn't going to go after it when it came up again. Too much of an arse ache. So I thought, Jesus, I'll try for it." He smiled. "And wouldn't you know I got the damn thing."

"And it's profitable?" Cronin asked.

"Profitable?" Wright puffed on his cigar and considered the question. "Depends on what you mean by profit. In accountant talk it sure ain't. But I have a different way of looking at profit. Am I ahead of the game, I ask myself. That's profit to me. And with this, I am definitely ahead of the game, you know, relative to where I'd be otherwise. The thing with this, see," Wright said with an impish grin, "is that even if *I* don't make no money, I've at least got jobs to give to my cousins, brothers, and sisters. I got half a dozen nieces and nephews working for me. My oldest boy and my daughter. They all drive and make a decent buck off it. So for me, it's worked out very good. Excellent." Wright nodded, seeming quite satisfied with the deal.

"So you saw Stewart at the bid opening and that was it?" Cronin asked.

Wright thought about it. "Except on TV," said Wright. "To be honest with you, I never cared for him that much. He was a radical liberal as far as I'm concerned. I'm not too big on the liberals, quite honestly."

"The city paid your bills on time?" Cronin asked.

Wright shook his head. "Always late. Always. They pay twice a year, always late," he said, swigging his root beer. "Last time, lemme see," he said, opening a desk drawer and pulling out an ink-stained ledger. "Last time, Christ, they paid nine weeks late. Nine weeks! I have to pay my leasing company on time. You think GM wants to wait around for its money because the city is behind. 'Hey, don't tell us your problems, pal.' My GM guy, that's what he tells me. Same with the gas companies. They want the money when you pump the gas. Shit, the city's got me in a hole all the time."

"But you get by?" Cronin asked.

"The trick is to keep the routes tight and the drivers pay reasonable," he said.

"Those are your biggest expenses, gas and the drivers?"

"Naturally, besides the leases on the vehicles," said Wright. "But there are a hell of a lot of others that add up. You'd be surprised. Insurance is wicked, of course, plus linkage payments, maintenance. It adds up."

"Linkage?" Cronin asked.

"Yeah, it's only, what, half of a percent annually but that's real money."

Cronin shook his head as though lost, feigning ignorance. He asked, "How does it work exactly?"

"Simple," said Wright. "You remember when the real estate boom was hot and heavy downtown? The pols, they latched on to linkage. If you wanted to develop a tower downtown you had to build housing in the slums. It was the price of admission. You don't like that, fine, screw, amscray. They had them lined up on City Hall Plaza begging for the go-ahead with condos, hotels, office buildings, you name it. Development here was a license to print money. And the city used linkage to cash in. The idea was they *linked* some business thing to some do-gooder project. A legal kickback, if you ask me."

Cronin knew the linkage law well. He had covered the issue when it was first proposed and he knew it applied only to large, downtown real estate projects. There was no provision within the law which would have permitted any linkage arrangement with a contract such as Wrightways had.

Cronin could barely believe what he was hearing. He wondered whether Wright might be lying. But the man was so open, so utterly guileless, that Cronin dismissed the possibility.

"Bear with me if you will," said Cronin, "so I make sure I understand this."

"Happy to help. You want a cold drink? Root Beer?"

"Please," said Cronin.

Wright reached over and opened the refrigerator. It was jammed with a dozen or more bottles of A&W. He pulled a couple out and snapped them open with a church key. Wright handed one to Cronin. He put the other to his lips and drank a third of it in one chug. He wiped his mouth and puffed on his cigar.

"I'm not sure I understand what linkage has to do with you," Cronin said. "You get the contract with the city to transport handicapped kids . . ."

"Sometimes we take 'em to events, or therapy or whatever," said Wright. "It's mostly to and from school but not strictly. When they have a special day at Fenway for the kids, we take 'em over. That kind of thing."

"So how does linkage affect you?" Cronin asked.

"See, I get the business so I have to do something in return for getting the business, same as a downtown developer," said Wright. "I pay much less, naturally, because of the scale. But it's along the same idea, see what I'm saying?"

Cronin nodded.

"So what do you do in return for the contract?"

"Well, everybody's different, as I understand it," he said. "I make payments to a homeless shelter. But the way it was explained to me was that other businesses pay to different things— to a housing fund or health clinics, what have you."

"Who exactly do you pay?"

"One of the shelters," Wright replied.

"Which one?"

"Well, it's not a shelter exactly, but something having to do with the homeless," said Wright. "It's called the Shelter Coalition Capital Fund."

"And that is what, exactly?" Cronin asked.

Wright shrugged. "Like I say, something to do with the homeless. A building or construction fund or some such. I never paid that much attention to it, to be truthful."

"You pay by check?"

"Of course."

"And where do you send the check?" Cronin asked.

"To the Fund," Wright said. "A P.O. box downtown."

Cronin was astonished by the simplicity of it. It was so clear now. Stewart was committing extortion yet the person being fleeced didn't know it. He merely considered it a legitimate part of the deal.

"Hasn't anyone ever told you that this was an odd arrangement?"

Wright was puzzled. "How so?"

"Hasn't anyone ever said it doesn't seem quite right to make these payments?"

"I thought it was screwy at first, no question. No question about it. Then it was fully explained to me," said Wright. "Stewart . . . he showed me the actual paperwork on the deal between Forbes Development and the city. Worth millions. They build the building on the water, the new bank. He gave me a copy to look at. Serious money there. My deal was peanuts compared. Peanuts. I pay, what? Let me see." Again, he pulled a ledger book out from a drawer and thumbed through the pages. "Here," he said, running his finger down the page. "I pay what amounts to a half a percent of the contract in linkage money. Since the contract total runs just shy of $1.9 million a year, that's linkage dough of eighteen grand and change."

"Who knows about this?" Cronin asked.

Wright regarded him warily. He puffed on his El Producto and said, "You're beginning to make me a little, how should I say, jiggy."

Cronin smiled. "I don't mean to," he said.

"Then why do you ask who knows about this?" Wright wondered.

"I'm curious whether your arrangement is common knowledge," Cronin said. "Whether anyone has ever questioned it?"

"Questioned it how so?" Wright asked.

"Whether it was legitimate," said Cronin.

Wright looked alarmed. "Hey, I pay the linkage. I get the kids to school. I get 'em home. I fulfill the terms of the contract."

"You misunderstand me," Cronin said calmly. "I wonder whether anybody has ever questioned whether the deal was legitimate from Stewart's end."

"Oh, Jesus," said Wright, as though suddenly realizing what

had happened. "Don't tell me. Hello federal." He shook his head as though defeated. "Vincent, my brother-in-law. He told me I was being jobbed. He said the deal stunk."

Wright's eyes beseeched Cronin for a sign that it wasn't so, for some indication that Vincent was wrong. The truth seemed, at that moment, to dawn on Raymond Wright.

"Weren't you ever suspicious?" Cronin asked.

Wright nodded. "When he told me not to talk about it with anyone, I was. He was adamant. He said that he was giving me a special deal, way below what others were paying, and if word of that got out he'd have to jack me way up. He said some people were paying one percent, even a point and a half."

Cronin took it all in.

"Am I in trouble?" Wright asked.

"You didn't do anything wrong," Cronin said. "Not knowingly, anyway. I can't imagine the DA would lean on you."

"Unbelievable," Wright said, shaking his head.

"I'd like your permission to write a story about this," Cronin said.

Wright shrugged. "Why not? I got nothing to hide. Stupidity's not a crime, is it?" And he laughed.

Under Massachusetts law, virtually every record pertaining to the financial status of a tax-exempt charity was public information. Before writing the story of Stewart's extortion of money from Wrightways, Cronin needed to be absolutely sure that the Shelter Coalition Capital Fund had been under Stewart's control. Instinctively, he was certain it was the case, but to publish a story he needed documentation.

At the Secretary of State's office, he found extensive records on an entity called the Shelter Coalition Inc., a large nonprofit corporation which served as a legal umbrella for dozens of shelters, soup kitchens, and other charities for the homeless throughout Massachusetts. Stewart had been chairman of the Shelter Coalition Inc., and he was listed as one of seven legal signatories—people empowered to spend funds on behalf of the organization.

The Shelter Coalition Capital Fund, Cronin discovered amid a pile of papers, was an entirely different entity, a separate charitable corporation. It listed Stewart as chairman and empowered Stewart only—no other person—to spend funds on behalf of the fund.

This was the smoking gun. It proved that Stewart controlled the money that Wright deposited into the account and could spend it any way he chose. The records indicated that the fund had taken in a total of $107,496 the previous year with an equal amount dispersed. In other words, Stewart had spent every cent taken in by the trust. How he spent the money was another matter, one which would require further digging. But it was clear from Wright's comments and from the records that Stewart had been running an illegal scam, that he extorted money from Wright under the guise of the city linkage ordinance, and that he had directed the money to be placed into an account over which he had sole control. The records raised an additional question: eighteen thousand came from Wright. What was the source of the remaining $89,000?

Cronin wanted to wait until he could find out how Stewart had spent the money, but Berman would not hear of it; he was crazed for the story. Berman was worried about the competition, worried that a reporter from the *Record* might somehow uncover the Wrightways angle and print it the next day. And besides, he argued that there was now a pattern of corruption on Stewart's part. No longer, said Berman, was there the possibility that the DiMasi's case was merely an isolated incident.

Cronin relented. He wrote a carefully worded account of his conversation with Raymond Wright, which appeared on the front page of the *Post* on Thursday, July 27. The headline read: "Contractor Charges Stewart with Extortion."

> *Former Councillor Philip Stewart apparently extorted funds from a Boston transit company owner with a city contract by convincing the businessman that the payments were linkage funds for the homeless, according to the businessman.*
>
> *For the past three years, Raymond Wright, owner of*

Wrightways Transit, who holds a $1.9 million city contract, said he made two payments annually of more than $9,000 to an account under Stewart's control.

Wright made the payments to an account under the control of the Shelter Coalition Capital Fund, he said during an interview. Records on file at the secretary of state's office indicate that the Shelter Coalition Capital Fund was controlled by Stewart.

Records showing that Stewart was the fund's chairman also indicate that only Stewart was empowered to disperse funds from the Shelter Coalition Capital Fund account.

The revelation of Stewart's arrangement with Wrightways is the second apparently illegal financial maneuver by Stewart reported within the past week.

The Post *reported last week that investigators are probing allegations that Stewart extorted more than $19,000 from a Boston catering concern with city contracts over a period of seven years.*

The charge that Stewart extorted funds disguised as linkage payments was made by Raymond Wright, owner of Wrightways Transit, which has a contract to transport special-needs students in the public schools. Wrightways principal function is to transport physically and mentally handicapped children to and from school.

According to Wright and city records, Wrightways won the contract three years ago. Wrightways was the only bid made to the city. As chairman of the council's Transportation Committee, Stewart passed on all transportation contracts, including those with the school department.

During an interview, Raymond Wright said that at the time he was awarded the contract he was summoned to Stewart's office for a meeting at which Stewart said that his obligation, having won the contract, was to pay a half of one percent of the contract amount in so-called linkage money to the Shelter Coalition Capital Fund. Wright said Stewart told him that the money would go for maintenance, rehab, and construction work.

116

Berman considered the story a home run. Now there were at least two scams, he told Roy Johnson, and if there were two, surely there were more. This bit of speculation from Berman seemed not to please Johnson. In fact, it brought a frown, dark and forbidding, to the face of the editor of the Boston *Post*.

CHAPTER

8

On a warm, sunny morning, the day the *Post* carried Cronin's article about Wrightways Transit, three dozen people appeared in front of the newspaper to protest the treatment of Philip Stewart. The demonstrators were young, in their twenties for the most part, though there were a half dozen among them who were in their fifties, even sixties. Demonstrations against the newspaper—its editorial position in support of abortion rights, its coverage of the Arab-Israeli conflict, its cancellation of an obscure comic strip—were common. Few had any impact at all on the paper or how it was perceived by its readers. But this demonstration, these demonstrators, were different. They presented a threat to the paper's reputation not because they were activists who worked as volunteers or paid staffers for the Shelter Coalition. The real threat to the *Post* was the man at the center of the demonstration, its organizer and leader, Father Patrick Boyle. While the demonstrators were dressed in blue jeans and cutoffs, tank tops and T-shirts, Boyle stood out in his priestly garb of black polyester slacks, bagged at the knee, cheaply made black tie shoes, and a black top with Roman collar.

Boyle was a thin, bearded, ascetic with deep-set eyes and an intense air. He squinted against the sun as he chatted with the half dozen reporters dispatched by television and radio stations to cover this event. This was news. For years, Boyle's causes had been the *Post*'s causes. Rarely had they disagreed on major issues. And, in fact, the *Post* had crusaded on its editorial pages (and some would say on its news pages as well) for the agenda enunciated by the Shelter Coalition and its legislative director, Patrick Boyle. Boyle was one of the best-known priests in the city, a man respected for his zealous commitment to the causes of the poor. For many people in Boston, it had been jarring to see the *Post* run two negative stories about Phil Stewart, a *Post* ally and at the top of the paper's unwritten list of political untouchables. But if Stewart had been at the top of that list, Boyle was next in line, and to see Boyle going so far as to organize a demonstration against the paper with which he had been so allied was also jarring in its way.

The demonstration was deeply embarrassing to the *Post,* and to Berman and Roy Johnson in particular. As editor, Johnson had absolute control over the *Post* editorial page, and he had used that power on scores of occasions when Boyle called and asked the paper to take one stand or another.

Johnson stood in an office on the building's third floor looking down at the demonstration, seething inside, furious not at Boyle so much as he was at Berman and Cronin for bringing this embarrassment on the paper. Johnson knew that the *Record-American* and the city's TV and radio stations—all competitors of the *Post* in the business of news gathering—would feast on this story, giving plenty of space and airtime to Boyle and making much of what would be perceived as a rift between the paper and the forces of Good led by Father Boyle. The *Post* was a paper with a liberal bent, and by letting that show through in its news pages, the paper had long since alienated conservatives in the city, including Republicans, many Roman Catholics, and blue-collar families who felt disconnected from the paper. The *Post* had its base among liberals, the very people with whom Boyle had the greatest credibility. If Boyle chose, he could harm the paper's reputation and perhaps even its circulation among those people.

As they walked a steady circle holding up banners reading "Honk if you hate the *Post*" and "Phil Stewart's memory lives," TV crews filmed the scene.

Berman, too, watched. Like Johnson, Berman was rattled by it. The city editor had known Boyle for nearly ten years. The two men had met in Central America when Berman was doing a stint as a foreign correspondent and Boyle was a missionary. They had stayed in touch when both men were back in Boston, though Boyle's interest in Berman was clearly related to what Berman could do in the way of publicizing Boyle's causes. Berman knew that Boyle was friendly with Roy Johnson and that the priest would go so far as to lead a demonstration at the paper was alarming to Berman. Berman thought Boyle a man of peculiar, though undeniable, charisma.

Berman had seen Boyle lead demonstrations before, most recently in Boston where he led marches for fair housing, welfare rights, jobs for the poor. He had also seen him lead demonstrations in Nicaragua in the late 1980s. In Managua, Boyle worked with a cadre of liberation theologists, priests whose missions took them into the poorest barrios where they ministered not only to the spiritual needs of the flock but to the social and political needs as well. These radical priests believed that to follow the teachings of the Gospel it was their responsibility to care for the poor practically as well as theologically.

There was something about Boyle that bothered Berman. Something hazy about his past. Though there had been literally dozens of stories done about him in local and national papers, magazines, and television stations, no one had ever fully explained the circumstances under which Boyle had left Haiti, where he had been working as a missionary after his time in Nicaragua.

In Haiti, Boyle had been a supporter of Father Aristide, long before the priest was elected to the presidency. Boyle shared Aristide's love of the poor masses living in squalid conditions in vast slums of Port-au-Prince. During the time Boyle had been in the country there had been much bloodshed. It had been common for innocent citizens who opposed the government to be shot down in the street by the army, or the Tontons Macoutes. And it was common for the people to retaliate against wealthy businesspeople and landowners, supporters of the Macoutes. In the parish where Boyle worked there were many instances where Macoutes were hacked to death with machetes, where businesspeople were subjected to "necklacing," a particularly savage form of torture where an automobile tire was placed around the neck, doused with gasoline, and ignited. When Boyle was recalled to the United States by the directorate of the Silesian Order, he refused, saying his mission was with the poor. Though the director insisted he leave, for his own safety, Boyle would not. Soon thereafter he was kidnapped by Macoutes, severely beaten and stabbed, tossed into a ditch on the city's outskirts, and left for dead. Miraculously, he was found by peasants who got him to a doctor in time to save his life.

"God would prefer I continue to make a bother of myself on earth," Boyle had been quoted as saying after he recovered. His willingness to remain in the country, his insistence that he stay with his flock and his subsequent shooting, resulted in a wave of flattering publicity and a hero's welcome when he returned to Boston.

In the years since his return, Boyle had plunged in to work on behalf of the poor and homeless. He had risen to the position of vice chairman of the Shelter Coalition. He had long waited for his opportunity to take what he viewed as his rightful place as head of the Shelter Coalition. He had felt a calling to the priesthood as a young man and for years he had felt called as well to be the leader of the poor of Greater Boston, the poor who lived amid such wealth. It was a crime, Boyle thought, a crime against man and against God. He had fervently believed since his return from missionary work that he would lead a quiet revolution here at home. He had patiently bided his time fully expecting that the degenerate Stewart would have retired by now.

But now that Boyle's chance had finally arrived, he feared that the vehicle of his revolution, the Coalition, was being heavily damaged.

Boyle feared he might be inheriting a burned-out organization, a shell of what it had once been. For the power of the Coalition was financial and political, and to attract money and exercise political muscle the Coalition needed the deep well of credibility it had always enjoyed. Stewart's activities were a grave threat to that credibility and Boyle knew it. The priest also knew it was in his self-interest and that of the organization to do whatever could be done to preserve the organization's reputation. If a perception took hold among the population that Stewart had been nothing but a venal crook who raped the Coalition, its sources of money—the public, major banks, corporations, and foundations—would dry up.

He and Stewart had been viewed as close associates and friends. Associates they were, but not friends. Very few people knew, in fact, that Father Pat Boyle had come to despise Philip Stewart.

"It is so very disappointing to me, after all of the good this institution has done, that for some inexplicable reason they now appear determined to destroy the legacy of a great man," Boyle told the reporters who had gathered before him outside. "I am frankly at a loss to understand the motive, but I understand clearly the effect: they're robbing a dead man of his reputation. And I find something particularly offensive about that. A man who devoted his life to seeking economic justice and who is unable to defend himself is a target of not character assassination but legacy assassination, I suppose you'd call it."

Boyle's assault on the *Post,* carried on a dozen radio news programs and several television news shows, brought a flood of angry callers who shared his sense of outrage. Throughout the morning, callers to various radio talk programs in town were apopletic. The lines were jammed with people waiting not to express disappointment in Stewart but to heap scorn on the *Post.* Hosts of the programs as well as the overwhelming majority of callers were incensed at the newspaper for sullying Stewart's name.

"It's a desecration, Jerry," said a caller to one program. "His body is still warm, in the ground a matter of days, and they commit a desecration. There's no other way to describe it, Jerry. What about the presumption of innocence, Jerry? What about that? He was never even charged with any crimes, never indicted, never mind tried or convicted. Never got his day in court, Jerry, and now this desecration."

When Berman heard what Boyle had said, he was distressed. "I cannot believe what I am hearing," he said. "Did anybody in this city do more for Stewart's causes than this newspaper?"

Cronin shook his head.

"Damn it, that pisses me off," said Berman, banging the desk with the palm of his hand and getting up to pace in the bullpen behind the city desk.

Cronin sat nearby. He shrugged. "What do you expect?" he asked in a reasoned voice. "These people have an image of Stewart that they've carried through the years. They revere him as some sort of chosen one and then, suddenly, their hero is gone. And on top of that, as though that isn't jarring enough to the acolytes, two weeks later, they're informed that the guy was a thief. They're being told that they worshiped a false god all this time."

"And in the meantime, who gets hurt?" Berman asked. "We do. In the meantime, the very institution that champions the causes in which those assholes believe, gets hurt. Let's not kid ourselves. This man can damage us. He perhaps more than anyone in town. He's got credibility. People view him as clean, unfettered. And we don't exactly start out with a huge reservoir of goodwill out there. People think we're a rung or two above used-car salesmen. We need every shred of credibility we can hang on to. And Boyle can hurt us. He goes on the tube wearing that Roman collar and people listen."

Berman's private line rang and he grabbed it. He listened and spoke briefly before hanging up.

"Boyle's in the lobby," said Berman. "Johnson's going to meet with him. He wants us there."

They gathered in Johnson's office. The editor was gracious when Boyle arrived. The priest shook hands with Johnson and Berman and ignored Frank Cronin. His face, pocked by acne, was flushed from the heat. He was sweating through his shirt, causing it stick to his back. He sat on an antique bench across from where Johnson sat in a rocking chair. Berman and Cronin sat on a sofa off to the side.

"I don't understand what's going on here," he said. "I must tell you I don't get it. Philip's reputation took a very long time to build, and now, suddenly, seemingly from nowhere, you people are out to destroy it in a week," Boyle said. "Why can't you permit his good soul to rest in peace?"

Johnson shifted in his seat, clearly uncomfortable.

"Sometimes when we follow the news, Father, the results aren't so pleasant," said Berman. "But the point is that in a sense it's out of our hands. It isn't discretionary. We have an obligation to follow the news, pleasant or not."

"But with all due respect," said the priest in a low voice, "you've gotten it wrong. I understand you have to print the news, but you have an obligation to get it right. And you haven't."

The room was still. Johnson knitted his brow. Berman's heart raced. The possibility that the stories were somehow factually incorrect was frightening. The worst thing for any newspaper was getting the story wrong.

"How do you mean?" Berman asked.

"You portray Phil as venal and greedy, as out for his personal gain," the priest said. "You don't explain the whole story."

"Which is?"

"That politicians commonly bend the rules for political fund-raising," said the priest. "Campaigns are very expensive. Your own paper has documented just how expensive and editorialized in favor of changing the way campaigns are financed. Here was a good man who, like so many other politicians, bent the rules to raise campaign funds, and you villify him."

Johnson and Berman were stunned. The idea that in his stories Cronin had missed the mark so wildly, that he had not reported that the funds were for Stewart's campaigns would be, if true, hugely embarrassing. Clearly, there was a dramatic difference between pressuring people for money for campaigns and extorting funds for personal use. Readers would be far quicker to forgive the former.

Johnson, his visage dark, glanced at Cronin, who started to speak in his own defense, but Johnson swiftly cut him off. "We're here so Father Boyle can have his say," said Johnson in a chilly tone.

"Look," said the priest, the voice of reason, "I deplore the business of political fund-raising, just as I suspect you people do. But the truth is that many politicians in this city and all across the country bend the rules. And so for me, there's a choice: adhere absolutely to the letter of the law and perhaps lose a man such as Phil Stewart from public life, or bend the rules and keep him in office doing so much good for so many people. To me, that's an easy call. The moral imperative demands that we do what we must do to keep him in office."

Boyle leaned forward on the bench. "Am I proud of the fund-raising techniques sometimes used by Phil? No. But don't you see a vast difference between fund-raising indiscretions and the kind of brutal extortion you have portrayed?"

There was a prolonged, uncomfortable silence in the room. Finally, Berman spoke.

"Why didn't you come talk with us after the first story ran about the DiMasis?" he asked.

"Because I assumed," said the priest, "that that was a one-shot deal." He shifted his glance to Johnson. "I didn't expect that the *Post* would mount a jihad against an honorable man in death."

"How can you be so sure of what you're telling us?" Johnson asked. "That it was for fund-raising?"

Boyle half laughed. He spoke softly, yet with a haughty air of certainty. "Well, because, as I'm sure your reporter must know"—and here Boyle turned and looked squarely at Cronin—"I was Phil's campaign treasurer. I handled all the money."

In the early morning, Cronin sat at his desk in the newsroom, alone. He could still feel the sting of Johnson's gaze from the previous afternoon. It was clear that Johnson believed Boyle's version of events. After Boyle had gone, Cronin told Johnson he did not believe that Stewart had been raising money for his campaigns. He could tell Johnson had not believed him. Even Berman had been shaky. How they could view what was so obviously extortion as fund-raising was a mystery to him. No matter, thought Cronin. It was clear that he would now have to dig deeper, that he would have to prove Stewart guilty of sins darker than fund-raising irregularities.

The city room was hushed. In the distance, Cronin could hear the police scanners crackling on the city desk. He took a yellow legal pad out of his desk and sat back, a cup of coffee nearby, and began making notes on the pad.

Suddenly, Cronin looked up and there, much to his surprise—it was not yet seven o'clock—was Lydia Wells, the woman who occupied the desk next to his. She was a young reporter—a "writer" was how she introduced herself, the term *reporter* was insufficiently lofty to suit her—and she had been given plum assignments since moving off General Assignment a couple of years earlier. She had yet to reach thirty.

For some reason she had taken a liking to Cronin.

"You're in early," he said cheerfully.

"I'm just leaving," she said. "I started this piece last night right after Letterman. I've been working on it forever." She slid on top of her desk and sat in a lotus position. "The piece seems too removed for me, so far. I wish it could have the spareness your stuff has. Your stuff is so . . . so . . . gritty," she said. "Close to the ground."

She glanced at the clock and saw that it was nearly seven. "I'm out of here," she said, rising and grabbing her bag. "I've got to get some sleep. But, hey," she said, turning back to face him. "I meant to ask you. These Stewart stories you've done, what's up with that?"

He shrugged. "Chasing various leads."

She tilted her head sideways. "But, like, I don't get it. What have you got against this dude? I mean, he's dead." She turned to go, and said, "Lighten up."

Many law enforcement people found it embarrassing to be forced to follow leads that emanated from news stories, but McCormack didn't mind in the least. He didn't care at all, in fact, where his leads came from. He was happy to have any information that might bring more order to his case.

And the Wrightways Transit article that Cronin had written certainly helped do that.

In a case such as this one, in fact, there was a distinct possibility that a front-page story in the *Post* about Raymond Wright being extorted without his knowledge might embolden others

who'd been held up by Stewart—with or without their knowledge—to step forward.

On the morning that Patrick Boyle and his followers demon-
strated outside the *Post*, Detective McCormack arrived at the
Suffolk County Courthouse for a meeting with Sloane about the
progress—or lack thereof—of the Stewart investigation. Mc-
Cormack carried a packet of papers in the pocket of his suit
jacket, papers that contained the notes he'd gathered from supervising his team of detectives investigating the case.

One of the sheets of paper contained McCormack's unofficial
list of suspects, people he had even a slight reason to be suspicious about. His instructions to his men had been, as usual, to
cast a wide net. He wanted to include every conceivable name on
the list and then winnow it down as the investigation progressed. The list, of course, included the names of Arlene Di-
Masi and her husband (who had boasted to a companion in a
North End men's club that he had done it himself, according to
a police informant; McCormack had great difficulty believing
this—DiMasi had never been accused of a crime in his life—but
one never knew).

Numerous other names populated the list, including another
councillor, Stewart's nemesis, a right-winger named Buster
Navarro, who'd opposed virtually every liberal initiative Stewart
had proposed during his career from an increase in welfare to
distribution of condoms in public schools. Navarro, upon hearing the news that Stewart was dead, had reportedly nodded his
head and said, "Outstanding."

There were other names, people who had been crossed by
Stewart during his career, some angry constituents in the habit
of writing him nasty letters.

But nowhere on the list was even a single name that made Mc-
Cormack feel like he had the killer in his sights. Nowhere on the
list was a name that made McCormack sit up and begin to as-
semble the pieces in his mind.

But he was not worried. He had been doing this long enough
to know that only the rarest homicide cases go unsolved. Mc-
Cormack was a patient man and he believed that they would get
their break in the case. Whether that break would come in

weeks, months, or years he did not know. Though he suspected, from past experience, that it would be sooner rather than later.

"So it seems," said Sloane, holding up a copy of the *Post* containing Frank's story about Wrightways Transit, "that your secret life theory may have something to it."

"It makes more sense than anything else we've got," said Mack.

Sloane nodded. "So we feel some confidence that this was not random?" Sloane said.

McCormack shrugged. "It has none of the signs," he said. "How many random killings have we seen in four years, five years?" he asked. "Two, maybe three that we've worked on," he said. "And they all have a messy scene and there's robbery and the people are drunk or on drugs and sloppy and they get seen by passersby or neighbors. They are messy. This is clean. Surgical."

"Anything new from the scene?" Sloane asked.

"Nothing worth anything," said McCormack. "The perp wears sneakers, Reeboks to be precise. Men's. No prints other than those of the deceased. Denim fibers."

"Nothing," said Sloane.

"Nothing," McCormack agreed.

"You worried?" Sloane asked.

McCormack shook his head dismissively. "Nah," he said. "Something'll pop up."

Sloane seemed skeptical. "I don't know," she said. "This has a funny feel to it."

"It does," said Mack. "I agree. But this"—he motioned toward Frank's story about Wrightways—"could conceivably lead somewhere."

Sloane nodded.

"I've got a subpoena going in this afternoon for the bank records of the Shelter Coalition Capital Fund. But you know how reluctant banks are to cough up documents."

"Could be a week or two before you get what you want," he said.

"So we'll go through those very carefully and see whether

there are any leads," said Sloane. "In the meantime, we keep interviewing friends, acquaintances, and neighbors."

Sloane sat back in her chair and folded her arms across her chest. "I must admit I am still not quite prepared to fully believe that Stewart was a bad man," she said. "I just have a hard time reconciling the public man with these indications of another, darker private side."

Believe it, McCormack thought. But he did not say it.

CHAPTER
9

It was fitting that the John F. Kennedy Library could be seen from the corner office occupied by *Post* editor Roy Johnson. Originally, Johnson had hoped the Kennedy family would realize its dream of having the library located in Cambridge, on a choice bit of Harvard Square real estate overlooking the Charles River. Kennedy had been a Harvard man, of course, and his administration had been populated by literally dozens of others. But Cambridge city leaders feared gridlock would result from the streams of tourists the place would surely attract, and they resolutely resisted construction of the library there. And so the building wound up on a point overlooking Dorchester Bay with a view of Boston Harbor.

Roy Johnson was also a Harvard man, and though he had not been a member of the Kennedy administration, he had covered the Kennedy White House for the *Post*. Through the years, the *Post* had supported the Kennedy family in their political ambitions. And no Kennedy had been more rabidly supported than Jack, and no *Post* reporter or editor had been more accommodating to Jack than Roy Johnson. He had known Kennedy since the late forties, had covered his first campaign for Congress in 1948. As a columnist, Johnson had been an ardent supporter of Kennedy's run for the U.S. Senate in 1952 against Henry Cabot Lodge. When Kennedy was elected president, Johnson had moved to Washington to head the *Post* bureau there. And his association with Kennedy proved magic, for access to the president and his men gave Johnson something enjoyed by few other

Washington journalists. Those had been Johnson's Glory Days. So prominent did Johnson become in Washington circles during the Kennedy years that he was hired away from the *Post* by *Time* magazine to become, initially, *Time*'s chief Washington correspondent and, later, the magazine's deputy executive editor. After Kennedy's death, he had maintained contact with other members of the family. Through the years, his Kennedy associations had given him a cache of sorts in journalistic circles. Johnson was not averse to doing a favor for the Kennedys now and again—writing a favorable column, making sure an editorial contained the Kennedy spin, influencing a news story so that it wasn't overly critical.

Johnson no longer fooled himself. He once thought of himself as a political player in Washington. It was many years before he realized that politicians worked him and feigned intimacy with him purely for what they could get out of the arrangement. Having seen his illusions for what they were, he had left *Time* and returned to Boston when the editor's position had come open at the *Post*. His plan was to live out his career in Boston where, as editor, he had some legitimate power. He had the final word on hirings and firings, on assignments, on who would be awarded a column, on promotions, on whether stories ran and where they were played.

Johnson was a worldly man—well traveled, elegantly tailored. He was of medium height and build, with thinning reddish hair, fair skin, and tortoiseshell glasses that gave him an academic air.

Though Johnson had been a confidant of Stewart's—at least that is what Stewart had led Johnson to believe—the editor had never before had to flex his editorial muscle on Stewart's behalf. For the truth was that Phil Stewart was one of those rare politicians who seemed above reproach and had never received bad publicity. The councillor's death had been a blow to Johnson, though hardly more than the news that Stewart had been involved in at least a couple of corrupt ventures. He had been shocked at the story of Stewart's extortion of the DiMasis and further chagrined at the *Post*'s report on Wrightways Transit.

He had thought the stories legitimate and fairly done. But he had recently been buried in an avalanche of criticism from people with whom it was important for Johnson to have a connection—the Kennedy's, the cardinal. He had received calls from them all—calls from four different members of the Kennedy family—urging him to lay off Stewart. It was fund-raising, they claimed. It was not pleasant or pretty, but it was a reality of politics. Stop persecuting a good man's memory, they urged.

He contemplated this from his corner office where he never failed to thrill at the site of the alabaster lines of the library across the way. He could ignore many of the calls that came to him pleading mercy for the memory of Phil Stewart, but ignoring the Kennedys was not something he did lightly. They had done so much for him through the years, provided him with a level of access and credibility he would otherwise never have enjoyed.

But beyond that it was through the Kennedys that he had met Gabrielle. He sat back in his chair, his hands clasped together and placed behind his head, reclining and gazing out at the bay. A smile came involuntarily to his face. Yes, he had met Gabrielle through the Kennedys and for that he would remain forever in their debt.

It had happened three years earlier, just six or so months after Johnson had gotten divorced from Miriam, his wife of thirty-one years. The break had not been in the least rancorous. Their marriage, they both sadly realized, had simply run out of steam. With their three children grown and happily off on their own, there was now no reason to remain together. Miriam had her life, Roy had his, and the two rarely intersected.

The summer after their breakup, Roy had been invited to Hyannis Port for a weekend. Among the guests were Henri Juenot and his wife and daughter. Juenot was one of the leading industrialists in France, the chairman of a conglomerate which owned three dozen companies throughout the world. He had once been in the diplomatic service, posted to Washington, where he had come to know members of the Kennedy family. Juenot was the product of immensely wealthy parents renowned for their generous support of artists and artistic institutions throughout France. They were also prominent Roman Catholics who had been regular guests of popes through the years.

But Johnson's interest that weekend in Hyannis Port was not in Henri Juenot or his wife, but in their daughter Gabrielle, who was then twenty-nine years old. Johnson believed that he fell in love with Gabrielle before he had actually seen her face, that he had fallen in love with a sublime, ethereal image. He had been seated on the terrace of one of the homes within the compound—Ted Kennedy's, he recalled—when he saw, across the expansive lawn, a woman walking alone toward the edge of the water. It was early evening, high tide, and the woman seemed to him, at first, to be a vision shimmering in the setting sunlight. She wore a long dress, a light gauzelike fabric, and as she walked he could see the outline of her long legs. Her hair was of medium length, thick, and the color of chestnuts, and she would patiently brush it away from her face as the sea breeze kicked up.

Johnson sat on the terrace, alone, sipping a drink and watching her move across the grass. He noticed she was barefoot. When she reached the shore on the far side of the lawn she stood for a moment in the breeze, her back to the setting sun, then she knelt, her head bowed. When she rose, Johnson was not sure but he thought he saw her make the sign of the cross. Had she knelt in prayer? he wondered.

She ambled back across the lawn and about halfway to the house she glanced up and seemed to notice him. She approached him, her face flushed. She was tall and so very thin. Her mouth was small, though her lips were full and red. Her eyes were bright and large, a rich blue, and he noticed that her cheekbones were high and pronounced. One of her teeth, on the bottom, was slightly crooked. He was relieved by this imperfection.

"You were watching me," she said pleasantly, as she approached him.

He was startled and not sure quite what to say, so he blurted the truth. "I could not help it," he confessed. "You are very beautiful."

"Ah, you are so kind," she said, blushing slightly and glancing away. "I am Gabrielle Juenot," she said, extending her hand. "And you are?"

He suddenly fumbled to place his glass on a small table by his chair and quickly rose to introduce himself. "Forgive me, please," he said. "How rude of me. My name is Roy Johnson."

"You are the newspaper man, no?" she asked.

"I am," he replied, feeling rather pleased that she knew who he was.

"That must be the most interesting sort of work, is it?"

Thus began the most glorious relationship of his life.

Roy Johnson had always been a rational man, never one who permitted his emotions to rule. Throughout his life he had taken the measure of whatever situation faced him, personal or professional, and made a careful, considered judgment.

But from the moment he met Gabrielle, from that weekend in Hyannis Port on, Roy Johnson was overwhelmed by a pure passion he had never before experienced. Initially, he thought it a lustful infatuation. But as time passed and as he began to see her more frequently—for dinner or lunch or a weekend stroll in the city—he became aware that his desire was not for her beauty, her body—though he greatly desired it. It was a far greater, more profound passion simply to be with her, in her presence.

He loved her, he realized, in a way and with a depth utterly unfamiliar to him. He revealed none of this to her, of course. He was, in fact, deathly afraid of spooking her, and he was sick with the thought that she kept company with him only to bide her time until a younger, more suitable man, a more appropriate marriage candidate, came along. But it soon became clear she was doing no such thing. Gabrielle, it turned out, loved him as well.

In those first weeks and months they spent time together he learned much about Gabrielle: that she had taken a degree in art history at the Sorbonne, that she had eclectic tastes that ran from El Greco to Paul Klee. When it came to the art world, Roy Johnson was on less than solid footing and he enjoyed learning from her, was grateful for her lack of pretension on the subject. He loved that she was a physical fitness fanatic, that she had been close to an Olympic-level skier until she tore the cartilage in a knee.

And he learned, most importantly, that at the center of her life, the thing that grounded her and from which she drew immense strength and joy, was her faith. Notwithstanding her disagreements with Church policy on matters such as birth control, she was a devout Roman Catholic who attended Mass four, even five, times a week.

Johnson had himself been raised a Catholic. But there was a problem. Both Johnson and his first wife were Catholics and they had married in a church ceremony. Though they were divorced, the Church still recognized their marriage as valid.

That Gabrielle would marry in a civil, not a religious ceremony, was inconceivable. The solution was obvious: Johnson would petition for an annulment of his first marriage, clearing the way for him to marry Gabrielle in the Church. Such a procedure had become common, and when Johnson initiated the process, he did some research and found that he could reasonably expect to have the marriage annuled in twelve to fourteen months.

But then came the bad news. During his first meeting with the pastor of his church, he got inklings that the Church was cracking down on annulments. The pastor told him a new man had been installed as vicar of the Tribunal of the Archdiocese of Boston. The man had come with a mandate to cut back on annulments. In subsequent meetings with his pastor and in phone conversations with influential Catholics he knew, Johnson learned that there was indeed a crackdown in the making. He was told that officials at the Vatican had been watching with mounting chagrin as the Church in the United States let the number of annulments get out of hand. It got to the point where the U.S. Church accounted for 80 percent of all the annulments granted in the world.

In Rome, this was regarded as a scandal. Making matters worse for Johnson was the fact that the diocese that led the United States in annulments was none other than Boston, the place that would first be targeted for far more stringent regulations.

This was terribly disheartening news for Roy Johnson and Gabrielle Juenot. Nonetheless, they proceeded. After sixteen months, the process had not budged. Worse yet, Miriam decided to oppose the annulment. She did not want her marriage, though dissolved under Massachusetts law, to be dissolved in

the eyes of God. Her opposition would only make it more difficult for Roy and Gabrielle. It was an intolerable situation for
Roy Johnson. His future with Gabrielle depended upon a judgment made by a cleric in an elegant Georgian manse in Boston
where the vicar and his staff were housed. And Roy Johnson,
who throughout his career had easy access to councils of power,
could not penetrate the walls of the manse.

Until Father Patrick Boyle came along.

On the morning after the encounter with Father Boyle,
Berman arrived at work to find a message on his computer
that Johnson wished to see him as soon as he arrived. After getting a cup of coffee, Berman headed to Johnson's office. Though
the *Post* building was modern, and the addition housing the city
room was only three years old, Johnson's office was furnished
with colonial antiques. His desk was made of heavy, dark ma-
hogany. There was a Shaker-style wooden bench, severe in appearance and as uncomfortable as it looked, against one wall.
Along another wall was an overstuffed sofa with hunter green
fabric. Recessed shelves were lined with books and displayed
Johnson's prized collection of antique decoys. Scattered
throughout the office were seven photographs of Gabrielle. The
two remaining walls were sheer glass, floor to ceiling.

When Berman entered Johnson's office, the editor was sitting
in a walnut rocking chair reading that morning's *New York
Times*. The stack of papers beside the chair indicated that Johnson had already been through the *Record,* the *Wall Street Journal,*
and, of course, the *Post*. Johnson dropped the *Times* on a coffee
table nearby and leaned back in his chair. He was wearing a navy
blue, lightweight wool suit. The pants were pleated, the jacket,
draped over the back of his chair, was double-breasted. He wore
black tasseled English loafers and yellow silk suspenders.

The two men exchanged greetings and Johnson queried
Berman about a couple of minor personnel matters. Then he got
to the point.

"What did you make of Boyle?" Johnson asked Berman.

Berman shook his head dismissively. "I don't believe him."

Johnson seemed surprised. "On what basis?" he demanded.

"Viscerally, I just don't believe him," said Berman. "In my gut."

"Seemed pretty goddamned persuasive to me," Johnson said in a gruff tone. Johnson's face tightened.

"How many pieces have we done on this?" Johnson asked.

"Just the two," replied Berman, who thought Johnson knew full well how many there'd been.

"Refresh my memory," said Johnson. "The first one . . ."

". . . broke the news that the feds had looked at Stewart," said Berman.

"That was the caterer?" Johnson asked. "The Italian woman?"

"DiMasi, yes," said Berman. "And yesterday. Wrightways Transit. That's it. Two stories. And Boyle calls it a jihad."

Johnson's brow wrinkled. He seemed to be trying to remember more. "You sure there wasn't another one?"

Berman laughed uncomfortably. "Of course I'm sure, Roy."

"Seems like more," said Johnson.

He knows damn well exactly how many stories there have been, Berman thought. Berman had given Johnson a heads up before the DiMasi story had run. He had heard nothing in return. Since Johnson was only involved in the day-to-day selection of stories when he chose to be, that was not unusual. The routine work of choosing which stories would run and, most important, selecting the six or seven stories which would get page-one play fell to Berman and three other editors. After the page-one calls were made each evening, Berman decided what stories to put on the Metro Front, the newspaper's second section, where much of the local and regional news appeared.

"No, it's been just the two stories," Berman said.

"Both on one?" Johnson asked, referring to page one.

Jesus, thought Berman.

"Yes, Roy, both on one."

"Below the fold?"

"Both below the fold, yes."

"Do we have any proof that the money was for Stewart's personal use?" Johnson asked.

Berman paused. "Personal as opposed to campaign funds?" Berman asked.

"Yes," said the editor.

"No," said Berman, "I suppose we don't have absolute, hard proof."

Johnson rose from his chair and moved to the window. After a moment, he turned toward Berman, placed his hands in his pockets, and said, "What's going on here, Howard?"

Berman gave a look of surprise. "With what, Roy?"

"Don't we customarily leave the dead alone?"

Berman considered the question for a moment, then he looked out the window, toward Dorchester Bay, and nodded his head toward the library building. "Not always," he said. "JFK has been trashed in death."

"Decades after his passing, Howard. This is *weeks.*"

"OK, Roy," Berman conceded. "It *is* soon. I have some slight discomfort with that. I'd prefer some more distance. But what are we supposed to do when Cronin comes in with a story—on the record from the victims and confirmed by the U.S. Attorney's office—that this supposedly pious man was under investigation? That he extorted money from a mom-and-pop catering operation? What do I say to Frank, other than nice job, when he then digs through the fucking records and uncovers an extortion scheme so brilliantly concealed that the guy being extorted wasn't even aware he was being ripped off?"

Berman was on the edge of his chair now, waving his arms wildly in the air, gesticulating, his face flushed, furious that Johnson was somehow calling into question the stories. But then, suddenly, Berman caught himself. "I don't mean to get excited, Roy, but these are nothing but great stories—that we have alone, let's not forget—and it bothers me, quite frankly, that you call them into question. We can believe that priest or our own reporter. I prefer to believe our own man, to be honest with you."

Johnson was motionless. He sat back in his chair, his hands folded on his lap. He studied Berman, then looked out the window over the rushing traffic and toward the library. A flock of herring gulls swooped lazily above the building in the balmy summer air. Johnson turned back toward Berman with a puzzled look on his face.

"What's Cronin up to?" he asked.

"How do you mean, Roy?" asked Berman, struggling to compose himself.

"What's his agenda?" Johnson asked.

Oh, what a fucking asshole you are, Berman thought. It was plain to Berman not only that Johnson was questioning the integrity of the paper's best reporter, but he was also subtly taunting Berman. The city editor would not be lured into such a trap.

"His *agenda?*" said Berman, his distaste for the word apparent. He smiled, thinly, and spoke in a crisp tone. "He's just trying to do what he's always done, Roy. Come up with good stories. That's all." Berman forced another smile.

The editor of the Boston *Post* shot a sharply disapproving glance at Berman.

He walked around behind his desk and put on his jacket. "I've got a meeting down front," he said, walking Berman out of his office. "Let's be careful on this, Howard. The man is dead."

D onald Deegan was asleep in the easy chair in his den when he was awakened by a tapping sound. He could not place it at first, but then determined that it was coming from the kitchen door to his house. He rose with some effort and shuffled through the den. It was dark outside, and he could see by the clock that it was nearly midnight. Deegan peered through the glass and made out the shape of a man. He flicked on the porch light and saw that it was none other than the Pious One, Father Patrick Boyle.

Deegan unbolted the lock and opened the door.

"We need to talk," said the priest.

"Ah, as civilized as ever," said Deegan. "Come in, padre. No advance call. You arrive at an inhospitable hour and without even the slightest pretension of a greeting. A joy to be in your presence."

It was as though Boyle had not heard Deegan. "I didn't want to be seen," he said, an apparent explanation for his arrival at the rear door under cover of darkness.

Deegan rebolted the door and led the priest into the den. Deegan sat and reached down beside the chair for the hose emanating from his portable oxygen supply. He placed the mouthpiece on his nose and mouth and took several deep breaths.

Boyle took a seat opposite Deegan without waiting to be asked. He was dressed in a T-shirt and black polyester slacks, bagged in the knees, worn shiny in the seat. He wore black canvas Converse All-Star high-top sneakers.

"Did he leave a document with you concerning me?" the priest asked.

Deegan regarded the younger man. So pious. Such an unpleasant fanatic. But Deegan had not responded promptly enough for Boyle's liking.

"Are you deaf?" Boyle barked.

Deegan laughed out loud. "Deaf?" he said. "Deaf, no. My lungs don't work too well, nor my eyes, legs, or cock. But my ears are fine, thank you for asking, padre."

Boyle did not so much as crack a smile.

"Did he leave a document?" Boyle asked.

"Not with me," said Deegan. "And even if he had, the law requires that his estate be probated before any asset is dispersed. Can't help ya, I'm afraid." He added with a smile. "Much as I'd like to."

Boyle leaned forward on his chair, his face growing increasingly tense. He used his hands and spoke slowly as though trying to communicate with a child.

"He left a letter in which he asks the Coalition board to elect me chairman," said Boyle. "He told me he placed it with you."

Deegan thought for a moment, as though trying to recall. "When did he tell you that?" Deegan asked.

"Recently," said the priest.

"What's your definition of recently?" Deegan asked.

"Last week," said Boyle.

Deegan nodded. "Last week," he repeated.

"And he said he'd written a letter recommending you to the board?"

"Yes."

"And he said he'd given that to me?" Deegan asked.

"The original," said Boyle. "He showed me a copy. I insisted on seeing the text."

Deegan wondered why Boyle had really come to see him, showed up unannounced at midnight at the back door. Deegan knew that Boyle, as vice chairman of the Coalition, was all but assured election by the board, which had been hand-picked by Stewart. Whether Stewart left a letter was hardly a matter of consequence, never mind urgency.

"Ah, yes," said Deegan. "I seem to remember something that may have been along those lines. Give me a day or two to look through the files and I'll get back to you."

Boyle nodded lamely, but did not move. He hesitated, then asked, "Did he mention the Capital Fund?"

Deegan took a hit off his air hose and considered the question. "In what regard?"

Deegan could see that Boyle was stuck. The priest did not know how much Deegan knew. He did not want to impart information through his questioning.

"Protecting it," said Boyle. "Protecting the assets."

"In what respect?"

"Protecting the assets from harm," said Boyle.

"You puzzle me, padre," said Deegan. "As Stewart's finance chairman, you would have knowledge of such matters."

Boyle was suddenly red-faced. "Those funds must not be put in jeopardy," said the priest. "I have plans for that money, every cent of it. A shelter to construct, an AIDS hospice, nutritional outreach, a wellness clinic, and more. Much more! I've waited my turn, Donald, and I won't be denied the opportunity that is rightfully mine to do good! I will not be denied that right!"

Deegan would now play father confessor. "Of course not, padre," he said in a soothing tone. "You should not be denied that right. But help me understand the context here."

"We had a goddamned deal," said the priest, "that I would gain control of the funds when he retired."

"Of which funds, exactly?" Deegan asked.

"All Coalition funds, but most importantly the Capital Fund."

Deegan shrugged, as though at a loss. "And what is it you would like me to do, padre," Deegan asked.

Father Boyle was calmer now. He spoke softly. He looked at Deegan as though regarding some lower life form.

"Larger issues are at stake here, Donald," said Boyle. "Be very careful. There is a greater good to be served and you would be ill-advised to be an obstructionist. Protect the funds, Donald. Just protect the funds."

Frank Cronin had worked with Scot Lehman in Tucson when they were both eager young reporters breaking into the business. After Tucson, Lehman went on to law school then to a job at the Justice Department in Washington, where he had specialized in white-collar organized crimes. Eventually he made his way to Massachusetts, where he joined the State Banking Commission's legal department, working his way up to chief counsel in only a few years. The two men had stayed in touch over time and got together socially every few months. On two previous occasions, Cronin had sought out Lehman on a story and Lehman had been eager to assist his friend. It was, of course, expressly contrary to the law for Lehman to reveal any of this information to Cronin. In fact, when Cronin had first started out in the business, he had been surprised by the frequency and ease with which people in government broke the law to help reporters. Prosecuting attorneys, legislators, and staff members of every conceivable government agency at the state, local, and federal level routinely ignored laws prohibiting them from divulging certain, supposedly privileged, information. He had so often been the beneficiary of such leaks that he did not complain, though he had sometimes thought that doing a story on just this phenomena would make for fascinating reading.

On the sultry summer day that Roy Johnson met with Howard Berman, Cronin sought Lehman's help in probing the life of Philip Stewart. Cronin needed proof that the money Stewart extorted was for personal use. And it was clear to Cronin that Johnson wouldn't publish another word about Stewart until there was such proof.

Lehman was familiar with the stories Cronin had written and had found the information about Wrightways Transit particularly intriguing, since it involved the banking industry and possible fraud. Within a matter of days, Lehman had culled out of the

Banking Commission's powerful computers two years' worth of activity on the Shelter Coalition Capital Fund account.

When he was finished, he called Cronin. Lehman sounded nervous on the telephone. He said he was sorry but he would not be able to talk about what he had found. Cronin was irked by this. The reporter pointed out that he had brought the original information to Lehman and that he would never have conducted a computer search had it not been for Cronin's spade work.

"I can't be seen with you," Lehman said, his voice edgy.

Cronin was now taken aback. "You're kidding, right?"

"Don't be so fucking cavalier, Frank," Lehman said angrily. "This is my livelihood."

Cronin could hear the fear in Lehman's voice.

"Look," he said, "I'm sorry. But this is very important to me. All I ask is that you give me the information you've got. Then I won't bother you again. I promise."

Lehman hesitated.

"You remember the Greek's in Roslindale Square?" Cronin asked. It was a hole-in-the-wall bar they'd been to a few times years earlier.

"How about we meet there after work and talk?" Frank asked.

"Jesus, Frank," said Lehman.

"I wouldn't ask you to do this unless it was extremely important," said Cronin.

Lehman reluctantly agreed.

"Do you think it's safe?" he asked.

"Absolutely," said Cronin. "See you there at six."

The Greek's was housed in a nondescript, one-story building in Roslindale Square, a bus stop directly in front. There was no sign on the place, no indication even that it was a tavern, but there was no need of a sign—beyond the locals and regulars, no one else ever darkened the door of the place.

When Frank arrived a few minutes before six, there were a dozen men at the bar. The place was long and narrow and erratically lit. The bar ran down the right side and on the left side were scattered tables of varying styles. Some round, some square, most with chairs, a few without. In the rear was a larger room with a pool table.

Frank went to a table in the back left-hand side of the room, set apart, protected by a corner of the wall and a cigarette machine that jutted out.

Frank went up to the bar, got two Buds, and brought them to the table. A moment later Scot Lehman arrived. He had removed his jacket and tie and looked furtively around the room as he made his way to the table. He was clearly nervous.

Lehman frowned and peered into the back room.

"You think this is safe?" he asked, yet again.

Cronin nodded, looking steadily at his friend.

"I need your word that none of this leaks to anyone, Frank," said Lehman.

Frank nodded. "You have it," he said.

"I could get fired for telling you any of this," said Lehman.

"Nobody will know," said Cronin. "Nobody will ever know."

"The DA's office doesn't even have this information yet, neither does the AG," said Lehman. "Nobody does."

Cronin studied his friend. Something was wrong here.

"This isn't like you," Cronin said. "You're scared of something and I don't think it's losing your job."

Lehman's jaw was tight. His eyes were narrowed, his brow furrowed.

"This doesn't feel good to me," Lehman said.

"All we're doing is having a conversation," said Frank.

"No, this"—and with that, Lehman clutched his notes— "This doesn't feel good to me."

Cronin looked puzzled.

Lehman leaned forward, hunched over the wobbly table, "There's something really wrong here." He spoke only slightly above a whisper.

"Something that scares you," said Frank.

Lehman nodded.

"What?" Frank asked.

Lehman shook his head. "I don't know," he said. "I don't know where it leads. I don't know what's underneath the layers of camouflage."

"What are you saying?" Frank asked.

Lehman began to speak and then caught himself. He took a deep breath. "Let me go through it with you," he said.

Cronin nodded.

Lehman glanced down at the notes and looked up at Frank.

"There's way too much activity in this account," Lehman said, "and the sort of traffic in it doesn't feel right. With a standard capital account you'd expect only a few deposits a year.

"There are deposits here in excess of $5,000 each, probably four or five times a month. The guy from Wrightways is in here, twice a year for each of the past two years. Each payment totals slightly more than $9,000."

"That's what Ray Wright said, nine grand and change each time," said Cronin.

"There's a freight company I noticed making regular deposits—five in the past two years," said Lehman. "There's a truck leasing company doing the same."

Two men got up from the bar and came toward their table. Lehman froze and leaned his arms over his notes. The men walked past and into the back room where they began playing pool.

"Usually with accounts like these, the charity is trying to maximize its investment while, at the same time, making sure none of it is put at anything more than minimal risk. So you'll usually see them in zero coupon bonds, Treasury bills."

"But some of this money is in risky ventures?"

"That's the problem," said Lehman. "You can't tell from this really where it is. It's going to a shell, a real estate trust where the true identity of the person or persons in control is camouflaged."

"Is that legal?" asked Cronin.

"In Massachusetts it is," said Lehman. "It's one of a very few states. And it was only a few years ago that the legislature changed the statute to allow them. They're controversial because it's a convenient way to hide illicit funds."

"How so?" asked Cronin.

"A real estate trust is actually very simple," said Lehman. "It's a legal entity that must file with the state like any other legal entity. Except the only name attached to it is a trustee—a front man basically. The entity that received most of the money is called Empire Realty Trust. The trustee is Donald Deegan."

This was very interesting—the man who discovered Stewart's body now turned up as the trustee on a secret Stewart financial deal.

"These sorts of trusts vary," said Lehman. "With some, the trustee is nothing more than a front, usually the lawyer who established the trust. But in other cases the trustee is also a beneficiary, though you can't readily determine that. The beneficiary or beneficiaries of the trust, the person who actually controls its funds, could be anybody. Deegan, Stewart, anyone. It can't be determined by viewing any public document. It also can't be determined what Empire owns. Could be a vacant lot, could be the Empire State Building."

"There's no way to find out the beneficiary?"

"Not through public records," said Lehman. "You'd need to subpoena records of the lawyer who established it."

"Why would a charitable organization seek to mask the true owner and why, of all things, would they invest in real estate?" Cronin asked.

"If the trust's assets are in fact in real estate," said Lehman.

The front door to the bar opened and three men entered. One who wore a suit, looked around as though searching for someone. Lehman's heart raced. But soon the fellow spotted whoever he was looking for playing pool.

"In the past two years, more than $1.3 million in cash has moved through this account," Lehman said. "That's in addition to the money from Wrightways Transit, from the freight and trucking companies. Cash. Numerous instances, and every single one under the $10,000 level that triggers federal reporting. Every one. Nearly all in the $9,500 range. All cash."

"Which means?"

Lehman's eyes were dark. He stared at his friend. "I worked on enough of these cases while I was at Justice to see the pattern," he said.

Lehman glanced nervously around the room. His face glistened with sweat.

"It's classic," Lehman said. "They were laundering cash.

Whoever was involved with this was laundering money, and substantial amounts. These aren't the types of people who you want to be dealing with, Frank. They're bad people, they hurt people without a second thought. Maybe Stewart crossed them somehow. Got in their way. And look what happened to him."

Lehman held Cronin's gaze. "Don't you get in their way, Frank," said Lehman.

"You're sure Stewart was involved?" Cronin asked.

"He's the only signatory on the account," said Lehman. "No question he was involved."

Cronin sat impassively.

Lehman grew agitated. "It's a brilliant criminal scheme," he said. "Philip Stewart, a man above reproach, was using a charitable account under his control to launder cash. There couldn't be a better cover for dirty money than the cause of homelessness and no better conduit than a man as far above suspicion as Stewart."

Cronin took it all in, savoring it, thrilled with the moment, with the rush he felt at the news. He had struck gold and he knew it.

10

Dockerty has been sighted in the city and the curiosity of Det. Thomas McCormack has been aroused. McCormack sat at his desk in the corner of a crowded room housing homicide detectives and ran his finger down a typewritten list of names. The list was a compilation of names collected by detectives during the course of scores of interviews. In each interview the detectives would seek to determine whether Stewart had any enemies. Researchers assigned to the homicide unit had also combed through Stewart's political history searching for any incident that might have caused someone to want Stewart harmed. The list included two members of the City Council with whom Stewart had frequently clashed. Listed as well were the DiMasis, a former employee at the Shelter Coalition, a mentally unbalanced individual Stewart had dismissed from a Council staff job, and several people who had been targets of Council committees he had chaired.

Mick Dockerty fell into the last category. His had been one of the first names placed on the list in the days immediately following the murder. An inmate at the state's maximum security prison at Walpole, a man who had been a police informant on and off for years, told investigators that Dockerty had confided in him two years earlier that he intended to kill Stewart. Such tips from convicts were notoriously unreliable, and McCormack had treated this one with indifference.

But Dockerty's name was kept on the list because he had, in fact, been fired from his job as a guard at a city jail due to an investigation by a Stewart-led committee which had concluded that Dockerty was probably responsible for the beating death of an inmate. Dockerty had at no point been under active investigation by the detectives probing the death of Councillor Stewart, but now that word came that Dockerty was back in Boston after a lengthy absence, McCormack wanted a closer look.

McCormack had received reports that a man fitting Dockerty's description had been seen in the neighborhood of Stewart's Moss Hill home. One neighbor who lived a half dozen houses up the street from Stewart called police to say he had seen the same man, whom he described as short and muscle-bound with closely cropped black hair and a diamond stud in one ear, several times in the vicinity of Stewart's home. Another neighbor said she had seen a man fitting that description park a black BMW several streets away from Stewart's and then walk down the hill in the direction of Stewart's home. She had seen the same man do that twice in three days, the woman said.

On the basis of this information, McCormack assigned two plainclothes officers to stake out the Stewart home. Two nights later, Dockerty appeared. He parked the BMW several streets away and ambled leisurely down the hill to Stewart's. He stood across the street and watched the house for just a moment, then he circled around the block to the back of the lot and looked through the row of hedges. He then returned to his car and drove away.

McCormack was puzzled. Was Dockerty looking to determine whether the house was under surveillance? Whether it was alarmed? What was he up to?

McCormack guided his Crown Vic on to Storrow Drive from Berkeley Street and headed out Boylston, past Fenway, along the Jamaicaway out to West Roxbury. He pulled off onto a side street and parked in a prearranged spot. A young detective, O'Toole, climbed into the front seat.

"He's still in the house," O'Toole said. "Been inside now for twenty minutes. I called you the minute he went in the door." The young cop paused and added, "I mean, I know whose house it is."

McCormack nodded his appreciation.

"My partner's watching the house now," O'Toole said.

"It's one or two streets over from here?" McCormack asked.

"Two," O'Toole replied.

"How long you on him?" McCormack asked.

"All last night," said O'Toole. "He was out to the clubs until closing. Then to the hotel."

"Which one?"

"Four Seasons," said O'Toole.

"Who was with him today?" McCormack asked.

"Stanton and Dix," said O'Toole. "Then we picked him up a few hours ago. Stanton said he was at the hotel all day. Worked out in the weight room, ate, slept."

Suddenly the radio on O'Toole's belt crackled. His partner's voice said, "He's on the way out."

"Gotta run," said O'Toole, jumping out of McCormack's car and racing to his own.

The BMW headed out of West Roxbury, through Jamaica Plain. McCormack, following O'Toole, who was tailing Dockerty, radioed to O'Toole's car: "I'm in the parade."

"Roger," came the reply.

Dockerty led them across Jamaica Plain, along Columbus Avenue toward the South End. In these neighborhoods, McCormack instinctively locked his car doors. His windows were closed, the air conditioner running steadily. Outside, along the dirty boulevard, people sat on the stoops of brick and cinderblock apartment buildings. Off to McCormack's right was a sprawling public housing project with its prison-style architecture and music blaring so loudly McCormack could hear it through tightly shut windows. As a young beat cop he had been assigned to this area and he'd chased dozens of kids into that project. But once inside it was like the catacombs. The residents who knew the tunnels always found a way to elude police. McCormack drove on, keeping O'Toole's car within sight. At the intersection of Columbus and Massachusetts Avenue hundreds of people were hanging on the street corners outside the sub and coffee shops, outside the liquor stores and bars.

Dockerty drove through more gentrified sections of the South

End, past well-maintained, bow-front brick town houses. But at West Newton Street he turned right and headed into a more run-down section. The farther he drove the more blighted the surroundings. Dockerty turned onto Pembroke Street, followed it to the end and parked on the street. McCormack was more than a full block back and could not see Dockerty, but when the detective saw O'Toole's car slip to the side of the road, he stopped, too. A moment later, O'Toole approached McCormack's car and spoke through the driver's-side window.

"He went into one-oh-three," O'Toole said.

"One-oh-three," McCormack repeated.

"Yeah."

"This is Pembroke, right?" McCormack asked, to double check.

"Pembroke, right," said O'Toole.

One-oh-three Pembroke. McCormack knew the address. He knew who lived there, upstairs over the first-floor soup kitchen.

O'Toole fidgeted. "What's up with this dude?" he asked.

McCormack shrugged. He wished he knew.

After a few minutes, McCormack got out of the Crown Vic. "I'm going for a walk," he told O'Toole. "Then I'm heading back. Stay with him, OK? Anything strange, call me."

"Roger."

McCormack walked slowly down the block, limping moderately, the pain in his leg tolerable this night. He felt lucky. He made his way past a doorway where two winos shared a bottle and where a third lay on the steps, asleep. He stood in an adjacent doorway and watched 103 for a few moments. In the hallway, he saw Dockerty and Boyle talking.

McCormack spent part of the morning reviewing a background report on Dockerty. The detective arrived at Sloane's office shortly after noon. He entered a back hallway, bypassing the reception area, through a small law library, past cubicles occupied by Sloane's staff, and into her office. She was speaking on the telephone when he arrived and she motioned for him to be seated at a long metal conference table. Sloane's quarters in the Pemberton Square Court House in Boston, two blocks to the rear of the State House, were similar to all of the other department heads in the office of the Suffolk County District Attorney. It was long and narrow, with one large dirty window overlooking a dreary courtyard nine stories below. Once a splendid garden, it had long since deteriorated into a parking lot for judges.

On the walls were brightly colored Lichtenstein prints. On Sloane's neatly kept metal desk were a half dozen family photographs, mostly summer scenes from Maine. One photo, her favorite, had been taken on the porch of the family summer house in Cape Elizabeth. There were her parents, Sloane, and her sister, Alice. It had been taken the night of their mother's fiftieth birthday.

McCormack pulled a sheaf of papers from a large manila envelope and laid them on the conference table. He pretended to review them as he half watched Sloane in conversation with a defense lawyer about a negotiated plea in a manslaughter case. She was wearing a navy blue raw silk suit, her skirt to the knee, black pumps, and her hair pulled back with a blue headband. She wore rimless glasses and little makeup and McCormack took delight in watching her, for he thought she was an exquisite beauty.

Sloane placed the phone in its receiver and looked up at McCormack. "You don't, by chance, happen to have any good news, do you, Mack?" she asked.

McCormack glanced down at his notes and began. "You remember the inmate I mentioned to you a couple of days after the murder?"

"The one claiming he'd heard someone planning to kill Stewart," said Sloane.

McCormack nodded. "We put him on the list, but you know how cons are. I don't think twice about it, though I send O'Toole over to see him, just to get it on the record. This character, Leach, says he was with a wiseguy named Dockerty some time back—over a year ago, now—and Dockerty told him he was planning to do Stewart."

"Did he say why?" Sloane asked.

"Leach told O'Toole he didn't remember exactly the reason . . ."

"Sounds almost honest, Mack," said Sloane.

"He says he remembered something about Dockerty saying that Stewart had shafted him somehow. That was all. Leach said Dockerty either never gave him more of an explanation or Leach has forgotten it."

"Did he say when this was?" Sloane asked.

McCormack shook his head. "Again, not clear," he said. "O'Toole gets the impression it's some years ago now. Which makes sense. I had some digging done on Dockerty and it turns out there's some unpleasant history between him and Stewart."

Sloane straightened in her chair, clearly interested in what McCormack was saying. "Oh?"

"Do you remember the guard at Deer Island who supposedly beat up the inmate who died? It was in '87. There was an investigation by the Council, suspicions the inmate was beaten to death. Remember that?"

"Dockerty was the guard?" Sloane asked.

McCormack nodded. "One of four escorting this kid," he said. "They all tell the grand jury the same story. That they're moving the kid to the infirmary and he falls down the stairs. But privately one of the guards tells our guys that Dockerty beat the kid senseless. Carey's his name, from West Roxbury. Dockerty has had some trouble before. Suspended a couple of times for fights with inmates. This other guard who talks to us says the kid, Carey, complained that Dockerty was shoving him along the hallway too hard and Dockerty punched him. Says he thinks that's the end of it. But then Dockerty pounces on the kid and before they can peel him off he smashes the kid up. Then shoves him down a flight of stairs."

"And the screws won't testify against Dockerty, will they, Mack?" said Sloane.

McCormack shook his head. "They protect their own, plus they're intimidated. Whether Dockerty explicitly threatens them, who knows? But he's a scary guy. About thirty, pumped up like Schwarzenegger. Walking steroid bomb. Plus, there's talk that he works on the side for some wiseguys in the North End."

"And Stewart's place in all this?" Sloane asked, a barely detectable note of impatience in her voice.

"The grand jury returns no indictments," said McCormack. "The guards walk. Naturally, the kid's family is outraged. His father knows Stewart and goes to him with the whole story. Stewart gets our files—he's not supposed to have access to them, but he has friends—and sets up a Council committee to investigate. He's chairman and he's not fooling around. This isn't window dressing. He calls a series of witnesses, including Dockerty, but because the committee doesn't have subpoena power, Dockerty and the other guards don't show. This pisses Stewart off even more. They go through a few days of public hearings, but the real work is done privately with our files. Stewart and a couple of the others are convinced Dockerty batted the boy around. The committee ends up calling for Dockerty's dismissal and he's axed soon after that."

McCormack frowned. "Then Dockerty vanishes. Within days, literally, he's gone. No trace. Then, just as suddenly, he reappears. Driving a new BMW, nice clothes, the works."

McCormack shifted his position in the chair. "We put a tail on him and night before last where is he but in the vicinity of Stewart's house."

Sloane screwed up her face. "How odd," she said. "What on earth for?"

McCormack shrugged.

"Strange," said Sloane, "but hardly a crime."

"There's something stranger," said McCormack. "Last night we tail him and he stops at two locations. At each stop for fifteen, twenty minutes."

He paused and looked at Sloane. "His first stop was in West Roxbury. He visited Donald Deegan at home."

Sloane's eyes widened and she cocked her head, taken utterly by surprise.

"After that, he drove to the South End and paid a call on Father Patrick Boyle."

• • •

McCormack was alone in his apartment at three A.M., listening to the steady hum from his window air conditioner. Outside the air was dense with humidity. He had been awakened by a thunderstorm around one and been unable to get back to sleep. He lay in bed in boxer shorts and a T-shirt, sweat dried around the neckband. He flicked on the bedside lamp and swung his feet onto the floor. He rose, unsteadily, placing most of his weight on his left leg, but nonetheless feeling the pain slice through his right knee.

"Jesus," he whispered, surprised as he so often was by the intensity of the pain.

He put on a pair of lightweight slacks and sneakers and went into the kitchen. He felt wide awake but not altogether steady on his feet. He squinted against the glare of the kitchen light. The Canadian Club was on the counter, a tumbler, nearly empty, at its side. He had had two or three, he could not recall which and was bothered by his failure of memory. It had not been a good day. At work, he had been unable to stop thinking about Stewart. He had arrived home a few minutes after seven that evening and gone directly to the liquor cabinet and downed his first, a full tumbler, no water, no ice. The liquid, the tawny color of a worn leather belt, calmed him and immediately had a slight taming effect on the raw nerves in his knee. He recalled that with the next drink he had downed two Percocets. Twenty-five minutes later—not yet eight P.M.—he had gone into the air-conditioned bedroom, stripped to his underclothes, and lay down on the bed. Two drinks, he thought. It must have been two. Two full tumblers. Then he was out on the bed. The next thing he remembered was the storm, claps of thunder, flashes of lightning, the torrent. He had tried to fall back into the bliss of sleep but his knee throbbed so and his mind was moving and he could rest no more.

On the sidewalk outside, he felt the familiar ache that came in his head from the combination of alcohol and painkillers. The air was still humid, though slightly cooler than it had been earlier. Thin vapors of steam rose up from the wet pavement. The neighborhood was quiet. McCormack could hear a car in the distance, out on the main road a quarter mile away. He moved slowly along the sidewalk in the gait he had developed after the shooting. He would step forward with his left leg, then move his right leg in an awkward motion that was half step and half drag, pulling it even with his left foot. He would repeat that over and over again. For McCormack, that was now what was loosely termed walking.

He struggled down to the corner, less than two hundred feet away. There, he paused and leaned against a fence. His knee throbbed. He wiped the sweat from his face and returned home. In the kitchen, he rinsed out the glass on the counter and poured it full of Canadian Club. He sipped it, enjoying the mild burn and the anesthetic effect. He sat down at the kitchen table and flipped on the radio. The all-news station mentioned something about Stewart and a scholarship being established in his name. Stewart. The detective could not get away from him.

McCormack thought of the man he had barely known but for whom he felt an abiding hatred. And when he thought of Stewart, he recalled the night when his life became one marked by physical pain.

His heart had pounded so hard on that night years before that his ears had rung. He had heard someone moving down the back steps and assumed it was Melendes. Melendes was a madman, drug dealer, a killer. There had been four of them on the raid and McCormack had been given this post downstairs by the rear door because it was the least risky. Safer certainly than trying to blast through the front door of Melendes's second-floor apartment with the portable battering ram favored by the narcotics detectives. These were young men with a wild look in their eyes and tight blue jeans, whose raids regularly put them in the line of fire. McCormack had accompanied them on the raid purely because their target, Melendes, was a suspect in a murder case.

For a man McCormack's age and condition it was madness to be out lurking around in the dark. He had been frozen with fear in the far end of the hallway and it did not occur to him at that moment, though it did many times later, that if it weren't for Stewart he wouldn't have been in that hallway. If Stewart had been a man of even modest honor, Thomas McCormack would have been in an office where he belonged. McCormack was a sedentary fellow, a thinker, a solver of mental puzzles, not a warrior. Throughout his career he had faced remarkably little physical danger. His gun had been unholstered for cleanings only and it had never been fired in anger.

McCormack had heard Melendes approaching and suddenly the detective had wheeled to his right in the hallway, revolver extended. He had been in a half crouch, the crouch he had learned so many years ago at the academy, but now he was trembling, his body shaking as never before. Melendes had come around the corner from the stairs and McCormack had been startled at how big he was, well over six feet. He had had a satchel in his left hand—the dope, McCormack thought—and a shotgun cradled in his right. McCormack could hardly believe his eyes: Melendes was going to put it down; he would put the gun down and surrender and McCormack would walk out the door and breathe the night air. He would go home and she would be waiting for him and they would talk about his day and he would avoid any mention of this insanity and she would never know that for a moment he thought that he was going to die at the hands of a lunatic without a shred of conscience. But as McCormack looked down the hallway, his finger on the trigger of the Glock .9 millimeter, he saw that he'd been wrong. Melendes hadn't been putting the shotgun down at all. He was lowering it, aiming it, and McCormack had found himself now staring down the barrel leveled at his chest just thirty feet away. He knew the weapon and he knew that the spray would blow a hole through him the size of a softball, and he could not let that happen. This no-good fucker was not going to end his life, not here in this filthy, rat-infested tenement.

McCormack had fired once, then again, and he saw that he had hit Melendes in the upper body somewhere, the shoulder, maybe even the chest, and he was spun sideways by the force of the slug and again McCormack thought he was safe, free! But simultaneous with his second round he had heard a third blast, and he had known it was not his and thought it must be from the shotgun, and then he was blinded for a second by the pain that seared him. When it hit him the trauma was so massive he could not locate it in his body, did not know whether he'd had his arm or his head blown off, but within milliseconds he felt that it was his leg and he looked down and saw that the fabric of his pants was gone and there was a mass of red.

And that had been all he remembered until he awoke sometime later and saw a nurse in white at the foot of his bed. Later still, a doctor told him that the good news was he would be able to walk again after physical therapy. The bad news was that his knee would hurt for the rest of his life. It had been as though there'd been an explosion in his knee, the doctor explained. It had been shredded by the blast, then painstakingly reconstructed by a surgical team working throughout a full day. From a medical standpoint, the operation had been a success. But now when he walked McCormack felt as though there was bone scraping against bone and it hurt him every day and every night, every waking moment, and he did not know how the pain could be conquered for any sustained period of time and now feared that it was unconquerable. It affected every aspect of his life. He could not exercise and so he grew heavier, and the heavier he grew, the greater was the stress on the leg. And it was difficult to be a cheerful, pleasant person whose company was enjoyed by others when the obsession of one's life was pain.

He had tried everything. Percocet, Percodan, Darvon, Stolichnaya. He had tried Halcion and Dalmane. He had tried various combinations during the day and at bedtime. Nothing worked.

It was indirect, to be sure. But there was no doubt that he would not have been in that hallway in the path of Melendes's savagery had Philip Stewart been a decent man. McCormack drained the Canadian Club and poured another, a half tumbler this time. He sat at the kitchen table clutching it, pleased that Stewart was dead.

CHAPTER

11

"It's much too nice to be inside today," said Sloane. "Can I talk you into letting me take you to lunch?"

Cronin was momentarily speechless.

"Try and contain your enthusiasm," she said with a hearty laugh.

"No, no," he said, fumbling for words. "I'm surprised. I didn't expect to hear from you." He brightened. "But I'm glad you called. Absolutely you can take me to lunch. I'd like that."

"Great," she said. "Meet you in half an hour at the corner of Charles and Beacon."

Cronin hung up the phone and found he was smiling. This is good. This is very good, he thought. He sat at his desk, staring vacantly into space.

The voice of Berman interrupted his reverie: "What are you so happy about?" he asked, sitting down on the edge of Cronin's desk.

"Oh, nothing." He rose and brushed back his hair. He put on a poplin sports jacket hanging on the back of his chair. "I'm meeting someone for lunch."

"Must be nice to have a tit job where you go out for lunch," Berman needled.

"Yeah," said Cronin sarcastically. "I try to do it every summer."

"Where to?"

"I don't know," said Cronin. "I'm meeting the person at the Public Garden. We'll maybe go over to Newbury Street."

"The person?" said Berman in lightly mocking tone. "This must be a female person."

Cronin laughed. "Howard, what are you, my chaperon? Yes, it's a female person."

"You're meeting an actual woman for lunch?" said Berman.

"An actual woman, Howard," said Cronin, "hard as it may be to believe."

"So do I know the actual woman?" Berman asked.

Cronin picked his car keys up off the desk and started walking toward the door. Berman followed. "Do I?" Berman persisted.

"It's Sloane, Howard," said Cronin as he walked.

"Sloane!" said Berman. "Is this about Stewart?"

"This is about lunch, Howard," said Cronin as he walked through the door.

Berman shouted after him: "Ask her about Stewart!"

While he drove, Cronin wondered, as he so often had in recent months, what had gone wrong. But he knew. He knew well. Though he loved being with her—found her beautiful, sexy, smart, and funny—the timing had been wrong. He had not been ready for something serious. As he weaved his way through traffic heading into the Back Bay, he thought perhaps that had changed.

Sloane hung up the phone and sat silently for a moment. There. I've done it, she thought. A little initiative goes a long way, her mother had always said. Sloane smiled. This is good. This is very good, she thought.

She rode the elevator to the first floor and began walking across Beacon Hill to Mount Vernon Street. Sloane walked slowly, enjoying the sunshine and thinking of this man who so attracted her. And who remained, in many ways, an enigma.

He saw her from a block away. She was crossing Chestnut on Charles Street headed in his direction. She was moving briskly now along the brick sidewalk of Charles Street, past an art gallery, an antique shop, and a bakery, under the lime green awning of a restaurant, past the outdoor fruit and vegetable stand in front of a small market. She arrived at the corner of Charles and Beacon, opposite him, waiting for the light to change, waving quickly in his direction. She wore a lemon-colored dress with white polka dots and a single strand of pearls. She crossed and they met on the other side of Beacon. They grasped each other's hands and quickly kissed.

"This is the nicest surprise I've had in a while," he said, grasping her hands and looking into her eyes. "You look wonderful."

She smiled at him. "Thank you," she said. "So do you."

Sloane had made a reservation at a new cafe on Newbury Street, an outdoor place that she had recently tried and liked. They strolled through the black, wrought-iron gate that led into the Public Garden, past scores of impeccably kept tulip beds. The wooden benches that lined the walkways that wove throughout the Garden were jammed with a lunchtime crowd that had purchased salads, hot dogs, sandwiches, and yogurt from pushcart vendors on Charles Street. Farther on, toward the center of the Garden, there were families sitting on the grass with picnics, children crowding around the organ grinder who sold balloons and popcorn. Frank and Sloane started across the picturesque footbridge that spanned the Garden's lagoon. Sloane stopped and leaned over the railing looking down at the Swanboats, long boats with half a dozen wooden benches facing forward and huge, freshly painted fiberglass swans in the rear, gleaming white in the sunlight, as college students in blue captains hats peddled the boats slowly across the lagoon, and around a tiny island. People on the boats tossed kernels of popcorn into the water for ducks and geese trailing along. Sloane and Cronin continued on through the Garden, exiting across from the Ritz and walking along Newbury Street. They took a table at a sidewalk cafe and each ordered a Caesar's salad.

"Hold the anchovies, please," Cronin asked the waiter.

"I'll eat yours," said Sloane.

"I forgot," said Cronin, with a laugh. "Anchovies. One of your little eccentricities."

"Don't be silly, Frank, it's you who's missing out," she said. "They're scrumptious—in the right place."

"Not alone?" Cronin asked.

"Oh, never alone," she said. "In salads, on pizza, that sort of thing."

"You haven't changed," he said.

"I should hope not," she replied, sipping her water. "It hasn't been all that long."

Cronin sipped a diet Coke. "I'm glad you called," he said. "I suppose this sounds lame but I had planned on calling you after your birthday. It seemed a little awkward back there on the phone."

He glanced up at her and she nodded her agreement.

"I don't think either one of us felt comfortable that night," he continued. "But I really am glad we've gotten together. It's been too long."

"Well, in the interest of full disclosure," she said, "I must confess that I've been tempted many times to call you but could never bring myself to do it. I suppose my pride wouldn't permit it. But now I thought, what the heck, you broke the ice with flowers on my birthday and it felt to me like sufficient time had passed so that we might find ourselves in different circumstances. And I'd been hearing your name quite a lot lately and that seemed a sign of some sort." She laughed. "Silly, isn't it?"

"Hearing my name from whom?" he asked.

"Oh, from Mack," she said referring to McCormack, "and mother has asked after you recently. A couple of times."

Cronin brightened. "How are your parents?" he asked with genuine interest.

"They're marvelous, thank you, knock on wood," she said. "Daddy has had a bit of heart trouble, nothing terribly serious, though he's medicated and a close eye is kept on him. Mother is, well, Mother! Still irrepressible, a tad annoying at times, but endearingly so."

Reflex suggested that Sloane, having been asked about her parents, in turn inquire about the well-being of Cronin's family, but she quickly caught herself. She had long since learned that when asked about family Frank dodged, shifting quickly to make sure the subject was changed. It was as though Cronin's life started when he entered Dartmouth in the fall of 1975. He didn't talk about anything prior to that. Ever. Sloane studied him. Did he feel any awkwardness not discussing his family? She was not sure. He was so well practiced at avoiding it that it was impossible to determine how he felt.

• • •

L unch passed in a lazy fashion that suited the day. It was Friday and neither had any pressing business that afternoon. At
other tables patrons finished and headed back to work. Tables
were cleared around them as they sat chatting over coffee. Finally, Sloane asked for and paid the check.

"If you don't have to get back," Cronin said when they got up
and began ambling down the street, "maybe you'd let me buy
you an ice cream cone?"

"But only if it is the tiniest ice cream cone ever," she said.

"I guarantee it," he agreed, as they strolled along Newbury
Street to the Häagen Dazs shop. They continued back to the
Public Garden, past the tulip beds and across the footbridge
spanning the lagoon. They settled on a bench in a quiet corner of
the park where they fell into comfortable conversation about
mutual friends, travel, books they had recently read. Sloane had
always found it remarkably easy to talk with Frank. He was an
attentive, sympathetic listener whose manner invited candor. After a while, she found herself talking about the recent frustration
of her work. She told him that the trial of the man who had murdered Benny Bennett had left her feeling beaten down.

"I don't know why, really," she said, looking puzzled and
brushing her hair off to the side of her face.

"You won it, though," he offered.

She nodded.

"I felt kind of empty when it was over," she said. "His wife
and daughters went off in a filthy old cab. Back to an apartment
over the liquor store. Back to where their view out the front window is of the sidewalk where Benny died. Back to a neighborhood where fourteen-year-olds riding by on bicycles might wave
at you or shoot you. I watched as their cab pulled away from the
curb by the courthouse and thought, 'They're headed home to
face this incalculable loss for the remainder of their lives. A husband and father, poof, just gone. Taken away from them by an
incredibly vicious individual.' I mean, think about the consequences of that act, of that punk pulling that trigger the second
time. These girls will have no father at their weddings, no grand-

father for their kids. And Mrs. Bennett will have no husband, no partner as she grows old."

Sloane glanced down at the bench and shook her head. He watched her as she frowned, the ends of her mouth turning down, her eyes averted. There was, he thought, no artifice about her. There was an openness, an honesty that deeply appealed to him. It was possible, he thought, to know who she truly was. She did not camouflage her life, masquerade as something she was not.

"The daughters," she said. "Oh, dear, how they have suffered." She seemed struck by the enormity of it. "They are such sweet girls. So well mannered and respectful. Not only of others, their parents, but of themselves as well."

She looked at Frank and said, "How do you deal with the trauma if you're thirteen years old?" she asked. "You know how kids are about their parents. Girls, I think, especially about their fathers. Their father was a strong man, a protector, invincible, as all fathers are in the eyes of their kids. And then this. The crushing loss of any semblance of innocence about the world. The sure knowledge at thirteen that there is true evil in the world."

"But you've given them something with the conviction," said Frank. "You've given them closure on his death. Legal closure. And I think that helps them work through it all."

"I feel worst of all for poor Benny," she continued. "He had lots of life to live. Lots of wonderful moments ahead. All lost. Gone. Spinning off into the cosmos somewhere. The unfairness of it all is getting to me. Benny played by the rules. He nurtured his family. He worked and saved. Bought and built a business. And from nowhere one night . . ."

She sighed.

"I used to love my job," she said. "But lately I wonder whether I shouldn't get out. Try something where not every case involves some unspeakable horror."

He nodded, understanding.

"It's one of the reasons, for all its obvious shortcomings, that I like journalism," he said. "The diet is wildly varied. You can be writing about tragedy one week, comedy the next. You can write about news or personalities or the human condition. I admire your steadiness and determination sticking to what you do day after day, month after month. I couldn't handle it, I don't think. It takes a toughness that most journalists don't have."

"You're nice to say that, Frankie," she said, "but toughness only works in certain circumstances. You need some luck, some breaks, and right now—as I'm sure you've noticed—we're getting no breaks on Stewart." She turned and smiled at him. "Other than following your leads, of course," she said.

"On Wrightways," he said.

She nodded. "Yes, quite incredible to me that Stewart not only managed to pull that off but had the cleverness and was bold enough to make it work. I can honestly say it's the first case of public corruption I've ever seen where the victim was unaware he was being fleeced."

She paused for a moment and asked, "You really don't think Wright knew?"

"No way," said Frank. "I sat there in his office and watched his reaction when I raised the possibility of what had been going on, and he was telling the truth. He was unwitting."

Sloane was comfortable talking with Frank about some things having to do with her work, though not others. They had long had a tacit understanding that whenever she talked with him about a case he treated it as a personal matter and never used any information she gave him for any news articles.

"Obviously we subpoenaed the bank records of the Shelter Coalition Capital Fund after your article came out about Wrightways," she said. "But you know how the banks are about subpoenas. They fight it overtly or covertly. They don't like the government snooping around in peoples accounts. So we've gotten some records but not all, and we haven't made any real headway in sorting through them yet."

Frank said nothing about what he had learned from Scot Lehman. He would have liked very much to be able to suggest to Sloane that she call Scot, but Frank had given his word to Scot that he would protect his identity and he would do just that.

Sloane had her own secrets, of course. Fresh in her mind was the conversation she'd had with Mack the previous afternoon when he had told her about Dockerty's visits to Donald Deegan and Father Boyle.

"What I don't understand," she said, "is how the trail could be so cold so fast. Nobody seems to have seen anything or anyone unusual. And there's been amazingly little that's bubbled up in the way of information from informants." Sloane sighed. "It's frustrating, particularly with the high-profile nature of the case, not to have really much of anything," she said.

Suddenly she shrugged it off. "Something will turn up, though," she said, smiling. "It always does. But enough about that."

"Yes, enough about that," Frank agreed. "What you need and what an afternoon like this demands is nothing less than a cruise. No afternoon this lazy should be allowed to pass without a quick sail around the lagoon."

He grabbed her hand and before she could respond pulled her up off the bench and led her to the dock. He bought two tickets and they took the front row on a boat occupied by parents and one child three rows behind them.

As the boat lazily turned around the island, Sloane, staring off toward the banks, said quietly, "I've missed you."

He was taken by surprise. His heart thumped hard. He turned to look at her but she was staring off toward the banks, away from him. He waited, expected that she would turn to look at him, but she did not.

"I've missed you, too," he said.

"You don't have to say that," she said quickly. "I didn't say it for that reason—for you to reciprocate. I said it because I want you to know how I feel."

She turned now and gazed at him, her brow knitted, her look serious, as though she were cross with herself for her honesty.

Late in the afternoon a warm breeze blew out of the south. Most of the families had left the Garden, and the Swanboat peddlers propelled nearly empty boats around the lagoon. A few couples lay back on the grass, staring at the sky and talking quietly. Sloane and Cronin sat on a bench in a corner of the Garden and watched several children about six or seven years old play nearby.

Sloane smiled at them. "Do you remember being that age?" she asked Frank.

"Sure," he said.

"Really?"

"Really."

"What do you remember?" she asked.

He thought for a second. "My mother," he said. "Being with her. I mostly remember going to work with her."

Sloane was startled by Cronin's mention of his mother. When they were together before, Frank had rarely talked about anything from his past life. That he had been unwilling or unable, whatever it was, to share himself with her had been a serious stumbling block.

Perhaps he was trying to signal to her that he had changed.

"What did she do?" Sloane asked, nervous that he would back away from the discussion. But he didn't.

"She was a waitress," he said. He laughed quietly. "The customers were crazy about her."

"I'd like to hear about that, about where she worked and what it was like," she said.

Cronin's voice was matter-of-fact, but she felt a thrill, when he began to speak, that he was willing to share this with her.

"She worked in a place called Misty's in Coaticook," he said. "It was a diner, really, with a counter in front, booths along the walls and some tables."

There was a long, uncomfortable pause. "She must have been quite a wonderful woman," said Sloane.

He looked down at his hands and nodded his head. "She made sure we were never deprived. She worked hard, of course. She would get picked up by another woman she worked with and she would take me with her for the breakfast shift. She had to be at work by six and I would go and sit in a booth in the back. After the breakfast crowd died down a little she would walk me a couple of blocks up the street to school, which I loved from the start. She was so pleased by any little success I had at school, and when I learned to read she reacted as though I was the next Einstein."

"She must have been so very proud," said Sloane.

He nodded that yes, indeed, she had been. "After school, I'd walk over to Misty's and go back to my booth until she finished up, usually around three o'clock. Except for Thursday, Friday, and Saturday nights when she'd work straight through the dinner shift. She never liked doing that because it meant I was up later than she wanted me to be, but she always said that she made as much on tips in three dinners as she did at breakfast and lunch Monday through Saturday. I don't know how much money she earned, but I know it wasn't much. She watched every penny, literally. We didn't have a car. I never remember her buying anything for more than, I don't know, I'd bet ten dollars. Literally. When I started hockey she got everything—and I mean every stitch of equipment—from friends who had older boys. Most of them were her friends from the restaurant. Sometimes we'd go to the movies, but that was rare. We didn't own a television, though we had a small radio on the counter. I think someone at work gave it to her. Everything went for food and electric bills and propane and other essentials.

"But what we had was more than enough. I always remember my mother being quite happy, and Chris and I never felt lacking in anything."

Sloane could hardly believe her ears. The subject that Sloane knew was most difficult of all for Frank was that of his brother, Chris. That Cronin had mentioned the boy without prompting amazed Sloane.

"We'd go to the library every Friday right after lunch at the restaurant. We'd walk down together and get new books, return the old ones, and go back to the restaurant, and she'd read me one new story before starting work on the dinner shift. And she read to me every night before I went to sleep, except the nights we were at the restaurant, and even there she would read to me if things got slow."

Sloane felt as though this was somehow a breakthrough for them. He was talking to her, comfortably and with ease, it appeared, about a subject he held close within himself. She took it as a signal that perhaps things had changed; perhaps he had reached a point where he was ready to take another step. They walked slowly together toward the corner of Beacon and Charles. The organ grinder was packing up to head home. The

shouting children were gone. The city seemed oddly, yet pleasantly, quiet. As they parted, Cronin asked whether Sloane
planned to be around over the weekend. She said she was. They
agreed to have dinner together Saturday night. On the way back
to her office, Sloane thought that they had been in love for quite
some time.

CHAPTER

12

When the silent alarm is tripped within the now-darkened home of the late Philip Stewart, an electrical signal is dispatched to police headquarters and relayed at once to plainclothes detective O'Toole. O'Toole is already aware that the house has been breeched, because he sits in his dark gray Ford Taurus sedan on a side street with a view down the hill to the Stewart house. O'Toole has tailed Dockerty this night from the Four Seasons Hotel to the Stewart house and watched as Dockerty disappeared around to the rear of the property. It is 10:40 P.M. on a pleasant summer evening. Within a minute of Dockerty's having disappeared from view, O'Toole receives the signal that the alarm has been set off. Dockerty knows nothing of the alarm, for it is the latest in electronic gadgetry, an invisible beam of energy that lays across the floor of the Stewart home like a shallow pool of water. It is impossible to evade. Any presence in the house heavier than a small dog will set it off.

Dockerty's break-in had been anticipated by McCormack, and O'Toole has explicit instructions in this case: he is to keep the house under surveillance and summon McCormack at once. With the compact cellular phone in his shirt pocket, O'Toole dials McCormack's beeper number, punches in his code, and waits. Less than a minute passes before McCormack is on the line.

"He's inside," says O'Toole.

"You're up the hill?" McCormack asks.

170

"Yes."

"What can you see?"

"Front entrance, front yard," O'Toole replies.

"His car?" McCormack asks.

"It's up the block from me, three, four hundred yards."

"You're between him and the BMW?" McCormack asks.

"Affirmative," says O'Toole.

"I'm there in five minutes," says McCormack, who was at his apartment, a short drive from the Stewart home.

Dockerty did what he had been instructed to do: upon entering the house, he removed a small flashlight from his pocket, picked his way carefully through the kitchen, followed a hallway to the living room, and sat down in an easy chair. Once seated, he clicked off the flashlight. The room was dark, and it took Dockerty's eyes a moment to adjust. He did not believe he had been followed. Dockerty was less sure about an alarm in the house, though he was betting there wasn't one. To be sure, however, he sat patiently and waited for thirty minutes to pass. Surely, if an alarm had been triggered, police would arrive within that amount of time. Dockerty was tempted, after the passage of twenty minutes, to proceed with his mission, but Bufalino had been insistent that he wait a full half hour. To Bufalino, a half hour meant thirty minutes, not twenty-nine and a half. And though Bufalino was very far away at the moment, Dockerty was determined to follow his instructions to the letter. That was why Dockerty had received this assignment, which could bring him a great deal of money. It was how he had earned Bufalino's favor.

Dockerty checked his watch. When half an hour had passed, he rose from the chair and went to the stairway leading to the basement. He clicked on the flashlight and went carefully down the stairs. The door to Stewart's home office was open and he went inside. The room was windowless, allowing him to turn on a table lamp and an overhead light without it being noticed outside the house. Dockerty's eyes had been used to the dark, and it took him a moment to adjust to bright light. He surveyed the of-

171

fice. There was a small love seat against one wall, a coffee table set in front of it. Beside it was an end table with a lamp. Nearby was a television set and against the far wall a desk. Dockerty paused briefly to get his bearings—he was looking for a spot six feet in from the front wall. He placed the coffee table face down on the love seat and pushed it across the carpet to the middle of the room. He then pulled a small jackknife from his back pocket and dropped to his knees. He moved rapidly along the wall using the sharp edge of the knife to pull carpet tacks out of the floor. When he had completed the row, the carpet lifted easily and he rolled it back eight feet across the room. Peeled back, the carpet revealed what appeared to be a tongue-in-groove hardwood floor. Dockerty estimated a point six feet from the wall and tapped the wood gently with his knife. His first few taps brought sounds reflecting solid spots. Then he tapped and heard a slightly different sound, not hollow exactly but not as solid. He pried at several pieces of wood, finding a slight crack and jamming his blade down between two slats. He worked the blade back and forth, loosening one slat. Finally, one piece, eight inches square, popped loose. He removed several other sections easily now and set them aside on the carpet.

With the wood out of the way, Dockerty could see a large brass plate held in place with a dozen screws. With another tool from his jackknife, Dockerty removed the screws and lifted the plate clear, setting it on the rug.

And there it was, just as Bufalino had said: a stainless-steel safe set into the concrete beneath the floor, built at Bufalino's insistence by Bufalino's men. Stewart had not objected. He had rarely used it through the years, so smooth and efficient had been their operation. The combination had been known to two men: Stewart and Bufalino. Now Dockerty had the combination and Stewart was in the ground, where he belonged.

O'Toole was itchy.

"What's taking so long?" he wondered.

McCormack shrugged. It was now 11:35. Dockerty had been inside fifty-five minutes.

"What's he *doing?*" O'Toole asked.

"Looking for something," said McCormack.

"What?" O'Toole asked.

McCormack shook his head.

O'Toole hesitated. "You think we should have just grabbed him?"

"Then we wouldn't know what he was looking for," said Mc-Cormack.

"What if he doesn't find whatever it is?" O'Toole asked.

"Then we haven't lost anything," said McCormack. "But if he does find it, he'll bring it out and we'll know."

Dockerty turned the small dial slowly, carefully. Five numbers. Tumblers aligned. Click. The cover of the safe pushed up ever so slightly. When Dockerty opened it he could see why: this large, stainless-steel air- and watertight case was full, packed to the bursting point, with cash money. Packets with wrappers marked "$10,000." The packs contained hundreds and fifties. Dockerty counted the packs, pulling each one out of the safe and placing it in a pile on the carpet. Fifty-seven packets: 570,000 U.S. dollars.

For Dockerty, now came the truly difficult part of his assignment, the part which most tested his willpower and loyalty to Bufalino. His instructions were to determine whether the money was in the safe and then, if it was there, to count it. He was then, Bufalino had ordered, to put it back in the safe, recover the floor, and leave. To Dockerty, this seemed senseless.

But Bufalino had insisted. Bufalino was self-educated. He had taught himself to anticipate, to think strategically. And he feared that if the police were aware of Dockerty, they would be intelligent enough to let him find whatever it was he searched for and then take him as he left the premises. If that was not the case, Bufalino reasoned, it would merely delay matters twenty-four hours, a small price to pay for caution.

Dockerty was sorely tempted. It seemed so easy. He could take the money, get into his car, and drive off. After delivering the goods he would be paid the 30 percent fee Bufalino had promised him—$171,000 in cash.

But Dockerty had not progressed to this point by ignoring Bufalino's instructions. He would do as he was told. And if the cops were unaware, as he felt sure they were, he would return the next night and take the money.

Dockerty made quick work of placing the cash back into the safe, screwing in the plate, replacing the wood flooring, and rolling back the carpet. He used the blunt end of an ashtray to bang the carpet tacks back into place. He returned the love seat and coffee table to their places. He shut off the lights and left the house, cutting across the backyard, through the privet hedge and circling back around up the hill to his car. He was opening the door of his BMW when three Boston police detectives, weapons drawn, suddenly appeared and ordered him to lay face down on the street. As he lay on the pavement, with one of the cops handcuffing his hands behind his back, all Dockerty could think of was that Bufalino was one smart fucker.

A patrol car was summoned and Dockerty was locked into the backseat, cuffs on his hands, manacles on his legs. His car was searched and, well concealed in the backseat, a gun was found—an Italian made .415 caliber, the type of gun used in the murder of Philip Stewart. Dockerty was removed to the Area D police station and placed in a holding cell. He refused to answer questions without benefit of counsel. He called a lawyer, a name Bufalino had given him, and he was charged with unlawful possession of a handgun. The gun was brought to the state police crime lab for tests to determine whether it was in fact the weapon used to kill Stewart.

Detective McCormack walked slowly through Stewart's house. He stood in every room looking around, waiting for something to strike him as out of place, as unusual. He went through the house once, twice, a third time. Finally, he went home, wondering what Dockerty had been searching for.

• • •

Through a contact at the FBI, McCormack had Dockerty's name run through the U.S. Justice Department computer—a cluster of massive mainframes containing every scrap of information the government had on all known organized crime figures and their associates. The file on Dockerty was not extensive but it was revealing. After leaving Boston in 1987, Dockerty had gone directly to Las Vegas, where he quickly attached himself to gangsters managing two casinos, one in Las Vegas, the other in Reno. Dockerty had started out as a bouncer at the Las Vegas casino, but he soon became an enforcer for the prostitutes the casinos employed. It was Dockerty's job to win the confidence of the girls, to get to know them, and to make sure they were not skimming profits. They were entitled to their share of any scores they made at the casino—half—but no more. The rules were clear, and broken at one's peril. Some girls tried to work side deals—meet a John at the casino, suggest they go elsewhere, and keep the full take for herself. It was Dockerty's job to see that that did not occur, and he enforced the rules with a ruthlessness rarely seen even in Las Vegas.

The Strike Force report, gathered from government informants, indicated that Dockerty had skillfully built a network of his own spies among the hookers, rewarding those who ratted on others and brutalizing those who violated the rules.

Dockerty's efficiency drew the attention of Joseph Bufalino, one of the key Mafia figures in the city. Bufalino was known as a smart man who kept to himself and preferred a quiet lifestyle to the splashy behavior favored by other leading organized crime figures. Bufalino lived modestly at the Sahara Hotel in a suite from which he ran his business ventures—gambling, prostitution, loan-sharking, drug dealing, and weapons sales.

The computer file indicated that Dockerty had worked for Bufalino directly since 1989. Dockerty had been arrested once on an assault charge and beaten it. That was the extent of the file, but McCormack's friend at the FBI put him in touch with an agent who had recently worked in Vegas for a number of years and knew the players there well. The agent told McCormack that he knew Dockerty had worked for Bufalino as a utility man who could perform a variety of functions, including bodyguard when there was a rash of violence among the crime families. The agent said that Dockerty lived alone in an expensive garden apartment in the desert, that he drove a Corvette, and had numerous girlfriends (one of whom had filed the assault charge against him).

The agent said that Dockerty would be unlikely to act as a free agent—to do anything unless he was instructed to do so by Bufalino. Certainly Dockerty would be unlikely to do something as significant as a murder on his own, the agent said. And that was the rub, thought McCormack. It was clear that Dockerty had a motive to kill Stewart, but if he really would only act as Bufalino's agent, then the question was, what motive, if any, did Bufalino have for wanting Stewart dead?

The ballistics report on Dockerty's gun was disappointing. "Inconclusive," McCormack told Sloane. Often that was the case in such matters. The report would state that the borings were "not inconsistent" with those found in the slug in the victim, meaning the tests could not prove or disprove that a particular weapon was used in the killing. Prosecution was always easier when ballistics could positively state that a certain gun was used to commit a certain murder. But inconclusive findings were common enough and could be overcome.

"I would suggest that we let it be known publicly that Dockerty is under suspicion and see what comes in," said McCormack. "See if anybody drops a dime."

"You know, somebody else who heard Dockerty say he planned to do Stewart," said Mack. "Somebody who might have seen Dockerty around the neighborhood. We can make sure his picture makes the paper."

Sloane nodded her ascent.

When Sloane had first started out in the district attorney's office, she had not liked this sort of approach. Initially, she had been surprised to find that prosecutors often leaked word that they were questioning a certain suspect in the hopes that it would produce additional evidence. She had worried that smart defense lawyers knew that such stories betrayed a weakness in the prose-

cution's case, making the defense reluctant in some cases to ne-
gotiate a plea. Why not try a case where the prosecution is essentially admitting it is weak, went the defense reasoning.

But Sloane had long since overcome her distaste for this
method of evidence gathering for the simple reason that, in a
number of cases, it had worked.

"So what do we do with this, just forget it?" Sloane said, motioning to the number of cartons of bank records that had been
delivered that morning in compliance with Sloane's subpoena.
The boxes contained several years' worth of data on the Shelter
Coalition Capital Fund's financial activities.

Mack waved it away.

"Forget it for now," he said.

"I suppose," said Sloane. "We're a little thin on the personnel
front right now, and I don't think we can justify doing much of
anything beyond zeroing in on our friend Mr. Dockerty."

"I agree," said Mack.

"So what are you going to do exactly to make sure his photo
gets in that newspaper?" Sloane asked.

"Get it into the right hands," he said.

"The right hands, Mack?"

"Someone I can trust," he said. "We can trust."

"Frank?"

McCormack nodded.

"I won't do it if you'd prefer that I not," he said.

"No, no," she said. "That's fine."

They fell silent for a moment and McCormack suddenly felt
awkward. "I respect him."

She had been staring down at her desk for the briefest moment and she looked up quickly. "I know you do," she said. "I
do, too."

From the top of the hill at Larz Anderson Park, Cronin could
see heat rising from the city streets. The jets taking off and
landing at Logan appeared elongated as they passed through the
shimmering waves of heat. From a distance, 747s had the look of
model airplanes passing in slow motion over a carnival mirror

that distorted its reflections. Cronin sat at a picnic table in a grove of trees next to the ice-skating rink. In the shade, with the slight breeze, the evening was bearable. Directly in front of where Cronin sat the huge field that sloped away from the top of the hill began. The grassy knoll ran down a quarter of a mile in a thirty-degree grade. On the upper reaches, children played.

Cronin liked escaping the urban din while at the same time being able to see much of the city laid out at his feet. The sounds he could hear were calming—children, with their yelps of delight and bursts of laughter; and the loving tones of parents. There was none of the assaultive urban noise that had so come to bother Cronin in recent years. He was soothed by the park, by its stately elms and firs; by the vast expanse of well-mowed fields that surrounded the pinnacle, by the gentle nature of people who gathered there.

McCormack arrived florid-faced and sweating. He sat heavily on the picnic bench next to Cronin, wordlessly handing him one of the two cold Buds he had brought. McCormack removed the jacket to his tan poplin suit and laid it over a corner of the table. His blue shirt was stained with sweat under the arms and on his back. He loosened his tie and sipped the beer.

He told Cronin that the full autopsy report revealed what police expected, that Stewart had died from gunshot wounds to the chest. One of the bullets pierced the heart directly, the other passed through the edge of the aorta. Tests showed that Stewart was shot from close range with a .415-caliber pistol, an Italian-made model that could be bought cheaply through the mail. There was no sign of forced entry, no indication of a struggle. The house had been scoured by investigators, but the only prints revealed were Stewart's. They had analyzed several bits of fabric but found nothing which provided even a hint of who the killer might be.

"But we think we've had a break," said McCormack, eyeing Cronin. The reporter seemed taken aback. He sat up straighter, his attention fully focused on McCormack.

"What can you tell me?" asked Cronin.

"The terms are the same?" McCormack asked.

"Absolutely," said Cronin. "I attribute nothing to you."

McCormack felt silly for having asked, but he wanted to be cautious.

"We're not sure here, so we've got to be careful," said McCormack. "We're looking at this guy. Carefully. We think he may be our man. But again, we're not sure. We need more."

"And you want his name out to help you get more," said Cronin.

McCormack nodded.

Cronin understood the game all too well. He didn't much like it, he never had, yet he had no choice but to play it. Reporters were used all the time—by politicians, businesspeople, law enforcement officials—to float ideas, to damage an adversary, and reporters and their editors were willing participants for a simple reason: competition. Cronin knew that if he didn't play, McCormack would go to the *Record-American* or one of the television stations. When Cronin had been a young reporter he had been put off by this practice, had even once refused to write a story because he saw it as a violation of a defendant's right to the presumption of innocence. Colleagues in the city room had laughed at him. Editors had scowled. The Constitution's guarantee that one is presumed innocent until proven guilty was nonsense in many cases, Cronin knew. If not in a court of law then certainly in the court of public opinion. Reputations were ruined by such leaks, but Cronin couldn't fight every battle.

"What's the name?" Cronin asked, pulling a notebook out of his back pocket.

"Mick Dockerty," said McCormack. "We brought him in on a weapons charge a few days ago. Illegal firearm. Unregistered. It gives us a chance to talk with him."

Cronin jotted the name down and paused. "Sounds familiar," he said. "Where do I know that from?"

"You remember when that kid got beat up very bad at Deer Island by the guard and they had the Council hearing and all of that, back in eighty-seven?"

"Dockerty was the guard?" Cronin asked.

McCormack nodded. "Good memory."

Cronin screwed up his face. "I don't get it," he said.

"Stewart ran the Council hearings that got Dockerty fired,"

said McCormack. "We think Dockerty waited for some time to pass and then got his revenge."

Cronin was nonplussed. "But you're not charging him?"

"Not now," said McCormack. "Not yet."

"So how should I write it?" Cronin asked. "That he's a suspect?"

"*The* suspect," said McCormack.

"Is he talking at all?"

McCormack shook his head. He wanted to tell Cronin that Dockerty had laughed about Stewart's death when they asked him about it, that he said he was glad he was dead, that he denied killing him but said he wished he had done it. But McCormack had to remember that though he liked Cronin, he had to maintain some distance. Cronin was, after all, a reporter.

"I'm going to pull the clips on the beating, but remind me of the basics of that, would you please?" asked Cronin.

McCormack told him the story essentially as he had told it to Sloane.

"So what's Dockerty been doing since then?" Cronin asked.

"Can't say," said McCormack.

"Can't say because you can't say or because you don't know?"

"Can't say."

"Where's he live?"

"Vegas, now," said McCormack.

Looking out over the city, Cronin saw that, as he and McCormack had been talking, lights in the downtown buildings had come on as darkness descended. Cronin saw that the children were gone from the grassy slope. He and McCormack were the only people left in the park, aside from a few young couples in the parking lot.

"Who's his lawyer?" Cronin asked.

"Delaney," said McCormack. Stephen Delaney was one of the best and highest-priced defense attorneys in town.

Cronin rose from the bench. "I'm going to head back to the paper now, to try and get Delaney to confirm that his client is a suspect. I want to get this in the morning paper."

McCormack understood. Cronin feared word leaking out to the competition.

"You have enough?"

Cronin nodded. "The fact that he's the suspect is enough, but then I'll cobble together some history from the hearings out of the clips. Background on the murder. It's plenty. But I better get moving to make deadline."

Cronin stopped at a pay phone near the park and called Berman to tell him he was on his way in to write a story saying there was a suspect in the Stewart murder. Berman, taking the call at the city desk, literally jumped for joy, thrusting his fist into the air as though he had just scored a goal in overtime for the Bruins against Montreal. Berman immediately huddled with other editors to remake page one. This would now be their lead story for the morning, bumping a leader about negotiations between the Serbs and Croats.

They would forget about trying to shoehorn anything into the first edition—the early papers printed before midnight and circulated upcountry. There wasn't time. The next edition deadline that mattered was for third—at 11:30 P.M. Two-thirds of the press run of 600,000 papers was for third edition, which circulated in Greater Boston.

After talking with Berman, Cronin was transferred to the *Post* library where he requested all available clips about Dockerty, the Deer Island beating, and the Stewart hearings into the matter. They would be on his desk when he arrived.

Cronin hurried back to the paper. He placed a call to the home of Stephen Delaney. The lawyer was not there, but his wife beeped him and he soon called Cronin. He would say little, but it was enough for a story.

Ninety minutes after he sat down to write, Cronin completed his story, which was headlined "Ex City Worker Probed in Stewart Death."

The story led the paper the following morning and caused a sensation in the city. Radio and television stations quoted from the *Post* account. Talk shows focused on the story and on Dockerty, who suddenly became one of the most despised men in Boston. Anger and even rage greeted the news. Some criticized the police and the DA's office for taking so long and for still not charging anyone with the crime. But the dominant emotion in the city was relief, a sense that finally the demon responsible for inflicting this terrible wound on the city had been found; that justice would be done. For in spite of the two *Post* stories— about the DiMasis and Wrightways Transit—Philip Stewart remained a beloved figure. In the wake of his death many people refused to believe the *Post* accounts of his corruption or ignored the charges entirely. The common reaction was not how and what Stewart had done, but anger at the *Post* for publishing stories that tarnished the dead man's image.

At the *Post,* there was an air of triumph that the newspaper had broken the story alone, that no other media outlet in the city had even a hint of it. Berman was ecstatic and even Cronin's detractors felt a grudging admiration for his work. Roy Johnson was delighted that his newspaper had the story. But also relieved. For this gave the story a new focus. No longer would the *Post* pursue Stewart's corruption. Instead, it was clear that Dockerty would have to be the object of their investigative work. Johnson communicated his feelings to Berman first thing that morning and Berman, in turn, conveyed Johnson's message to Cronin.

But Cronin was not ready to shift gears quite so quickly. He surprised Berman when he told him he had one more major incident involving a corrupt act by Stewart. He said he needed a little more time to put it together. He assured Berman it would be worth the wait.

CHAPTER

13

Cronin crossed School Street, just down from the Parker House, and thought he noticed a familiar face out of the corner of his eye. He glanced again through the morning crowd hustling to work in downtown Boston, and saw that it was indeed the dreaded Joe Skash, a reporter at the *Record-American*. Like so many other reporters at the *Record,* Skash bullied and intimidated sources, usually government officials, threatening that if information was not leaked to him he would humiliate the person in the *Record*'s political column.

Cronin normally cut through the alley from School Street that led to Court Street and on to City Hall, where Skash manned the *Record-American*'s bureau. Cronin assumed Skash was headed to the Hall, but he also wanted to make sure Skash wasn't following him. It would not be the first time a *Record* reporter had followed someone from the *Post* working a big story. Rather than turning into the alley, Cronin headed down School Street another half block and turned left through the crowds onto Washington Street. As he did so, he glanced over his shoulder and saw Skash hurrying after him. Skash looked as he always had. He had a porcine face, round, pinkish, and sweaty, with a blunt snout.

Cronin suspected that Skash was following him to see what he might pick up on the Stewart story. Cronin had heard that editors at the *Record* were incensed that the *Post* was beating them so thoroughly on the story. He continued along Washington toward City Hall, then, abruptly, made a sharp right onto State Street, past the Old State House, then turned right again on Congress. After making the turn, Cronin sprinted down a half block to get well ahead of Skash. Cronin continued briskly along to Post Office Square. He paused momentarily before turning a corner and had a clear view of the sidewalk along Congress Street. There was Skash hurrying along, appearing from a distance to be laboring. Suddenly, Cronin had an idea. He continued along another block, walking slowly enough now so that Skash was sure to keep him in view. Cronin walked into the side entrance of the U.S. District Court, went through the metal detectors, and walked the length of the lobby where he waited in a crowd for the interminably slow elevators. He made sure now that Skash did not lose him in the crowd. He rode to the seventh floor and walked down to the office of the court clerk, where he had often researched federal cases he'd written about. The system was simple and far more efficient than at the state courts. He would write out the names of the cases he wanted, note the carrel number at which he would be sitting and, within ten or fifteen minutes, the files were delivered.

Cronin asked for files on a case he knew little about except that it had been a lengthy proceeding with numerous pretrial motions. The case involved the city of Boston, so Skash might plausibly believe it had some bearing on the Stewart matter. After filling out his order slip and handing it to one of the clerks, Cronin sat down at a vacant carrel and took his notebook out of his back pocket and began making notes.

Fifteen minutes later, a clerk arrived with a large cardboard box and placed it on the carrel. Then he brought a second box jammed with files and then a third. He and Cronin joked about the size of the task the reporter faced. For the following hour and ten minutes, Cronin read through random sections of the files. Then, he rose and returned to the counter where he told the clerk that he suddenly remembered he had to be somewhere else and would not be returning until the following day. Clerks were far less prompt about retrieving files and so, as was the custom, Cronin knew the files he had ordered would sit on the carrel for a while.

As soon as Cronin left, Skash marked down the name of the case. And for the remainder of the day, as Cronin went about his business unhindered, Skash began drowning in a sea of worthless paper.

Cronin took a seat in the far corner of the Public Records Division of City Hall. He laughed to himself at the contrast between this operation and the federal court down the street. At the courthouse, records were well cared for. There was a system that worked. Here, at City Hall, there were a few Public Records Division employees who lounged around throughout the day listening to a loud radio and waiting on people only when the spirit moved them. It could be a distinctly unpleasant experience if you were uninitiated in the byzantine ways of the division. But it was perfect for Cronin. The records clerks knew he was a reguler and let him help himself to anything he wanted, for that meant the clerk need not stir.

Cronin sat in front of a series of cabinets that held files from the City Council. Included within those files were records of when members of the Council traveled out of the city and for how long. Few people outside the Council knew or cared that such records were kept. Cronin had heard about the practice years ago, and it had recently occurred to him that such information might be useful. The records were required by ordinance, as it was once explained to Cronin. Some years back, he thought in the postwar period, there was a rogue city councillor who was reelected year after year, took the full salary for the job, as well as whatever else he could collect for various "favors," but did no actual Council work. In fact, he lived for much of the year on Cape Cod, rarely attending Council meetings. To spite him, a group of councillors drafted an ordinance that required any member of the Council traveling beyond the city limits for more than two nights to log that information with the city's Public Records Division. The ordinance required that any councillor out of town two successive nights or more in excess of six times a year was to have his pay reduced by some fixed amount per trip over the limit.

Supporters of the ordinance argued that the new law would encourage councillors to stay at home where they were available to constituents. And the record-keeping requirement would ensure a full and accurate accounting of any absentee councillor. Every now and again through the years, councillors had lapsed in their record keeping. But just a few years earlier the *Record* had run a series of articles on councillors who were often out of the city without reporting it. Several had far exceeded the six times a year limit on two-night or more stays away from Boston and should have lost pay as a result, but did not. It was one of those absurd statutes that should long ago have been changed, but no one on the Council was politically brave enough to initiate it. Whenever someone even hinted at doing so opponents on the Council would cry out that such a change would make councillors less available to serve their constituents. Ever since the *Record-American*'s exposé, councillors had dutifully filled out the forms required.

As he thumbed through the file cabinets, Cronin saw that the records were kept chronologically, not by councillor. So he could not pull one file on Stewart for a given year and note the dates of his absences from the city. Instead, he would have to go through every file for the year searching for Stewart's name.

Without the list he had folded in his pocket, his task would have taken him days, perhaps a week. But the list would make this fast work. He looked around and saw that nobody was near him. The clerks were gathered around the Xerox machine, on top of which sat a boom box blaring Paula Abdul.

Cronin smoothed the single sheet of paper out on his lap. There were seven lines of figures on this page that had arrived in his mail, with no note, and no return address. It was untraceable, but Cronin knew it had come from his friend Scot Lehman at the State Banking Commission. Each line included a left-hand and a right-hand column. In the left-hand column was a date, in the right-hand column an amount of money. The date was when Stewart had made a withdrawal of funds to his own name from the Shelter Coalition Capital Fund. And the right-hand column listed the amount he had withdrawn.

Jan. 17 ....$7,000
Mar. 3 6,000
Mar. 29 6,000
Apr. 21 8,000
Aug. 7 9,500
Sept. 19 7,000
Nov. 9 8,000

In all, during calendar year 1992, Stewart had withdrawn $51,500 to his own name. Cronin had no doubt that those at the bank processing his withdrawals assumed he was using the funds for some purpose connected with one of the shelters, if they gave it even a moment's thought. But why would they? Why would anonymous bankers think to even question the activity of a man with Stewart's reputation?

Cronin began thumbing through the files, searching for specific dates. The first checked out. On January 17, it was recorded that Stewart left Boston for four nights. The second worked as well. On March 3, he left town for three nights. And the third: on March 29, he left again for four nights. April 21 it was for four nights, August 7 for a week, September 19 for three nights, and November 9 for four.

The pattern could not have been clearer: Stewart was withdrawing funds from the Shelter Coalition Capital Fund to his own name and then leaving town.

The question now was where was he going and what was he doing with the money. That he would take such large amounts of cash for such short trips suggested to Cronin two possibilities: either drugs or gambling or both. But it was hard to imagine Stewart having a serious drug problem—if he had, it quite likely would have been noticed. But a gambling problem could be concealed more easily.

Cronin took his information back to the *Post* and typed up a brief memo laying out what he found. He took it in to Berman and waited while the city editor read it over. Cronin wanted to run a story laying out the details of Stewart's withdrawals and his trips. To his disappointment, Berman expressed little interest.

They were in Berman's office at lunchtime. Berman was tired. He had been up throughout the night before, supervising coverage of a hostage situation in which all survived, not much of a story. Berman was dressed in wrinkled chinos, a T-shirt, and socks. His heavy beard looked as if it had not been shaved in four or five days. He was eating a cheeseburger club sandwich and drinking a large Coke.

"Is this you talking now, Howard, or is this Johnson's voice speaking through you?"

Berman frowned. "Thanks a lot, Frank. Like I'm a fucking mouthpiece for that asshole."

"So you are speaking for him?"

Berman put his sandwich down on the desk and swung his legs onto the floor. "You know, Frank, the amazing thing is that I almost agree with him on this one," said Berman. "I do think there is greater news value in who killed Stewart and why than in what Stewart's secret life might have been. And I particularly think the questions of who killed him and why contain vastly more news value than this"—Berman reached over and waved Cronin's memo in the air—"which is a long ride from conclusive about anything. A long ride. How do we know he didn't spend the dough on food for the shelters for Chrissake? How do we know the money and trips are related? It could have been coincidence? It was perfectly legal for Stewart to withdraw money from an account he controlled. It was perfectly legal for him to take a few trips. So we should do a story saying he withdrew money and took trips, all of which, by the way, Mr. and Mrs. Reader, is entirely legal. So what's the point of the story?"

"Of course we should pursue the killer and motive," said Cronin. "But Howard, you've got a room full of people out there. It doesn't have to be me. We've got an investment in me writing about this man's other life. Let's not blow that now just because Roy is getting calls from the fucking Kennedys."

Berman banged his desk with the palm of his hand. "That is *not* why I want to shift gears on this story, and goddamnit you know me better than that, Frank."

"But Howard, isn't it obvious that we can work on both angles simultaneously? That we can chase Dockerty *and* stay on Stewart's hidden life?"

Berman was tired and exasperated. "Frank, I'm not stupid," said Berman, wearily. "I know we can pursue both. But *you* can't pursue both, and I have to decide which aspect of the story you're more valuable on. And to me, that's a no-brainer. We *need* you to track down Dockerty and who he is and why he did it and all that. We just need you to do that for us."

Cronin got up from his seat and paced the office. He was silent, his head down, hand on his chin. He stopped and faced Berman. He started to speak, thought better of it, and went over and closed the door to Berman's office. He went back and stood directly in front of Berman and spoke softly.

"Howard, I want you to know about something else I'm working on," said Cronin. "Another angle. It's just kind of developing."

"What is it?" Berman asked.

Cronin hesitated. "I'm not sure exactly what will become of it," said Cronin. "As I say, it's just developing—in my mind I'm trying to put it together."

"Is it good?" Berman asked.

"If the piece pulls together it would show that Stewart's corruption caused someone's death."

Berman suddenly perked up. "Who is it?" he asked. "What happened?"

"I can't really talk about it yet," said Cronin. "I'm working on it now, collecting string. It'll take some time."

"How close are you to having it?" Berman asked.

"A week maybe" said Cronin. "It's very sensitive."

"Source sensitive?"

Cronin nodded.

"Who is it?" Berman asked.

"I can't tell you that right now, Howard," Cronin replied.

"It's Sloane," Berman declared, a broad smile breaking out across his face.

"It is *not* Sloane, Howard," said Cronin.

"But it's not your guy? It's a new source?" Berman asked.

"Yes," said Cronin.

"Reliable?" Berman asked.

"Unimpeachable," said Cronin.

Berman folded his arms and put his feet back up on his desk. "Johnson will freak," he said. "Freak. He'll go nuts. He'll say it's overkill. He sent me a message after news of Dockerty broke."

Berman searched quickly through papers on his desk and handed a single sheet to Cronin. It was a note from Johnson to Berman which said: "Stewart is dead, buried and destroyed. Enough."

Cronin shook his head. "I'm not so sure that's true," he said.

"Then they better dig him up fast," said Berman.

"Have you noticed that they are going ahead with the dedication this weekend of the elderly housing in Hyde Park?" said Cronin. "They're changing the name to the Philip Stewart Housing Complex," said Cronin. "Yesterday, they changed the name of a street in the South End to Stewart Way. And two days ago, they held a fund-raiser in his name for the Shelter Coalition. You know who was there? Kennedy, the mayor, the cardinal, the presidents of Edison, the phone company, on and on and on. This is a fund-raiser for the very organization which he was using as a cover to launder money. The same organization he was stealing cash from."

"But those people didn't know all that, it's not been proven," said Berman.

"But they did know that he extorted money from the DiMasis and they did know that he stole money from Wrightways Transit and they still went," said Cronin. "He's far from destroyed. People don't want to believe these things about him. They see a story or two and they put it out of their minds. They say it was an aberration. Whatever. They make sure the reputation is preserved."

Berman settled back in his chair and paused a moment. "Frank, of all my reporters in this room, you know as well or better than any that we can do the stories but we cannot go into every heart and mind and instruct it on how to feel or think about Philip Stewart."

Cronin rubbed his face with both hands. He was tired, frayed.

"You're right, Howard, I know that," said Cronin. "But let's not forget that he was an evil man. He hurt people."

• • •

The more Cronin thought about it, the more pleased he was that Berman had no interest in his story on Stewart's withdrawal of funds coinciding with dates he left town. It occured to him that the information would be of great interest to the law enforcement group that had convened to unravel the mystery around Stewart's death. He knew from his friend Scot Lehman that the state attorney general, Malcolm Sears, had put together a working committee to plot strategy on Stewart that included Sears, Lehman, Sloane, McCormack, and Ben Palmer, head of the Boston office of the U.S. Justice Department's Organized Crime Strike Force.

Cronin thought it interesting that McCormack had kept the group's existence secret from him. Cronin did not know that Sears had sworn each member of the ad hoc committee to complete secrecy—Lehman had told Cronin of the group's existence before that happened. Sears had told them he would prosecute anyone who broke the silence. Since then, Lehman had been unwilling to talk to Cronin about the group's work.

But now Cronin had information he was certain the committee did not have. The correlation between Stewart's withdrawing funds from the Shelter Coalition account and his trips out of town was tantalizing. But Berman was right, it proved nothing. It wasn't clear what Stewart did with the money or where he went. Or even if the money and the absences from the city were connected, though Cronin felt sure they were. Nonetheless, he could prove nothing with what he had. There was a point at which being a reporter was nothing but frustration. Law enforcement officials had vastly more access to information than journalists.

Cronin contacted McCormack and they met at Larz Anderson Park. Cronin turned the list matching the withdrawals with Stewart's trips out of town over to the detective. McCormack thanked him but said nothing about any possible connection between what the police were investigating and these facts. But the detective thought immediately of Las Vegas. Where else did one go for three or four days with thousands and thousands of dollars?

Cronin also told McCormack that on the list of those making deposits to the Shelter Coalition Capital Fund was a freight company which Cronin assumed had a contract with the city and a truck leasing company. Cronin said he suspected those were scams similar to Wrightways Transit.

"So why don't you go after this stuff?" McCormack asked.

"There's only so much I can concentrate on at any given time, and I've got other stuff," he said. "It would be a shame for this to go to waste."

McCormack found this news extremely interesting. Just a few days earlier Cronin would have considered the information he was giving to McCormack to be the basis for dynamite stories. Now he was on to something else.

"You got something good?" asked the detective.

"Could be," said Cronin.

"Something we might be interested in?" McCormack asked.

Cronin shrugged.

McCormack shifted in his seat. He didn't like trying to pry information out of reporters.

"I hear the heat's on you over there," McCormack said.

Cronin was surprised McCormack knew that. "You know how it is," Cronin said. "You step on a toe or two and the usual suspects howl."

"The cardinal called Johnson, eh?" said McCormack.

"Kennedy, too," Cronin said.

"Kennedy?" McCormack said. "How come?"

"To complain we were being too tough on Stewart."

McCormack nodded. "Chappaquiddick," said the detective.

Cronin didn't get it.

"It all goes back to Chappaquiddick, twenty-five years ago," said McCormack. "Mary Jo drowns and the senator's political career is on the line. Stewart wasn't an elected official then, but he was a budding activist with strong connections to the left and the news media. He pitched in, went to bat for Teddy."

"When you put two and two together on this, all I ask is for a head's up," said Cronin. "OK?"

McCormack didn't respond right away. "I'm in an awkward position," said the detective. He did not want to say that he had taken a pledge of secrecy in the presence of the attorney general. He would feel too foolish.

"Oh?" said Cronin.

McCormack sighed. "It's complicated," he said, "but I'm sure we can work something out."

CHAPTER
14

When Cronin had last been to her home, Sloane had lived in a condominium on Chestnut Street, on the flat of Beacon Hill. Since then, however, Sloane's grandmother had died leaving Susan her home in a leafy suburb just outside the city. When Cronin pulled into the driveway and drove back through the woods, he found a white clapboard farmhouse, a rambling, secluded old place. As Cronin pulled his car to the side of the gravel driveway and walked around toward the back, he saw what was obviously a new wing constructed of glass and wood stretching out toward a flagstone terrace next to a pool.

He carried a bottle of Silverado Chardonnay to present to Sloane and walked through the yard and on to the back terrace. He called through the screen doors of the porch: "Please tell me that the owner of this spread is some industrialist traveling in Europe and that you are house-sitting," he joked. "Please tell me that."

She came through the door wiping her hands on an apron. She was wearing pale yellow silk pants and a white shirt with a design of brightly colored hot-air balloons. Her hair was pulled back and she had a slight sunburn on her face. He was struck by her loveliness.

"Welcome," she said brightly. "And I'm sorry to disappoint you but I actually own this place due to an accident of birth."

"This is," he said with a look of wonder, "unreal."

"I suppose it's a bit too much, but I had no wish to sell it," she said. "I don't think Grammy would have approved."

He presented her with the wine and she saw that it was her favorite. "How thoughtful, Frankie," she said with delight. She reached up and wrapped her arms around his neck and kissed him.

"Thank you," she said softly. "Shall we have some?"

"Whatever you have opened is fine with me," he said.

"Oh, no," she said walking quickly to a kitchen counter, "I insist on this." She uncorked the wine and poured two glasses. They each took a sip and pronounced it delicious.

"I love this space," he said.

"Thank you," she replied. "When I got the house I realized that the kitchen hadn't been touched since the fifties, literally. Everything was ancient and it just seemed so dark and out of date that I couldn't stand it. When Grammy was here it was fine—it was *her* kitchen and it suited her. But I wanted . . . this."

"This" was a large combination kitchen and sitting room. On one wall were the refrigerator, sink, and dishwasher. On an island just a couple of feet away was the gas stove. The cabinets were cherry with glass panes. Past the island was a brick fireplace and chimney that acted as a kind of buffer between the kitchen and sitting room where Sloane had a dining table, sofa, bookshelves, and a television and stereo system built into the wall. The sofa, easy chair, and curtains were a bright orange, the walls white.

"The fireplace is great," said Cronin.

"There was a wall there," said Sloane, "separating the kitchen from a sort of mud room that wasn't really used. I knew the chimney ran up through there and so I asked whether if the wall was taken down we could open up the chimney and the architect said they could. It was lovely during the winter to be sitting by the fire and watching the snow mount up outside. I must spend ninety percent of my time in this room."

But this was an evening to be outside in the warmth of the summer air. The sky, with the sun descending, held a few puffy clouds the color of overly ripe raspberries. They stood on the terrace looking out over the pool, down across an easily sloping lawn to a red clay tennis court. Beyond the court was a grove of trees and, beyond that, Cronin could see the outline of a pond.

"Can you swim in there?" Cronin asked, pointing toward the pond.

"Oh, sure," she said. "It's warm around the shore and near the surface, but cooler the deeper you go. It's fed by a cold underground spring that runs off the Concord River. Jump in if you'd like."

"Would you mind?" he asked.

"Oh, please, not the least," she said, turning and heading back through the kitchen. "Here," she returned and handed him a fresh bath towel.

He headed down the hill with the towel slung over his shoulder, glass of wine in his hand. Cronin walked past the tennis court, which had been recently brushed, on toward the pond. There was a small stand of trees at one end where he took off his madras cotton shirt, shoes, chinos, and underwear. He set them in a pile next to the tree beside his wineglass and glanced back up at the house to make sure he could not be seen. He stepped into the water, walking gingerly until he was deep enough to push forward and begin a leisurely swim. The water was bracingly chilly the farther out he got and he dove down deep, to perhaps fifteen feet without hitting bottom and felt icy cool water there. He surfaced and continued on in a steady stroke until he reached the other side. The bottom was sandy there and Cronin supposed that sand had been trucked in through the years to create a beach, perhaps for Sloane when she was a child. He swam back across, guessing that the pond wasn't any more than two hundred feet long and half that wide. He reached the trees where his clothes were piled and sat down on the grass naked, then stretched out on his back and stared up at the sky. It was growing steadily darker now and the colors of the clouds were more muted.

Cronin sat up and sipped his wine. He lay back again feeling cleansed, and ready for this evening. For he knew a crucial time had come. He knew that he faced a test with this woman of whether he was able to engage in normal human connections, to feel love for her and to express that love. He did not feel burdened by such thoughts as he so often had in the past. Perhaps he had been baptized into a new life now and had a second chance.

He toweled off and dressed. As he walked back up toward the house feeling cool and revived, he knew that he was ready for this evening that was too long overdue.

They ate on the flagstone terrace at a black, wrought-iron table. The dinner was a treat—tasty swordfish, rice and salad, dessert of Häagen Dazs strawberry ice cream, and, to cap it all off, a half-bottle of chilled Perrier-Jouet champagne. It was dark when they finished, but they sat quietly on the terrace, sipping the sparkling wine, candles flickering in the slight breeze. Soon they were chased inside by a few pesky mosquitoes. Cronin rinsed the dishes and placed them in the dishwasher while Sloane sponged off the table and counters. She brewed decaf and they took their cups into the den, a cozy, walnut-lined room, and relaxed in easy chairs on either side of the stone fireplace. Sloane put James Taylor on the stereo and they chatted idly for a while. In time, they fell silent.

"I was thinking last night about our conversation at lunch yesterday," she said. "I'm not sure I've ever heard quite the same tone in your voice as when you were reminiscing about your mom. It sounds like you were a very happy child."

Frank considered this for a moment. He nodded. "Very happy," he said, looking into her eyes and smiling. "Life was simple then, and very good. I remember one summer in particular. One magical summer that I'm sure was the happiest time of my life. We went to an inn on Cape Cod. I don't even recall the name, but it was one of those grand old places with great wide porches and a beautiful formal dining room. And the guests were mostly old and *so* civilized. And I remember the room we stayed in together in a kind of dorm for the people who worked there. My mother worked as a waitress at this place, but she worked in the evening so we had every day together all summer long. And I remember it being beautiful every day except maybe one or two, and we would go to the beach, she and I, and play in the sand and swim and it was all so perfect. So idyllic. And I think I thought that that was what life would always be like."

He laughed. "What did I know. I was only five."

He paused, recalling that time so many years ago. "I remember very distinctly that we left there the day after Labor Day, very early on a cool morning. I remember walking along into the town to catch the bus. She held my hand and in the other hand she carried a big duffel bag with all our stuff. We rode up to Boston; it was still quite early and we hadn't eaten yet, but we couldn't eat at the station there because things were too expensive in Boston."

He shook his head, half smiling. "I remember her saying that. So we finally ate when we got to the bus station in Concord, New Hampshire. Anyway, we continued north on the bus, up across New Hampshire and into Vermont, and finally, in the evening, we pulled into Coaticook. We got off the bus and were shivering and it felt like in just one day—in just a bus ride—we had traveled straight from summer to fall.

"Our trailer was set in a clearing a quarter mile up from the Cold River, at the end of a dirt road. It was actually a very nice little place for us, certainly not fancy, but more than adequate. It was about the width of a bus, as a matter-of-fact, and it had a very cozy feel to it. I'm sure I'd be shocked at how flimsy it was if I were to go back and see it now, at how thin the walls were, and how everything was on top of everything else. There were three rooms: a kitchen with a fold-out counter that we ate on, and my room and my mother's room."

He held out his hands and glanced at Sloane, not even a slight hint of self-pity evident on his face. "When that is what you know, it can be a very happy place. I never yearned for space or privacy or anything but what we had."

He smiled a contented smile, and sat back, silent now.

"How come you never mention your father when you recall those days?" Sloane asked.

"It was a happier place when my father was gone," he replied, staring down into his glass. "He was a huge, hulking man. A logger, had been the son of a logger, and logging was all he knew, all he cared to know. He was kind of a drifter, a drinker.

"When he visited, which was infrequently, my mother would

be frightened. There were a couple of times, very late at night, when me and my mom were sleeping, when he would show up at the trailer. I'm sure he was drunk those times. He would bang on the doors and windows, demanding that she let him in. And she would have no choice."

Sloane was shocked by this, sure she knew that some horrible violence was done to his mother and just as sure that he would not tell her the details.

Cronin paused for a moment remembering one night when his father forced his way in and pushed her down the hallway to her bedroom. Frank had come out of his room and had seen her cowering with fear. He was ordered back into his room by his father and he heard his mother imploring him to be quiet for the sake of the boy. But Frank heard everything—every harsh, obscene whisper, every creak of the springs. He heard the headboard banging against the wall, so quickly and hard that he thought it might break through. And he heard his father make a scary sound, a loud noise like an animal.

When his father left that night he heard her crying in her bed, and he went from his room to her and she held him so tightly she was hurting him and she cried and told him she was all right, she was fine and she loved him, she said, more than the sun and the moon and the stars.

Frank got up and left the room. Soon he returned with a drink in his hand. His brow was knitted as he sat down in the easy chair. He hunched forward, sipped the drink, set it aside, then clasped his hands, as though in prayer. He spoke quietly.

"My mother went food shopping every Wednesday evening because that's when she got a ride from a neighbor, Mrs. Wensink. It was a snowy night. She considered not going. She mentioned it to me. But it was arranged that Mrs. Wensink would pick her up at a certain time and there was no way to change that. We did not have a telephone. If we had had a phone I think she would have called Mrs. Wensink and canceled. Because of the snow."

He sighed softly and sipped his drink. "Logging trucks always go too fast. They're always overloaded. They roar down from the camps, bulging with huge trees stripped of their branches, accelerating around curves. I've gone back and researched this a bit. To satisfy my own curiosity, really. I've just felt the need to know. They may not have heard much of anything. Probably never knew what hit them. The driver, I found out, had had a snout full of ale, and was rushing to Maxwell Paper with an overload. The visibility must have been very bad. The snow swirls in these storms and there was a clearing nearby where the wind could get up a good head of steam and whip the snow into a blinding frenzy. He must not have seen them because he didn't so much hit them as rode up over them. Crushed Mrs. Wensink's Dodge. It spun off to the side and down an embankment and into the trees. The coroner's report said both women died instantly."

Sloane sat in silence, stunned. Her eyes burned and a tear slipped down her cheek. She crossed to him and held him and found that it was she who needed holding. He had been through this a thousand times, a million times, in his mind.

He did not tell her, he supposed he did not need to, that it had devastated him and his brother. After she had been buried, a lady from the provincial government drove them on the interstate to a gray house in a subdivision that would be their transition into the world of foster care. It was to be the first of too many foster homes. The boys wanted to be in Coaticook, back with their friends, but there were no foster homes available just then willing to take two children. The thought of splitting the boys up was raised with Frank but he dismissed it. It had been just weeks before the accident one night in the restaurant when she thought both boys were asleep, he heard her talking with one of the other waitresses. "He's not strong, like Frankie," he heard her say about Chris. "Frankie is strong and wise, full of common sense. Chris is a sweet child, but not so lucky as Frank."

She had said, "Frankie's got to look after that boy."

•   •   •

Sloane's embrace was fierce. She had settled on his lap, curled herself on top of him, her face buried in his shoulder. She sobbed. Her face was warm and wet with tears. He felt calm. He held her and kissed her hair. After a while, she stopped crying. She sat up and wiped her cheeks and her eyes. She held him at arm's length, clutching his biceps with her hands. She held his gaze. "I am so very, very sorry," she said. "It's heartbreaking, Frankie. I wish there was something I could say or do. Something."

He smiled at her. "There is something you can do," he said. "You can take a walk with me."

They went out through the glass doors leading to the terrace where they had eaten dinner and walked past the pool, down beyond the pond. There was a path that cut through the woods and led onto a sprawling tract of conservation land and a series of trails used for cross-country skiing and horseback riding. A huge yellow moon hung in the sky illuminating the path. The night air was warm and smelled of an earthy fragrance.

They ambled along the path, past a meadow that was so bright in the moonlight it appeared artificial. Beyond the meadow, near the point where Sloane's property abutted the conservation land, there was a large sloping rock where they stopped and sat down. They looked up at the moon and listened to crickets. The sound of a barn owl came from not far away.

"Are you OK?" she asked him tenderly.

He squeezed her hand. "I'm really fine," he said. "Really, I am. I've had twenty-four years to deal with this, remember. I've been living with it for most of my life and I've long since adjusted. I've long since come to terms with it. Life goes on. I try very hard not to dwell on it. There are times when I do. Naturally. But I fight hard the temptation to be absorbed by it because the self-pity that comes from dwelling on it is overpowering. It's druglike. And when you're under its power then nothing is your responsibility. You become a victim, and when you become a victim you start laying off responsibility for your own life on other forces in the universe. I hate that."

The truth was that he did feel sorry for himself, as much as he tried not to. He of course did not tell Sloane about the dream.

201

That he had long since come to terms with his mother's death was true in a sense, false in another. It haunted him, but he could not say that to her.

It was clear to Sloane, however, that he had not entirely put it behind him. He was scarred by recollections of his father and his mother, of a marriage where there was violence and neglect. Was it any wonder he had difficulty with intimacy?

"I want to make the best of my life, Sloane," he said. "It's my only chance. I know that. I'm trying to live as though I truly understand that. That's why I want so very much to try to make it work between us. I honestly do. And I know you must be suspicious of that. You have reason to be. But I believe that I am ready now. I don't know whether it will work, but I want to make a good-faith stab at it."

"Oh, Frankie," she said. "That's really all one can ask, isn't it? That we *try.* I mean these things are terribly complicated in a way. But in another respect it's *not* very complicated at all. It really comes down to whether we're willing to make an effort. And Frankie, I *do* believe there's something here, something between us. And I am so very, very happy to hear you say you want to try, because there *is* something, I feel it so strongly and I think you do, too, and goddamnit, Frankie, we've got to give it a chance. We can't let it die of neglect. That would be a dreadful sin."

They embraced there on the rock, kissed tenderly and held each other. They ambled back along the moonlit path, his arm around her shoulder, hers around his waist. Every now and again they would pause and he would look into her eyes and she would touch his face and they would kiss gently.

It was very late when they returned to the house. They were both exhausted. They stretched out on the sofa together and soon he had fallen asleep. She moved carefully out of his embrace and went to a guest room to get a blanket. She placed it over him and stood looking down at him. She went to bed feeling very much in love.

CHAPTER

15

The L1011 turned onto the runway, accelerated smoothly, lifted easily off the ground, and rose steadily into the sky over Boston. When Cronin glanced out the window and saw the city recede he felt a palpable sense of relief. He was happy to be out of there.

He felt Sloane squeeze his hand and he turned to look at her smiling face. She held up a flute of champagne. "Cheers," she said. "Here's to a great little vacation."

He clinked glasses and they sipped their drinks. "And here," he said, "is to the genius who had the idea for all of this."

"Thank you," she said, beaming.

It had happened so fast. She had seen on Saturday night that he needed a break. On Sunday afternoon, she had made a few phone calls—to a couple of her deputy prosecutors, the airlines, and a hotel. Everything clicked.

This, she thought, is meant to happen.

She sat down with him early Sunday evening and told him she had a surprise birthday present for him, but that he had to be willing to take a week off from work. He noted that his birthday was two months away and she said it was an early present. He asked why it required a week. She wouldn't say. She said you either trust me or you don't. He laughed for the first time all day and picked up the phone. He called Berman and asked for the week off.

This was not an easy call for Berman. Since the murder of Councillor Stewart, Cronin had been his lead reporter, his only reporter, in fact, to break any news on the case. To let Frank go at a time like this increased the likelihood that the *Post* would get beaten on some aspect of the Stewart story.

But there was another consideration for Berman. Roy Johnson had put tremendous pressure on Berman to back off on Stewart coverage. And if Cronin were away for a week it would seem that Berman was yielding to the pressure, thereby getting Johnson off his back. For the moment at least.

The risk of not having Cronin around was worth taking, Berman decided. He told Frank to go ahead and take the week off. Berman hoped that in a week's time, he would get the old Cronin back.

On Monday, before going into the office early, Sloane told Frank to go home and pack a bag and she would pick him up at his apartment at noon. He was not surprised when they drove to the airport. He *was* surprised when they boarded a flight to San Francisco and were seated in the first-class cabin.

During the flight they chatted and drank more champagne. They ate some of the fruit and cheese served with lunch, and Sloane dozed off. While she slept, Cronin read a magazine and sat gazing out into the sunny sky.

In her sleep, she had shifted in her seat and her head came to rest against his shoulder. She slept so soundly that her mouth opened slightly as she breathed. When the flight attendant had disappeared, he placed a gentle kiss on her forehead.

After landing in San Francisco, they caught a small plane headed down the coastline to Monterey. They rented a car at the airport and Sloane drove them down 17 Mile Drive to the Inn at Spanish Bay, on the Monterey Peninsula. It was early evening, Pacific time, when they arrived. Their room was spacious and elegant, furnished with a king-sized bed at one end, a sofa and easy chairs at the other. In a wall by the sofa was a fireplace and the hotel staff had built a fire before their arrival and brought in a supply of wood. The far wall of the room was glass from floor to ceiling, end to end. Sliding glass doors led out to a large private balcony. Directly below were dunes and wild sea grass, but just beyond was the spectacular pounding Pacific surf, and as the day grew late the sun began to set on the horizon. In the clear sky the sun appeared to be an absurdly large orange ball, so huge it was as though Hollywood's special effects teams had been at work, but standing in each other's arms in the increasingly cool evening air, Cronin and Sloane knew this was real. In the room when they arrived was a bucket with a chilled bottle of Taittinger that Cronin popped open and poured. They stood on the balcony sipping their wine and quietly watching the sun slip ever so slowly below the horizon. When it had finally disappeared and the evening descended, they moved back inside. They left the balcony doors open to hear the crash of the waves. In their room the fire crackled.

Standing in front of the fireplace, Frank took her in his arms and they embraced. They kissed over and over again. After a while, he unfastened her pants and dropped them to the floor, running his hands along the upper portions of her legs, front and back. Sloane put her head back, her eyes closed and took a deep slow breath. His hands were big and strong but he was so patient and gentle with her. He took his time, never hurrying. He would do anything and everything to please her and she thought of what they were about to do together and she felt a shudder of excitement.

He unbuttoned her shirt and took it off her. He unfastened her bra and felt the smoothness of her skin. He undressed himself and embraced her again and they moved to the bed. She had him lie on his stomach and she straddled him and began to massage his back. She pressed firmly and worked the muscles in his upper back and along his shoulders. She took her time and massaged until he was completely relaxed. And then they switched positions, with Frank on top of her massaging her back. Soon, she was on her back and he was above her and they kissed.

The room was dimly lit by the fire and the reflection of the rising moon off the black ocean water. It was enough light for them to see each other clearly.

They kissed some more and rolled over on the bed and then Sloane was atop him and he was inside her and she felt his hardness and she moved her hips back and forth in a steady rhythm and in time she was coming in slow waves. And then he was on top of her again, between her legs and soon she felt him inside of her and she felt a flush of warmth and a sharp snap of pleasure within.

"I love you," he said to her.

"And I love you," she said.

"I think I've loved you for a while," he said.

"I'm sure I've loved you for quite a long time," she said.

They never made it out of their room for dinner. They shared an apple and crackers that Cronin had left over from the flight. And they went to sleep, finally, exhausted at midnight, three o'clock Eastern time, wondering whether they could ever get enough of each other.

After a day on the West Coast they felt as though they had been away a week. After three days it felt like they'd been gone a month. They walked the beach in Monterey and Frank accompanied Sloane as she played the famed Pebble Beach Golf Links, just a few miles down the coast from Spanish Bay. He watched carefully as she swung, trying to learn from her, but the few shots he hit were comically poor. Her form seemed perfect on each swing, compact and powerful. She repeated the same motion over and over again and hit one straight shot after another. They walked the course in the late afternoon and in spite of whipping winds, she negotiated her way around one of the world's most famous layouts in an impressive eighty-four strokes.

They had drinks on the terrace at the Lodge at Pebble Beach and dinner in a restaurant in Carmel which had a retractable roof that refused to close when the rain began. The waiters and maître d' struggled to crank it shut but it would not yield, and when they scanned the tables for someone more muscled they settled on Cronin and he happily pitched in, but when he pulled on the crank with all his might he snapped it off to groans from the staff and applause from the patrons, some of whom were either drunk enough or laid back enough to sit in the downpour and finish their meals.

Cronin and Sloane were neither. They headed back to the Inn, soaked and chilled. They got out of their wet clothes and took hot showers, then draped themselves in terrycloth robes provided by the hotel. They sprawled together on the couch facing the fireplace, he caressing her neck. Soon, Frank reached down and undid the belt that held Sloane's robe in place. It fell open and he reached down between her legs and felt her warmth and moisture.

They made love in front of the fireplace and slept that chilly night with the balcony doors open and the sound of the surf and rain lashing down outside. The storm brought with it unseasonably cool air and they spent all of the following day in their room, in front of the fireplace.

Feeling sluggish from the day, they went out for a long, vigorous walk when the clouds drifted away early that evening. Their route took them along the sea at Spanish Bay and up past Pebble Beach to Cypress Point, where thirty- and forty-foot cliffs stood above the Pacific. They saw seals and sea lions in the water below and stumbled onto the Cypress Point Club, where they saw deer tracks on a fairway. They walked on and on, faster and faster, building up a sweat until they broke into a jog and circled back around, down through the pine forest just inland on the peninsula and back to the Inn. They went to the gym, where they were the only patrons, and worked on the Nautilus machines for forty-five minutes and then plunged into the outdoor pool just as darkness was falling.

They showered and dressed and dined at a table by the huge fireplace in the main dining room of the Inn. They voraciously ate appetizers of smoked salmon and a main course of rack of lamb with asparagus and new potatoes. Sloane ordered a bottle of 1982 Silver Oak Cabernet Sauvignon which Cronin sipped and pronounced "the damnedest wine I've ever tasted."

The next day they checked out and drove south along the highway rising up into the hills just south of Carmel, driving with towering forests on both sides until suddenly, the forest on their right was no more and there was only open ocean, hundreds and hundreds of feet below. Big Sur. Dizzyingly high cliffs that plunged into the surging Pacific. The road was carved into the cliffs at points and any misstep with the wheel meant the end. Along the way they noticed an occasional private home perched on the cliff, stunning places that were homes to movie stars.

They drove mesmerized by the views and calmed by their steady movement south where the air was warmer. They had intended to stay at the Ventana Ranch in the hills but decided to press on south to Santa Barbara. They checked into the Four Seasons and spent the final two nights of their vacation there. During the day they drove around and explored the area, and Cronin, who had never before been to Santa Barbara, fell in love. It was, he said, the perfect place for them to live.

Sloane laughed. "But what would we *do?*" she asked.

"We could teach," he said, meaning the University of California at Santa Barbara.

They were having dinner at a small, informal Mexican restaurant in town.

"I'm absolutely serious," he said. "What's holding us in Boston? Let's just go. We're free to live wherever we want. Why not give it a try?"

She was taken aback by this. What was Frank saying? Was he, in his circuitous fashion, trying to tell her something? Why couldn't he simply say that he thought they should be together?

Clearly it was the implication of what he was saying. Sloane thought maybe it was the lawyer in her that valued directness. Ambiguity held little charm for her. She wanted to call him on it, to stop him right then and there and prod him to explain what he meant, to share with her his view of what they should be. But she did not feel the moment was right. And she let it pass.

In bed that night she said to him, "Now I know we have a serious adult relationship."

"How's that?" he asked.

"Because," she said, "we're in bed to sleep not for sex."

After breakfast they took a stroll on the beach, then returned to the hotel and relaxed by the pool. After baking in the sun, Frank got up to swim and, as he did so, she watched him carefully. Standing at the pool's edge, he was tall and fit looking. He wore a baggy, lime green bathing suit that hid how slim his hips were. His stomach was flat, his chest and upper arms well muscled. His shoulders were broad and strong. He dove in and swam at a steady pace, rolling his head back and forth, side to side, in rhythm with his long, powerful strokes.

As she watched, she wondered about him. She thought about a brief conversation they'd had their second night at Spanish Bay. In front of the fireplace she had asked him what he wanted out of life. She had expected he'd make some sort of joke to escape having to answer. But he had not done that.

"The same thing everybody wants," he had replied. "Health. Happiness. A family. Rewarding work." He had shrugged and added, "What else is there?"

She had pressed. "But above all else, what?" she had asked. He had not hesitated.

"A family," he had said. "Above all else, I want a family." He paused, then said, "That's what it's all about, isn't it?"

He had made it sound so basic, so simple. For all the intricacies of life, for all the complications, that's what it came down to.

"Isn't that what you want?" he had asked.

She did not speak. She merely nodded her head in affirmation. Yes, indeed, she had thought. That is exactly what I want.

They lay on the beach in the late afternoon. The sun was headed down. Santa Barbara seemed quiet, tranquil.

They lay together on a blanket on their stomachs. The sound of the surf crashing onto the shore had lulled them both into sleep. Frank soon woke and lay reading a magazine. He thought Sloane was still sleeping but she stirred and moved closer toward him. She reached over and took his arm and brought it across her shoulders. He squeezed her.

"You OK?" he asked.

"I'm afraid sometimes," she said. She surprised herself with her bluntness.

He turned to her, surprised himself. "You? Afraid?"

She smiled, but she was quite serious.

"Of anything in particular?" he asked.

"Of things going wrong," she said without hesitation. "Of bad things happening."

"What sort of bad things?" Frank asked.

"Oh, you know," she said. "The usual bad things."

"And what are the usual bad things?" he asked.

"The things that shatter people's happiness," she said. "Terrible things. Like what happened to Alice."

This surprised Cronin. For as long as he had known her she had protected this part of her life, guarding the memory of her sister, steadfastly avoiding any extended discussion of her at all.

"Do you think about her much?" Cronin asked.

Sloane nodded. "Quite a lot," she said. "Not every day but just about. I mean I don't linger over it, but I recall her in flashes, in moments of the day. Different things will trigger it. Little things. If I see what are obviously two sisters together or if someone talks about her sister or if I encounter someone named Alice or if I talk with my mother or father.

"Or sometimes when I'm at home and I look up at the wall in the living room or in my bedroom or my office and see one of her paintings. Those wild strokes, slashing, vibrant strokes that were so much Alice, so energized and colorful and playful. I think of her then and I think quite happily about her life, but then I also think what a terrible loss to us all, to the world, that Alice is gone."

She stopped to compose herself.

"Every now and then," Sloane continued, "when I think of what happened to Alice it frightens me. It proves that terrible things do happen in life. Sometimes it's hard to trust happiness, I think."

He enveloped her in his arms and held her for a long moment. He wanted to tell her that everything would be OK, that bad things would not happen to her, but he knew that sort of talk would serve no purpose.

"Sometimes sharing the burden helps," he said.

• • •

They went swimming in the early evening and sat on the beach drying off.

"You know," she said. "I feel OK talking to you about Alice, telling you about her. I can't help but ask if you feel OK talking to me about Chris?"

Cronin thought about this. He nodded.

"Of course I do," he said. He reached for her hand and squeezed it. With her now he felt some kind of liberation he had not experienced before. He felt free to share almost anything with her now.

He watched some children down the beach playing Frisbee. Here and there along the sand couples strolled together. Though late in the day it was still pleasantly warm.

"Christopher was very small when he was born," Frank said. "He was anemic and unbelievably tiny. I think he weighed something like four and a half pounds when he was born. They wouldn't let him out of the hospital right away. My mother was home for about a month before they'd discharge him. He had to build up his weight and strength. And we would go every night to the hospital to visit him. I will never forget as long as I live the first time I saw him. I was only six at the time, and we walked into the Intensive Care Unit and there he was in a sort of clear plastic box, with tubes in his nose and an intravenous needle stuck in his thigh. And his face was scrunched up and he was screaming his little head off. And I knew when I saw him he was terrified. He was scared to death. And my very first thought was, 'This is my brother. I should be able to do something so he doesn't cry. To comfort him.' "

Sloane sat propped up on her elbows, listening intently. "Alice was protective of me that way," she said. "It's a nice instinct older brothers and sisters have."

He gazed out to sea and remembered leaving the hospital that night with his mother and standing at the bus stop in the rain. Her hair was matted down on her forehead and she grasped Frank by the arms and appeared for a moment as though she were angry. And when she spoke she did so with an intensity he had never seen in her before.

"Listen to me now, Frankie," she had said. "That little guy in there needs us. Frankie, he's got no one else. He's all alone in this world without you and me. He's our family and there is nothing more important. Do you understand me, darling?"

And Frank understood. In spite of his age, he grasped what she was saying. Somehow, she had transferred her madness and intensity to Frank.

"Did you spend a lot of time together, you two?" Sloane asked.

"For years we were inseparable," he said. "We were very different, but we had a rapport that was telepathic, I think."

"How were you two different?" she asked.

"Physically, for one thing," said Frank. "I was always much bigger than Chris. He was very small for his age. And he was a nervous kid, skittish around people. He had a hard time with school, too.

"But we were a very happy, contented family. We had one another. And that was a lot. The three of us got along so well. We never argued, never fought. There was no tension in the house."

"Come on!" said Sloane, "don't you think you're romanticizing just a bit?"

Cronin laughed. "No, really, it's true," he said. "We had the greatest life. Chris and I would go to work with Mom on Thursday, Friday, and Saturday nights and I would read stories to him in the back booth. Sometimes Mom would give me some money and I would take Chris down to the movie theater or the arcade to play pinball.

"In the summer, as I got older, I would caddy at the golf club where the executives from Maxwell Paper played. We saved some of the money I made but every week my mother would let me spend a little on Chris and myself. I always bought him something, candy, an ice cream cone."

"Sounds like the perfect childhood," she said.

He smiled and nodded. "It was in a way," he said.

But Chris had a difficult time of it, Frank recalled. He had been a poor student and not much of an athlete. And he had had a stutter that was the source of frequent mockery from other children.

Frank had told Chris to ignore the children who made fun of

him. His mother had explained that that was hard for Chris to do. "His feelings are easily hurt," his mother had told him. "You have to understand that Chris isn't as strong as you are. He's frightened sometimes. He's fragile, Frankie, do you know what that means?"

"Something that's fragile could break easily," Frank had replied.

"Exactly," she had said. "That is why you have to always care for your brother, darling. Always. And I know you won't let me down."

"I won't, Mom," Frank had said. "I would never do that."

The next day, when they bordered the plane at LAX bound for Boston, the lightness Frank had felt all week seemed to dissipate. He was not eager to get back to the East Coast. The city where he lived held no charm for him anymore. It pretended to be something it was not, and though he had once accepted that pretension as reality, now he knew the truth. It was not a place he wanted to be anymore. Not a world in which he cared to live. It suddenly occurred to him that he wanted out.

16

Somehow, McCormack had known it would come to this. The police had wanted to question Dockerty in detail but the defense lawyer, Delaney, would not allow it. Delaney had said, after his first interview with Dockerty, that his client possessed an alibi. He said that Dockerty did not wish to disclose the nature of that alibi unless it was necessary. Detective O'Toole, upon hearing this, laughed out loud at Delaney. McCormack had not laughed.

The entire focus of the investigation into the murder of Philip Stewart was now on Dockerty. Detectives carrying his photograph had gone door to door in the Moss Hill neighborhood, and four neighbors swore they had seen Dockerty in the area, though none could state positively that they had seen him anytime before the murder took place. All had recollections of seeing him since the killing. Records showed Dockerty had checked into the Four Seasons two nights after the killing, but police theorized that he had been at some other hotel and moved.

It was not the strongest of cases, though clearly Dockerty had motive. The prosecution would also make a deal for the testimony of the inmate who had heard Dockerty say he intended to kill Stewart. The prisoner's credibility on the stand would be crucial at trial. The weapon would help, of course, as would the fact that Dockerty had broken into the Stewart house. The prosecution would speculate in an opening argument that Dockerty had come to Stewart's house on the night of the murder looking for something and killed Stewart in the process of searching.

It was not the strongest of cases but it was better than no case, and no case was what the prosecution had without Dockerty. And law enforcement officials in the city, the police command staff, in particular, were happy to have some case, any case, so long as it served to reduce the heat on them.

Dockerty was their man.

Until, that is, the lawyer Delaney was informed late in the afternoon that his client would be formally charged with homicide the following morning. When Delaney delivered this news to his client, the lawyer was startled by Dockerty's response. Dockerty claimed that he really did have an alibi. He said it was airtight. He explained to Delaney that he had held back from using it because the use of the alibi would result in Dockerty's going back to prison for a short stay for a parole violation. He had held back the alibi in the hope of getting off entirely. But now that he was about to face a formal charge of murder, Dockerty told his lawyer, he wanted the authorities told of his alibi.

He told Delaney what it was. Delaney conveyed it to the DA's office, and, to the astonishment of senior police officials in the city, the alibi checked out.

The truth was there was no way in the world Dockerty could have committed the murder, for on the night Philip Stewart was killed, Dockerty had been in a Providence, Rhode Island, jail. He had been en route to Boston, had stopped off in Providence and gotten into a beef at a bar. And he had had no intention of going back to face the charges. The arrest constituted his third parole violation, which would land him back in prison for an additional nine to twelve months.

The investigation would now have to take on a new direction. McCormack was ready.

The attorney general of the Commonwealth of Massachusetts, Malcolm Sears, convened the meeting in his sprawling suite on the twenty-first floor of the state office building. Sears occupied a corner office which held a sweeping view east to the harbor, the airport, and the ocean beyond, and west and south out along the Charles River. Directly below him was the glittering gold dome of Bulfinch's Massachusetts State House and across the river was more Bulfinch handiwork—the spires on the houses of Harvard. Sears sat at a conference table, his back to the window. He was joined by Tom McCormack, representing the homicide units of the Boston Police Department and the Suffolk County District Attorney's office; Scot Lehman, general counsel to the State Banking Commission; Ben Palmer, head of the Boston office of the Organized Crime Strike Force of the U.S. Justice Department.

Sears intended this to be an intensely private meeting. These disparate divisions of law enforcement had joined forces secretly to investigate the subterranean activities of Philip Stewart. McCormack believed, and had convinced Sears and Palmer, that the most intelligent way to produce a new list of suspects in the murder was to fully probe Stewart's crooked dealings.

"Find the wronged party and we find a killer," McCormack had said.

Sears had been reluctant to get involved, but with the apparent violation of state banking laws, he had had no choice. Sears found himself in an uncomfortable position. He was a moderate Democrat in a state where voters in Democratic primaries tended to be quite liberal. And Sears was working furiously to head off the candidacy of a liberal Hispanic woman who was making rumblings about opposing him in the next primary. In Sears's efforts to keep her out of the race, he had won the support of no less a liberal leader than Father Patrick Boyle.

That very morning, in fact, Boyle had telephoned Sears and impressed upon him the importance of keeping private any further damaging information gathered concerning Stewart.

"The need for secrecy is paramount," said Sears, starting the meeting. "The point of our efforts is not to humiliate this man in death but to apprehend a killer."

Sears opened the file on the table before him. He glanced down at a sheet of paper. "As the detective has capably noted at our earlier sessions, this is an unusual case. No prints, no fibers, no forensics of any value," he said. "No witnesses. Nothing."

"Clean," said Palmer. "It has all the marks of a professional strike. In, bang, out. No traces."

"Except the weapon," said McCormack.

"It's not what you'd expect," said Palmer, "but it worked."

"So we have ruled out the possibility that this was in any way random or a crime of passion?" said Sears.

McCormack nodded.

"We have no choice," said Palmer. "No forced entry, no struggle, nothing to betray the killer. This was thought out."

Sears fidgeted, his mind drifting from the merits of the case to the politics. He ignored Palmer.

"I want to say emphatically that we are examining and will examine the late councillor's, ah, dealings exclusively to the extent that they may bear on his death," Sears said. "Period. This will not become a romp through his private life. We all understand that?"

There were nods around the table. It was embarrassing. McCormack, who'd never had any dealings with Sears before this case, was now convinced the man was a fool.

"The point has been made ad nauseum, Malcolm," Palmer said. "Let's try and solve the crime, shall we?"

Sears's back arched. He was offended by Palmer's manner. And his implication. Sears was about to respond to Palmer but thought better of it. He thought if he did, he ran the risk of reading an item in one of the political columns about his overzealous efforts to protect Stewart's reputation. There would be speculation why. Who in the room would quietly lay that information on one of the city's political writers? Sears wondered as he glanced around. Who wouldn't? he thought.

Sears directed his gaze across the table to Scot Lehman and nodded.

"Empire Real Estate Trust is the key," said Lehman, "and it's now clear he was in violation of the state banking codes . . ."

". . . not that that matters given the parameters of our mission," Sears interrupted.

Lehman seemed annoyed. "Well, it speaks to character, doesn't it? But, strictly speaking, you're right, it's not what we're about here."

"Strictly speaking *nothing*," said Sears, clearly miffed. "It's not what we're about here period."

Lehman paused, then continued. "The records subpoenaed from Stewart's counsel, Mr. Deegan, and from his personal estate reveal that there were two trustees, not one, as we thought, as the record indicated. Stewart was one. The other, we now know, was Mr. Deegan."

Lehman paused to let this nugget of information settle in. Sears sat glumly at the head of the table, mute. McCormack, slouched to one side, his chin resting on his fist, raised his eyebrows.

"He shows up in at least three places, by my count," said Palmer, leaning forward over the table. "One, he's attorney of record on establishment of the trust. Two, he is trustee on the trust. Three, he discovers the body." And four, Palmer thinks, but does not say aloud for fear the information will somehow leak, there are letters in Stewart's files. Letters from Deegan to Stewart. Nasty letters. Letters one could even characterize as threatening.

"The rather disturbing news," Lehman said, his voice dropping an octave so that he was speaking with a kind of respected hush, evidently for the dead, "concerns what we have uncovered about the beneficiaries of the trust. There are two. One is Councillor Stewart. The other is a man named Joseph Bufalino."

Lehman glanced over at Ben Palmer, the federal Strike Force man, who nodded his head in confirmation. "A notorious character in the rackets," said Palmer.

"The pattern is well established," Lehman continued. "Large amounts of cash washed through the Shelter Coalition Capital Fund, moved into Empire, and dispersed through Empire by Bufalino and Councillor Stewart."

"How much?" asked Sears.

"Over a seven-year period nearly $4 million," said Lehman.

"All cash?" said Palmer.

"All cash," said Lehman.

The room fell silent. There could be no doubt whatsoever. The most beloved political figure in the city, the slain hero, had been a money launderer for the Mafia.

Sears sighed heavily. Lehman sat back in his chair, his report complete. McCormack remained still. Palmer moved some papers around.

"It's not clear how much Deegan knew," said Palmer. "He wasn't listed as a beneficiary, but he might have been one, de facto. I'm disinclined to give him the benefit of the doubt."

"And he declines to talk," said Sears.

"We spoke to him right after the murder, naturally, because he discovered the body," said McCormack. "Nothing about any financial dealings, certainly. Nothing since then."

He'll never say a word, thought McCormack. Not to the law. McCormack knew Deegan and he knew that, above all, Deegan hated cops; he hated state and county prosecutors and especially federal prosecutors. He hated strike force people, and the FBI and auditors from the IRS. He despised them all for they had conspired to ruin his life and had, by and large, succeeded. He would never talk to anyone official, no matter how he yearned to talk, to unburden himself about the Evil One.

"What about Bufalino?" Sears asked.

"His main businesses are gambling and drugs, thus the need to scrub the cash," said Palmer. "He used some of it to buy legitimate businesses—restaurants, auto dealerships. And he has extensive stock holdings—through straws, of course."

Sears interrupted, seeming suddenly annoyed. "I'm listening hard," he said, "but I'm not hearing a motive for murder." His tone was accusatory. "Am I missing something?"

Jesus, thought McCormack.

Palmer looked at him with knitted brow.

"With that much money going back and forth there's always room for murder," said Palmer. "Who knows what happened between them? How the deal might have soured?"

"So the point is?" asked Sears.

"That under all these thick clouds of smoke there may be fire," said Palmer.

"There was regular contact between the two," said McCormack, meaning Stewart and Bufalino. "He made regular trips to Las Vegas. Stays at Bufalino's hotel. Hangs around with him some. This we get from people in Vegas."

"Stewart was a big gambler?" Lehman asked.

McCormack nodded. "He liked to gamble. Always lost. Didn't care because it wasn't his money, obviously. But he also spent money on women and possibly men, too, we hear."

Sears was annoyed. "That has *nothing* to do with anything," he snapped.

McCormack eyed the attorney general. "It places him in Las Vegas," he said. "In contact with a known organized crime figure. With an expensive gambling habit. Probably an expensive prostitution habit." McCormack paused. "As Ben says, sometimes when you have these unstable elements compressed together, it's combustible."

Lehman nodded in agreement.

"We find who he screwed over, we find a killer," said Palmer.

Sears grimaced.

McCormack was in trouble and he knew it. He had heard that the commissioner suspected him of leaking grand jury minutes to Cronin. And now Sears seemed wary of him. And Malcolm Sears was the type of attorney general who would salivate at the thought of indicting a cop. It would help him knock the steam out of his liberal primary opponent who charged him with being too cozy with police.

But McCormack was beyond caring about his own career. He saw very clearly the truth about Philip Stewart and it was just as he had long ago suspected. Worse, in fact. McCormack wanted the truth out. It was that desire that compelled him to meet secretly with Frank Cronin and recount for him the details of the meeting with Sears, Palmer, and Lehman. McCormack did so in spite of the explicit warning by Sears against anyone at the meeting revealing any details outside the room.

Cronin returned to the *Post* with the information McCormack had given him and drafted a story, the meat of which was contained in the first several paragraphs:

> *State, county, and federal law enforcement officials are investigating what they believe to be links between former Councillor Philip Stewart and a prominent orga-*

nized crime figure for clues to who might have murdered the councillor and why, according to a law enforcement source.

Officials have evidence indicating that for seven years Stewart participated in a scheme to launder cash generated by organized crime activities—including gambling and the drug trade—the source said. Officials believe that Stewart laundered the funds through an account ostensibly intended for the Shelter Coalition. Stewart was chairman of the Coalition and held control of Coalition accounts.

Investigators to date have been stymied in their probe of Stewart's murder. The scene yielded no clues of any use in the matter, police have said.

Investigators now believe that if they probe what appears to have been Stewart's extensive corrupt activities, they will be led to the killer.

Cronin printed the story out and went to Berman's office and handed him the sheet of paper. Berman's eyes bulged.

"The *mob?*" Berman said in disbelief.

Cronin nodded.

"Money laundering?" Berman asked, incredulity overtaking his voice.

Again, Cronin nodded.

Berman stood at his desk, ran his hand through his hair while he read it again. "This is astounding," he said.

He stared intently at Cronin. "You're sure?"

"Absolutely," said the reporter.

"A law enforcement source?" Berman asked. "A source. This is your guy?"

"Yes," said Cronin.

"Can't we get confirmation?" Berman asked. "Make it plural?"

"I'm worried about the competition," said Cronin. "Any call we make to check on this widens the circle of those who know. Right now it's a tiny circle. Part of my arrangement with my guy is that I may not call anyone else in the small circle for confirmation. I agreed to that."

Berman nodded. He understood. Reporters made such deals all the time. Sources held the cards, after all.

"Let's go see Roy," said Berman.

They walked along the edge of the city room, past the city desk and the assistant editors, past the bullpen filled with reporters, past the copy desk where the editors' mission was to wring every ounce of life from a story, and on back to the corner to Roy Johnson's office. He was on the telephone and his secretary asked them to wait until he was finished. Time passed. Five minutes, ten. Fifteen, twenty minutes. Finally Johnson was done. Berman was sweating. Cronin was tense.

There were no preliminaries. Berman handed the sheet of paper with Cronin's lead to the editor, who read it over slowly. When he was done, he glanced up at both of them, a dark scowl covering his face. He was about to speak, thought better of it, and read the words on the paper again. This time, when he was done, he removed his reading glasses, placed them on his desk, and rubbed his eyes. When he spoke, his voice contained a note of impatience. "A single-sourced story that ties the man to the *Mafia?*" he said, making the notion sound preposterous. He glared at Berman, then Cronin. "We're going to destroy the man's memory for all time based on one source?" He frowned. "The hell we are."

He tossed the piece of paper on the desk.

Berman glanced at Cronin then back to Johnson.

"Frank's source has been unerring from the start," said Berman.

"Who is the source?" Johnson was asking Berman, not Cronin.

Berman blushed, embarrassed he did not know.

"He doesn't want anyone to know," said Cronin, attempting to rescue his friend. "That was his stipulation from day one, Roy. I thought it was a reasonable thing to agree to."

Johnson shook his head. "Fine," said the editor. "Protect him all you want. But we're not running this story based on a single source, period, never mind one that is unknown to us."

"We can't get confirmation," Berman said. "The source stipulated that Frank not call anyone else involved in this."

Johnson threw up his arms and looked at them as though they were stupid. "Then we don't have much of a story, do we?"

"But the story's good," said Cronin. "It's true."

Johnson was impatient. "Without confirmation that story doesn't make our pages," Johnson said in a tone that indicated they were dismissed.

Berman could not bring himself to yield.

"Roy, there were probably a half dozen people in the meeting where this was discussed," said Berman. "If the law of averages applies, each one of them will tell two people who in turn will tell two more. Within a few hours dozens of people in town will know about this, which means the *Record* may find out today. If they do, they won't worry about a single source."

Johnson was slouched in his chair, feet up on his desk, hands held as though in prayer, pressing his fingertips against his lips. He wanted to think about this very carefully. He wanted to make the right judgment and he wanted to make that judgment independent of his personal interests. Boyle had phoned him only the night before. Ostensibly, the priest was calling to report a slight bit of progress on the annulment application. The new vicar, it had turned out, had not only been a seminary roommate of Boyle's, but the two men were close friends as well.

Johnson's heart pounded each time Boyle called. But he believed that he was capable of separating his personal interests from professional judgments. Many senior editors similarly fooled themselves.

Then Boyle had turned the conversation to the damage being done to the Shelter Coalition's reputation, to its ability to raise funds, to help the poor.

Johnson ignored Cronin altogether. He looked hard at Howard Berman. "The story's not running, Howard," he said. "Is that clear? Philip Stewart is dead and whether he was associated with the Mafia or Mother Teresa is now of little consequence. Period."

"Jesus, Roy, I don't agree," said Berman.

Johnson cut him off. "I understand that. You've made your case. The answer is no. Now let's get back to work."

• • •

Donald Deegan was not a well man. When asked to discuss the case by investigators, Deegan, speaking through his attorney, said he was too ill to be interviewed. He made it plain that without a subpoena from a grand jury, he would have nothing to say. Whatever he told the authorities would find its way into the newspapers, he knew. And he was a private man.

This was a clear signal to investigators that Deegan could not speak for fear of self-incrimination. Deegan knew he would be foolish to answer questions from law enforcement officials. But he nonetheless had a powerful itch to talk to someone about the case. Anonymously. For he wanted to contribute to the destruction of the memory of Philip Stewart, his old friend and confidant. And an opportunity to do just that occurred when Frank Cronin suddenly appeared at Deegan's door.

CHAPTER

17

To the outsider, Boston was a city of sophistication and grace. It was a cultured place that, more than any other American city, had about it an aura of Europe, the Old World. But those who had long lived in Boston knew better. Those who had been born in one of its balkanized neighborhoods and had not migrated from west of the Charles River or south of the Blue Hills knew Boston for what it really was: a city of ethnic tribes and class envy; a bazaar of assorted hatreds; a city where vengeance was a common goal; a place where most ethnic groups at least mistrusted and often despised most others.

Cronin had learned during his years as a reporter in Boston that often the motive for a person's willingness to help a reporter dig up information damaging to someone else was simple revenge. This was of course the case in other cities as well. But no where else did it have the intensity of Boston, where wrongs and perceived wrongs and slights were not only not forgotten; they were put away in a special place and cared for, occasionally brought gingerly into the sunlight, like fine silver, where they were polished, burnished to a high gloss. In Boston, they have always loved to hate.

It was true of everyone in the city, what was said in the old joke: What's the definition of Irish Alzheimer's? You forget everything except the grudges.

When working on stories with any sort of political bent to them, Cronin made it a habit—never with any success—to seek the views of one Donald Deegan, former city councillor, state representative, and three-term congressman. Deegan had been a promising young politician back in the postwar years when he had graduated from Boston College and BC Law School. He had successfully prosecuted a number of high-profile cases as an assistant in the Suffolk County District Attorney's office and on the strength of his record there, had sought and won a seat in the Massachusetts House from West Roxbury. After two terms in the State House he had run citywide and won a council seat on his first try. Deegan was different from the old pols of that era, most of whom started their careers during the Depression. The old-timers emphasized personal political service, a kind of politics that was on its way out. Deegan worked larger issues with skill. Rather than getting Mrs. McGillicuddy a turkey for Christmas, he would push for the state to pay for a program for turkeys for thousands at Christmas. Deegan understood well the significance of the Boston vote to any politician running statewide and he held Beacon Hill hostage for the programs he most wanted for the city. In just a few terms as a state representative, Deegan had been able to bleed the state of tens of millions of additional dollars for Boston.

When he ran for Congress from a newly formed district that included all of the city and a smattering of suburbs, Deegan won easily and headed to Washington. Through the good offices of soon to be House Speaker John W. McCormack of South Boston, Deegan was the only freshman member of the House to win a coveted seat on the Ways and Means Committee, where he used his role to bring contracts to Massachusetts companies.

After a single term, Deegan was reelected with a record 86 percent of the vote in the general election. But soon after he returned to Washington he began to feel a financial pinch that had begun during his freshman term. He would fly home each weekend to work the district. On Monday he would fly back to Washington, working long days and spending nights at his Capitol Hill apartment. He found the schedule backbreaking and the rewards few. In fact, he learned that the job was costing him money. His office budget fell well shy of covering all of the travel, staff, and other expenses he incurred. Other members of the House experienced a similar crunch and most members, many well-to-do to begin with, coped. But there were always a few who could not resist the temptation to supplement their incomes. Deegan did not initiate the corruption. He was approached, initially, by a man who owned a small engineering company on Route 128. The fellow was seeking to sell guidance systems for a new generation of small missiles to the air force. The man offered Deegan $10,000 if he could secure the contract. Deegan was able to do so—it turned out the firm was destined to get the contract, anyway—and pocketed the cash. He was approached by others, subsequently, and performed similar services.

But in the midst of his third term Deegan grew bolder. Instead of waiting for eager businesspeople to offer money, Deegan asked for it. It worked the first few times, but then he propositioned the wrong person; a man who went to the FBI and cooperated in a sting of Congressman Deegan. He was indicted on the eve of his reelection campaign and defeated. He was promptly tried in the federal court, convicted, imprisoned, and suspended for five years from the practice of law. He served eleven months at Danbury and returned to Boston penniless, a broken man.

One thing about Boston, though—it took care of its own. A Boston lobbying firm, run by an old friend of Deegan's from his days in the Massachusetts State House, quietly hired him. For all the disgrace he had suffered, Deegan still had a number of contacts in Boston politics, many of whom engaged in practices similar to those which brought Deegan crashing down. The difference between him and them was simple: he got caught. But in addition to influence he could exercise on behalf of clients through friends in the Massachusetts House and Senate, Deegan was also just as bright as he had ever been and his strategic political sense remained keen. He could plot strategy on behalf of a variety of clients—from a major insurance company to the tobacco lobby—quietly, without ever emerging from the political shadows. And that is how his career had gone, and rather profitably, at that, since his return from federal prison.

Deegan had become the ultimate inside player. He had contacts everywhere that mattered in Boston politics—in the Council, the mayor's office, important city agencies, the police department, the DA's office, and in the State House. He made it his business to know who was doing what to whom—politically—and why, at any given moment in time. When the racing industry wanted to know whether the climate was right on Beacon Hill to pass new legislation expanding racing dates, they went to Deegan. When members of the high-technology council wanted to know when to seek a cut in the capital gains tax, they went to Deegan. When the police commissioner wanted to know which member of his command staff was fucking a reporter at one of the TV stations, he called Deegan. That Deegan's name was barely known to the public, and remembered largely by old-timers who recalled his trial, was an advantage to him, for it permitted him to operate with the anonymity that suited him best. Deegan didn't know everything about Boston politics. But he knew more than anyone else.

Most reporters in town knew who Deegan was but few had ever spoken with him. He was considered a relic of sorts, a practitioner of the old style of corrupt city politics who had long since been out of the political loop. But Cronin knew from the best political reporters at the *Post*—those who covered the State House—that, in fact, Deegan was wired. Cronin had tried on occasion in the past to speak with Deegan, but the lobbyist despised reporters.

Councillor Philip Stewart had been a man of Boston. Deegan was such a man, as well, and Cronin believed Deegan, more than anyone else in town, might be able to make sense of Stewart's double lives.

Deegan was at home, battling emphysema. Cronin learned that he had basically stopped working and that the chances of his continuing his lobbying business seemed slim.

Cronin arrived in Deegan's West Roxbury neighborhood early on a humid summer afternoon. Cronin got out of his car and walked to the house, rang the bell, and waited. Soon, Deegan emerged from a room on the first floor. He was dressed in green striped pajamas and a dark blue robe, and he shuffled along the floor, carrying a small box with a thin plastic tube that ran from the machine to his nose. He opened the door and immediately, without a word, turned and began shuffling back through the living room toward a sun porch where Cronin could see a hospital bed had been set up.

Cronin followed slowly along. When Deegan reached the sun porch, he sat down, gingerly, in a large, red-leather chair that dwarfed him. Cronin could see that his eyes were wide and he was struggling for breath from having crossed then recrossed the living room. Deegan looked pale and uncomfortable. The old man waited until his breathing had steadied before speaking.

Cronin started to introduce himself but Deegan stopped him. "I know who you are," he said. "I've been expecting you." A wide smile appeared on Deegan's face. Another moment passed before Deegan had fully caught his breath. When he did so, he spoke more easily. Deegan adjusted the tube that led to his nose and was held in place with a piece of plastic that wrapped around his head, just over his ears.

"I've read your articles," he said. "Very good." He nodded. "The Evil One unmasked."

Cronin was surprised by Deegan's characterization. He thought Deegan and Stewart had been friends.

"Of course, no attention has been paid," he said. "To the articles. You understand that, correct?"

Cronin didn't know quite what to say. "I suppose not much," he offered weakly, though, in fact, they had been followed up on by the TV and radio stations and had been the subject of the talk programs.

Deegan half laughed and coughed. "Don't flatter yourself, son." He waved his hand in dismissal of Cronin knew not what. "Jesus, they pay no attention," he said. "A couple of indiscretions is how it's viewed. He overstepped his bounds, they say. Once or twice. Nobody's perfect." He coughed. "Look at the whole record, not just one or two blemishes. You see? This is the thinking. This is how they rationalize."

Deegan reached to his side and grasped a long hose that led to what appeared to be a larger oxygen tank at the foot of the bed. At the head of the hose was a mouthpiece, which he capped over his nose and mouth and held there for a long moment.

"You think you've damaged him, don't you?" Deegan asked.

"Some," said Cronin.

Deegan spit out his words. "You're pissing in a big ocean with a tiny dick," he said derisively.

Cronin was taken aback momentarily. Then he said, "So how come the reaction from the powers that be?"

Deegan eyed him. "Let me guess," said the old man. "Heat from the Kennedys, of course. The cardinal, probably. The meek and pious Father Boyle. And the mayor." He smiled. "How'm I doing?"

Uncanny, thought Cronin.

"No, in fact, it's easy to dope out," Deegan said. "There's a basic leftish constituency in the city. The do-gooder crowd. They're not powerful in numbers but they have muscle. The Catholic left, basically. They believe one thing: that they are morally superior to thee and me and everyone else." Deegan again combination coughed and laughed. "In my case perhaps they're right. In yours I don't know. But imagine your binding notion in life being moral superiority to the great unwashed?"

He reached for the hose once again and let it revive him.

"This was Ray's crowd, the Flynn people," he said. "We are poor and dedicated and we are better than you! Their attitude shrieked. And imagine when the president sent Ray to the Vatican. Nearer my God to thee!"

Cronin took out his notebook and his pen.

"Put that away or get out," Deegan barked. "I'll talk for your education only. No quotations. Period."

Cronin held up his hands in a gesture of retreat. He put the notebook and pen back in his pocket.

"You believe he had a secret life," said Cronin.

"I *know* he did," said Deegan. "The Evil One. Of course. I know it. He relied on me for guidance. He confided in me. He called upon me to review his financial dealings. I knew him well, which is why I acquired, through the years, a powerful distaste for the man. They ought to develop a scale to measure the distance between reputation and reality. His was more out of whack than anybody ever, I'd guess."

"Was he always that way?" Cronin asked.

Deegan considered this. He cocked his large, ever-so odd-looking head and reflected upon it, a look of pleasure on his face. He liked this question for some reason. Wanted to do it justice.

"Did you know that he'd been a cop?" Deegan asked.

Cronin shook his head no.

"Most people don't know that," said Deegan. "Most people, in truth, know little of him, except the aura. The halo exempted him from scrutiny through the years. He didn't last long. It was up in Lowell, sometime in the fifties. He'd just gotten out of the service and needed work. He'd been an MP in Germany and it seemed a natural move. He lasted less than a year, as I understand it. Some incident. There was talk it involved a woman. Other talk it was dough." Deegan shrugged as if to say, What does it matter? "But that's how things so often are here, isn't it? There's a history, but nobody knows for sure what it is. There are intimations, hints, shadows, a background buzz, but no heart of the matter. No meat. It's all so slippery so often. No paper, no records, and nobody who knows. And if they do know, they don't talk."

Deegan coughed and reached for the hose. He laughed and exclaimed, "Welcome to Massachusetts politics!"

Deegan shook his head. "Yes, he was always like this and no he wasn't. He was straight when he first got involved in community organizing. This was after Lowell, after he'd quietly left the police force. He wound up in Boston working for a veterans organization building low-income housing. In the sixties, he became a liberal convert. He bought it all—women's rights, affirmative action, forced busing, unilateral disarmament—you name it. And why shouldn't he have? He found out that by being with these groups he got laid more than he ever had in his life! When he beat the booze he really went bad. When he was a drunk, his life revolved around booze. But when he stopped, he looked around and discovered women on a grand scale. He started thinking with his dick!"

Deegan laughed. "Jesus he loved the young ones, college girls. This was a few years ago, now. When he was in his fifties. No matter the cause they were there: hunger marches, demonstrations against the banks on red lining, the Sandinistas, welfare, whatever. But it all turned ugly with the intern in his office, the girl who went nuts, back twelve, fourteen years ago. You don't recall? She was a total political junkie. It was all she cared about. Went to Emmanual and worked in his office for an internship. Beautiful girl. Gorgeous. He said the only thing to do with her was to 'jump on her and stay on her.' He was doing her in the office just about every afternoon. A stiff prick has no conscience. She'd do anything he wanted, if you follow me. When she graduated she was under the impression she was going to go to work for him. She was into these hunger programs and nutrition in the cities and whatnot. The usual."

Deegan reached for the large hose again and breathed deeply.

"Naturally, he didn't hire her," he said. "And she went nuts. Had to be hospitalized. Her parents wanted to sue him but he made some private settlement. And you know who knew all about this? The Meek and Pious One himself: Boyle. Did he do anything about it? Nahh."

Deegan lifted himself from the sofa and shuffled slowly off to the bathroom. When he returned, he placed himself carefully in his seat.

"I don't mean to denigrate his political commitments," said Deegan. "They were real. That's why he was such an enigma. He did God's work and he didn't steal at first, but he was always looking for opportunities. He had about him the air of a prospector."

Deegan leaned back and caught his breath, resting his head on the back of the sofa.

"When someone is smart and careful, the way the Evil One was for so many years, it takes a very long time for anyone in the political community to figure out that they've gone bad," said Deegan. "So who knows when he did his first side deal. But about six or seven years ago there was a feeling I got that something was up. He'd bend a rule here and there—use campaign money on his vacation. Some inquiries about IRS regulations. Hints. But enough. You see, he had a predisposition to go bad. Most don't. Most pols are straight. Others who'd like to take advantage don't have the balls. Very few have the predisposition *and* opportunity. He had both. When he started using Shelter Coalition money for campaign expenses, a few thousand here and there, I raised it with him. Too late. By that point, he thought of it all as his own: he raised the Shelter money and the campaign money and they were all of a piece—to keep him in office to continue doing God's work. This was his view. With such a view, anything one does is kosher. Comprende?"

Cronin asked Deegan how the truth of what Stewart had been could be so at odds with the perception of him?

Deegan's face lit up. His splotched, pallid countenance took on a glow. He liked this question, too, in part because he saw it as revealing a political naïveté on Cronin's part.

"Perception is reality in politics," said Deegan. "People vote based on their perceptions of politicians. How they perceived Stewart may have had little to do with the reality, but what does it matter? Voters act on what they see, not on what is.

"Stewart was a niche player," said Deegan. "In business it's all the rage now. Find a product niche and you thrive. Stewart had the saint niche in Boston, the beyond-reproach niche, the sacred cow niche. His rise from the gutter was a story so ingrained in the political consciousness of the city it was unquestioned. He went unexamined and unchallenged for years on the strength of a myth. Ahh, but it was a myth the culture fostered, wanted to believe, needed to believe.

"The truth is that you can never really know whether a man with power is liked until he no longer has power. Then you know."

"What happened to the girl?" Cronin asked.

"Moved away," said Deegan. "I heard she got out of the hospital and went to California with her family."

"I don't understand something," said Cronin. "Why have the Kennedys tried so hard to muscle my editors, even the publisher?"

"He was part of the extensive Kennedy damage control network," said Deegan. "People always got it wrong about the Kennedys, saying they had such a great political organization.

That was never so, except in sixty when the old man bought the election. They always had weak opposition, that was their secret. Except for Eddie McCormack, of course. No. The Kennedys' secret was not a political organization but a ready-made, seamless damage control network anchored by Church people. Always anchored by the clergy."

Deegan took a quick hit on the hose.

"Think about it," Deegan continued. "There's always a Roman collar around when there's a Kennedy in trouble. Some of them are sycophants, others are recipients of Kennedy family largesse. Stewart was part of the network, like Boyle. Both got federal funding for various pet projects: soup kitchens, vaccination programs, community housing, whatever. Federal funding that came through thanks to the Kennedys. Stewart profited handsomely from his Kennedy association over the years. And the Kennedys, well, what can you say? Dole out federal bucks, keep the pumps primed and you've got a nice, tight network out there for when you stumble. And if you are a Kennedy you have stumbled, do stumble, will stumble. The network supplies the imprimatur of goodness when a Kennedy has been naughty."

Deegan smiled. "And then there are the complicit journalists," he said, savoring it. "The ones whose careers have been helped along by their association with the Kennedys. They play their hands. Quietly. And so when a Kennedy is in trouble, the network rallies. There are testaments to their piety—the cardinal; recollections of the family sacrifice and suffering—the mayor; indications of their good works for the least among us—Father Boyle; and a journalist to make sure its wrapped into a neat feature package, with color photos of the senator's new wife, of course—Johnson."

Deegan sucked some air down.

"You think he was shaking down more people than have been reported?" Cronin asked.

"Course. Course," said Deegan. "My guess is he needed big money. For something, I don't know what. He'd disappear regularly from the hall, every month or so. There was a messenger who'd deliver tickets from a travel agent to Stewart's office. The tickets were in some staffer's name. Las Vegas. But then the staffer would never leave. Stewart would take the tickets and go."

He pointed to the living room, toward a radiator against the wall. "Reach behind there for me, like a good fellow," he said. Cronin went into the next room and did as instructed. He pulled out a package of Marlboros hidden from the nurse who daily visited Deegan. Matches were tucked inside the wrapper. Deegan reached down and switched off the oxygen machine, something he did each time he smoked to prevent an explosion. He removed a cigarette, lit it, and asked Cronin to return the rest to their hiding place. He took a drag and exhaled. "Know who their latest suspect is?" Deegan asked.

Cronin shook his head.

Deegan smiled. "You're looking at him," he said. He held the hose in place for a half minute.

Cronin was indeed surprised, but masked it this time. He was disappointed that McCormack had not told him that. He wondered what else McCormack was keeping from him.

"Are you serious?" Cronin asked.

"Certainly," he replied. "They told my lawyer. There are some personal files of Stewart's they subpoenaed which show he owed me money. Which is true. For consulting. Forty-three thou. He never paid. This is going back three years now. He just wouldn't pay. It made me very angry. I wrote him a few nasty notes—one *very* nasty. One might read it as a threat. The feds found it in his files."

"You know who hated Stewart to the core?" Deegan asked. Cronin shook his head.

Deegan smiled and his eyes widened with delight. "Your pal, McCormack."

"I don't get it?" said Cronin.

"Of course you don't," Deegan replied. "He's told you everything but that, I suspect."

Cronin was unpleasantly caught off-guard.

"Don't be so surprised," said Deegan, cupping a cigarette in his hand. "It's relatively easy to figure out. I know the police department well. There's talk around. Process of elimination. Who knows enough to get this stuff out there, who's willing to tell. I made an educated guess and your expression confirmed it for me. Thank you very much, and remind me to play poker with you in my next life."

Cronin did not want his silence to be read as confirmation that McCormack was his source. "You're assumptions may be wrong," said Cronin. He smiled. "Facial expressions don't always tell the full story."

Deegan wheezed and laughed. "Too late, young man," he said. "Cat's out of the bag. But who cares. I can't do any damage with that information. At least, not any damage I'm interested in doing."

Cronin took a deep breath. Deegan was getting on his nerves. The air was heavy with humidity and, now, with the smell of cigarette smoke. And Deegan was saying things Cronin did not quite grasp. Cronin hated being surprised about his sources, hated learning things about them that might effect their veracity or their motives that he did not know.

"So he's your source on this, eh?" said Deegan, savoring his triumph. "Ever wonder why? Ever ask him why he's been so free with information? Or don't reporters look to the source anymore? It used to be that was a factor. A guy had an ax to grind, well, maybe his inside dope wasn't so good after all."

Deegan grabbed the hose and sucked down some air.

"The standards are different now, I take it," said Deegan, taunting Cronin. But the reporter had no interest in fighting this old man.

"Why did he hate Stewart?" Cronin asked.

Deegan smiled again, rather pleased with himself that Cronin had acknowledged his ignorance.

"You don't know, do you?" said Deegan.

"I don't know," Cronin acknowledged.

Deegan waved his hand in the air. "There's no shame in it, really," he said. "It is not well known. Very few people know it. Fewer know why."

Cronin was still, waiting.

"McCormack is a very intelligent man," said Deegan. "Much smarter than the average cop. He was unusual in his intellectual curiosity. It made him stand out in the department. He worked his way up through the ranks. He earned a law degree and, essentially, dedicated his life to his work. You know, of course, he had no children."

Cronin nodded.

Deegan coughed hard and fought to get his breath.

"Do you know the command structure?" Deegan asked.

"Generally," said Cronin.

"Commissioner, appointed by the mayor," said Deegan. "Superintendent for each of four general areas. A cabinet of sorts to the commissioner. Then eight deputy superintendents. These are the elite positions of the command staff. Theoretically, at least, in the twelve superintendents and deputy superintendents you have the best and brightest of the uniformed force. Most of the time, it is from within these ranks that a new commissioner is chosen. Rare to do otherwise."

Deegan reached for the hose and applied the mask. As he did so, he pointed toward the living room and nodded to Cronin. The reporter retrieved the cigarettes, lit one, and returned the pack. Deegan exhaled with delight.

"As you know, the current commissioner is among those exceptions," said Deegan. "Ernie Donohue is a pleasant man, a deeply religious fellow, and a moron. He has no business being commissioner and would never have been chosen had not his boyhood friend become mayor. What is not widely known is this: Donohue was not the mayor's first choice for the job. McCormack was."

Cronin was stunned.

"You had no idea," Deegan said, smiling. "Everyone assumed the mayor wanted a close friend as commissioner. That's what got written from day one. But it was wrong. The department was too haywire for anything but a pro. The mayor knew this. He said the police department for him could be like Vietnam for LBJ. He talked around quietly to people in the know—law enforcement people, judges, lawyers, cops. And one name kept coming up when he asked about competence: McCormack." Deegan wheezed and laughed. "Nobody mentioned Donohue. Nobody!"

He reached for the hose and applied the mask to his face, waiting a long moment before resuming.

"So the mayor sits down after talking with quite a few people about this and thinks it through. First, he wants the best available person because the more successful the department is the better it makes him look. Second, he expressly does *not* want a close friend in the job because that boxes him in if there's ever trouble. If you're mayor you can't distance yourself from an old pal whose commissioner. And if something is really screwed up, you can't fire him because that's an act of disloyalty. So he settles on McCormack. Privately, this is. He's about to submit McCormack's name to the Council for confirmation, but before he does so he speaks confidentially with McCormack and Stewart. McCormack to make sure he will accept the position and Stewart, as chairman of Public Safety, to make sure he'll let it out of his committee for a vote on the floor. These were anticipated to be two very simple discussions."

Deegan placed the mask on his face and sat back in the chair, breathing deeply. He appeared tired, and paler.

"McCormack was bowled over. According to the mayor, terribly moved. He accepted, of course, said he would serve with the greatest of pride and give it his best. The mayor told him to keep it quiet. McCormack asked permission to tell only his wife, and naturally the mayor agreed.

"Then the mayor spoke with Stewart, who reacted very badly. He didn't know McCormack, he said. He said he assumed all along it would be Donohue. He praised Donohue up and down, talked about how important it was that the mayor have someone he knew personally, like Donohue, in that job. It went back and forth, on and on. The mayor explained why McCormack was the right choice. Stewart was skeptical. Then hostile. He grew agitated. Said he didn't know him, didn't know if he could trust him. The mayor asked him to think about it over night. The next day it was worse. Stewart was enraged. Said the mayor had blindsided him, given him no indication it was to be anyone but Donohue. They argued in the office for a couple of hours. It got very heated but Stewart never backed down. He said he'd bottle it up in committee, hold hearings, drag it out, and make sure there was no floor debate or vote for months. The mayor knew he could do it, of course, and, in the end, Stewart won. The mayor backed down. At that point there was nobody else but Donohue. Nobody the mayor trusted."

Deegan clamped the mask on his face and closed his eyes. He slumped back in the chair, seeming exhausted, and took in oxygen for several minutes.

"I get tired in the afternoons," he said. He was subdued now and seemed to take no pleasure in the telling of the tale.

"The mayor called McCormack in and broke the news to him. He told him the whole story. Told him exactly why he wasn't getting it. Told him Stewart had been like a madman. The mayor asked whether there was some history of a problem between them. McCormack said there was not. Though he told the mayor he suspected that Stewart had some side deals working and he thought perhaps Stewart was afraid that if McCormack was commissioner those deals might be jeopardized." Deegan coughed from deep within his chest; a nasty, raw sound.

"The mayor wanted to hear none of that, of course, and it was all over," said Deegan. "McCormack went home to tell his wife. Evidently, she was heartbroken over it. Which, naturally, made it much worse for him. She had the cancer by then.

"And, of course, McCormack is getting no younger at this point and not exactly a prime physical specimen, and he should, by all rights, have some cushy spot, but he is back out on the street doing murder investigations after this," said Deegan. "He quit as chief of homicide out of disgust. Couldn't work for a commissioner who he knew shouldn't have the job. So he went back to being one of the boys on homicide. And one night he joined in a drug raid a man his age shouldn't have been on. Shotgun blast, his knee's gone. Blown out. Constant pain. Thanks to Stewart."

The air was thick and steamy. All of the windows in Deegan's downstairs were closed. Cigarette smoke hung in the air, a bluish cloud slow to disperse. There was a languor to the day. Deegan was damp with perspiration. He was pale. He looked unwell. The two men sat together for a long time in silence. Finally, Cronin broke it.

"Who hated him?" the reporter asked.

Deegan laughed. "You mean who do I *know about* who hated him?"

Cronin nodded.

"Could be others, for all I know, but I'd have to put myself in that column. Your pal, Mack, of course. And this one will surprise you, perhaps greatly: the Meek and Pious One must be counted on that list." Deegan thought about this for a moment and then nodded his head with certainty.

Cronin was jarred by this, shocked. "Boyle despised him, in fact," said Deegan. "Because Boyle, you see, is a true believer. He's like the Jesuits who tramp off to the third world to abet the Left. Social and economic justice man. He'd tear the whole god-damned building down and start over again. To each according to his need."

Deegan regarded Cronin. "You are surprised by this, no?"

"I must admit I am," said the reporter.

"But it makes perfect sense," Deegan said. He was animated now, excited that there was perhaps a logic to all of this that had not been explained before. "Boyle *knew*," Deegan said. "Don't you see? Boyle *knew* at least some of what was going on. He kept the books. He was in charge of the money. He *knew*. And he was repulsed by it. And he wanted Stewart's position. And you know what? Now he's got it. Elected this morning as chairman of the Shelter Coalition. It's his show now."

Deegan held out his arms as though signaling that it was all so terribly obvious, as though to say it's right there in front of you as plain as anything could possibly be.

"Ask yourself who stood to gain the most by the Evil One's demise. There's no question that it was the Meek and Pious One."

Deegan began to laugh, shaking his head in disbelief as he did so. He laughed harder and harder and interrupted it only briefly to say to Cronin, "And the fuzz haven't got a fucking clue."

Frank Cronin considered Deegan. In a certain light, he seemed gnomelike, otherworldly.

"Maybe you're too cynical," Cronin said.

Deegan turned his head quickly to the side and regarded the reporter with suspicion.

"Cynical?" he said, with mock indignation. "Cynical, you say?"

He knitted his brow and eyed Cronin. "Is this naïveté authentic or a posture?"

Cronin was silent.

Deegan waited a moment.

"Perhaps it is authentic," said Deegan, a trace of pity in his voice. He took hold of the lifeline and breathed deeply, then set it aside.

Cronin was startled by Deegan's gaze, which was now angry, glowering. When he spoke, he did so with an air of contempt.

"What is it that you are looking for?" he asked. "Some sort of *truth,* is it? Perhaps you seek an honorable man?"

His laugh was harsh, derisive. "An honest soul?" He shook his head dismissing the notion. "Not in this town. Not in this town. In this town everybody's got something to hide. Everybody's got an angle."

F rank Cronin had read the entire *Post* clip file on Boyle. There were scores of news stories in which he was mentioned, articles reflecting his work on behalf of the poor. There were stories where he was involved in fighting for low-income housing, for community health centers, for integration of housing projects, for school busing, for AIDS hospice funding, for more welfare funding, and virtually every other liberal cause of the day.

But there were other stories as well, long profiles, most of which had been written several years earlier after Boyle had returned from Haiti. The profiles all struck the same thematic chords, all portrayed Boyle as a courageous man of principal who had dedicated his life to the cause of the poor. He'd been lionized as selfless, fearless, a man who had willingly sacrificed his own personal comfort and physical safety for the greater good.

The most interesting profile of all, it turned out, had been written by Howard Berman back when Berman had been covering the political upheaval in Haiti. Berman's story offered the notion of liberation theology as an explanation for Boyle's commitment to a revolutionary social and spiritual movement. Liberation theologists believed it their responsibility to minister not only to the spiritual needs of their flock but to their social and political needs as well. It often meant taking sides in nasty interethnic or interclass struggles. Through the subtext of Berman's article, Cronin got the impression that beneath Boyle's pious exterior lived a righteous fanatic.

Cronin recalled several instances when Berman had expressed privately a measure of distrust for Boyle. That night, after the paper had been put to bed, Cronin asked Berman about the priest.

"He's a strange mix," said Berman. "I always found him to be cold and withdrawn. He has this burning passion for populist issues and I've no doubt whatever that it's sincere, but his concern for the people gets lost when he's dealing one on one. People to him aren't individuals; they are, collectively, a cause. He's very awkward, you may have noticed. He is not easy around people. And he is utterly shameless in the way he uses people. I hear from him only—and I mean without exception—when he wants something from me, usually coverage of some story he's involved with."

"What did he do in Haiti, exactly?" Cronin asked.

Berman rolled his eyes and shook his head. "That's the question. I'd love to know. I have my suspicions."

"What do you know and what do you suspect?"

"I know he was dedicated to the revolutionary cause, to prayerfully resisting the Tonton Macoutes and politically battling the vestiges of the Duvaliers. That he was a devoted follower of Father Aristide's. He headed a health project, worked with children with typhoid fever, which was common, and organized an immunization effort that didn't go anywhere because the vaccines were stolen by the army before they reached their destinations. He was one of a number of missionaries who worked with Aristide. A very suspicious man, Aristide. Paranoid and virulently anti-American. Boyle was the only American he trusted."

"Boyle became a liberation theologist while in Haiti?" Cronin asked.

"Before he got there," said Berman. "Boyle had been down in Peru as a missionary for a couple of years and came in contact with Gustavo Gutierrez, kind of the father of the liberation theology movement. By the time Boyle got to Haiti he was completely committed. He'd bend my ear about it time and time again. Early on, Rome supported the movement, seeing it as a logical extension of parish ministry, but through the years, as it took on an increasingly political hue, the Vatican began to crack down. That was fine with Boyle because it meant he was an outsider even within his own Church, and he is most comfortable as an outsider, a provocateur militating for change."

"The Church leaders complained they were Marxists," said Cronin.

"And a lot of them were," said Berman. "There were Marxist overtones to liberation theology movements in El Salvador and Nicaragua, certainly, and probably in Peru and Brazil, too."

"And Haiti."

"And most definitely Haiti. They supported redistribution of the wealth, land reform. They were anticapitalist. What divided them was the issue of violence, whether force was appropriate and under what circumstances. Some of the priests were pacifists, but there were others who argued that if their mission to serve the people included organizing others to take up arms against the oppressor, then so be it."

"And Boyle?"

"He was very careful," said Berman. "He knew then that he would have a life after his missionary years and I think he knew that any involvement in violent acts would scar him, diminish his future effectiveness back home. But if I had to bet, I would bet that he at the very least looked the other way and perhaps even abetted violent acts."

"Why do you say that?" Cronin asked.

"Because he would regularly disappear for days at a time, once for a couple of weeks, into the bidonvilles—the sprawling 'tin can cities' that choked Port-au-Prince and were populated by the wretchedly poor souls. And after a while, the pattern became obvious: he would disappear and before he would return, there would be some bit of violence, an assassination of an army or government official, a kidnapping of a wealthy businessperson or, worst of all, the necklacing of an informant."

"You think Boyle condoned that sort of thing?" Cronin asked.

Berman considered this.

"I remember a ride in the back of a truck from the countryside back to Port-au-Prince," said Berman. "I had been out on a story and ran into him and he offered me a ride back. The roads are hopeless, of course, so traveling any long distance can take all day. We sat together chatting for, I don't know, ten or twelve hours. And he seemed more relaxed than at any time I could recall. He talked incessantly of *pep la*—'the people.' Everything was *pep la*. And the essence of what he said was that any act could be justified if it was for *pep la*."

"Any act?" Cronin asked.

"That was the message," said Berman. "I don't remember his exact words. But you know what I do remember?" Berman sat forward as though recalling some long suppressed memory. "We were talking about the necklacing of a regional government official in the farming village we had just left. This was a youngish guy with a family, a nobody, a functionary. He had been burned and his body left in the town square. Horrible. The heat, the stench, covered with flies, the widow screaming and wailing. And I will never forget the look on Boyle's face when we were talking about that murder. He said it had been demanded by *pep la*. And then he smiled."

CHAPTER

18

Bufalino was 2,800 miles away but he knew they were talking about him or would be soon. He had known since Dockerty was arrested that he was under suspicion, that his financial dealings with Stewart would soon be revealed. Probably in the press, he thought. They would leak to a reporter and he would write that they were looking into the possibility that Stewart had links with organized crime figures. Bufalino would be named.

These thoughts had given him a migraine and prompted him to call Kristee. He tried to get these unpleasant notions out of his mind as he reclined on the sofa in his Sahara apartment living room. His tan slacks were down around his ankles and Kristee was on her knees between his lizard-skin loafers.

Bufalino was explicit in his guidance to her. He instructed her at various points to slow it down or speed it up; to move harder, or softer. Like others in Vegas, Kristee did what Bufalino wanted. She worked him as she had countless times before. She was diligent and patient and knew he would reward her for it. Usually it was $150, though she had caught him in more expansive moods when he had given her double that and invited her to stay afterward for a cocktail. She had liked that. She liked the ambiance of his suite—the musky maleness of it, the chrome trim on the ultramodern furniture; the wild splashes of color on the huge paintings, the lush, white, wall-to-wall carpeting; the sparkling cleanliness of it all; the spacious living room with its ersatz fireplace, well-padded sofa, and easy chairs; its oversized color television; its smoked-glass coffee table. On one end of the room sliding doors led to a balcony looking out seven stories above the hotel's pool, with a view beyond to a sprawling emerald golf course that looked somehow unreal in the dusty brown of the desert. Kristee was most comfortable in the living room, where Bufalino usually held their appointment. She found the bedroom, a darkened space with plum-colored draperies and bedspread, not altogether comforting.

Bufalino leaned back on the sofa, his shirt unbuttoned and spread away from his chest to keep the shirttails out of Kristee's eyes. She could smell his cologne—an almost overpowering scent coming off the thatch of black hair that covered his abdomen, chest, and back. He looks like a fucking gorilla, she had thought the first time she saw him: squat, powerfully built, and covered with hair. Once, arriving early for an appointment, she had seen him douse himself with cologne, shaking the contents of the dark green bottle onto his thick hand and spreading it across his chest and stomach, then between his legs.

Soon, she fell into a rhythm that she sensed pleased him and it was not long before his body stiffened and then, with a powerful shudder and a bestial grunt, he fell limp.

When she was done, she went into the bathroom and switched on the overhead heat lamp to get warm. On days when he liked her to work naked she would soon be covered in goose bumps from the blasts of frigid air that filled the suite. Bufalino kept the air-conditioning on full force. While it was often well over one hundred degrees in the desert outside, it was barely sixty in Bufalino's rooms.

In the bathroom, Kristee wiggled into a black minidress from Victoria's Secret. It highlighted her athletic figure. She was blessed with an appealing form which she had made even more attractive through rigorous aerobic training. She was five-six, slim and firm. She was not a striking beauty, but she was cute— too cute for her own taste. She preferred glamorous over cute and was not flattered when Bufalino had told her she looked like the Flying Nun.

In high school she had become so proficient in aerobics that she had become an instructor, and had worked for a year after graduation in a suburban Dallas health club, but it was not long before she realized that without a radical change she would be poor, or on the verge of poverty, for the rest of her life. She hated nothing more than the poverty in which she had been raised; loved nothing more than money. In the two years she had been plying her trade she had learned the business well and prospered. She had her own condominium in the city and she drove a convertible. She worked out nearly every day, was selective about her customers, and had repeatedly tested negative for HIV. All in all, she was quite happy with her life.

"If you don't have plans, stay for a drink," Bufalino said, as she emerged from the bathroom. "If you don't have plans."

"Oh," she said. "No. That sounds good."

Bufalino went into the bedroom and emerged a moment later with a giftbox. "A little something for you," he said, handing her the box. She was delighted. Only once before had he surprised her with a gift and it was when he had given her tickets to some fight at Caesar's Palace that she could have cared less about. She had taken a friend with her who was impressed with the ringside seats.

"You didn't have to do this," she said.

"I wanted to," he replied. He smiled, flashing his pearl white, capped teeth. He was not unattractive, she thought. His eyes were an icy blue, not warm, but a nice color that looked good with his well-trimmed black hair. His nose was thick and long—"like his dick," she had once told a girlfriend who dissolved in gales of laughter. His complexion was imperfect, but not as bad when he was tanned.

"It's so thoughtful," she said, as she lifted the lid and placed the tissue paper to one side. "I can't tell you how nice this is."

She removed the garment and found that it was a black dress, identical to the one she was wearing. She held it up and laughed.

"Sit here," he instructed. "Relax. I'm going to clean up, then we'll have a drink."

• • •

As he showered, Bufalino recalled a meeting with Stewart, seven years earlier, at which they had struck a deal. Bufalino had heard back then from some of the girls that Stewart displayed an eclectic sexual appetite. Bufalino also learned from his people on the floor that Stewart dropped fairly large amounts of cash—and it was all cash, he never asked for credit—at the blackjack table. Bufalino knew the casino's regulars and he made it a point of introducing himself to Stewart. They would have drinks when Stewart came to town, usually four to five times a year for three or four days. Bufalino introduced Stewart to some women whose particular talents would, he knew, be well suited to Stewart. Three women who worked as a team became a favorite of Stewart's for years thereafter. Stewart came to like and trust Bufalino. Later, as the years passed, Stewart once drunkenly expressed an interest in young men as well. With well-concealed distaste, Bufalino arranged to have Stewart's wishes fulfilled.

Stewart had grown too arrogant for his own good. The change had been subtle but noticeable to Bufalino, who paid attention to such things. On his last two, maybe three, trips to town, Bufalino noticed that Stewart's appetite for cocaine, always considerable, had grown. He demanded more women and complained about their willingness or ability to satisfy his needs. Kristee had heard from some of the girls that Stewart had lately displayed a violent streak. Bufalino saw that Stewart had grown arrogant, that the affable manner he had effected through the years was wearing off. Stewart had grown increasingly militant in his insistence that his share be raised. Twice in a year's time he had called Bufalino and demanded a bigger cut. Each time he threatened to undo the arrangement. Bufalino, while working gingerly to calm Stewart down, seethed with rage at the man's impudence. They had an arrangement that was exceedingly profitable for all concerned, an arrangement that had been *agreed* upon in a face-to-face meeting between Bufalino and Stewart.

Bufalino had learned a great deal about Stewart, more than Stewart was aware. Before proposing the arrangement, Bufalino had quietly had Stewart checked out in Boston. When he learned of Stewart's reputation as a revered figure, he made his proposal. Bufalino knew that Stewart controlled the finances of a loose conglomerate of shelters for the homeless in the Greater Boston area. Each shelter, Bufalino had been pleased to learn through his research, maintained independent accounts at separate banks. What Bufalino did not know, not that it mattered, was how Stewart made the money which he so freely distributed in Las Vegas. It was obvious that Stewart was running some sort of scam, an indication to Bufalino that Stewart might be receptive to his proposal. Bufalino had explained to Stewart that he ran a business which produced a substantial amount of cash—he did not volunteer any more details about his business and Stewart didn't inquire further. As Bufalino toweled dry, he recalled the scene vividly. He and Stewart had been sitting in his living room having coffee.

"My proposition is what I like to think of as just good business. Old-fashioned business," Bufalino had said. He had allowed himself a tight smile. "I've noticed in the business publications recently they sometimes call it a 'win-win' situation. Meaning in such a deal as this I win and you win also. Both parties win. They write about this as though it's some revolutionary concept from the Harvard Business School. 'Win-win.' It implies that there's a type of deal where somebody wins and somebody else loses."

Bufalino had paused for effect. "Maybe there is," he had said, sipping his coffee. "But short term only. Because in the long run, business relationships—partnerships—only work when they are profitable for both parties. Notice the word I used? Partnership. I use it deliberately. It's not a word I use loosely. I can say truthfully," said a man whose life depended upon deceit, "that I can count on one hand the number of times I've entered into a partnership. The reason is trust. One little word that is a massive idea. Rare is the man I have met who I could trust."

Bufalino sat up straight on the sofa, then leaned forward and placed his coffee cup and saucer on the table in front of him.

"Phil," Bufalino had said, in a hushed tone, "you are a man I can trust. As I sit here, I look at you, look you directly in the eye and I know you are a man I can trust. These are serious matters." He had paused, his gaze fixed on Stewart, to let the gravity of what he was saying sink in. Bufalino was not like so many of the others. He was more intelligent, and for all the baseness with which his life had been filled, he was more sophisticated. He wanted to convey a message without threatening or seeming to threaten. "Fuck me and you're dead," others would have said, but Bufalino would never stoop to such coarseness. He wanted those with whom he did business to fear him, certainly, but not to hate him. He had seen others who were hated come to unhappy ends, victims of accumulated bitterness.

"These are *very* serious matters," Bufalino had continued. "In my business, trust is everything. Without trust, there is nothing. Worse than nothing. Without trust there is hell, the deprivation of a man's freedom, confinement to a cage. That is the result of a breakdown in trust. I know men who have met that fate. To me, it is worse than death. That is why trust is the soul of a partnership. Do you follow what I am saying?"

"Clearly," Stewart had replied quietly.

"And I can trust you, Phil? You assure me of that?"

"Absolutely," Stewart had said without hesitation. "Absolutely."

Bufalino nodded as he hesitated for a moment to let Stewart's assurance sink in. "Good," he had said.

Bufalino had risen and poured coffee for Stewart, then for himself. He had returned to the sofa and sat down. "Our arrangement, as I envision it, is simplicity itself. My business, as I've said, generates amounts of cash that are awkwardly handled by banks. I need accounts where cash can be deposited and legitimized by having been on deposit in the accounts of an enterprise unlikely to draw scrutiny from law enforcement. Once the funds are deposited, I need an arrangement where money can then be easily dispersed, at the behest of a single signatory. I assume, given the nature of your charitable work and your standing in the Boston community, that you have both accounts with reputable banks and relationships with major officials at those banks." Bufalino, of course, knew this was true.

Stewart nodded. "Naturally," he said. "I control the funds for more than forty shelters and soup kitchens in the Boston area. I'm chairman of the Homeless Coalition and run all the fundraising. I also personally sign off on all major disbursements."

"And relationships with bankers?" Bufalino had asked.

"Too many," Stewart had said, with a laugh. "Many of the banks contribute to us and a number of major players at the banks have become friends. They contribute to my campaigns, as well. And I'm embarrassed to say that though I've been meaning to consolidate our accounts for the sake of efficiency, we currently have something like a dozen or more accounts scattered around. There may be as many as twenty, in fact. Accounts were set up for different shelters or different projects through the years and we never streamlined."

Bufalino, through his research, knew all of this, of course. He knew, in fact, that Stewart controlled the disbursements from no fewer than twenty-three bank accounts at seventeen different institutions. In spite of his knowledge, he listened patiently to Stewart, pretending this was all new to him.

"Phil, I propose that you chose a bank executive whom you know and trust. That you call on this person for a private visit, perhaps in your office. Perhaps first invite them to accompany you to an event of some sort where his public association with you would be flattering to him. I suggest that you tell him this story, or something like it: you say to your banker, 'I have a friend, a longtime friend, a boyhood friend who went down the wrong path somewhere along the line.' You sit with him comfortably, Phil, as you and I are now doing and you say to him something along these lines, you say, 'My friend got mixed up with the wrong crowd. He makes his money on sports betting'— you could say he is a bookmaker, if you wanted. 'Illegal sports betting. Not huge amounts but he's made a comfortable living for his family, sent his three kids through college, and, in fact, has a daughter, his youngest, who is doing a residency in neurology at UCLA Medical Center. His family, needless to say, has no idea that their income is derived from illicit means. They believe that my friend is in the food brokerage business because for years he has operated out of the office of a friend who owns such a business.' You're opening yourself up to this person, Phil, and you say, 'I cannot reveal my friend's identity but I can tell you that he is in his advancing years. His health is not perfect. And he is plagued with guilt about his life. He has developed a burning desire to help others. He wants very badly to contribute to our shelters. And, frankly, we need his money. You know what the impact of the economy has been to our fund-raising. The guilt-money of the eighties has all but dried up. Yet the need is no less urgent. Those poor souls out there wandering the streets, thousands of them betrayed by society or by their own minds, desperately need help. At the very least, we owe them shelter and a hot meal. They need my friend's help. But there's a hitch: He will only donate in cash. He's afraid that anything else would flag the IRS.' You say to this banker, 'I want to help my friend. I want him to be able to contribute his money which will, in turn, do a tremendous amount of good. I'm asking you to make it possible. I'm asking you to quietly pave the way for regular deposits of cash to be made into designated accounts which I have already opened. No deposit will exceed $9,999, under the amount where federal notification is required. The deposits would occur every few weeks or so. I know I am asking you to look the other way on something that is, technically speaking, a violation of regulations. But I am asking you to do it, in total and complete confidence, only because I know how much this money could help people who are on the margins of our society.' "

Bufalino had paused. A slight smile had appeared on Stewart's face. "Quite a performance," he had said, admiringly.

"I wonder whether such an approach might work with one of your banker friends?" Bufalino had asked.

"I can't imagine that they would turn me down," Stewart had said. "I can think of a couple who I am sure would do it with no problem."

It had begun modestly enough with a few thousand dollars a month being washed through a single bank. With Bufalino's couriers shuttling the cash from Vegas to Boston, over time, Bufalino pressed Stewart into expanding the operation. Stewart's routine had been to write checks disbursing the money to several different corporate shells, all of which were controlled by Bufalino. Stewart would divert his personal share into a private account he kept, though it was ostensibly a miscellaneous fund for the Shelter Coalition. On average, one cash deposit was made into each account about every three weeks with each account laundering about $160,000 annually. For seven years the arrangement had worked flawlessly. Then Stewart got greedy. Rather than negotiate a new deal, which Bufalino would have been willing to do, he simply doubled his take, announcing it to Bufalino after the fact.

That act had broken their covenant. Bufalino had already taken steps to establish a backup operation through a businessman in Philadelphia who had access to various legitimate accounts. He moved to expand that relationship after Stewart's breech. Bufalino had nothing more than harsh words for Stewart at the time, and though he continued the relationship he began cutting back on the amount of cash he shipped to Boston. He would never again trust Stewart.

When Bufalino had heard rumblings that Stewart had drawn the attention of the U.S. Attorney's office in Boston, he feared the worst: that Stewart would offer to testify against Bufalino in return for leniency. This had alarmed Bufalino, whose fear of incarceration was paralyzing. Stewart knew little about his operation, but he knew enough to convict him of money laundering. And with Stewart's reputation, Bufalino knew he would be doomed in a federal trial in Boston.

Bufalino gazes out across the golf course, past the dusty brown of the desert to the shimmering sun that bakes the distant landscape. He thinks about Stewart beating him out of the money, of Stewart deceiving him. The idea seems so preposterous to Bufalino. That a man such as Stewart would outmaneuver, outthink him, even for a moment, was embarrassing. He did not know precisely how much Stewart had embezzled from him, could not know until the next quarterly accounting of Empire Realty Trust, but Bufalino's own calculations put the figure somewhere in the neighborhood of $550,000 to $600,000. Stewart had not taken his share of that money, his fee; he had taken *all* of it.

With thoughts of Stewart, there stirred within Bufalino an overwhelming sense of rage. Bufalino seethed. I must be made whole again, he thought. He felt an overwhelming compulsion to exact retribution. That Stewart was dead was not enough. Bufalino had to have the money back, he had to win! He had been unable to sleep nights, he had not been himself. It was not the money itself, it was a matter of pride. He had to have the money.

But how to get it? Bufalino assumes it is in the safe, although he cannot be entirely certain of that. If it is not in the safe it is surely lost to him forever. He will not know whether the money is in the safe until he sends Kristee to Boston to visit Dockerty. She will find out whether Dockerty discovered the money, whether the police have seized it.

There is a problem for Bufalino, and he contemplates it from his air-conditioned perch high above the desert. If the money is there, how does he get it out? Who could get into the house and get out with the money? Who could possibly have a plausible reason for going into Stewart's house? For taking money out? Who would be willing? Who could pull it off?

Bufalino thinks he knows.

CHAPTER
19

Sloane felt their relationship had experienced a breakthrough. She felt they had reached a level of trust with each other that they had never before achieved. Frank had been able to let down his guard with her as never before.

They were both aware of the change. At Sloane's house one evening after a dinner of pizza and Cokes, Frank had remarked upon it.

To Sloane, the difference was manifest in the ease with which he now spoke to her of his brother. On the occasions when she brought up the subject of Chris, he did not clamp down. He seemed far more willing than ever before to lift the lid off his past.

"That must have been wonderful, to be so close to your brother," Sloane said to him after they had consumed the pizza.

"It was," he said. "Absolutely. But things were never the same after I went away to college."

"How so?" she asked.

"When I first went to Dartmouth, Chris would visit just about every weekend. That first year he came on the bus every Friday up through Christmas. Then it was every other weekend. Then in my sophmore year it was one weekend a month, and then, after that, well . . ."

He shrugged. She waited, determined not to press him.

"Chris had always been a timid boy, easily frightened, but now he seemed afraid of his own shadow. His guidance counselor said he seemed prone to depression. His only happiness came from his music. He was a fairly skilled guitarist and I thought that if he pursued music with some intensity it would build his self-confidence. And he did work hard at the guitar, but he let everything else in school go. His attitude wasn't very good and his grades were terrible."

"Did you try and talk to him?" she asked.

"I talked to him time after time after time," said Frank. "I talked with him on the phone, I went up to Coaticook to see him numerous times, I talked with teachers and administrators about him, all people I knew and they all understood his background and the circumstances he'd grown up in and they all bent over backwards for him."

Frank shook his head, saddened by the memory.

"But he'd kind of drifted too far off track. He thought everyone was down on him, thought everyone compared him unfavorably with me, thought no one took him as an individual on his terms. He quit high school at the beginning of his senior year and went to work in a record store in town."

Sloane had a pained look as she listened.

"It wasn't the greatest, but he seemed happy for a while. This was around the time I was graduating and things were going very well for me. I had been chosen in the National Hockey League draft by Boston and I considered giving it a try. But I had a great professor in math who convinced me that it would be a dead end. He urged me to go to business school at Dartmouth. He said it would mean I would have many choices of careers, and that I would have a chance to make a good deal of money and maybe be my own boss if I found something I was really good at. And he also said—he knew me pretty well—it would give me the wherewithal to help Chris out. That really clinched it for me, so I applied to Tuck and was accepted, and I was excited about the prospect of going."

"So why didn't you go?"

"Because without any warning at all Chris announced he was moving out west and the whole plan kind of blew up in my face."

"Why?"

"Because I felt it my responsibility to go with him."

256

"That seems a bit extreme, doesn't it, Frankie? I mean, he was an adult at the time, wasn't he?"

"Something had gone wrong between us. I had not seen or felt it happening, but we had been drifting apart. I felt terribly, terribly guilty. After graduation I went back to Coaticook and I was startled by Chris's appearance. He was slight, as always, but he had taken on a pallor that made him look sickly. He seemed to accentuate this by wearing all black just about all the time—black jeans, black T-shirts or sweatshirts, black boots. His outlook was dark and he had about him a kind of pseudo-sophistication. He was a seventeen-year-old kid with a world-weary attitude, as though he had been exhausted by life. He resented the hell out of me because I had managed to escape Coaticook. That's all he talked about, when he talked. Much of the time I got one-word responses from him. Or merely shrugs.

"I think I knew throughout college that I should have brought him with me to Hanover, found a foster home for him there, or had him live with me. *Something.* To leave him behind was a very bad mistake. It was a betrayal."

"Chris and three of his friends had formed a band and one of the guys knew somebody who knew a club owner in Tucson. Somehow they got it into their heads that if they went out there they would get work in the club and end up with a recording contract. It was insane from the beginning. I tried to be as supportive of Chris as I could, but this scheme was out of thin air."

"They were chasing a dream," Sloane said. "That's not such a bad thing to do."

"Maybe," Frank said, sounding unconvinced. "Anyway, I was supposed to start Tuck in September, but in August the boys took off for Tucson. I couldn't just let Chris go like that. I did everything I could to persuade him to stay. I told him we would move to Hanover together, that I would get him lessons with a member of the Dartmouth music faculty, that things would be great. He was unmoved. So I had a choice: I could go to business school or I could follow my brother and do whatever I could to help him."

"So you went to Tucson," she said.

"So I went to Tucson. Drove to Tucson. The boys in a beat-up old Chrysler, me in a well-used pickup I had bought after graduation. Somehow I found out that the Tucson newspaper was owned by a Dartmouth alum. It was the only connection, however remote, I had there, so I went to see him. And he gave me a job as a police reporter working from six at night until two in the morning. It was my illustrious start in journalism.

"I wanted to get a two-bedroom place and have Chris live with me, but he would have none of that. The band members found a cheap rooming house and all lived on the same hall. They got work in the club they'd been told about. But it was as bar workers, hauling ice and beer, cleaning up.

"Then, all of a sudden, the band broke up. Two of the guys headed back to Coaticook, and one stayed on in Tucson. Chris told me out of the blue he wanted to go to Boston, said he had heard a lot of new bands were forming there. I quit the paper, we packed up, got in my car, and headed for Boston. To make a new start."

CHAPTER

20

O'Toole was startled when the silent alarm in the Stewart house was tripped. He had not seen anyone enter the house, had in truth been dozing in the front seat of his unmarked car, parked up the hill from the house. It was a balmy night and O'Toole was alone. McCormack had insisted that the house be kept under surveillance.

O'Toole beeped McCormack right away and the lieutenant called back within a minute on a cellular phone.

"Someone's inside," O'Toole said.

"Who?" McCormack asked.

"Don't know."

"Did you see anything?"

"Nothing out front," said O'Toole. "He must have come in the rear."

"See a car or anything?"

"Not from my vantage point."

"Stay where you are," said McCormack. "I'll be right there."

Patrick Boyle had parked on the side street at the rear of the Stewart house. Wearing a light windbreaker over a T-shirt, Boyle left his car and approached the Stewart property from the rear. He paused, gazing at the gray, Cape Cod–style house, then he set off across the yard, brushing against the hedge. He took the key that had been provided to him and opened the back door. He walked quickly through the kitchen and descended the stairs to Stewart's office. Unlike Dockerty, Boyle was not particularly skilled with his hands. He clumsily yanked the carpet tacks out, slicing the rug in several locations in the process. He was on his knees working hard, sweating. Finally, he had removed all of the tacks along the front wall. He struggled to roll the rug back the requisite six plus feet.

Boyle worked the blade of the knife into slivers of space in the wood floor beneath the carpet, but several minutes passed before he was able to remove enough sections to see the outlines of the steel plate. He unscrewed, then removed the plate and set it aside. Boyle wiped his face on his T-shirt and paused before turning the dials on the safe.

"How long have they been inside?" McCormack asked upon arrival

"Ten minutes maybe," said O'Toole.

"You stay here," said McCormack. "I'll cover the rear."

"Careful, Lieutenant," said O'Toole.

McCormack ignored the comment.

McCormack sat in the Crown Victoria, across the narrow side street and down a hundred or so feet from the rear of Stewart's yard. The detective wondered for a moment whether he had placed himself in harm's way. He wondered whether there might be some dangerous criminal, someone like Dockerty, inside. He wondered whether he should be prepared for a violent confrontation. But he dismissed those thoughts. McCormack knew who was inside.

Boyle turned the dials to the numbers he had memorized and the safe door pushed up an inch or two. The priest opened the door and saw the cash. He immediately began removing the banded stacks of bills and setting them in piles on the carpet. Each time he thought he might have reached the bottom, there appeared another layer of money. He had never seen anything like it. After removing everything, he counted the packs—fifty-seven in all, $570,000.

Boyle got up to leave and realized he had nothing in which to carry his treasure. He went upstairs to the kitchen and rummaged around in the cabinets until he found a plain brown paper shopping bag with handles. He found a grocery bag and placed it as a liner within the shopping bag, returned to Stewart's office, and filled it with the money. It was nearly full and surprisingly heavy. Boyle placed the bag by the office door and set about the task of closing and locking the safe. He did so hastily, however, and failed to use the tacks to secure the carpet against the wall. He failed, as well, to move the sofa and coffee table back into position. In truth, Boyle did not care whether anyone discovered the safe. For him, it no longer served any purpose.

McCormack watched as the priest, lugging the shopping bag, cut through the hedge and walked alongside the road. Boyle walked down a half block and set the bag down on the pavement next to a dark Ford Tempo. Boyle fished keys out of his pocket, opened the passenger side door, and hefted the bag in onto the floor of the car. As Boyle walked around to the driver's side, McCormack pulled up and got out of the Crown Victoria.

Boyle glanced up, startled.

McCormack looked down through the window and saw the bag—and saw its contents.

Both men stood still, silent, frozen for the moment. Finally, McCormack looked up across the roof of the car at Boyle. The priest's expression seemed to be a mixture of concern and annoyance. Most people, confronted by police under such circumstances, would be frightened. Many would panic. Such was Boyle's arrogance, however, that he remained calm.

"You know, Father, we have laws against going into other people's homes uninvited," said McCormack. "It's known as breaking and entering. In this case, breaking and entering in the nighttime. And even worse, since you took something of value, burglary. People have been known to receive lengthy terms of incarceration for such crimes."

Boyle replied in a tone contemptuous of McCormack.

"I am here on a private business matter, detective," he said, "that is none of your concern."

"It's my concern when someone goes to the scene of a recent *unsolved* murder, spends time in the house, and then leaves with an awful lot of somebody else's money."

Boyle flashed a look of anger.

"On the contrary, detective, this is not someone else's money. This money belongs to the people, to the poor. As you're well aware, Phil was chairman of the Shelter Coalition and I am now his successor. These are Coalition funds which he kept at home for safety and convenience." The priest gestured toward the inside of the car. "I'm merely retrieving those funds."

"Kind of strange to keep that amount of cash in someone's house, wouldn't you say?"

"Unorthodox," said the priest, "but I don't think that's a crime in this country, is it, Detective?"

Boyle broke into an arrogant smirk.

McCormack was impassive.

"He was mistrustful of banks, Detective," Boyle said.

McCormack thought for a moment. "Who told you where to find the money, Father?" McCormack asked. "Who are you splitting it with?"

Boyle tried to conceal it, but a look of surprise appeared on his face.

"It could be very messy," McCormack added, "if it became known who tipped you, who you're splitting it with. Who you're an agent for."

Boyle's face turned red, McCormack thought with embarrassment, but he quickly learned it was from anger. When the priest spoke, spittle came from his mouth.

"And it could be very messy for you, Detective, if it was known how you carried a grudge against Phil ever since he deprived you of the commissioner's position. Very messy if it was known how deeply you hated him, how much of a motive you had. What did you care? Your wife was dead and gone. Your life had gone haywire. And you had to drag that leg around every day, a reminder of him. It fits together too nicely, Detective."

McCormack just stared at him, taking it all in. He made no reply.

"Leave it alone, Detective," said the priest. "Nobody wants this pursued any further. The department brass is on to you. They want it to fade away. Everybody wants it to fade away. He's gone. We both know that he was a very bad man. He neglected his duties, neglected his constituency." Boyle glanced down into the car. "I'm going to rectify that, Detective. That's what I'm called to do."

Frank Cronin and Howard Berman met after work at Doyle's Cafe in Jamaica Plain. After a lengthy discussion with Mc-Cormack at Larz Anderson Park, Cronin had phoned the paper and asked Berman to meet him. In the smoky bar, they had beers, and, to Berman's surprise, Cronin smoked a Marlboro Light he bummed off a waitress.

"What's with the butt?" Berman asked.

Cronin exhaled off to the side. "Every once in a while," he said. "It helps my nerves."

Berman was taken aback.

"Your *nerves?* I didn't know you had any. Since when is there a problem with *your* nerves?"

"There's a lot going on," Cronin replied.

"With Sloane?" Berman asked.

"With a lot of things," Cronin replied.

Berman sipped his beer and waited for Cronin to speak.

"This is bizarre," Cronin said, "but I know it to be true. I have it from an unimpeachable source. Last night, Patrick Boyle was seen leaving the Stewart home with a shopping bag full of money—hundreds of thousands of dollars, I am told."

"*What!*" Berman fairly shrieked.

Cronin nodded. "It's true. Evidently there is a safe in Stewart's house that the cops had not found before. Dug into the concrete basement floor."

"This is nuts," said Berman. "It's crazy. I don't believe it. You're guy has gone off the deep end."

Cronin frowned. "It's true, Howard," he said.

Berman finished his beer and leaned forward across the table. "What the hell is going on here, Frank?"

"Stewart had some kind of scam going, some major scam

where he was laundering money," said Cronin. "This must have been proceeds from that."

"So why wasn't Boyle arrested for burglary?"

"Because he claimed that it was Shelter Coalition money that Stewart just happened to keep at home and he was claiming it as the leader of the Coalition."

"And they believed him?" Berman asked.

"What choice was there?" Cronin asked. "There was no proof to the contrary."

"But for God's sake he was taking something of great value out of the house of a man who was recently murdered, whose murder remains unsolved. *Christ!* At the very least, the *very* least they should have taken him in for questioning, gotten some answers on the record."

Berman shook his head in utter amazement. "My God, Frank, what's going on here? Who the hell was the cop who let him go." Berman asked the question with a note of incredulity in his voice.

Cronin looked away and suddenly it dawned on Berman.

"It was your guy," Berman said softly.

Cronin nodded.

"Jesus," said Berman. "I don't like this, Frank. This doesn't feel good to me. There's something wrong here. We've got to push on this thing. We can't sit on this. I don't care what the terms are with your man, this goes in the paper. We'll source it, protect his name, but the incident itself has got to see the light of day. It *has* to. First, we need a quick piece on the facts of what happened. We'll source it. That Boyle entered the house, spent X amount of time inside, and came out with what sources estimate to be X amount of cash."

"Why the rush?" Cronin asked.

"Because something as bizarre as this is going to get around, and if it gets around the swine from the *Record* will sniff it out," said Berman.

"And the second thing we need to do?" Cronin asked.

"Is go deep on Boyle," said Berman. "We'll do it as a profile of the heir to the Shelter Coalition mantle, but we want to look carefully at his, shall we say, dark side. Agreed?"

Cronin nodded. "Let's go," he said.

But the following morning when they met with Johnson to discuss the stories, the editor of the Boston *Post* nixed both ideas.

"He's dead and buried," said Johnson. "We've done enough. More than enough. We're through with the whole dirty business."

Johnson was emphatic. Cronin left the meeting while Berman remained to argue with Johnson, but it was no use. Johnson's mind was made up. Berman and Cronin had no way of knowing, of course, that Johnson's view had been colored by a visitor he had received at his home the night before. A visitor who spoke to Johnson about his pending application for an annulment, a visitor with a stake in there being no further stories of the sort Berman and Cronin wanted done. And after the session at Johnson's home, the editor was hopeful and the visitor satisfied. Father Boyle, in fact, left Johnson's house feeling rather pleased with himself.

Frank Cronin wanted to tell Sloane about a crucial moment in his life, an incident back in high school.

Chris had gotten picked on a lot in junior high and high school. Partly it was his size and his stutter, but it was also that he had a somewhat effeminate manner about him that invited ridicule.

It had happened after hockey practice one night. There was an assistant coach, a priest named Father Turgeon who for some reason had it in for both Chris and Frank. Turgeon was a huge man, noticably bigger even than Frank. Turgeon had played semi-pro hockey and had been more of a tough guy than a skater. Frank had always given him a wide berth. In the scrimmage on this night, Turgeon filled in for another player and played opposite Frank. But Turgeon wasn't as quick as Cronin and Frank got the better of him.

After the scrimmage Frank noticed the priest in the stands talking with Chris. The shield of fiberglass surrounding the rink prevented Frank from hearing what they were talking about, but it did not appear pleasant. Frank went over to them and asked what was up.

"He sassed me," Turgeon had said.

Frank looked at his brother and asked if that was true. Chris said it was. Frank asked why. Chris looked down at the floor, reluctant to answer. And then he said, "He c-c-called me a f-f-f-faggot."

Turgeon called him a liar. Frank said he doesn't lie to me. Chris never had.

Frank was very angry but he thought the smartest course would be to go get the head coach. Frank turned and began walking away, back toward the ice, and was almost at the gate when he distinctly heard this priest call Chris a little asshole.

He went back and confronted him and told him he didn't allow anybody to talk to his brother that way. Turgeon told Frank to go fuck himself and started storming off toward the locker room. As he did so, Frank reached out to grab his arm. He wanted an apology for Chris before Turgeon went anywhere. Just as Frank touched him, Turgeon wheeled around and punched Frank, knocking him to the ground.

After being knocked down, he had gotten up and moved toward Turgeon, hunched in a boxing crouch, his fists high. Then suddenly he shot a left hand forward, nailing the priest on the jaw, staggering him momentarily. Turgeon dropped his hands ever so briefly, but it was long enough. Frank flashed a right, landing it just above the priest's eye, tearing the skin and sending blood down, covering his eye.

Suddenly, players on the ice noticed what was happening and moved toward the boards, hurrying in single file through the gate leading out to the bleachers, jockeying for the best view. Coach Hunter saw what was happening and rushed over to intercede. But he was too late.

For at that moment, Turgeon threw a clumsy left which missed its target and allowed Cronin to bring a thunderous right hand that landed on the priest's cheekbone, snapping his head back. Cronin moved closer and threw a quick left followed by a right uppercut which landed full bore on Turgeon's jaw, breaking the bone and sending the priest crashing to the ground, unconscious.

When the priest landed, he struck his head on the cement floor. He was in the hospital for some time after that. Frank had been suspended from school and the hockey team. And there had been a court session where he had been charged with assault. He had been very lucky that his coaches and teachers stood up for him. But he was placed on probation nonetheless, and was technically guilty of a felony. Because of that, he was forced to put off going to college for a year. The magistrate said if he kept his nose clean for a year he'd seal the record, so that it would be as if the incident never occurred.

Frank had applied for early decision to Dartmouth and gotten accepted; now he had to delay it for a year. That had pained him because he saw going away to school as his escape from the confines of Coaticook where he was seen as the poor, pitiable foster child.

So instead of going off to school, he did what his father before him and his father before him had done. He took a job as a logger and headed for the big woods.

He wanted to tell Sloane that the part of it that really frightened him was that there had been something within him urging him to keep punching until he had beaten the very life out of Turgeon.

CHAPTER
21

Cronin could not sleep.

The story that was demanding to be written was in his head now, forming and reforming itself. In his mind he wrote it, then rewrote it, then tore it up and started over again. He had promised Berman that this latest one would be his finale, the story that told it all. He had grown sick of it, of all the lies and deceit. The city reeked of dishonor. He was sick of the likes of Boyle and Sears and Roy Johnson and Deegan and sickest of all of Philip Stewart who seemed larger now in death than he had been in life.

Cronin was filled with nervous energy. After midnight he got out of bed and went for a long jog through the quiet streets of his neighborhood. At home he showered and changed. He drove to the *Post,* arriving shortly before two A.M. The city room was empty, save for the night assistant city editor asleep at the city desk. The scanners were on low to avoid disturbing his slumber. In Cronin's far corner of the room, all was quiet. He was wide awake and felt not the least bit tired.

He sat at his desk, slouching in the chair, his feet up on the desk, thinking the story through. Soon, he was sitting up, tapping an outline onto his computer screen. Then he began drafting the story. He wrote in fits and starts, shaping the first four hundred words of the story. He wrote and rewrote for ninety minutes with increasing frustration. Each lead he drafted was clunkier than the one before. They conveyed little of the pathos at the heart of the story. It was close to four A.M. when he got up from his desk and ambled upstairs to the cafeteria, bought coffee and an apple, and returned to his terminal. Then it occurred to him that the story would work far better if he wrote it not as a news story but as a feature. He considered this, working through the progression in his mind. The story would have a softer feel to it, but that might be appropriate, he thought.

He started over and soon found a rhythm. This was it, he thought. It was a strange sensation, writing without notes, purely from material in his head. When he was finished, he did not reread what he had written, as was his custom. Rather, he shipped the story to Berman's computer and went home to go to sleep. When Howard Berman arrived later that morning, he sat down at his terminal and read the story.

> *Robert thought he had broken through. Things had never gone well for him. It seemed he had always had to struggle, with little to show for it.*
>
> *But then, in the spring of last year, Robert felt that he was on the verge of turning his life around. Or so it seemed for one sweet, brief moment.*
>
> *For years Robert had struggled with a substance abuse demon. He had fought it and been beaten down, time after time. But then, finally, Robert seemed to have it licked. He had been clean for nearly six months, all through a dark and bitter winter and into a bright and glorious spring.*
>
> *Robert's recovery was helped immeasurably when he became involved as a volunteer aiding others fighting addiction. He proved a deft teacher, an inspiring example.*
>
> *Robert dedicated his life to helping others who had suffered as he had. And he believed that if he continued to work with substance abusers, he would have the strength and motive to remain sober forever.*
>
> *Robert's big break came when he was told about a job opening for a counselor at the city hospital substance abuse outreach program. The head of the program said Robert was perfect for the job.*

According to a member of Robert's family, who wished to remain anonymous, Robert was the first choice of officials who ran the program. The final hurdle for the job was an interview with Councillor Philip Stewart, chairman of the Council committee that oversees the outreach budget.

Robert's family members said that during the interview, instead of being quizzed about his abilities, Robert was bluntly told by Stewart that he would not be given the job unless he paid Stewart $10,000 in cash.

Robert told Stewart that he did not have anywhere near that amount of money. Stewart said he would give him one week to raise it.

Robert was unable to do so.

Stewart was murdered four weeks ago. Police have questioned a disgruntled former city employee, Mick Dockerty, in connection with the case. Dockerty has not been charged with the murder.

Law enforcement officials are currently investigating what they believe to be links between Stewart and organized crime. Officials have evidence indicating that for seven years Stewart participated in a scheme to launder cash generated by organized crime activities—including gambling and the drug trade. Officials believe Stewart laundered funds through an account ostensibly intended for the Shelter Coalition.

In the wake of Stewart's death, the Post *reported that the United States Justice Department had investigated allegations that Stewart had extorted tens of thousands of dollars from a North End catering company.*

Arlene DiMasi, who with her husband, Gabriel, owns Napoli Catering, said during an interview with the Post *that Stewart had extorted approximately $19,000 over a seven-year period. She said that Stewart told her that if they did not pay him they would lose their city contract.*

The Post *subsequently reported a second apparent scam run by Stewart in which the former councillor extorted funds from a Boston transit company owner with a city contract by convincing the businessman that the payments were actually linkage funds for the homeless.*

Raymond Wright, owner of Wrightways Transit, holds a city contract to transport special needs students in the public schools. Wrightways principle function is to transport physically and mentally handicapped children to and from school.

According to Wright, and banking records, Wrightways paid an account under Stewart's control some $54,000 over a three-year period.

Added to the list of Stewart transgressions is now the case of Robert. A family member says that after the extortion demand by Stewart, Robert grew depressed, then despondent. Within weeks, he was back on the substance that he had struggled so valiantly to defeat.

On the night of June 2, 1992, Robert went to the attic in the apartment building where he lived. He tied a thick rope to a rafter and hanged himself.

Robert is not his real name. The young man's family requested that his true identity be protected. But he died, says a member of his immediate family, "at the hands of Stewart." The late councillor, said Robert's family member, "might as well have put a bullet in his brain."

Robert's relative, who lives in the Boston area, said Robert was precisely the kind of person Stewart had a reputation for helping.

The murder of Councillor Philip Stewart has thus far stumped law enforcement officials. Dockerty, formerly of Roslindale, once worked as a guard at the Deer Island House of Correction. He was alleged to have beaten an inmate who later died. Hearings into that death chaired by Stewart resulted in Dockerty's dismissal.

Police investigators have said they have few clues in the case. Police say that Stewart was on the screened-in porch of his Moss Hill home on the night of June 26 listening to a Red Sox–Yankees game while drinking a can of Moxie and smoking Pall Malls. He was shot twice at point-blank range. He was wearing slacks, a golf shirt,

271

and a sleeveless sweater. Police have said the crime scene
was undisturbed.

Berman sat at his terminal, a cup of coffee in one hand, a half-eaten bran muffin on his desk. He was dressed in dungarees and a work shirt and his hair was still wet from his morning shower. He was clean-shaven. He read the story for a third time. Every so often he would strike a single key and move farther down into the text. Once he got past the midpoint in the article, Berman sped up his reading.

He went back and read the story again. Rarely did a story produced by one of his reporters jar him, but this one did. Berman was touched by the poignancy of it, revulsed by Stewart's base indecency. How terribly, terribly sad that this young man had come to such an end. Stewart, Berman thought, had been a vile man.

So this was the story Cronin had said he was working on. It was a giant spike through the heart of what remained of Philip Stewart's legacy.

Cronin arrived at noon to review the article with Berman. They went into his office and closed the door. Outside the glass wall, reporters and editors buzzed through the room, discussing stories, arguing, fighting over assignments.

Berman sat down behind his desk and Cronin took the seat opposite. Berman's tone was heartfelt. "Frank, this is a sensational story," he said. "You've done an unbelievable job. You can imagine when I read it, I mean, I was floored. I had no inkling. I mean, how did you find this guy?"

Cronin looked down, staring at the floor for a moment. "I have an arrangement, Howard, with the source," said Cronin. "I've given an ironclad guarantee that I won't talk about the source in any way or about Robert in any more detail than is in the story. I made that agreement to get the story and I feel bound to stick by it."

Berman nodded. "No problem," he said. Then he thought for a moment. "No problem with me," he added. "But I wonder what Roy will say. My suspicion is he'll have problems that the story hangs on a single source. You cite 'a' family member, 'the' family member. Never family members, plural. So before we go in to see Roy, let's cover a few things."

Cronin nodded.

"How good is your source?" Berman asked.

"There could be no better source on this story," Cronin replied.

"A member of the family?" Berman asked.

"Yes."

"Not some distant cousin?"

"No, Howard, not some distant cousin."

"Parent, sibling, spouse?" Berman asked.

"A member of the immediate family," said Cronin.

Berman seemed annoyed. "Frank, I'm trying to prepare you for the editor of the newspaper," said Berman. "He won't like this line of yours. Let's not forget that as the editor he is entitled to know who the source of your information is. The *Post* policy is that if he asks you must answer him."

Cronin shrugged.

There was an edge in Berman's voice. "What's that supposed to mean?" he asked. "You don't care?"

"It means there's nothing I can do about his desire to know my source," said Cronin. "I cannot reveal my source. I cannot reveal anything more about Robert than is in the story."

"You know the rules," said Berman. "An editor is entitled to know the identity of a source."

"That policy is enforced on a selective basis," said Cronin. "He can invoke it or not. Nothing's written in stone. Either you believe my story is right or you don't, Howard. That's what it comes down to."

Berman studied Cronin's face. The reporter seemed impassive.

"Nobody has more faith or trust in you than I do, Frank," said Berman, meaning it. "That's not the issue. To get the story in the newspaper, Roy's got to give his OK."

Berman and Cronin sat silently in Roy Johnson's office while the editor of the *Post* read the story. He did not appear happy. He removed his glasses and looked up at Cronin. "Very moving," he said. "It's a tragedy." He shook his head, seeming genuinely touched.

"I wonder though . . ." he said, his voice trailing off. "Are we being fair?"

"To whom?" asked Berman.

"To Stewart, of course," said Johnson. "Many good people cherish his memory. Are we fair to that memory?"

"What's unfair?" Berman asked.

"Is the implication fair, I wonder," said Johnson.

"In a very real sense Stewart pushed this kid to his death, Roy," said Berman.

"I don't disagree," said Johnson.

Suddenly, Johnson switched gears. He placed his hands together, fingers stretched out, as though about to pray. He tapped his hands against the front of his face and then spoke. "The single source issue again," he said. Johnson glanced hopefully at Berman. "Have we raised this?"

"Ah, yes," said Berman.

"And?" Johnson asked.

"And it's something I can't reveal," interjected Cronin. "I made a commitment. I reveal the source's identity to no one. I reveal nothing more about Robert than is in the story."

That trademark calm again, thought Berman, who was now quite nervous himself at the palpable tension that filled Johnson's office.

Suddenly, Johnson was flushed with anger.

"You've got *one* source," he said, his face reddening. "And this newspaper is supposed to supply the definitive destruction of this man's reputation less than a month after he's put in the ground on the basis of a single source which you refuse to identify in the privacy of this office to the editor of this newspaper."

Johnson, leaning forward in his seat, glared at Cronin.

Berman wanted to intercede, but was frozen for the moment, groping for something appropriate to say.

Cronin nodded. "It makes me sound completely unreasonable, doesn't it?" Cronin said in a soft voice. "But consider this. Many times in the past we have published stories where the source was a step or two or *three* removed from what we were writing about. Very infrequently do we have a member of the family of someone we're writing about as the source on a sensitive story. But here, we have one. What more do you want than my absolute assurance that the source is unimpeachable? That the story is accurate in every detail?"

"Have you considered the damage this will do to Stewart's legacy?" Johnson asked.

Cronin did not respond.

"It will be the definitive destruction of the man. Mark my words," said Johnson. "Are you sure that's what we want here?"

"Why not?" Cronin replied without hesitation.

Johnson stiffened. "Because we're not in the demolition business," he replied, spitting out his words.

Cronin screwed up his face as though he didn't get it. "But we're supposed to be in the truth business," said Cronin. "And the truth is that he was an evil man . . ."

"He had a dark side," Johnson interrupted.

But Cronin plowed on, ignoring the editor. "He hurt people. He was a fraud. He was greedy, venal, corrupt. This story illustrates that. It's the truth."

"The truth is a tricky thing, Frank," said Johnson. "It is also true that he did God's work for the Shelter Coalition . . ."

"Like stealing their money and using it to launder mob cash," said Cronin.

Berman froze. Cronin's subtly mocking tone seemed dangerously close to some invisible line. But it seemed to strike Johnson in the gut. He sat back in his seat and placed his hands behind his head. Had he given up? Berman wondered.

"It's overkill," said Johnson. He turned toward Berman, ignoring Cronin, and said, "Let's hang on to it. Think about it a few days. All right, gentlemen?"

Ordinarily, this was the final word, a signal to Berman and Cronin to leave. Berman rose but Cronin did not move. Both editors looked at the reporter, waiting for him to speak.

"I think we need to run the story, Roy," Cronin said quietly.

"We may do that," said Johnson dismissively, "but I think we need to turn it over in our minds before we decide."

"We have the story now," said Cronin. "It's an exclusive. It's the best story we've had on this case. We don't sit on stories like this. In the time I've been at this paper it's never happened. Why now?"

Johnson looked closely at Cronin. He did not seem so much angry as curious.

"I'm uncomfortable with the story and would like to sleep on it," Johnson said. With that, the editor stood up abruptly, a clear signal they were dismissed. Berman moved to the door. Cronin did not budge from his seat.

"We should run the story, Roy," said Cronin. "Tomorrow. Maybe the next day. It should run. It must run. We have an obligation to get it out there."

"Come on, Frank," said Berman, who wanted nothing more than to get himself and his reporter out of Johnson's presence.

"And you should know that if we aren't going to use the story, I'll take it elsewhere," he said.

"Oh, *Christ!*" said Berman.

Johnson stood motionless, then sank slowly into his chair.

"What's that supposed to mean, Frank?" the editor asked.

Johnson's secretary suddenly appeared in the doorway. "Sorry to interrupt," she said, "but there's been a shooting in Roxbury, Howard, and they need you on the desk."

"I'll be back," Berman said. "Don't anybody do anything they'll regret," he said, catching Cronin's eye.

After Berman left, there was an awkward silence in the room until Johnson repeated his question.

"What's that supposed to mean, Frank?"

Cronin spoke carefully, his words measured.

"It means, Roy, that if we're not going to run the story I'll go to the *Phoenix,* the *Ledger,* somewhere, to make sure the story sees the light of day. It's an important story and we both know it. A crucial piece of the Stewart puzzle. People have a right to know about it."

Roy Johnson pulled himself forward in his seat. He was red-faced with anger. "You mean to tell me that you're threatening me that . . ."

Cronin cut him off. "I'm not threatening anyone," he countered. "I'm merely telling you my contingency plan."

He paused and stared hard into Johnson's eyes. "Especially in view of you're having been compromised on the story."

Johnson was thunderstruck. He turned purple with rage at the accusation. He pulled himself forward and pointed at Cronin, jabbing his finger in the reporter's direction.

"Who the fuck do you think you're talking to, mister?" he demanded.

Cronin was still. He did not blink.

"This story is too important to have it compromised at this stage, Roy," he said.

Johnson could barely control his fury. And he grew even more furious as he saw Cronin's placidity. He was about to dismiss Cronin from his office, to suspend him again, perhaps even fire him when, suddenly, from deep within, Roy Johnson felt the sharp stab of his conscience. In a moment of sheer panic, he pulled himself back and looked at Cronin in horror. He thought in a flash of Gabrielle, of the annulment application, of Boyle's intercession on his behalf.

My God, Johnson thought, he knows! In a situation where most people would be paralyzed by anxiety, Cronin was composed. He knew. He had to know.

Johnson had somehow convinced himself that the conflict was no conflict, that he could be an even-handed judge of stories even as he was privately in Boyle's debt. The test of whether something was wrong, he had always believed, was whether one would be embarrassed by its being known publicly. Johnson suddenly felt deeply humiliated.

How could he know? How could he have found out? But that didn't matter now. What mattered was the truth and Cronin knew. He was a reporter, after all, a digger; he knew many things.

Suddenly, Berman was back. The city editor glanced from one man to the other and wondered what had transpired during his absence. Berman was pleased Cronin hadn't been thrown out of Johnson's office.

"So where are we?" Berman asked.

Johnson regarded Berman. Johnson was deflated. He wanted

277

the meeting to end. He wanted Cronin out of his sight. Johnson turned to Berman and asked, "So what should we do?"

"If you're asking me, I have no problem with the story," said Berman. "Yes it's a single source, but this is Cronin we're talking about. He says the source is A-one, gold." Berman shrugged. "How can you do much better than a member of the immediate family?"

"You're saying we run it?" Johnson asked.

"Absolutely," said Berman. "A great story from our best reporter with a top-shelf source? How can we go wrong?"

The following morning the story ran on the Metro Front of the Boston *Post*. Not putting it on page one was Johnson's way of saving face on the matter. Cronin did not care where it ran, so long as it ran. He was pleased when he saw it. Even more pleased over the ensuing days when it became clear what the public reaction was. A few Stewart diehards denounced the story. But in general, the people of Boston were aghast. The story was the subject of extensive follow-ups on radio and TV news reports. Radio talk program lines were jammed on the subject with one caller after the next expressing horror at the rank nature of Stewart's corruption. Thousands of Bostonians found it hard to believe that they had been so completely fooled by Stewart. There was astonishment that he would so brazenly steal and that he had somehow lived another life without even the slightest detection.

What had been left of Philip Stewart's reputation was now in shreds. Frank Cronin, understanding this, at long last felt a measure of satisfaction.

The story caught Detective McCormack's eye for another reason. He read the article over and over again and, still, there was a small portion of it that did not make sense to him. He went to Sloane's office and they sat at her conference table.

"You've read this?" he said, placing the article on the table.

"So sad," said Sloane, shaking her head in sorrow. "To be so admired in public and such a monster otherwise. It all has a rather eerie quality to it, the whole thing, don't you think, Mack?"

McCormack nodded, but that was not what he had in mind. "Did anything in particular about the article catch your eye?" he asked.

She considered the question. "Other than the obvious—the tragedy of the young man's life—nothing really, Mack, why?"

McCormack smoothed the newspaper out on the table in front of him. He reached into the breast pocket of his sport jacket for his reading glasses and put them on. He was moving in an oddly deliberate manner, close to slow motion. Something is askew here, she thought.

He spread the paper out with both hands and leaned forward over the table for a better view of the print. He began to read. "Police investigators have said they have few clues in the case. Police say that Stewart was on the screened-in porch of his Moss Hill home on the night of June 26 listening to a Red Sox–Yankees game while drinking a can of Moxie and smoking Pall Malls. He was shot twice at point-blank range. He was wearing slacks, a golf shirt, and a sleeveless sweater. Police have said the crime scene was undisturbed."

McCormack stopped reading and looked up at Sloane. He removed his glasses and held them out to the side in his right hand.

"Anything strike you?" he asked.

She'd been sitting with her arms crossed, listening carefully. "Nothing, really, Mack," she said. "Though the Moxie can seems an odd bit of detail."

"Did you know about it?" McCormack asked.

"Know *what* about it, Mack?"

"That it was there?"

She thought a moment. "No, I don't think I did, really. If it was in the report I missed it."

She held up her hands as if to say, what does it matter?

"Did you know about the radio?" he asked.

"Yes, surely," she said. "It was stated in the report that there was a side table with radio, cigarettes, and matches."

"But the report said nothing about a baseball game on the radio," said McCormack. "The radio was off when the body was found."

She felt chilled, suddenly, a vague sense of foreboding. She sounded annoyed when she spoke. "What is it, Mack? What's your point?"

McCormack watched her closely. He asked, "You didn't tell him about the Moxie can?"

"I did not *know* about the can," she said, "until now. I would have guessed that you had told him, but by your tone I see you didn't. Surely another investigator *did* tell him."

McCormack shook his head. "No," he said softly, strain evident in his voice.

"You can't be certain of that, Mack," she asked.

He chose his words carefully. "I was the first person on the scene after the body was discovered. I personally put the empty can into an evidence bag, marked it, sealed it. When I left the house, I put it into the trunk of my car with some other items. When I got downtown, I retrieved the other items, but not the can. It evidently rolled under a box in the corner when I was driving. I forgot about it. Until this morning when I read about it. I went out to the car and it was still in my trunk."

Sloane's eyes narrowed as she listened. She responded coolly. "The EMTs preceded you," she said. "Surely they saw it."

"I called them both this morning," said McCormack. "Frank never talked with either one of them."

They met that evening at Larz Anderson Park. McCormack had called and said it was extremely important that they talk. When Cronin arrived, McCormack and Sloane were waiting for him on a bench past the skating rink. The night was hot. McCormack's shirt was soaked. His tie askew. Sloane looked composed but worn. Both seemed withdrawn. When he saw their eyes, he knew why they had come. Both were frightened. McCormack held a copy of the *Post*. He handed it to Cronin with the final paragraph of his story circled in red.

"We'd like you to tell us how you came to know these details," he said.

Cronin held the paper and looked from McCormack to Sloane before looking down at the newspaper. He glanced at the paragraph. He looked from McCormack to Sloane and back.

They were both sitting, looking up to where he was standing, waiting expectantly.

"A source," said Cronin.

Sloane stared at him. McCormack looked away. The detective spoke with sadness. "That's impossible," he said.

McCormack turned back and looked up at Cronin. "I never told anyone about the can. It wasn't in the report."

Cronin sat down on the bench beside Sloane. He leaned forward, elbows on his knees, his head resting on his hands.

"Not you," said Cronin. "I had another source. *Have* another source. The only living soul who would know for sure about the can and the Sox game."

He turned sideways and looked at them, then looked away again.

"My source," said Cronin softly, "is the person who killed Philip Stewart."

CHAPTER

22

McCormack's kitchen was spotless. The table, against an open window, was set with one place, a small plate, a bowl, knife, fork, spoon, and paper napkin. There was not a dirty dish or utensil or glass or pot or pan to be seen. The sink, white enamel, gleamed. The counters, on either side of the sink and to the left of the refrigerator and stove, were shiny. The room was done in yellow and white—yellow curtains, white stove, refrigerator. The wallpaper contained a pattern of small, yellow and white flowers, carnations and daisies. There was a captain's chair in front of the single place setting and two other chairs around the table. The floor was linoleum, white and yellow squares, as gleaming as any on a TV commercial. There was a small portable television set on top of the refrigerator. In a corner, leaning upright, was a wooden cane. On a side wall was a photograph of McCormack's late wife. On the counter next to the microwave, Cronin saw a copy of his story about Robert.

As soon as they had arrived, McCormack had filled a copper tea kettle and set it on the stove. Their drive from Larz Anderson to McCormack's had been brief and wordless. Now they sat silently waiting for the kettle to whistle. In the meantime, McCormack set out cups with a tea bag in each. He placed a bowl of sugar on the table alongside a quart of milk.

When Cronin had broken the news, Sloane and McCormack had been profoundly shocked. Sloane had felt sick to her stomach at first. McCormack experienced a flash of dizziness. Both were speechless. What could they say? How could it be possible?

When the initial wave of shock had passed, Sloane had gathered them together and insisted they go somewhere private. She suggested McCormack's and he assented. They needed a place to talk, she had said, away from officialdom. There was already in place an unspoken agreement that this news would be shared with no one.

The water boiled and McCormack filled each of the three cups and set the kettle back on the stove. Sloane was the first to speak.

"There's lots that needs learning, Mack," she said, "and Frank will be our teacher. So let's set about it, shall we?"

There was no question that Sloane was in charge now. On the inside, she was in a state of turmoil. But on the exterior, she was collected, confident.

"One raises the most obvious question," said Sloane. "Not that one expects you're prepared to answer, but if you don't mind, could you tell us who your man is?"

"You know I cannot do that," said Cronin.

"And why the hell not?" asked McCormack. "To protect your *source?*" The word dripped with sarcasm.

Cronin looked down into his tea and did not respond.

"We could end this right here, Frank, if you would simply tell us who it is," said McCormack, impatience in his voice. "We're talking about a capital crime. Doesn't that weigh against journalistic codes? A man has been murdered, you know who the killer is, yet we're sitting around having tea?"

This tack would go nowhere, Sloane knew.

"There's a great deal one would like to learn, Frank," she said. "Such as how this came to be. And when? He approached you, I suppose, for whatever reason."

McCormack was vexed. He half laughed in frustration. "This is not complicated," he said. "It is simple. A murder has been committed. We"—he indicated Sloane and himself—"are responsible for bringing the killer to justice. This is our sworn duty. You know who the goddamn killer is. I don't think you have any choice, legally or morally, but to tell us who it is."

Cronin sipped his tea. He rose from the table and walked back and forth across the room, hands in his pockets.

Sloane tried but was unable to smile. She felt unsettled and

283

hoped she didn't sound it. "What can you share with us," she asked, as brightly as she could, "that will allow us to put the pieces together in the sort of tidy package for which lawyers and policemen have such a fondness?"

Cronin leaned against the counter, looking at her, struck by her beauty, her straight white teeth, thick, dark hair, her pretty legs, primly crossed. Cronin reached across the counter and picked up the *Post* containing his story about Robert and placed it on the table halfway between Sloane and McCormack. She searched his face for an explanation.

"What's this got to do with the killer?" McCormack asked.

"Everything," he said.

Sloane and McCormack looked at each other. McCormack took a deep breath. Sloane, strands of her hair falling out of place onto her forehead, turned back to Cronin.

"Everything," she repeated.

Cronin nodded his affirmation.

"And by everything you mean what, exactly, Frank?" she asked.

"That the story and the killer have everything to do with each other," he said.

She leaned forward solicitously. "I don't mean to be tedious, Frank, but I'm awfully thick at the moment and being a lawyer I *do* like things spelled out rather explicitly. You understand?"

He nodded.

"So help me get all of this information straight in my dull but orderly little lawyer's mind," she said. "You mean to say, I take it, that the story and the killer are related?"

"Yes," he said.

"So that would mean that whoever provided you with the information on the story claims to be the person who took the life of Councillor Stewart. Is that correct?"

"Yes."

"I see," she said, turning and looking at McCormack.

She stirred her tea, reflecting for a moment.

"Your man, Frankie," she asked. "Young or old, black or white, rich or poor, insane or not?"

Cronin was impassive. Remarkable how he can sit without

speaking and not be made uncomfortable by the awkwardness of the silence, she thought. A trick he learned as a reporter, no doubt.

"My curiosity is killing me," she said. "I want to learn, Frank. Truly I do. I want to understand your man. *Why* is always the ultimate question, isn't it? Why does a person kill? The categories are few and the parameters narrow. Who commits murders? In the city they kill for drugs. For money. For the fun of it. Husbands kill wives. Drunks kill their pals once in a while. What else is there?"

Sloane pushed her hair back on the side. Her eyes widened and she extended her hands to her sides, palms up. "Go look at my caseload," she said. "That's what it consists of. Do I exaggerate, Mack?" she asked, turning toward the detective. He shook his head.

"But *this,* this is different," she continued. "I wonder about this man and who he is and what drove him to this."

"What does it matter?" Cronin asked.

"It matters," she said. "In the eyes of the law and the eyes of God. It matters *why* he took the life of another."

He shook his head. "I can't help you," he said. "I'm sorry."

Sloane nodded. "But I believe you can, darling," she said, unembarrassed at the term of affection she used in McCormack's presence. "You can go and talk with your man and ask him our questions yourself. And you can return and enlighten us. And perhaps, through you, we can make some progress."

Cronin placed his teacup on the counter next to the sink. McCormack got up, rinsed it out, and placed it in the dishwasher.

"You would have to begin by telling him he will be treated fairly under the law if he turns himself in," said McCormack. "You might urge him to come in."

Sloane frowned. "But you need not pressure him," she said.

Cronin saw no alternative but to agree. He said he would make a phone call and set up a meeting. He left the apartment and walked three blocks to a convenience store. He was about to use the pay phone there, thought better of it, and walked across the street to a gas station. He went into the phone booth there. He was back shortly with the news that a meeting was set for that evening. He knew, of course, that he would be followed. He did not expect that it would be McCormack, but he was sure other detectives would be on his tail. And he was just as sure that their plan was to wait until he arrived at the meeting place, and then arrest the killer. Sorry, Frankie, no choice in the matter. You understand.

At home, Cronin shaves, then showers. He is about to dress but he feels fatigued and lays down on his bed instead. He shuts his eyes and relaxes his body. He wakes with a start, glances at the clock and sees he has been asleep twenty-five minutes. He dresses in gray slacks, loafers, a blue button-down shirt, a quiet green rep tie, and a blue blazer.

It is dusk when he drives along the Jamaicaway headed downtown. He drives at a moderate speed and soon spots the unmarked cruiser tailing him. He changes lanes a number of times and the cruiser, a dark blue Crown Victoria, does the same. Though it is three cars back, Cronin can plainly make it out to be the police. He speeds up and it does the same, slows down and it follows suit.

He has been briefed by McCormack and Sloane on how to behave with his man, on what to ask and how to query him, on when to apply a bit of pressure and when to back off. He crosses Brookline Avenue and drives on to the Riverway, the sprawling hospital district to his right, the leafy Emerald Necklace to his left. He goes left on to Boylston Street and stops at a light a block from Fenway Park. He can see the huge scoreboard in right field and notes that Mo Vaughn is coming to bat. It is the middle of the game and the streets outside the park are deserted except for vendors selling peanuts and Red Sox pennants. The light changes and Cronin pulls forward, and as he does so, through his open window, he hears the swelling roar of the crowd. He switches on his radio—he knows readily what station the Sox are broadcast on—and hears Joe Castiglione reporting that Vaughn has lifted a towering blast into the seats in straightaway center field, the deepest point in Fenway.

He enters Storrow Drive and sees that the unmarked cruiser

follows. Are there other officers in the area? Nearby, perhaps, but none on his tail, he can see that. They will not think he is aware of being tailed and, for that reason, he believes they will have one car following and another as backup, for the apprehension.

It is pleasant along Storrow Drive, with the Charles River to the left. He swings off Storrow at Arlington Street and cuts across Beacon Street and Commonwealth Avenue. He goes right on Newbury Street then immediately turns into the Ritz parking garage on the left. He leaves his keys with an attendant and walks across Newbury and enters the Ritz lobby by the side door. He has already phoned a reservation in his name into the Ritz Cafe for that evening. He is expected.

But when he enters the building, instead of going left into the Cafe, he walks unobtrusively across the lobby and ascends the single flight of stairs in the back right corner.

The police have stopped farther up on Newbury, past the garage, and double parked in front of an art gallery. As soon as Cronin enters the building, one of the detectives gets out of his car and walks up the block to follow him. The detective enters the hotel only a minute after Cronin, but, already, it is too late. The officer looks around and does not see his quarry. He walks down to the far end of the lobby and enters the bar. He peers around but does not see Cronin. He goes to the Cafe and looks around the room. The maitre d'hotel asks if he might help the gentleman. The officer says he is looking for his friend, Cronin. Ah yes, says the headwaiter, he has a reservation and is expected momentarily. Perhaps the gentleman could wait in the lobby?

But Cronin has used this precious time wisely. He has walked along the hushed and carpeted corridor on the second floor that connects the hotel to the Ritz condominiums. He has descended another staircase in the lobby of the residence building, a full half block from the hotel, and he has slipped out the side door and walked briskly across Commonwealth Avenue. Once across, he disappears into a maze of side streets on the flat of Beacon Hill and slowly wends his way down to the Charles Street MBTA station, where he catches a train. Forty minutes later, he arrives home.

• • •

The following morning they are back, by prearrangement, at McCormack's. Everything is the same. The kitchen is spotless and bright. The story about Robert lays on the counter. McCormack pours coffee this morning instead of tea. No mention has been made of the previous night. McCormack and his men had been puzzled when they lost Cronin. Had he intentionally slipped them? Had it been inadvertent? Had Cronin gone somewhere in the hotel to meet his man?

Sloane was again in charge. She appeared tired. Her hair was still wet from her shower, shiny black and neatly clipped. She wore a sleeveless tan shift, her muscular arms in evidence.

"Tell us about your man, Frank, why don't you," she began. "What's up with him? I suppose he must be in terrible turmoil carrying this burden around. He is tormented, I'm sure."

Cronin considered this and shook his head. "No," he said. "Not much if at all. I wouldn't say he's totally at peace with himself, but he's reconciled to it. He feels justified."

Sloane jerked her head to one side in a look of surprise. "Justified?" she said. "How's that?"

"This is going to sound strange to you," he said, "but this is the explanation he offers. I convey it to you as best I can."

And with that, Cronin, speaking as the killer's advocate of sorts, told them of Hammurabi's Code.

In the early days of the twentieth century, a small group of French archaeologists digging in the dust of Iraq unearthed a spectacular stele of black diorite. It was more than seven feet high and nearly that wide at its base. At the top is a carving of Shamash, a Sun God, sitting on a throne. The carving shows Shamash handing a code of laws to King Hammurabi of Babylon. Chiseled into the stone below the carving of Shamash and Hammarubi are the 285 provisions covering civil, criminal, and commercial law that comprise the code. It was one of the earliest established bodies of law in the history of man, Cronin explained. And it remains the earliest and best preserved codification. The significance of the code would be hard to overstate. For what Hammurabi did was not merely to issue a series of random rules, but to codify laws into a coherent whole, into a system based on logical principles.

Hammurabi did this, Cronin continued, after consolidating the various kingdoms of Mesopotamia under Babylonian rule. He gained a reputation for competence as both an administrator and a warrior. He was also considered a champion of scholars and writers, and he was far ahead of his time. Under the Code of Hammurabi, women could own businesses, buy property, and if a man divorced a woman she was entitled to the return of her dowry and he was required to pay child support.

Sloane listened intently. She was amazed by Cronin's ease with the material. It didn't sound to her at all as though he had heard this pitch from his man the previous night and was now passing it along. She recalled, in fact, earlier conversations with him in which he had mentioned various aspects of Babylonian history and culture. It had been an area of interest to him in college, he had once told her.

The Code of Hammurabi was best known through history for its severity, he said. The punishment for many offenses was death. For Hammurabi's was a system based on *lex taleonis*— the law of retribution.

"This principle is frowned upon by our society, but it is one with exceedingly deep roots in human nature," said Cronin. "The desire to see that one who harms us is harmed in like degree is woven into our souls. In our culture, though, we've fled from that. It's considered a baser instinct today. But if you look back across the historical spectrum, you find we are the most lenient society in history—before or after Christ. More than any society in history, we permit grave injustices to go unpunished or minimally punished."

Cronin stopped and gazed down at the table. He looked from McCormack to Sloane, studying her closely, then sipped his coffee. It was cool.

Sloane could not take her eyes off him. She gave him a quizzical look. "You're on his side, aren't you, Frankie?"

He did not reply, did not dispute her.

"You're writing a prescription for anarchy," said McCormack.

Cronin turned toward the detective. "What recourse did Robert's family have?" he asked. "Under our laws."

"Well," said the detective, fumbling for an answer. "They could have brought in evidence of the attempted extortion of Robert. Presented that."

Cronin shook his head at the lameness of the answer. "They've lost a member of the family because of Stewart," said Cronin, his anger rising, "and their recourse under our system is they get to sit down with an FBI agent or police detective who couldn't be bothered with their case and say that Stewart attempted to extort them. And the lawman says, 'Well, doesn't seem like much evidence to me. The word of a kid with a shaky history against a vaunted member of the City Council.' So the answer to my question is they had no recourse. They swallow the bilge and keep quiet is their recourse."

Cronin drummed his fingers on the table, slowly, quietly. "To be forced to accept this unspeakable fate is barbaric. Yes, one must accept the normal hurts of life. But grave assaults on a person that alter the course or quality of one's life? Then there's a right to strike back. If for nothing else than to retrieve a part of ourselves that has been taken away. What about the man who kills the rapist of his daughter? The woman who walks into court and fires six rounds into the man who sexually abused her son? Sometimes what is taken from us is so precious that we have a moral right to take something back in return."

"And so what is it that Robert's family should be able to take from Stewart?" McCormack asked. "His life?"

"More than that," said Cronin. "His life, yes, but of what great value was that? He was an older man and not well. I don't suppose he would have lived an awful lot longer. I think something more valuable should be taken from Stewart: his reputation. His legacy. Those are enduring things. Immortal things, so much more precious, in some ways, than life.

"We ought to understand why rational people commit acts that are considered irrational under our civil and moral laws," Cronin continued. "In fact, what could be more rational than to respond proportionally to someone who has broken your life. Robert's family would be considered outlaws, immoral for acting against Stewart. In fact, it was Stewart who was immoral. It was Stewart who broke the laws and violated the public trust year after year after year. And yet *he* is seen here as the victim. I say Robert is the victim. Sometimes laws are unjust. Sometimes a person's conscience dictates that they act outside the civil law."

"Unfortunately," said McCormack, "we don't get reimbursed every time we're nicked."

Cronin looked at McCormack in astonishment.

"*Nicked?*" he said, his face and neck reddening. "You call that getting nicked? It's a catastrophe. Stewart took away the most important thing in that family's life; destroyed a boy's life, robbed him of whatever fighting chance he might have had, and that's getting *nicked?*"

He was furious. He drew himself up to his full height, his fists dangling at his sides. The veins in his neck bulged. Both McCormack and Sloane were taken aback.

"You just don't get it, Mack," he said. "This boy who was the object of such love is gone. Forever."

Sloane's hands trembled.

She went to her office and made a phone call to the head of the Public Records Division for the Commonwealth of Massachusetts. She told him that she needed whatever information was available on one Christopher Cronin. She spelled it. She did not have a middle initial or an address, she said. She said she believed he had died sometime in the previous year. She said the matter was urgent.

Twenty minutes later, he phoned her back. Three men named Christopher Cronin had died the previous year. Two were in their eighties. One had been twenty-three years old.

The twenty-three-year-old, she said. That's the one. The man said he'd been afraid of that. Unfortunately, it was one of those cases where the records were virtually nonexistent. No exact date. No cause. Only that he had been buried at St. Joseph's Cemetery in Boston.

Sloane made a second call, this one to the cemetery office. She spoke with an older woman there who kept the records. Sloane explained what she was looking for and the woman said it would take a few minutes to find.

Sloane drove rapidly through the city streets, outbound on Storrow Drive along the Charles River, past Fenway Park, out along the Riverway past Jamaica Pond. She turned into the entrance off the parkway and pulled in behind a small stone administrative building.

Inside, there was a reception area and a small office. The woman with whom Sloane had spoken on the phone was the only person there. Sloane introduced herself. The woman was businesslike. She asked Sloane for identification, which Sloane provided.

"You understand these are private records, property of the archdiocese," she said. "These aren't open to the public, though we always cooperate with police. Diocesan policy."

Sloane said she appreciated the help.

"Though, in truth, we rarely get requests for any of these records, really," she said. "Usually people come in here looking for the location of a plot. Perhaps it's a long-lost relative, old friend, whatever."

Sloane was tense. "You have the information I phoned about?" she asked.

"Right here," said the woman, indicating a large, dark green cloth-bound ledger book spread open on a table.

"You see, we note the name and the plot," she said.

The woman pointed out the entry for Christopher Cronin. On a single line was listed his name and number of his burial plot. There was also a notation near the end of the line which appeared to be "OB."

"What does this mean, here?" Sloane asked, indicating the notation.

"Other burial," said the woman. "We have always kept records of other members of the same family that might be buried here. OB 307 means there's a relative in section 307. Each section of the cemetery contains three rows of eight plots, twenty-four in each section."

"I wonder," said Sloane, "do you by any chance have other information you keep elsewhere? Anything at all might be helpful to me. Date of death, cause of death, that sort of thing?"

"We're not required by law to display any of this information, you know," the woman said. "The Archdiocese policy is to aid law enforcement, though we are not required."

"I understand perfectly," said Sloane, "and I do so appreciate your help, but I would dearly love to see your other records."

The woman thought a moment. "When you return from viewing the grave, perhaps," she said, "but I have files that must be dealt with right away."

"Of course," said Sloane.

With instructions from the record keeper, Sloane drove on a windy, unpaved road around a small stone chapel to a section shielded by tall oaks. Section 307. She looked at the name, Jocelyn Cronin, and her heart ached. She thought of the woman Frank had so lovingly described, thought of the tragedy of her early death, of two boys being left alone in the world. She placed her hand on the stone, a grayish hue flecked with black. She thought of her own mother and how deeply she loved her, how unthinkable her death would be.

Sloane sighed as she walked away. She soon found section 327, the newest part of the cemetery. It was distinctive in its fashion, with newer headstones, more flowers for the more recently dead. She saw a headstone taller and thinner, more elegantly chiseled than the others nearby. Most were a light gray, while this was in charcoal. The inscription read simply, Christopher Cronin, 1969–1992. She thought of the boy Frank had described. She thought about the precious child, feverish, who would lie on the laps of his mother and brother; she thought of the little boy who was moved like a piece of furniture, from one home to the next and on and on after the death of his mother; she thought of a stuttering boy, effeminate, an outcast who found refuge in his music. And last of all she thought of Frank and what he had lost. In this ground beneath her feet was all that he had loved in his life. They were in boxes, both of them, covered now by dirt, under tons of ground, gone forever and ever.

She returned to the office and asked, once again, to see the other records.

The woman hesitated.

"Please," said Sloane. "It would be so very helpful."

"Come with me," said the woman. She retrieved a set of keys from the desk drawer and led the way outside and around to the rear of the building. She unlocked the steel door, snapped on a light, and descended a half dozen steps. The woman unlocked another door and they entered a large cool room. On all four walls were shelves, floor to ceiling, and ledger books neatly arranged, with notations on their spines. The room was poorly lit.

"May I see the entry on Jocelyn Cronin first?" Sloane asked.

The woman reached down a lower cabinet. She pulled out a dusty ledger, sought a particular page, and handed it to Sloane. Sloane read the entry. Jocelyn Cronin had been buried in February of 1975. It noted that she had suffered an accidential death, that it had been in Coaticook, Quebec. It stated that she was survived by a husband and two children, Francis and Christopher Cronin. Sloane lingered over the entry for just a moment.

"If I could see Christopher Cronin, please," she said.

The woman led the way off to a dark corner of the room. She reached for a flashlight on a table and aimed the beam at a particular shelf. She moved the flashlight down, down, then stopped. She reached up and lifted a hefty volume and placed it on the table. She thumbed through it and ran her finger down a page.

"Here," she said. "This is the main set of books. It's more complete. The set upstairs is just there to guide people to the right plots. Here it is."

Sloane moved directly in front of the book and leaned over for a better look. The line was halfway down a page. Each entry was written in blue ink. Chris's entry indicated that he had been born on May 1, 1969, and died on June 2, 1992. It indicated that his home was Boston and that he was survived by a brother. In the column under the heading "Cause of Death," there was a blank space. Sloane thought that curious. Every other entry included a cause—N for natural, A for accidental.

"I wonder why this is blank," Sloane said, pointing it out to the woman. "Seems curious when all the others are filled in."

The woman looked more closely and suddenly tensed.

"Sometimes a mistake is made," she said. "I must head back up-stairs so if you're done . . ."

Sloane was about to close the book when she noticed some initials at the extreme right end of the line on which Chris's entry was written. The initials were tucked by the binding of the book and difficult to read. They were written in black. Sloane aimed the beam of the flashlight at the initials. They appeared to be "boh."

"This notation here," she said to the woman. "What does it signify?"

The woman reached for the ledger and literally attempted to pull it out of Sloane's hands.

"Excuse me!" said Sloane, yanking it back. "I am examining this record."

The woman was flushed with anger. "These are private records and I hereby order you to leave. I've been more than courteous but you must leave."

Sloane shook her head. "No," she said. "Those initials. What do they mean?"

"Please leave," said the woman. "You . . ."

Sloane's face darkened. She moved toward the woman. "Tell me what it means, damnit!"

The woman paled. She looked stricken. The room was hushed. Sloane moved so close her face was only inches away from the woman.

"By own hand," said the frightened woman. "BOH is 'by own hand.' He committed suicide."

23

By the time Sloane returned to her office, Frank had already spoken with McCormack. Cronin agreed that he had no alternative but to do what Sloane and McCormack had asked—to convey to the killer their desire that he turn himself in. Cronin had two conditions: that he chose the place and that only Sloane and McCormack know anything about Cronin's association with the killer. McCormack agreed.

McCormack told Cronin he needed to carry a small audio device which would allow McCormack to stay in touch with him and permit Cronin to call for help, if necessary. Cronin was reluctant but McCormack insisted.

The meeting would take place that night on a golf course in a Boston suburb. This was not a charade Cronin was dragging them through. Since he could not utter the words that spoke the truth, he had to have them see with their own eyes, to reach the truth on their own.

Cronin, Sloane, and McCormack drove together in McCormack's Crown Victoria out to the suburb. The sun had just gone down. During the drive, Cronin guided McCormack from the Mass Pike to back roads that led to a small development that bordered the golf course. Sloane was silent for all of the twenty-five minute trip. The development was set in a heavily wooded area. The night was warm and when they turned into the parking lot, the only sounds were sprinklers watering the lawns.

The agreement was that Cronin would walk through the woods and across part of the golf course to reach the cabin; that McCormack would come if summoned. Sloane, unarmed, was to remain in the car.

"Good luck," said McCormack as Cronin was about to start off through the woods. Cronin nodded.

Frank Cronin looked at Sloane, searching her eyes, but she turned away, unable to meet his gaze. I love you, he thought, and surprised himself as he almost involuntarily voiced the words aloud.

He headed off, through a thicket of trees, across one fairway, through the rough and more trees, across another fairway, past a marsh and, finally, to the woods where the cabin was located. Cronin entered the cabin. It was a single room, sixteen by twenty, which had originally been a satellite maintenance shed. Now it was nothing more than a pine box with Cronin inside. There was a single wooden stool next to an empty, upside down nail barrel, which served as a table. There was a stubby candle and a book of matches. Cronin lit the candle and dripped wax on to the wooden table. When it pooled, he stood the candle up, anchoring it in the soft wax. The candlelight cast a warm glow at its center but an eerie light beyond a few feet. Shadows were distorted. Cronin's head, cast against the ceiling, seemed freakish, monstrous.

The sound of crickets surrounded the cabin. In the distance, he thought he heard a screech owl. He placed his face in his hands.

Oh, dear God, he thought, what have you done to me? He thought of her and Chris, when he was a baby. He thought back to before that when it was just him and his mother on Cape Cod at that place, he forgot the name and even the town. But he remembered that summer, remembered those days, long and glorious days with her. He had had her all to himself! What sweetness it had been. He remembered how happy she had been when the baby was born. He thought of them as the perfect family, in absolute harmony. And they had been. He was not recalling it with a false fondness. It had been the truth. They had, in this life, on this earth, enjoyed true bliss. It had been theirs, they held it, grasped it to their breasts and treasured it. And in a fleeting moment, it was gone. Forever.

And he knew that now.

Everything in his life had turned brittle and been smashed to smithereens.

It was all too much for him, the thoughts, the stinging pain of those memories. He sat on the stoool and tears streamed down his face and he began to sob quietly at first, then he began to shake and cried harder, beyond his control.

He had forgotten that he was wearing the audio device that McCormack had placed on him.

In the car, at the first sounds of weeping, McCormack had made a move to go to him, but Sloane had held him back. She, too, cried, but only briefly. She quickly gathered herself.

McCormack and Sloane set out through the woods walking slowly, feeling their way through the darkness. Soon their eyes adjusted and the moonlight guided them through the woods and across the golf course. McCormack moved along as best he could, but in uncertain terrain his leg weakened quickly and the pain was sharp. Sloane was fit and strong and moved easily while McCormack would step forward with his left leg, then move his right leg in an awkward, dragging motion. After only a few hundred yards his knee was on fire. In a few minutes, the cabin was in sight, perhaps eighty yards away. They could see the yellow light spilling out the half-open door.

McCormack spoke in a gentle tone to Cronin over the wire. He asked whether Frank was all right. Cronin said he was OK.

"Is the man who killed Stewart in the cabin, Frank?" McCormack asked.

There was a long pause. Then Cronin replied, "Yes."

Sloane and McCormack advanced on the cabin. They entered and Sloane saw Frank's tear-streaked face, his eyes swollen, the man she loved, broken.

McCormack looked around the tiny room that contained the killer and saw that Frank Cronin sat on the stool, alone.

CHAPTER
24

Sloane was awake all night. At first light she drove to Mc-Cormack's house. He, too, had been awake throughout the night. He made coffee and they talked.

They made a pact.

At 8:30 A.M., Detective Thomas McCormack drove to the retirement board and signed seven pieces of paper that began the formal processing of his retirement from the Boston Police Department. Later that morning, as a courtesy, he visited briefly with the police commissioner to tell him he was through. He said he was too tired to continue.

McCormack turned over all of his files, including a sanitized version of the Stewart case, to his deputy. Early that afternoon, he returned home, packed a large suitcase, locked up his apartment, and got into his car. He drove out of Boston, headed west to California. He thought maybe he'd go back out and visit his sister in San Diego. But he'd take his time. He would meander, stopping off here and there, taking in the sights. He hoped the drive would consume a month, maybe two. In that time, he would make or receive no phone calls. He would make sure no one in the world knew his whereabouts.

He knew that the whispers when he was gone would be that he had been forced out for failing to crack the Stewart case. He was sure that's what the papers would say. But he didn't care.

• • •

Susan Sloane submitted her resignation at nine A.M. to the district attorney. She did it in person. She told the DA that she was worn down from the job, too tired to continue. She met briefly in her office with her closest and most trusted assistants, had a tearful good-bye, turned her files over, and left.

Late that afternoon, a courier arrived at her home. He had her sign for a package, handed it to her, and drove away. She ripped open the Federal Express envelope and found another envelope with her name on it, scrawled in Cronin's handwriting. Her heart beat harder as she tore open the envelope, raced to the terrace, and sat down to read.

My dearest Susie,

I have such terrible regrets in my life.

I regret that I did not find you in a different place and time and circumstance. What love we have had for the briefest whisper. I love you with all of my heart and soul and I have prayed to God to provide some chance for us to be together in our lives, but my prayers, I fear, cannot now be answered.

I regret that what I have dared to imagine cannot be realized. For I have imagined a life together for us. A life of great beauty and peace. Have you imagined it, too? In my mind I have seen us on summer days on a deserted beach, talking and planning. Savoring the greatest of life's pleasures—anticipation of future happiness. I have imagined children. A boy and a girl, bright and lively and demanding and so well and fully loved that their lives burst with promise. A family. Loving one another as well as we can and forgiving each other our mistakes and misdeeds.

All is lost now because I failed at the one truly significant mission in my life—caring for my brother, Chris. I loved him more than I loved my own life. Our mother entrusted me with that sacred task and I failed. I failed her. I failed Chris. I failed myself. Now I have failed you.

The Greeks recognized hundreds of years before the

birth of Christ that there is only one thing God cannot do. "This only," wrote one of the Greek thinkers, "is denied to God: the power to undo the past."

The past is fixed, carved into the stone of history. It cannot be altered. I live with mine, at times obsessed by it.

I'm sorry you could never know my dear mother.

She would have loved you, I am sure.

You must be wondering: why?

I can only say that something inside compelled me to do it. Whether it was the memory of my mother's passionate plea to me, I do not know. It was not something I did on the spur of the moment. I considered it carefully over time. That makes me more culpable legally, I know. Premeditation. Morally, too. But I cannot trim here. I can only tell you the truth and hope that in the telling you understand. I don't expect you to sanction what I have done, but I hope that in your condemnation of my act that there is some understanding. It would pain me to think that you would not try, at least, to place yourself in my position for a moment, to understand what drove me to it.

Chris was my responsibility. I tell you now that I did the best I could and it was not good enough. Things went spinning out of control so many years ago. It seems like a lifetime ago, now.

He was such a good boy. I loved him so. I can honestly say that now. He was getting himself back on track. He had been beaten down by it for so long and then, suddenly, he fought his way back. The counselor's job was perfect for him. He would have helped a lot of people. He said in his note that he considered coming to me for the money to pay Stewart. But he decided against it because he felt I had too strict a moral code and would not give him the money.

Ironic, isn't it?

He said in the note that he begged Stewart for the job. He offered to pay him in installments over time. He offered more money than Stewart asked for. He said the job

301

meant saving his own life. He said Stewart laughed at him.

I cannot confess this sin I have committed. A priest friend reminded me recently that to receive absolution in the confessional, one must be truly remorseful. I am not. I wish I were. But I would do it over again. I am sure that is not what you wish to hear from the man you love and who loves you so hopelessly. But it is the truth.

Had we lived in an earlier time, what I did would have been neither a sin nor a crime. More than 2000 years ago, under the Code of Hammarubi, revenge was sanctioned in the civil law and by the gods.

So I look back upon what I did knowing that at some moment in time—on this earth, beneath this sky, under the gaze of this God—there were men who were wronged who struck back and were not condemned for it; who killed and did so with the approval of the state and the gods.

So I go on with my life such as it is. I am mournful, but don't imagine that I am tormented by what I have done. I am not. I am no Raskolnikov skulking around in terror, tormented each day by the vile act that he has committed.

I must say that the deepest regret I feel is the shame of having been involved in such a deception. I deceived Howard, though I never wrote a word in any of the stories that wasn't absolutely accurate. They were good stories that unmasked Stewart for what he was.

I very much regret having deceived Mack, though I think I did not have a choice. I never placed anyone else in serious jeopardy. No other person was ever in danger of being tried, never mind convicted, for this crime. Dockerty spent a few days in jail, but he was held on a weapons charge unrelated to the killing anyway. It is important to me that nobody else endured suffering intended for me.

Worst of all, of course, is that I deceived you, whom I love. I know that it means you will never again trust me and that makes me sadder than I have ever been.

As you read this, I am bound for foreign lands.

Within a week, I will send you an address through which I may be reached. If it is your wish that I return to face charges, I will do so. I know enough about the law and this particular situation to know that there is no evidence that could ever convict me. Except, ironically, this letter. What you do with it is up to you.

Please know that I love you, and that I ache for you each moment of every day, saddened immeasurably by the thoughts that we will never experience what might have been.

With all of my love,
Frank

She looked out over the pool and the garden, out beyond the pond to the trees. She felt the burning in her eyes. She went to the house for a pack of matches and walked slowly down the slope to the pond, to the spot by the tree where she had seen him swimming that night not so long ago. She knelt on the grass and lit a match. She held the flame beneath the letter until the paper had caught fire. She turned it this way and that, letting the flame climb up the sheets, consuming his words. When the flame approached her hand she let the letter flutter to the grass where it soon burned itself out. There was only ash now and she took it and she scattered it upon the water.